PRAISE FOR CHRISTOPHER RICE

Bone Music

"A stellar and gripping opening to the Burning Girl series introduces the tough, smart Trina Pierce, a.k.a. Charlotte Rowe, who survived a childhood of murder and exploitation to discover there might be another way to fight back . . . Readers will be eager for the next installment in Rice's science-fiction take on *The Girl with the Dragon Tattoo*."

—Booklist (starred review)

"*Bone Music* is a taut and gripping thriller that's as bleak and harsh as the Arizona desert. It never lets up until the final page. Rice has created a great character in Charlotte Rowe."

—Authorlink

"A simply riveting cliff-hanger of a novel, *Bone Music* by Christopher Rice is one of those reads that will linger in the mind and memory long after the book itself has been finished and set back upon the shelf."

—Midwest Book Review

"Christopher Rice's first Burning Girl novel weaves a complex, suspenseful, gritty tale with grace and energy that turns the tables on the female victim trope."

—RT Book Reviews

Blood Echo

"An undeniable page-turner . . ."

—Library Journal

"Rice has something to say about the devastating effects of childhood trauma and what makes a monster . . ."

—*Kirkus Reviews*

"Strong sequel . . . Rice combines bloody violence, complex characters, and high tech in a dark tale that will leave readers wanting to see more of [Charlotte Rowe]."

—*Publishers Weekly*

"Christopher Rice has written a suspense-filled, forceful second entry in his series, a well-balanced thriller with deep-delving characterizations. *Blood Echo* is filled with a complex cast of characters imbued with both good and evil, as well as a good man who walks the thin line between."

—*New York Journal of Books*

"A deftly crafted novel by author Christopher Rice, *Blood Echo* is an inherently riveting read with a wealth of unexpected twists and turns right down to its nail-biter finish."

—*Midwest Book Review*

Blood Victory

"Cyrus's true story unravels to dramatic effect. Fans of paranormal suspense will be well satisfied."

—*Publishers Weekly*

"The third Burning Girl thriller has action aplenty for superhero fans."

—*Kirkus Reviews*

DECIMATE

OTHER TITLES BY CHRISTOPHER RICE

DECIMATE

CHRISTOPHER
RICE

THOMAS & MERCER

Published by Thomas & Mercer, Seattle

www.apub.com

Amazon, the Amazon logo, and Thomas & Mercer are trademarks of Amazon. com, Inc., or its affiliates.

ISBN-13: 9781542032742 (hardcover)
ISBN-10: 1542032741 (hardcover)
ISBN-13: 9781542032766 (paperback)
ISBN-10: 1542032768 (paperback)

Cover design by M.S. Corley

Printed in the United States of America

First Edition

This one's for Eddie Shine,
whose San Francisco summer program first
introduced me to the power and mystery of the
woods when I was a child.

PROLOGUE
SHADOWS

Fourteen Years Ago

Claire followed her brother into the woods because she was afraid he wouldn't come back if she didn't go with him. They were only two years apart in age, but up until that camping trip, which would shatter their family, she'd assumed she would always be his protector.

In the wild, Poe tended to flip over large rocks without pausing to see if a snake was coiled underneath, to head in the direction of strange noises with a confident stride, arms swinging, backpack bouncing, heedless of whatever animal might be lurking past rustling branches. His curiosity had frightened her from the moment he first learned to walk. At ten years old, he loved the world so fearlessly she worried its sharp edges would one day result in an injury that crushed his spirit.

And so she went with Poe into the dark that night because if he took a wrong step, she'd be there to pull him from the waters of the lake their father had described in seductive detail before nodding off next to their illegal campfire.

"Trees go right up to the edge," their dad had explained, one hand outstretched, eyes glazed from the shots of Wild Turkey he'd promised their mom he wouldn't drink during the trip. Back then, with his shoulder-length hair and heavy beard, he dressed the part of the naturalist he'd always wanted to be, not a guy who spent most of his days installing drywall for house flippers who'd just relocated from Los Angeles to Spokane. "No docks. No beach. No real shore when you get right down to it. Just this almost perfect bowl of clear water surrounded by gorgeous pines. And you don't have to deal with any boaters because nobody's going to hike in a bunch of equipment through all that. Some days, when the light's just right, you can see down forever."

Lake Michele, it was called, and the description made Poe's round blue eyes blaze in the campfire's glow. "Can we go tomorrow, Dad?"

"Next time, kiddo. Mom's watching the clock and wants us back before Sunday."

He'd fallen asleep in his folding chair next to the fire's last embers. And because Claire knew her brother, she knew he would wait and try something reckless. So when she heard him sliding out of his sleeping bag later that night, she reached through the shadows and grabbed his arm with the same force she used to keep him from stepping off a curb before the signal had changed.

"Come with me, Bear," he'd whispered in response.

Most of the time, her little brother's nickname for her—a product of the way his toddler-aged mouth had rebelled against hard consonants—made her feel loved, but out here in Glacier National Park, it made her think of the black-and-white pictures she'd seen in her father's dog-eared paperback copy of Jack Olsen's *Night of the Grizzlies*, a true story about a series of fatal bear attacks in the 1960s. Not only had he kept the book hidden in the shed, he'd also underlined passages and made notes. This made her feel good. It meant that even though her dad always pretended to be unafraid of the wild, he was privately assessing the risks.

But tonight, thanks to the Wild Turkey, he'd be no help unless she woke him. And if she woke him, she'd pay a serious price with her brother, who was still her best friend.

"There's a full moon," Poe whispered. "We'll be able to see down forever."

The way he repeated their father's words, his exact intonations, made Claire feel like some anxious outsider to the intrepid spirit that united the men in their family and left her and her mother on the margins, dismissed as whiners and crybabies. If she hadn't been roused by his movements, he might have slipped off and come back without her knowing, and then she wouldn't have been faced with this choice. But now she knew, so she had to go.

Their father shunned traditional campsites, dismissing them as overused trash magnets, and so the minute they left the little clearing where they'd spent the last two nights, branches started scratching at their Gore-Tex jackets and they had to step over giant rocks every few feet. The slow going made it easy for Claire to reach out and break a branch every now and then, marking the path back for when it was time to turn around. After a half hour of strenuous hiking, Poe's excited chatter started to take on the same refrain, most of it attempts to assure her they hadn't made a terrible mistake.

"It'll be cool, Claire. Timmy Preston's always bragging about how his dad took him to Europe last summer and he saw the Eiffel Tower and stuff and now I'll be able to tell him we saw all the way down to the center of the earth and all we had to do was drive to Montana."

"The lake's not that deep."

"How do you know? You haven't been there."

"No lake is that deep, Poe," she said.

"I think there's one in Africa or something."

"There isn't."

He was baiting her, of course. They all knew she was the only member of their family who read Wikipedia for fun. There was no point in getting into a dispute with her about geography or history. But she played along because it was preferable to letting the quiet of the vast forest close in around them.

3

For most of the trek they'd been ascending a gentle slope. Everywhere their flashlight beams landed revealed thick brush.

Poe came to a sudden stop.

His beam had landed on a rock ledge several paces ahead. As she caught up to him, she saw the seven-foot drop just beyond. If he hadn't lowered his flashlight at just the right second, he might have broken his leg.

"Poe," Claire whispered. "We need to go back. Seriously."

"No, look."

Beyond the drop-off, a steep but manageable slope descended toward shadowy trunks. Between them, water sparkled in the moon-light. Poe reached back and took her hand. He aimed his flashlight at her stomach so that it sent a soft glow up onto their faces without blinding them.

"OK. Make you a bet," Poe said. "If we can't see all the way to the center of the earth, then—"

He never finished the sentence.

The earth under their feet shook with enough force to send gooseflesh up Claire's legs. Her flashlight was ripped from her hand, the beam bouncing wildly as it sailed through the branches. Then she felt like she'd been punched in the stomach and her head yanked side-ways, as if someone had pulled hard on her straw-colored ponytail.

In the next instant, she felt her brother's chest slam into hers. The same force that had torn her flashlight away had driven the two of them into a half embrace. The rush of hot air on her face was his breath, she realized. He was screaming, but his scream was drowned out by a thunderous growl that seemed to come from everywhere and nowhere at once. Her feet had left the earth. Since their bodies were intertwined, she realized his must have too.

They were flying.

Her ears popped like they sometimes did on planes.

A landslide, she thought.

But when Claire slammed back to the earth with enough force to knock the wind out of her, Poe was gone, and there was no tidal wave of mud and debris. Broken branches rained down, shorn leaves slapping her face. The pain of the impact was delayed, and then it spread. Her right shoulder felt like it had been torn open. The throbbing in her head became a tightening vise. She felt swarms of something crawling under her skin, scrambling to break free.

She blinked, saw tangles of shredded and dangling limbs overhead, but it looked like there were two sets of everything. And one set was moving.

She was hit by a light so blinding it stole time itself.

The next thing she knew, the deafening roar had been replaced by a helicopter's blades, and she was staring up at several neat fluorescent rectangles. The floor underneath her rocked. She was high above the earth as medics conversed frantically over her body. A tight band across her forehead kept her immobilized. Now the pain was like spreading fire beneath her skin. She had a terrible fear she'd been burned, but when she jerked her head as much as she could against the restraint, she saw the arm of her jacket was shredded, not scorched.

She couldn't turn her head enough to see who was next to her, but she figured it was Poe. When she tried to cry his name, she coughed up grit instead. Dirt. There was dirt in her throat from the force of the blast. It speckled the inside of the oxygen mask covering her nose and mouth.

Claire closed her eyes, remembered what she'd seen before the blinding flash had claimed her, after she'd slammed back into the earth—two sets of branches in the air above. One set had looked like it was moving away.

Shadows, she realized. It was the branches and then their shadows. Whatever the source of that impossibly bright light, it had moved toward them through the woods before drowning them in white. And these shadows, and the light that followed them, had come after the terrible blasts of air that had sent her and Poe flying off their feet. Like the light had been seeking them out after knocking them down.

This seemed important, and she wished she could share it with the EMTs right then. But she was coughing, and the mask wasn't helping, and when it was pulled from her and she felt someone wiping at her mouth, darkness claimed her again.

She heard her father's voice next.

"I saw it my damn self. It lit up the whole damn lake, and now you're going to tell me—"

"We'll do some more extensive tests, Mr. Huntley, but for now she needs to rest," another man said.

She opened her eyes. She was in a hospital, and the man who'd just spoken was the doctor examining her. The touch of his cold, gloved fingers was dulled by the drugs in her system.

When he saw she was awake, his brown eyes met hers, but there was something remote and suspicious in his gaze. "Hi, Claire," the doctor said, and at this, someone shot up out of a chair in the corner of the room and rushed to her side.

Her father took her hand. He was about to speak when the doctor said, "Claire, can you remember anything about the attack?"

Attack. The word came close to describing what had happened, but not close enough. Force, power, wind, light. If it was an attack, it had been waged by the earth itself. "Light" was all she could manage, a rasping whisper that made her sound ninety years old. When she spoke, the excruciating pressure in her temples started up again. She closed her eyes. The pain lessened only a little, so she opened them again.

"Look, she's got no bite marks." The piano-wire tension in her father's voice told her they'd been having this debate for a while. Bandages wrapped his right forearm. Some sort of injury. When did he get injured?

6

The next thing Claire knew, her father was following her doctor out of the room, arguing furiously under his breath. She glimpsed a uniformed park ranger standing in the hall outside. He looked back at her with an expression she couldn't read, as if she'd become a source of both mystery and dread for them all.

An attack. Bite marks. They thought a bear had done this, and maybe that was the case. And maybe the light was something that had happened in her head. Maybe she'd whited out instead of blacking out. She wasn't sure.

And she wanted to sleep. The next time she woke up, she asked about Poe, and the nurse told her that he was fine. He'd broken his right arm and she'd broken her left. They made a pair, you see. Wasn't that funny? But Claire didn't laugh, because both of her arms hurt like the devil even though only one was in a cast. Every time she woke up, she had a few good minutes before her head started throbbing like her brain needed more space than her skull allowed. And each time she woke up, her memory of those moving shadows seemed more distant, farther away. Just some trick of her mind resulting from the powerful swat of a bear's massive paw against her head.

Whited out instead of blacking out. That had to be it.

But even then, through her drugged haze, through the confusion of being wheeled in and out of MRIs and other giant machines meant to peer deep into her body in search of injuries people couldn't see, she wanted to tell them about the shadows, but her next visitor was her mother. She looked exhausted and disturbed but explained in a soft and gentle voice how their father was to blame for everything that had happened, that he'd been terribly irresponsible to bring them that far out into the woods, that far from help. She didn't ask for Claire's opinion, didn't ask for Claire's version of events. Claire was relieved. This meant she didn't have to talk about her father's drinking or his falling asleep by the fire and how far he'd taken them from a trail or a real campsite. But it was always that way with her mother. Always easier to let her tell you what to do. The downside was that she would also tell you what to think and feel.

When Claire woke next, her mother was gone, and she could hear her father down the hall, arguing with everyone, it seemed—Claire's mother, the doctors, a man who might have been the park ranger she'd glimpsed through the door to her room. "It wasn't a *goddamn* bear, for Christ's sake," he kept yelling, and when they asked him what he thought it was, his answer shocked her. "Something we don't understand," he'd fired back. "Something *none of you* understand!"

The anger in her father's voice had given way to a pain that made her chest get tight. She prayed the pain medications would take the feeling away.

Eventually, she told herself, the tests and the examinations would find a claw mark or some evidence of a bite. Maybe even a patch of fur caught in her hair or her clothes. Then her dad would have no choice but to accept the truth.

They never did.

And in the end, her dad's version of the truth tore them all apart.

I

The Crash

Life and death are one thread, the same line viewed from different sides.

—*Laozi*

1

Poe Huntley makes his way up the aisle of the crowded plane. Every few rows, he spots the guy who stabbed him in the gut and changed his life. *Makes sense,* he thinks. The stress of traveling for the first time in a year has stirred up old phobias.

In the months after it happened, he saw his assailant on every crowded sidewalk, in every snaking checkout line at Duane Reade. His AA friends thought this was nuts. They'd heard the story many times: how he'd been so high on the subway ride to the Bronx that night that he'd hallucinated spirits fluttering outside the windows of the train, all of whom looked and sounded just like Dua Lipa. How he'd been awake for forty-eight hours by the time the knife plunged into his belly. The point was, would he even recognize the man if he saw him again?

Yes, Poe insisted. Drawing faces was his passion; the part of his brain that remembered noses, eyes, and eyebrows still worked even after he'd firebombed it with eight balls of coke and whatever else the most attractive guy at the party had offered him.

But he knows the flashes of bushy eyebrows, equine jaws, the little peeks of serpentine neck tattoos he keeps spotting among the male passengers are all just products of his anxiety. He only boarded a few minutes ago and already he's sick of making awkward eye contact with any guy who looks remotely menacing.

Instead, he focuses on the harried mother he's stuck behind. Her two toddlers, both of whom are trying to take each empty seat they pass, are angel-faced cuties, but they're slow, and Poe would really like to use the bathroom before takeoff. One of the downsides of getting sober is his new addiction to caffeinated beverages.

As he zombie-walks toward his seat, his mind drifts back to that dingy apartment building in the Bronx. He feels the blood pumping through his fingers in a wet, warm rush, remembers his dim amusement over the fact that the guy who'd just stabbed him was running away, abandoning his own apartment.

Poe had wanted to cry out, *You're the one who lives here, dude,* but he couldn't manage words, just a gasping, dry cough that was more astonishment than fear. One minute they'd been arguing about the money he'd been sent to collect. Next thing he knew, he was on the hallway carpet, hands soaked red. He didn't black out, never lost consciousness. No white light. Just a searing pain that felt like a charley horse traveling the entire left side of his body, seizing even his neck in its twisted grip. Then came the sense he might have soiled himself before he realized it was the feel of his blood pooling in his groin and the crack of his ass.

During the hours he'd spent in the ER afterward, he heard every other word the doctors said because his own thoughts kept drowning them out: *Something's over, and if it's not my life, it's the way I've been living it.* The last time he'd spent that amount of time in the hospital, he'd been ten years old and helicoptered in with a mouthful of dirt and a broken arm and a headache so bad he thought his skull would split. Everything had gone to hell soon afterward thanks to so-called decisions made by the so-called grown-ups in his life. This time, Poe was the grown-up. This time he could draw himself a new story. In short, he could clean up his act.

And that's pretty much what he's done.

Sobriety has been good for him, but it's also exposed a part of himself he's been drowning for years, something that's led him to fill the notebook in his backpack with pages full of entries that would probably get him institutionalized if his sober friends discovered them. But the notebook will either save his relationship with his sister or sink it, and their relationship's been on life support ever since she threw him out of their mother's funeral for being a babbling, sketched-out mess. So he'd say the chances this trip will be either a success or a failure are pretty even. He reminds himself of his real purpose. To share information. That's all. What Claire chooses to do about it will be her choice and not his.

Poe makes it to his aisle seat, exchanges a nod and a smile with the woman who's already settled into the middle of their row. Her cherry-red pantsuit has silver buttons so big you could serve hors d'oeuvres on them, but she's briskly unpacking her laptop, which means her penchant for bright colors isn't a sign of a chatty nature. *Excellent.*

He tugs his phone from his jeans pocket. Claire's got classes all morning, but he wants to text her something gentle and sweet, something no response required. Something that makes this whole trip seem a lot more normal than it is.

She seemed happy when he first emailed a few weeks before. Probably because she'd thought he was dead. Didn't know a thing about the stabbing, but she knew how he'd been living since he was fifteen. When he told her he'd racked up a year of sobriety, that he had things to make up for, things to make right, she warmed to the idea of a visit, and this gave him hope.

He's about to start typing when a text pops up.

I'm getting uncomfortable. When are you telling her?

Poe sighs so loudly the woman next to him glances his way before refocusing on her computer.

The notebook he plans to present to his sister that night wouldn't have a single entry in it if it weren't for this guy, his Eyes on the

13

Ground. Maybe Poe should be more patient with the guy's discomfort over what's to come. He stops short of thinking of him as a spy. The title suggests subterfuge and deception when all they've done is share information Poe didn't have access to in New York.

> I'll tell her everything in just a few hours and I will keep your name out of it. Don't worry.

> U won't be able to keep my name out of it. Just let me know as soon as you tell her so I can explain. Deal?

> Deal.

No little dots. No response brewing. Safe to put the phone away for now. He pulls his backpack from under the seat, roots through it for the little Moleskine notebook he splurged on. Now that he's settled into his seat and committed to the six-hour trip, he needs to rehearse his presentation down to the last word. What he has to tell Claire is almost as nuts as the things their father's been shouting on YouTube ever since that night in Glacier National Park.

The difference is, Poe has proof. A mountain of it.

And that's good, because his sister's a total ballbuster who won't accept anything less.

———

Claire Huntley is usually eager to approach Leonard Doyle's office door. When he's not in a meeting or on the phone, he leaves it open, a message to the students of Arcadia Heights High that they're free to call on their guidance counselor whenever they're in crisis.

She's not a student, but she's brought him plenty of her dramas over the years. After her mother announced she wouldn't pursue treatment for the cancer that had spread through her body, Claire practically took up residence on his cushy office sofa. But even before then, she'd been determined to make him her mentor from the moment he'd addressed her orientation session for new teachers. "What I've learned in all my years in secondary education is that none of us are broken, just molded," he'd said to a rapt classroom of eager young hires. "And we can continue to work the mold for as long as we're alive. The key isn't genetics or our past; it's strong hands."

Molded, not broken, she'd written on the inside cover of her shiny new planner that night. Leonard had been describing the many students who'd passed through his office over the years, but Claire had wanted to believe it was true of her as well.

And Poe, she thinks now.

Leonard looks up from his laptop. He has a face like an illustration of a man who would have been used to market candy to children in the 1950s, before various human predators made the idea seem creepy. A long mouth that smiles easily, a round dimpled chin, and apple cheeks. Everything about him seems fatherly, if you don't use Claire's actual father as a comparison.

But the smile he gives now is strained. He's as uncomfortable with this visit as she is.

Ironic, since he requested it last night by text.

His blinds are slightly cracked and angled down, pouring the late-morning sun into a fierce river along the baseboard behind his desk. The hedge just outside his windows is ablaze. When Claire moved to Southern California with her mother after her parents' divorce, the year-round sunlight felt like a relentless bully compared to the short gray fall and winter days up in Spokane. Now she treasures it. It expels shadows, reveals potholes and other destructive traps the Pacific Northwest likes to shroud in rain and mist.

15

The office is one of the more spacious on campus and crammed full of upholstered furniture more suited to a family's romper room. The intent is to relax students into dropping the defiant poses they've been tricked into believing make them more mature. Today, Claire has no plans to kick back. She's not a teenager. And occasionally, given their age difference and the paternal nature of their relationship, she has to find subtle ways to remind Leonard of this.

"Have a seat," he says.

"On a schedule today, I'm afraid. I've got juniors next and—"

"Poe's coming. Is that tonight?"

"This afternoon, actually."

"Meeting him at the airport?" he asks.

"Can't."

Leonard nods, probably taking note of her succinct answers. "Is he staying with you?"

"He's taking an Uber to a Travelodge close to my house."

"Smart. I mean, you're confident he's sober, right?"

"Says he's got a year."

It's his emails that have convinced her. When he was in the thick of his addiction, he'd often send her reams of discursive nonsense he'd composed while sleepless and high. He called it poetry; Claire called it word salad, which didn't stop her from printing out the emails and going through them with a red pen looking for coded signals he was in danger, maybe being held hostage by some lowlife he'd fallen in with. A fruitless endeavor, considering her brother had chosen danger as a lifestyle at age fifteen. But since he reestablished contact, his emails have been clear and to the point, and so have the first, hesitant texts they've shared. That said, every time she sends one, she braces for a response that would make William Burroughs proud. So far, he's stayed in Hemingway territory. Concise and to the point.

"Still, good thinking. On your part," Leonard says.

"You know we had this conversation yesterday, right?"

Leonard clears his throat, settles back into his chair.

"Thalia Vale," he says.

"It's a difficult situation," Claire answers.

"I'm aware. I've been monitoring it."

"OK. Good."

"Delete the account, Claire."

Dammit, she thinks, and even though it feels like a defeat, she pulls his office door closed behind her. "Who told you?"

"No, no. I'm not playing that game."

"With all due respect, it's not a game. I'm a grown-up, and I'd like to know who betrayed my confidence and—"

"Oh, cut it out. We don't fraternize with students on social media outside of specific school-sponsored Facebook groups. It's school policy."

"Which it's not your job to enforce."

"Claire."

"She's being groomed, Leonard."

"We're looking into the rumors. We know there's been a shift in behavior."

"And dress. And eyeshadow. About five layers of it. And she's not going to tell you a thing."

"Why's that?"

"Because you're a man."

"But she'll tell you everything if you impersonate a teenager on Snapchat?"

"It's going pretty well so far. She's been bragging about the gifts men have been sending her. One of the guys is from Long Beach, she thinks. I should have names before long."

"Real names, no doubt. Just like the one you're using with her. Have you reached out to the parents?"

"The mom's not in the picture, and the dad says everything's fine and offered to take me out sometime and help me relax."

"Gross," he whispers.

"Listen, Leonard. Can we talk about this after Poe leaves? I'm sorry if I—"

"Delete the account, Claire, or I'm going to Principal Pearsons."

"You're not serious."

"I am very, very serious. Arcadia Heights is lucky to have you, and I won't let you mess that up with a stunt like this."

"Nobody's there for that girl. Nobody."

"You're not either. Some teenager you invented is."

Claire feels her cheeks flush. "An Amazon gift card for fifty dollars and a Samsung Galaxy. I think she's doing cam shows, but I can't prove it. Anyway, that's what one of the guys bought her. Figured you should know since you're taking over her case."

"We'll all keep an eye on her. In the meantime, have you tried buying her coffee? You've got a talent for sneaking up on these things the right way. They trust you."

"Five times. She's not having it. Why do you think I went the Snapchat route?"

"I'll see what I can do. And I'll keep you updated *if* you delete the account."

"See you later, *Dad*."

"If we bring your dad into this, we'll be here all day."

On any other day, this remark would have earned him a laugh. Not today. When Claire steps out into the hall, she almost runs smack into Deanna Ruiz, who's clearly been eavesdropping. The fact that she wears her nurse's stethoscope over her chest doesn't make her look any less like a frightened younger version of herself.

"Traitor," Claire mutters.

"Don't be mad." As Claire heads for her classroom, Deanna matches her step for step.

"Too late," Claire says.

"Claire, it was crazy. I had to tell somebody you'd actually listen to. I'm just your drinking buddy, apparently."

"I did listen to you. I just didn't do what you said. There's a difference."

"Are you deleting the account?"

To keep Deanna from following her into her classroom, Claire turns at the door to face her.

"Come on, Claire. I'm worried about her too, but this is too far. If you get found out, someone'll think *you're* the criminal."

"I was just trying to get names."

"Was. Past tense. So you're deleting the account? Great!" Deanna smiles and bats her eyelashes.

"I'm considering it."

"This is about Poe. You're stressed out he's visiting and—"

"I have a therapist, thanks."

"Yeah. And when was the last time you saw him? Oh, that's right. Three months ago. Just so you could get your . . ." Deanna raises one hand and moves it back and forth like she's shaking a pill bottle to see how many are left inside.

"*That* was too far," Claire whispers.

"Maybe," Deanna whispers back, eyes to the linoleum. "Sorry."

"I'll delete the account. But if she ends up being a *Dateline* episode, I'm taking you and Leonard to her funeral."

"*Claire!*"

She closes her door before Deanna can follow her inside.

Once she's shut up in the relative quiet of her empty classroom, she heads for her desk and unlocks the drawer in which she keeps her purse. Suddenly it feels like a liability having the pill bottle on campus with her, now that she's made the mistake of confiding in a colleague about it. She can count on one hand the times she's had to swallow one of her little blue friends on school grounds.

Her bigger mistake, she thinks, was falling in with Deanna's Girls' Crew. Someone with Claire's past should only make friends in controlled, sober situations, not over big fruity cocktails at the Cheesecake Factory.

Deanna and her friend Charmaine, a PE teacher and coach of the girls' softball team, had formed their little social group in response to the controversial news that some of the male teachers had a guys-only soccer team they were using to build comradery, which, according to several students who ran into them in the park, was also where they'd come up with a crude ranking system for the most attractive female teachers. In the interest of female solidarity, Claire had finally accepted one of Deanna's invitations and somehow wound up with that thing that had always eluded her up until then—work friends.

Then she'd started telling them too much about herself.

Leonard had called it "opening up."

After a few weeks of letting her hair down over Tropical Tiki Punches, Claire had slipped and revealed how her father had done his best to inform anyone who would put him on their wacko podcasts and YouTube channels that something terrifying and unearthly had happened to her and her brother during a camping trip when she was twelve. That the brief flash of white light that had knocked her and Poe off their feet and left them with baffling injuries wasn't the result of a bear attack he'd failed to prevent, as the authorities believed, but some sort of paranormal event that traveled light-years just to screw up their camping trip.

For what it's worth, Deanna had texted her the next day, I did some Googling and you seem super grounded for someone who was abducted by aliens. Claire had laughed for what felt like a solid minute. It was good to laugh with someone about that part of her life. God knows her mother had never found any of it amusing.

Fast-forward to her admission to Deanna—and Deanna only—that she was on medication to manage the strange anxiety attacks that had been with her ever since that night.

What had she been thinking?

She wasn't an addict. Never took a pill preemptively—only once an attack was underway to stave off the worst of it. And it wasn't easy, since the attacks came on without warning.

Things had improved during college and her first years of teaching. And that had tricked her into thinking she'd made some progress, that nuking herself with Ativan every time she felt the familiar combo of disorientation, dizziness, racing heart, and strange phantom pains had started to have a cumulative effect.

Then came that night about a year ago, when it suddenly felt like someone had torn her stomach open in the middle of a dinner date. She can't decide which memory's worse—the pain, or the embarrassment as she rushed away from the table, convinced she was suffering from instant food poisoning and was seconds away from going full *Exorcist*. But in the end, it was only pain. Terrible, deep, stabbing pain on her left side, so bad she'd gone for a medical exam a few days later, even asked for a pregnancy test just to be sure. Even though her risk of that was lower than dirt. Everything came back clean and negative. No burst ovarian cyst. No intestinal blockage. Just pain from out of nowhere. Pain from her brain, as she'd come to call it.

Deanna's comment stung because the truth is, Claire hates the pills, wants nothing more than to be free of them. Hates how many psychiatrists have patiently listened to her describe her episodes over the years before pointing out how they're atypical for panic attacks. How panic attacks often remain centered in the chest, accompanied by the obvious physical symptoms of hyperventilation—an angry tingling throughout the limbs—whereas her episodes have involved a dizzying array of physical sensations. She hates that her MRIs have always come back clear. She wants an explanation or a source that

21

can be identified, zeroed in on, and treated, but the diagnosis most doctors resort to always feels like a cop-out.

Unspecified traumatic brain injury caused by possible animal attack as child.

Whatever the cause, the pills—the usual benzos, as Dr. Fitzsimmons calls them—stave off the worst moments if she can get to them in time.

And now someone at Arcadia Heights High knows she carries them with her all the time.

She wants to stash them in the car, but the thought of freeing them from the confines of her purse is disturbing. What if Poe sees the bottle later that night? As distant as their relationship has been, she's always been the finger-wagging big sister, and he the screwup lots of men want to screw. Will he feel betrayed if he finds out she's been on medication the whole time? That so much of the unsolicited life advice Claire used to shove down his throat by email was courtesy of a therapist he knew nothing about?

What does it matter? She's not the one who has to fly cross-country to make things right. She's the one who nursed their mom during her dying days; Poe's the one who crashed her funeral like a deranged street musician.

Maybe she's got things to make up for eventually.

But Poe goes first, no doubt about that.

She'll fight him on that point if she has to.

And her drugs come from a doctor, so there.

He's not even here yet, she thinks, *and we're already fighting in my head.*

Claire walks out to the car, tucks the pill bottle into the armrest, and then heads back inside to teach American History II.

———

Instead of trying to lose himself in one of the dozens of movies and TV shows offered by the seatback video monitor, Poe's settled on the moving air map instead. There's something pleasantly hypnotic about watching the icon that's supposed to be their plane as it blips its way across square states toward the Nebraska-Colorado border.

As he tries to think of scientific-sounding alternatives to phrases like *psychic connection*, words his sister might be able to swallow, he listens to the playlist he's been putting together over the past year, another suggestion from his AA sponsor, Benton. The man's a former Broadway chorus boy who turned to meth once he realized his career would expire in his late twenties, and he often lectures Poe about how it's our job to preserve our positive memories, and the easiest way to do that is by refreshing them through music. "Hooked on a Feeling" has been a favorite of Poe's since he was nine years old, but he's already listened to it twelve times since takeoff. He first heard it during a family trip to San Francisco, pumping from the outdoor speakers at Pier 39, where the opening chords made his mother rise off their bench and start moving her hips like she'd had a few drinks, heedless of the other tourists shooting looks her way. It was the last time he could remember seeing the woman happy; it was the last time they were all happy together.

Insane of him to go to her funeral. They hadn't seen each other or spoken since he was ten, but he'd told himself he had to go for Claire, with whom he'd stayed in touch through the occasional email and text over the years. But he knew it wasn't going to be easy, and so, like most active addicts, he'd turned an uncomfortable situation into a disaster. He'd fortified himself with a bottle of wine, a couple of lines, and a Xanax. Or maybe two—his memories of that day are like a watercolor left out in the rain. On the bus ride down to LA, he wrote a poem that he thought was genius and moving, and then suddenly people were getting up and leaving the service as he read it. But mostly he sees the despair and anger in his sister's eyes as she demanded he leave the reception. In this moment, he'd rather see anything else, but sobriety is about learning to let the drumbeats of shame and self-hate run like an underscore beneath your otherwise-pleasant waking moments until the drummer gives up and gets tired.

He forces himself to focus on the air map, forces a few slow, deep breaths into his lungs, and after a minute or two, he's feeling zoned out and comfortable for the first time since takeoff. Then a businessman several rows away stands and starts up the aisle in Poe's direction. The guy looks familiar, but the familiarity's uncomfortable, like several shots of espresso hitting Poe's gut at once. The man wears a rumpled, tie-less suit and sports a salt-and-pepper sidewall haircut. Artful stubble hides a weak chin. They smile at each other the way men who've been in tawdry situations together smile the first time they see each other in public. It's more eager eyes than upturned mouth, a hesitant invitation. *Can we speak to each other without speaking of* it?

Poe riffles through hazy memories of drunken nights, tries to work his way around the edges of countless blackouts.

Marvin. Or Martin.

Something to do with banking.

An old friend of the boyfriend Poe cut ties with as soon as he was out of the hospital and on his way to the first rehab he could find that didn't require insurance. The guy used to visit Danny's unfinished loft space in Alphabet City as Poe sketched in one corner by the light of the battery-operated lanterns they had to resort to whenever some new piece of wiring shorted out. Which was often.

It had all seemed so romantic and exciting in the beginning, so simple. So indicative of his ability to survive by finding new opportunities.

Poe, almost out of living situations in the Bay Area, had gone to a music festival in Berkeley in his best slutty *Midsummer Night's Dream* getup—mop of bleached-blond hair sprayed up and threaded with gold ribbon, addict-slender torso covered in glitter body paint, rhinestone nose ring to match the studs in his ears, and presto, out from the crowd came the confident grip of a man who looked like he could play the heroine's stalwart dad in a teen horror movie. Danny Wernicke was his name, and his hobbies were traveling and sleeping with guys in their twenties. Two nights of frenzied, drug-fueled sex later, Poe was being offered connections in the New York art world and a place to live in one of the most expensive cities on earth. Cue a trance remix of some catchy tune about independence and playing by your own rules and off to the Big Apple he went!

Those first few weeks, he'd been more than content to play the part of the hippie-dippie NorCal artist Danny had imported from out west, more than happy to draw quick sketches of Danny's strange cross-section of visiting friends (and smart enough not to ask them what they thought of the sketches when the wine stopped flowing). But when men like the one headed toward him now kept visiting their place each night, bouncing on their heels, making vacuous small talk that seemed more frantic than cheerful before Danny sent them on their way with a lingering handshake, Poe could no longer ignore the shrill voice in his head.

Your sugar daddy's a drug dealer, bitch.

Danny's art world connections never materialized. His drug world connections kept coming. The friends weren't friends; they were clients. And six months later, after more than one comment implying he'd be homeless if he didn't, Poe agreed to run late-night errands for Danny so long as they involved the money and not the product, a distinction that had mattered so greatly to him in the moment he'd gone hoarse demanding it. Alas, it didn't prevent him from getting stabbed. Maybe if he hadn't been inhaling the very product he had sanctimoniously refused to tote around Manhattan, things would have turned out less bloody.

Benton likens the types of decisions active addicts make as "riding a bullshit train through fields of crap and pretending it's all sunsets and caviar."

After a year of looking back on his old life with clear and sober eyes, Poe can't disagree.

The guy who's headed toward him now, however, has had a few. The smell of booze wafts toward Poe, and he's sure that if Marvin-or-Martin stops at his seat, he'll either recount some embarrassing, messy episode that Poe can't remember, or, worse, he'll ask Poe to set him up with a drug connection once they land in LA.

Poe's thinking of graceful ways to cut any conversation short, when there's a sound like a cannon going off outside the plane.

The shock rattles every bone in his body. He tastes the dirt of Glacier National Park in his mouth, hears the roar that came from nowhere and everywhere. Shadows shoot up the cabin. He thinks they're cast by a flock of large birds sweeping past the windows. But birds can't fly this high.

Pieces of something, he thinks.

Like everyone on board, Martin-or-Marvin has stopped what he's doing and has turned to look in the direction of the terrible boom. The right engine. A hole opens in the roof above the guy's head, and a second later, he's plugging it. Everything from his torso on up's been sucked out into the atmosphere, leaving his legs limp and dangling. Wind screams through the little cracks, and soon similar holes have opened down the length of the plane, spearing the cabin with shafts of sunlight. Loose papers swirl, and a flight attendant who was racing up the aisle to investigate the cannon sound is now holding on to the seatbacks on either side of her for dear life. The nearest passengers, he sees, are holding on to her too.

Pops like rifle fire sound above the train-whistle chaos of a depressurizing cabin, followed by the appearance of smaller veins of light. Icy blasts of air coat his neck and the parts of his arms his T-shirt leaves bare.

Oxygen masks erupt from the overhead compartments like soldiers ready to attack but tethered hopelessly in place.

Above the screaming wind he hears passengers shouting, but they all have one word in common. *The engine! The engine!* The woman next to him is bent over, hands clasped, sobbing. Because he can't think of what else to do, Poe reaches up and grabs her oxygen mask, then grabs the back of her neck, rights her head. She doesn't resist. A strange man's sudden touch is nothing compared to the plane's assault on them all. Once he's got her masked, he sees the teenage girl in the window seat, who's been listening to her earbuds the whole flight, already has hers on, and she's thrown herself back against the seat, eyes screwed shut, as if offering herself to this nightmare so she doesn't have to endure another second of it.

Outside the window, a plume of red-hot flame shoots across the cornflower blue. What's left of the engine, he realizes. Pieces from the explosion are what had just punched holes through the plane like it was a paper target at a shooting range.

The jet starts wobbling like a surfboard on rough seas. Every molecule of air it had been cruising through only seconds before has decided it's an invader that must be repelled.

Poe grabs the armrests with enough force to send throbbing pain up his arms. He should be grabbing for the oxygen mask dangling above him, but this idea enrages him. It's stupid and childish, but putting the mask on feels like a demoralizing surrender.

He's gripping the armrests as if they connect him to something solid, but suddenly the floor drops out, and it feels as if the air is trying to eat them all alive. Anything he does now is a futile, useless gesture, he knows. The words he thinks next bubble up from deep within his soul, as if coming from some instinctive part of him that's been quietly preparing for death throughout his life but without his consent.

Claire, he thinks with shocking clarity—as if he's calling out to her, as if she's only a few feet away and might not know how bad this is, and he needs to warn her they might never see each other again.

The last time he was assaulted by a force like this, they were together. Now she's miles away and he is plummeting out of the sky, and his rage at this gives way to a desire for her touch, and a connection between them he's only begun to fully understand.

Love you, Bear.

———

There are three American history teachers at Arcadia Heights, but Claire's the only one who devotes an entire week to John Jacob Astor's failed attempt to establish a global trading empire on the Pacific coast. One of its bloodiest chapters, the battle between members of the Clayoquot tribe and the crew of the American trading vessel the *Tonquin*, has the sort of *Game of Thrones*–level spectacle required to hold the attention of media-saturated high school students.

As she gears up to describe the final explosive act, she notes with satisfaction that all eyes are on her, and no phones are being secretly swiped under desks. They're wide-eyed and stunned as she reveals how one of the few surviving crew members lured the recently departed natives back to the ship after their brutal attack by pretending to gesture for help, only to light the ship's powder magazine the second the raiding party boarded, blowing the sailing vessel and the hundreds of people on it to smithereens.

She's been using a timeline of that day's events she had written on the whiteboard before her meeting with Leonard. When she notices there's a misspelling in one of the entries, a little of the wind gets knocked out of her. She left out the first *o* in Clayoquot.

Claire uncaps her dry-erase pen, and suddenly it feels as if there are knives inside her wrists, the blades angled up her forearms. The same throbbing pain she got the last time her mind wandered on the treadmill at the gym and she had to grab on to the display at the last second or risk knocking out her front teeth on the belt.

Her heart races. She thinks of the pills in her car, curses the haste with which she removed them from easy reach.

This is going to be a bad one, she can tell. Maybe the worst that's ever happened on campus.

Her mind wants to drop the pen, but its tip meets the whiteboard instead. Against her will.

An invisible force yanks on her right arm. Her heart is racing, but it feels like all her blood has surged into the right side of her body. She thinks, at first, the whiteboard is moving; then she realizes she's moving, just not under her own control.

Clawlike tension in the back of her neck erupts into a tingling across her scalp. The phlegmy sounds of her inhalations through her nostrils are new. When she's in the throes of an attack, her body rejects the idea of breathing entirely—"Because if you don't breathe, then you don't exist and you can't be hurt," a therapist once told her—but in this moment she's gulping air, sucking it through her nostrils and her mouth.

"Ms. Huntley?" a student asks from behind her, voice so halting and hesitant she can't tell which one it is.

But she can't turn. She can't turn because her arm is flailing.

And then it's over.

It wasn't just the worst attack she's ever suffered at school; it was the worst one she's ever suffered, period. Worse than the one when her stomach felt torn open. She'd been able to keep control over her body then instead of spasming wildly in front of students whose respect she had to work tirelessly to maintain.

If it was worse, maybe it was different, she thinks.

When she turns to face the class, she feels the urge to ask them how her face looks, if one side's drooping, but that would turn this already awful moment into an excruciating one. So she asks Kim Johnson, who always watches her like a hawk in search of opportunities to earn extra credit, to preside over class for the next few minutes, says she'll be back shortly. When she stumbles out into the hallway, she hears the laughter her students have been holding in. Feels slightly grateful they waited until she left the classroom to ridicule her.

In the bathroom, Claire does the tests she learned years ago: raises both arms in front of her, closes her eyes, then opens them again to see if her arms are still level or if one of them has sunk or lifted, all signs of some sort of stroke or circulation issue.

Her hands are perfectly level, and so is her face.

It's the pills, she tells herself. *The attack was worse because I knew I couldn't get to my little blue friends in time.*

And even though it makes her feel shameful, she hurries down the hallway, then out into the blazing Southern California sun toward faculty parking. Downs one of the pills with the mostly empty bottle of water still wedged in the cupholder. She's never done this before, taken a pill after an attack and not during its onset, and it feels like she's breaking some cardinal rule she's maintained in order to prevent the pills from taking over her life.

From turning her into an addict like her brother.

She checks the clock on her phone—11:50 a.m. She's only got about fifteen minutes of class before the lunch bell rings.

When she finally steps back inside the classroom, she finds the pill's done little to tamp down her embarrassment, especially when the laughter and whispers stop and all heads swing in her direction.

"Where's Kim?" she asks.

"She went to get the nurse." Ben Pade is glaring at her like the answer should have been obvious, but Ben's one of those teenagers who talks to everyone like they're a waiter who's late with his order.

"Why?"

"Um, for *you*, Ms. Huntley."

"Sorry, guys. Been feeling a little under the weather and took some medicine this morning that didn't agree with me."

It's the best she can do, and it's not good enough. No one says anything.

"Ms. Huntley," Ben says, "who's Bear?"

When she gives the boy a puzzled expression, he points to the whiteboard behind her.

That's when she realizes she didn't just suffer a little spasm. She actually wrote words. They're huge and run over the timeline she wrote on the board that morning before class.

love you bear.

She's barely had time to process the words when the bell rings. Claire turns, finds herself staring at Deanna and Kim in the doorway. She starts for them, getting ready to explain, when suddenly it feels as if the ground's been yanked out from under her and she pitches face-first to the floor as her students scream.

2

"You've never written anything before?" Deanna asks.

She slides the blood-pressure cuff up Claire's arm. Claire's not the largest woman, but everything inside the nurse's office feels kid size, which makes her presence here seem inappropriate. Deanna's just allowed her to sit up after forcing her to lie flat while she checked Claire's forehead for bruises. It didn't matter that Claire assured her that she'd managed to break her fall with her hands.

"It's 'cause I put the pills in the car," Claire answers.

"Why are they in the car?" Deanna pumps, watching the gauge.

"I put them there after our little exchange this morning."

"Ah, so it's *my* fault."

"I didn't say that."

"But you're not answering my question."

Claire blinks. She's gone from feeling sidelined by her attack to worried Deanna will notice the numbing effect of her quick trip to the parking lot. "What question?" Claire asks.

"Have you ever written anything during one of your attacks before?"

"No."

Deanna's eyes cut to hers briefly; she waits for Claire to say more. *I've never lost my footing that fast and hard either,* she doesn't say.

"It's like you said. It's nerves about Poe's visit. Bear was his nickname for me when we were kids."

"That's sweet. OK. You're elevated but not tachycardia levels, so why don't—"

A fierce pounding shakes the door. When Deanna turns to open it, her mouth looks poised to scold, but she's silenced by the sight of Leonard, white-faced and staring at Claire as if he expected her to be missing a limb. He must have heard about her incident at the whiteboard. Still, this reaction seems extreme.

"What's Poe's airline?" he asks.

Nobody speaks for what feels like an eternity. Then Deanna mutters "Oh no" under her breath, a recognition that Leonard's question is the last anyone wants to hear when a loved one is somewhere high over the country.

The next thing Claire knows, she's running for her car while Leonard and Deanna race through the hallway alongside her and Leonard blurts out some explanation about the news alert that just came through on his phone. The words *dropped off radar* lance through her like a sword.

"I need to go," Claire keeps saying, thinking only that whatever is happening, she cannot fall apart twice on school grounds.

But Leonard steers her into the principal's office instead, where they find their boss riveted by something on her laptop. As Leonard starts to rapidly explain how her brother is aboard "that plane," that her classes need to be covered for the rest of the day, Claire turns the computer around before the woman can snap it shut, hits "Play" even as Linda Pearsons rises and gently grips her arm, repeating Claire's name with soft but building concern.

The video is shaky camera-phone footage taken from some suburb with a rigid line of mountains in the background. For the first few dizzying seconds, the plane's descent looks almost normal. Then the amateur videographer zooms out, and Claire can see thick black smoke pouring from one engine, the jet's misshapen tail, and its strange, zigzagging flight path. The worst part is the mild-mannered, quizzical conversation of the people filming as they speculate on whether or not the plane is in trouble.

My brother's in there, she wants to scream. *My brother's inside that thing and you're talking about it like it's a drunk bird.*

It brings back memories of a horrible TV special she made the mistake of sitting through when she was in high school, about the crash of that United Airlines flight back in the '80s, the one that hit the runway so hard it somersaulted, its fiery impact filmed through a chain-link fence before it exploded. She remembered the computer animation of the doomed flight's careening path through the sky after it lost hydraulics. Knew the minute she saw the shaky video that a similar fate had struck Poe's plane. A total loss of control.

A text vibrates the phone in her pocket.

It will be Poe, she thinks. *It will be Poe telling me he missed the flight and he's fine.*

It's her stepsister, Melissa.

Where are you? 911

Claire types back, At school watching. Going home.

Meet you there, comes the response. It's not a question.

Leonard and Deanna chase Claire as far as the parking lot, but they don't pursue her all the way to her car. When Claire peels out onto the oak-shaded street, she catches a glimpse of them in her rearview mirror, shaking their heads in shock, and feels guilty for abandoning their offers of help. But the urge to get far from school grounds, far from the devastated expression on Leonard's face and the video on that laptop screen, was like a starving person's appetite.

She'll stay off the freeways, she tells herself now.

No way in hell is she going to the airport.

She's seen that movie. The one where the hysterical relatives, refusing to accept facts, pour into the terminal as if the airliner they know is doomed will somehow magically pull up to the arrival gate with their loved ones inside. It never ends well, so she's got no interest in starring in it.

She can feel something worse than panic bubbling up inside her, something that feels like despair, something that makes her want to shout the word *no, no, no* over and over again as she pounds the steering wheel. But hysteria is the province of her father, and she is her mother's daughter, and her mother had a rule: *When you are in pain, make a plan.*

She is going home to meet her stepsister and her husband, who are already on their way to her house. That is the plan.

Until then she will grip the steering wheel with as much focus as she can manage.

She will do the only thing she can in this moment.

Drive.

———

After the hooded men banished him from his hometown, Vernon Starnes returned to the abandoned cabin he'd spotted in the woods years before because he knew there were plenty of quaking aspen nearby. Aspen wood, his mother had taught him, was good for carving, and carving is what she'd encouraged him to do instead of killing things. He could inflict his "strangeness," as she called it, on wood and whatever he made from wood but not anything with skin, fur, or blood. That was their deal, and if he broke it, she took his knife and tools away for two weeks.

And for most of her life, right up until she'd collapsed in the kitchen during breakfast one morning, it had worked. She'd made her jewelry from the stones they'd collected from mountain peaks and streams, selling it to the tourists who came to town during the spring and summer months and lingered around the display cases she'd wheel out and park in front of their home just off Pine Street where the shops were. Meanwhile, he would carve out back, keeping his strangeness concealed from strangers.

But his mother's been gone months now, and with each passing day, it's getting harder and harder not to use his blades on living things. He carves more than he used to, and that helps. He's added shelves and even a chair to the ruined interior of the cabin he's called home for months. And he's started making bigger versions of the little dolls he's fashioned all his life. He kills to eat, the way she taught him, and steals the things he can't make for himself. But the desire to plunge his knife into an animal just to see what happens as the life slips from its eyes and goes to some other place, or to find out why it makes some sounds when it's in pain and not others . . . It's not just a desire anymore. It's a need.

He's near the top of the ridge an hour's hike from the cabin, hacking into an aspen's white trunk with a stolen ax, when he hears screaming. There have been times since his banishment where he's been sure he heard his mother talking to him. But this is something else. This is a high, piercing sound that doesn't belong in the woods.

It's coming from the sky.

The plane is descending fast—level, as if it's planning to land way up here in the peaks of the Rocky Mountains. It looks almost normal. Vernon's a man whose definitions of normal have always been fluid. He's also never flown in a plane. Never even been inside an airport, and so he's never seen big planes like this one take off or land. All his life he's lived in remote places. In Spurlock, the town he and his mother called home after they moved out of Uncle Johnny's house, people spoke of Denver and Boulder as if they were exotic, foreign lands. His mother could never manage to say the name of either without equal measures of fear and wonder.

But the thing that strikes him now is the plane's logo. Up here, where the trails are unmarked and the nearest official campsite is a day's hike down pine-shrouded slopes, the plane's cheerful logo is a searingly bright, man-made artifact from another world. The word ASCENT in silver letters against a background of the same bright blue that coats the entire fuselage—it screams wrongness. Way up here, a human creation shouldn't be this visible, this close, this damn loud.

Then he sees that one of its two engines doesn't look like the other and is trailing smoke and fire.

At the top of the slope, he's greeted by a view of the little valley he'd explored that morning. It looks like the pilot might be trying to aim for it. Even Vernon, who's never flown before, knows that would be a terrible mistake.

Maybe not a mistake. Just a last-ditch effort by someone out of options.

But as Vernon watches it all unfold beneath a clear blue sky, watches birds take flight from branches as the plane's wailing and screaming gets closer, he knows he should get the hell out of there. Because if that plane makes anything like a landing, then these mountains will be full of dazed, freaked-out people wandering around asking for help. And if there's one thing Vernon can't do—and he knows good and well there's plenty more than just one thing—it's help people.

Before he can turn, one of the wings clips a mountain peak. The plane spins sideways like a top, keeps flying, then slams into a pine-shrouded mountainside, sending an orange bloom toward the blue sky. The impact rattles Vernon's teeth, shakes the earth underfoot, kicks his body back so far he becomes painfully aware of the entire length of his spine.

The explosion echoes across the valley. The ascending fireball turns blood orange as it climbs, the color of the sun rising through wildfire smoke.

And then the only sounds are damp crackles. They seem small, but Vernon can hear them from this far away, so the fires are large and spreading. Even if they seem puny compared to the plane's wailing descent and the terrific explosion of its impact.

No way could anyone have survived that, he thinks.

And that's good, he thinks next, because that means if he can dodge the flames, he can take their stuff. Because a defining fact of Vernon's life during these last few months of banishment is that he's desperately in need of anything he can't carve.

Vernon is no stranger to fire. As a child, he watched more than one decimating blaze creep over the mountainsides toward the town where he grew up. During the summer months, he would hike up to Newton Dam after his mother nodded off so he could catch a view of the blazes that raged down valley. But this conflagration is different. It's scattered. The cold at this altitude will keep it from uniting into a full-scale inferno, he's sure, and so he moves ahead with confidence.

But he's not prepared for the wall of eye-watering stench that hits him as he nears the first suitcases. Jet fuel, he figures.

The plane slammed sideways into a mountain slope. Whatever wasn't consumed by the initial fireball was blasted down the mountainside toward where he's standing now. Upslope, a large section of fuselage burns fiercely, sending a thick black plume toward the dome of blue overhead.

The suitcases are mostly split like melons, disgorging swells of clothes both bright and dark. Clothes he doesn't need, so he walks past them carefully.

If he's going to make off with some good stuff, he'll have to stash his ax somewhere, he thinks. Then he almost laughs.

Who up here is going to steal it from him? Certainly not the man and woman dangling from a bank of seats that somehow landed upside down on a pine tree stripped of most of its branches by the blast. Their hands are still linked. And he doubts he'll lose his ax to the woman lying facedown several paces away, her shock of bleached-blonde hair blowing in the same wind that tosses her bright floral-print dress up over her thighs. He's pretty sure the occasional soft squishes under his feet are body parts, so he takes care to keep his steps light but quick. Others will be here soon. Drawn by the smoke, or the fact that this world's so damn connected now people everywhere will realize this plane fell clean out of the sky.

He sees a fierce throb of light through the smoking trees up ahead that he figures must be part of the plane, some piece of electrical equipment puking sparks out onto the mountainside. There might be something useful there.

Finally, it comes into view, stopping him in his tracks.

There are two airplane seats, and it's clear the row used to have a third but it's been ripped away by the impact. A woman is strapped into one of them. She wears a bright red pantsuit with big silver buttons. Her head's turned to one side as if she jerked it back at the last minute before slamming into the earth. The closer he gets, he can see the reason her head looks tilted back is because half of her face is missing. What's left behind is mangled gore, but bathed in the dancing blue shimmer next to her, it looks no more real than a poster for a freak show in carnival lights.

Vernon has no name for the shimmer that occupies the seat next to the woman's corpse.

Bright tendrils rise from the cushions and the seatback like smoke, each a fierce shade of silver blue he's never seen before in nature. Brighter than the sky overhead, darker than the crayon he used to draw river water as a boy. *Aquamarine.* It's the blue of the stones his mother loved, the ones he tried to save her with. Another few steps and he sees each fluctuating tendril houses a kaleidoscope of silvers and blues, and he gets the sudden nauseating feeling that if he stares into them too closely, he might lose all sense of himself. In a film, a sight like this should be accompanied by strange choral music. But up here, its only soundtrack is the hisses and crackles of the surrounding fires.

Then he sees the glowing silver handprints. They match, one on each metal armrest. They emit more undulating tendrils.

This seat was never empty, he thinks. *Someone was in it, and they were gripping those armrests as the plane went down, and then whatever happened, they turned into this.*

The word *ghost* is on the tip of his tongue, but it's like no ghost he's ever seen in a picture book or film. No face, no screaming O of a mouth, no reaching arms. No silhouette or outline that looks vaguely human. Instead, it looks like a sea anemone made of heavenly blue smoke.

Vernon reaches for the nearest tendril. It recoils like a shy snake, a pocket of normal air forming around his finger. He's disappointed. Its colors are so inviting, so soothing, he'd expected contact with it to produce that same experience. Then it occurs to him to reach for one of the handprints. The density of the radiance rising from each one might be too concentrated, too sluggish, to pull away from his touch in time.

As he bends forward, he sees the shimmer draw back from his head, but as it draws back, something else peels away from it. A slender thread of luminescence made up of something that reminds him of dandelion seeds blown free, only they're glowing. And moving toward him with determination. Dazzled, Vernon lowers his arm, standing as still as he can as the particles twist and somersault through the air on a path toward his face. Then, with a jolt, he realizes they've vanished.

Then he sees them appear again. They're directly under his nose, pulsing toward him and away, riding the tides of his breath. Up close, peering down his nose at them, he can see that what at first looked like dandelion seeds are actually tiny clusters of smaller blue particles that shimmer as they orbit each other. It's their fluid movement that dazzles him. Along with their color.

The particles are riding his inhales and exhales, staying close to his nose and mouth, as if they're waiting for him to breathe them in. Waiting for an invitation to enter his body.

He inhales, quick, sharp, deep.

A shock of freezing cold fires up both nostrils. His throat pops open, every muscle going instantly lax, forcing him to suck air like a drowning man even though he doesn't feel remotely breathless. Then it's like a blade has been driven through the center of his forehead, and that's when Vernon becomes convinced whatever he just inhaled is about to split his skull like the broken suitcases all around him were split by the crash.

Even though his eyes are screwed shut from the pain, he sees something. He sees twisted storefronts, the windows intact but their frames bent, and the frames look the way wood looks after Vernon's whittled away at it for hours. There are no signs on the windows, but their shapes, even contorted, are vaguely familiar.

Spurlock, the town he was forced to leave. But it's like a vision he might have dreamed, and so he figures the shock of whatever the particles had just done to his body kicked a stray fragment of a nightmare to the front of his brain.

He forces his eyes open.

His hands are glowing.

The roaring pain in his skull collapses into a blissful rush down his body. While his eyes were closed, while he battled the vision of his hometown, he bent forward without realizing it, and now he feels like he's just taken the greatest, most longed-for shit of his life. All the tense connections of muscle and bone inside him have softened into something pliable, like stalks of wheat swayed by gentle winds.

At first, he thinks the glow is the reflection of the airplane seat's weird magic on his skin. But that's not right. He's emanating a more muted version of the same radiance. Not in thick, undulating tendrils. This is a tight, skin-hugging layer of bright silvery blue.

He thrusts his arms out to better see them. The gesture sends some kind of energy wave into the air in front of him. He can't see it, but he can see its effect. The glowing airplane seat and the one attached to it, the one containing the corpse of the woman in the red suit, are hovering off the ground and farther from him than they were before, as if he pushed them away and then up with his outstretched arms before freezing them in place when he did.

Their sudden levitation knocks the corpse of the mangled woman in the bright red pantsuit to one side. Her right arm and shoulder now dangle over the armrest; what's left of her curly brown hair drapes the shorn-off side of her face. Her seat's coated in the same silvery-blue light that's been pulsing off the empty seat next to hers since Vernon was drawn here. But the behavior of this glow is different from the swaying, rising tendrils next to her. This radiance comes from Vernon's outstretched hand, and it covers the seat the same way it now covers his skin.

The seats are coming back to earth now, like the slow turn of a steering wheel that's been abandoned while a car's in motion.

In his mind's eye, he sees them rising again.

And they do. They rise on his mental command. And Vernon hears his own gleeful, stuttering breaths.

Higher and higher the seats rise, one still glowing with heavenly light, the other containing slumped remains whose grotesque form seems less and less suited to this divine moment.

He's tired of looking at the woman. She doesn't belong here. She's a distraction. Vernon imagines the seat belt around her waist popping open, and it does. Imagines her sliding forward out of the seat, and she does, falling to the ground with a wet smack.

Now he can focus.

Focus on the fact that with one quick inhale he has plugged himself into some source, some current, that makes him feel light as a feather on the inside, while giving him the power to move objects with his mind. But it's the familiar color that brings with it the most joy, that suggests none of this was an accident.

It's the color of the aquamarine she brought me that day, he thinks.

Vernon was ten, maybe eleven, he's not sure. They'd been hiking a creek bed close to the base of Mount Antero, his mother in search of the occasional glimmering polished river rocks she enjoyed using in her work. She always kept her hair short and parted on one side so she didn't have to hold it out of her face while she was bent over her worktable or reading the homeschool textbooks aloud with him. She was standing in the creek, the clear, cool water flowing around her rubber boots, as she sifted through the shallows with gloved hands.

"It's aquamarine, Vernon." Saying his name in that warm, enthusiastic way that always made him feel safe and seen. "It's very rare to find it way down here. You have to go to the top of the mountain to find it. A storm must have washed it down. Isn't it beautiful? Stones have much longer lives than we do, and so if we keep them close, if we can care for them, they can protect us."

A crawling feeling rises up the back of his neck now, new and seemingly separate from the lightness in his body, a sense that he's being approached. When he turns, he sees only more wreckage and low, guttering fires. Then he hears a gasping sound.

He spots the source several feet away, a man in smoke-blackened jeans and a shredded, bloody dress shirt, still tethered to his seat gasping for breath in between coughs. He can't tell if the man's face is covered with soot or if he's actually that burned. When the man opens his eyes, the whites glow bright against his charcoaled skin. He lets out a bellow that combines anger and fear, as if his only hope for survival is to make Vernon look his way again.

The sound reminds Vernon that a man's every emotion sits atop a bend of dangerous and destructive anger. It reminds him of the grunts and moans made by the men who drove him out of town, the ones who dropped their voices to growls so he wouldn't recognize them, which meant he knew them, had probably known them most of his life, the men who assured him if he ever set foot in Spurlock, Colorado, again he'd end up six feet under it.

Vernon's only thought is that he must stop this sound. That it has no place in this perfect moment his mother has sent him from heaven.

Later, he'll realize that he made the moves in his mind. But in the moment, they're all just pieces of the same thought: *Shut the fuck up.*

With a soft pop, one of the jagged metal spines snaps free from the levitating seats and flies through the air, spearing the bellowing man straight through his open mouth. Head pinned to the back of his seat, mouth agape and frozen around the metal spear's width, the suited man's breath leaves him in a series of rasping, high-pitched whistles.

Vernon is still dazzled by the ease of what he's done when, a few yards away, something darts behind three intact windows in a gnarled piece of the plane's sidewall.

It can't be a survivor. The shadow moves with too much energy and speed. Sprightly, childlike. As he moves closer, he sees that the fragment of fuselage rests against an incinerated tree stump.

Vernon raises his hand, studies its glow, reminds himself that this gift, this gift that has come down from heaven, means he no longer has to be afraid. Even of ghosts.

Then, beyond his fingers, he sees a little boy in a big puffy orange jacket with a mess of blond hair staring back at him from inside one of the smoke-blackened windows. There is accusation in the child's eyes. The boy turns and runs. Just before he vanishes, Vernon wills the window to explode outward and it does. But there is no living boy or ghost on the other side, just a smoking, jagged hole revealing the skeletal remains of a tree and the deformed engine parts beyond.

Vernon turns to the gift from his mother, uses his newfound power to tear the seat that smokes with heavenly blue light free of the one that once contained the corpse of the woman in the red suit. Liberated now, his gift from heaven, his mother's gift for him, floats above him, ready to be claimed. Perhaps the ghost of the little boy knew this and it's why he was angry with Vernon. He knew that the plane was brought down by a gift Vernon's mother had sent him from heaven.

By the time he crests the slope and reaches the trees from which he first saw the plane tearing out of the clear blue sky, Vernon hears the approach of helicopters for the first time. But by then, he's moving deeper into the forest. From a distance, it probably looks like the shimmering airplane seat is Vernon's North Star, and that makes perfect sense, he thinks, driving it forward, because he plans to follow his mother's magic all the way home.

3

Claire is several blocks from her house when she sees a little boy's face staring at her in the rearview mirror, so close she can practically see up the kid's nostrils.

She screams and slams into a parked Volvo.

The airbags don't detonate, but the crash is loud enough to draw the attention of several people in the park nearby. A muscle-bound guy in a tank top starts running toward her.

She's got no choice.

She has to medicate now. What she just saw was impossible. The boy's face was so close to the glass he would have to have been leaning forward from the back seat and staring right into the mirror to be reflected that way. But there's no little boy in the car with her. Just her neglected pill bottle. She pops the armrest, dumps three—*no, let's go with four since we're actually, literally losing our shit right now*—little blue pills into her palm and gulps them down with a swig from her water bottle, barely feeling them in her throat as they go down. Then someone's knocking hard on her window, and she averts her eyes from the glass as she pops open the door with one hand.

"Ma'am, are you—"

"My brother's on that plane."

The excuse tears from her like the ones she used to make to her mom when she got a B minus. It fills her with shame, like she's using this sudden tragedy to distract from the fact that she just had her first fender bender in years, even though she's barely had time to process said tragedy.

The man's demeanor changes from defensive to piteous. "Oh God. Ascent Air? Oh my God. I'm so sorry." His tone twists her gut worse than the hallucinations, worse than the video she watched back at school. She couldn't bring herself to turn on the radio while she drove, and this guy's got more news about the crash than she does, and it's clearly bad.

Smartphones, devastating the world one instantly delivered tragedy at a time.

Claire steps from her car, lets him put a hand on her shoulder to steady her.

"I'm sorry," she says. "I'm just trying to get home. Is the Volvo yours?"

"Yeah, but who cares. It's a dent."

"I'll give you my insurance."

"Forget it. I'll give you a ride."

"No, I'm just a few blocks. I'll walk."

"Well, at least let me park you. We can't just leave your car like this."

She's not even sure what he means until he tugs her keys from her hand. For a second, she thinks he might be about to steal her car. The man backs her car away from the tail of his, revealing she's left several dents, not just one, and a clawlike scratch to boot.

And then she sees the little boy again. He's not inside her car; it's like he's contained within the passenger-side window and everything behind him is a veil of fog, but when he slams his little fists against the glass, they make no sound, and his screaming O of a mouth is silent too. And she recognizes him. He's nine years old with a mess of blond hair, wearing that bright puffy orange jacket she used to make fun of. Poe.

Her little brother is somehow trapped inside a reflection.

Which means she has finally gone nuts.

"No!" she screams.

She whirls and stumbles right into the path of a car that blares its horn as it swerves to avoid her.

She spins back toward the sidewalk, but the thought of hallucinating again is more terrifying than being run over, so she throws her hands over her eyes. When her toes knock into the curb, she steps up onto the sidewalk, listening as the man cuts her engine and steps from the car, her keys jangling in his hand.

"Ma'am."

"What's the latest?" she asks. "About the plane."

She summons all her courage and looks up at him. His mouth is slack. She feels sorry for him. One second he's working out in a beautiful sunlit park, the next he's comforting some crazy lady whose sudden intrusion into his day has made a disturbing headline uncomfortably real. But his expression makes something else clear. He's got an answer to her question, and he doesn't want to give it to her.

"Ma'am, I'm *so* sorry," he finally manages.

Crashed, she thinks. Realizing some foolish part of her thought the footage she'd seen on the laptop might end some other way. An emergency landing, maybe. Something other than death. Or insanity. She closes her eyes, feels the hot sting of tears; then something's pressing against her chest. It's her purse. She forgot it inside her car.

"Ma'am, are you sure you don't want me to—"

She starts for her house, quickens her steps, hoping increased circulation will pump the Ativan through her faster, sending a dousing spray across the hallucinations that caused her little fender bender. But she's avoiding the windows of every parked car, eyes glued to the pavement as she walks.

Glass is suspect now. Glass is where her new and spreading crazy has taken up residence.

When Claire's mother moved her from Spokane to California after the divorce, when it became clear Poe would stay with their dad, the woman became a veritable tape loop of facts about why their new home would be better than the last. And one of the items on that perpetual list of perks was the abundance of sweet-gum trees in their new neighborhood in Eagle Rock, close to where she'd landed a job as an office manager at Occidental College. The trees, she promised Claire, were some of the few in Southern California that put on a brilliant display in autumn, their fat palm-size leaves papering the sidewalks and making piles big enough for children to play in.

It's the trees Claire focuses on now as, covered in sweat and feeling as if she's run ten miles, she walks the rest of the way home. She's doing her best to savor the pleasant dampening effect their canopy of orange branches has on the fierce California sun, to count her careful footsteps to keep within reach of the nearest mailbox or fence post. Breathing five counts in and ten counts out, it takes all the energy she has to marshal the steady pose of a woman whose mind isn't falling apart by the minute.

The first time Claire injured herself enough to draw blood in front of her new stepsister, Melissa went for the first-aid kit without pausing to grip Claire's injured hand or pelt her with a dozen questions about how and where it hurt. Claire's parents had always greeted every injury as if it were a four-alarm fire, so for a while afterward, she interpreted her stepsister's wordless competence as cold dismissal. In the years since, she's come to understand that quickly dispensing a needed solution is Melissa's way of showing love and concern.

It's what she's doing now as she meets Claire on the sidewalk in front of the little Craftsman house Claire inherited from her mother, guiding her inside with one arm around her waist. No words or invasive questions, just smooth, forward motion in the direction of comfort and shelter. It was the way of Melissa's late father too, an economics professor who gave Claire's mother the stable and reliable marriage her father couldn't. Efficiency without effusiveness.

Claire can't bring herself to tell Melissa that she almost got run over, because she was terrified of what she might see reflected in the front windows of the house.

Melissa's stocky husband is brewing coffee in the kitchen. Claire could count on one hand the times she's seen Phil Hasteck in anything besides a rumpled men's dress shirt and chinos, and now isn't one of them. Melissa, she notices for the first time, is wearing the black cashmere blazer and skirt she reserves for buyers who aren't interested in seeing any listings under a million. The thought that her stepsister and brother-in-law might have abandoned important clients to help Claire makes her eyes well. But she can't attempt conversation. Four pills in one gulp would be enough to knock her on her ass in any other circumstance, but she's yet to feel their narcotic pull. She will, though. Any second now, she's sure.

"Bedroom," she says.

Melissa nods, navigates them through the kitchen. As Claire's escorted past him, Phil turns, reaches out for her. She's never seen the man's lantern-jawed face so twisted by grief, not even when Claire's mother died. But Melissa keeps moving Claire through the kitchen, and that's when Claire sees the living room television has been tuned to CNN and is playing the same video she saw back at school.

Suddenly she's standing next to the bed and staring down at the gleaming hardwood floor her mother thought was such a perk of this quaint little house as Melissa draws back the comforter Claire had straightened just a few hours before. It feels rude to sink down on top of it, given how primly Melissa arranged it for her. But Claire's incapable of much else, and Melissa doesn't seem offended. Once Claire's curled into the fetal position, her stepsister's hand comes to rest gently on her shoulder. It lingers there. Claire can't bring herself to turn over and look at her, convinced Melissa will morph into some terrible hallucination of Poe the second she does.

How terrible was it, though? she thinks. *He just looked like a little boy.*

A little boy trapped inside glass.

"Tell me," Claire says.

"Claire, let's get you some food or something to—"

"Just tell me the latest."

After a long silence, Melissa asks, "Is there any chance he missed it?"

"I texted him at a stoplight. Check my phone. The password's 4312."

She can hear the unvoiced question her stepsister might ask in any other circumstance. *You haven't checked since then?* To which Claire could only respond with, *Going insane distracted me.*

"A friend of his from New York," Melissa says. "Some guy named Benton. He's not in your phone book, but he says he just heard the news. Is that the boyfriend? The drug dealer?"

"No, that was Danny. Benton's his AA sponsor."

"What's an AA sponsor?"

"Someone he checks in with. Like a sober support system kind of thing. He would know if Poe hadn't got on the flight."

A short pause. "He says he's here for you."

Which means he knows Poe got on the flight.

"Who else?" Claire asks. When her stepsister doesn't answer, Claire resorts to her nickname. "Missy?"

"He's not here, Claire. He didn't text."

"Tell me what they're saying on TV."

"Claire, why don't I call Dr. Fitzsimmons and—"

"Melissa, please."

The mattress dips as Melissa sits on the side of the bed. Her grip on Claire's hand tightens. "They're saying there was a distress call from the cockpit around 12:40. They said the left engine came apart and the cabin was depressurizing and . . . The people on TV are talking about hydraulics being severed by pieces of the engine . . . Claire, it's really bad. I mean, I could lie to you and tell you that it isn't, but it is—"

Melissa's not usually a crier, and in this moment her tears sound like an angry struggle.

Now Claire's squeezing her hand. Even amid the terrifying events of this day, comforting others comforts her.

"Bomb?" Claire asks.

"Maybe," Missy croaks. "The crash site's in the mountains. They just got there with helicopters. I don't want you watching any of it. I'm sorry the TV was on. When I saw you outside, I just ran out to get you and forgot to turn it off."

"I need you to cover all the mirrors in the house." Claire says it quickly, before she loses her nerve.

"Mirrors?"

"Yeah, I'm sorry, it's just . . . it's like a stress reaction I'm having right now. The sight of myself is just . . . I can't take it, so if you could just . . ."

"Of course, sure."

"And the windows. Draw all the shades."

"Sure."

Melissa's weight leaves the bed. She is relieved, no doubt, to have a clear set of instructions.

And then Claire's alone. Alone with the full-length standing mirror she uses to check herself after she finishes getting dressed for work each morning. The door opens and Melissa enters with a stack of bath towels draped over one arm, and Claire watches silently as she drapes one over the top of the mirror and adjusts it as if it's a design element and not a completely ridiculous concession to a state of mental collapse. Then Melissa turns, and Claire realizes her mistake. By lying and saying it was her own reflection she wanted to avoid, she's let

Melissa believe covering the top half of the mirror will be sufficient. But by then Melissa's dropping the roman shades over both windows.

"How's that?" she asks when she's done.

Claire wants to tell her it's not enough. But that would sound completely nuts.

And she would rather feel that way than sound that way.

And there is a part of her—a part of her that's possibly been emboldened by the spreading effect of the Ativan—that wants to leave the mirror exposed, just to see what happens.

"I'll get the others," Melissa says, then leaves the room.

"Thank you," Claire whispers.

She tells herself not to, but she can't resist. She slides her feet to the floor, approaches the mirror, then tugs the towel away.

She's staring at herself. She looks wrecked, like she did that one morning a few years ago after she drank way too much at Melissa and Phil's Memorial Day party and ended up chewing her Uber driver's ear off about her crazy alien-hunting dad. But no little Poe pops up behind her in that puffy orange jacket, the one she used to say made him look like a traffic cone. It was his San Francisco jacket, they called it, because he wore it during their last big family trip together. And whenever they called it that, no matter where they were or what they were doing, Poe would jump his feet apart and make a triangle with his arms above his head. But what would really crack her up was how he stuck out his lip and furrowed his brow whenever he struck the pose. "Is that your traffic-cone face?" she'd ask him, and they'd all laugh until they could barely breathe. That trip was their last happy memory as a family. And she's always wondered if that was part of why Poe had stayed centered mostly around the Bay Area during his nomadic wanderings as a grown-up.

The relief of not hallucinating is replaced by the weight of grief.

Claire, it's really bad, she hears Melissa say.

If he *was* a ghost, perhaps he was just passing through.

Claire raises her hands to her mouth to hold in the sob.

Acceptance. By accepting that he's gone, the hallucinations have stopped, but with acceptance comes an awful, irreversible truth. Her brother, taken from her on the eve of their reconciliation. She'd dreamed they'd go to movies together again, stay up late talking about their problems. Try to find ways to do more sophisticated and grown-up versions of all the things they'd loved to do together as kids.

When she looks in the mirror now, the details of her bedroom are blurred, fading, replaced by a cloudy white.

It's fog.

She backs away from the mirror. Something is emerging from the fog, near the faint reflection of her torso. She sees knotted, weathered boards extending away from her, and there he is, farther away this time, but in the same orange jacket. His messy blond hair tousled by winds she can't feel. He jumps, landing with his feet apart and his arms in a triangle over his head.

The mirror flies backward.

She's kicked it before she could stop herself. It collides with the wall behind it, shattering into several big pieces and dozens of smaller ones. Poe falls with it, as if some single version of him, now divided into pieces, is racing toward the other side of the shards as they fall and separate. Melissa's arms are around Claire suddenly, and she sinks to the floor sobbing. In one of the shards of glass, child Poe seems to back away far enough for his entire face to come into view. His face falls, cheeks pouting, and he turns and walks off into the fog. The sadness in his eyes seems as real as the floor beneath her.

A second later, the fog vanishes from the glass as if it has left with him.

4

The airplane seat crashes to the earth.

Vernon looks down at his hand. He's no longer glowing.

His power didn't just fade; it ended as abruptly as someone flipping a switch.

The impact looked hard enough to do further damage to the thing, but it holds together, and Vernon can see the radiance acts like a pliable, luminescent skeleton.

He gasps for breath. Suddenly, it's as if the thirty or so minutes he spent connected to this miraculous current as he hiked away from the crash site has resulted in a cumulative exertion that's decided to exact its entire toll in a single moment.

It's over, he realizes. *Whatever it is, is over.*

But the seat still glows.

So it can't be *that* over.

The woods between the crash site and his cabin got denser as he traveled, but it was easier going than usual since he could now snap thick, clawing branches out of the way with his mind. A few black helicopters roared by overhead, but none circled back or seemed to zero in on the glowing light moving through the woods. Maybe the overstory was thick enough to keep it hidden, or maybe it doesn't glow as bright from way up there as it does down here on the ground.

He's got to get the thing under some kind of cover, though. If the people searching for the crash site spot his gift from the sky, they might come and try to take it from him. Then it occurs to him he's got no idea how much the seat actually weighs. If it's got to fly through the clouds, how heavy can it be?

When he approaches the seat and its radiant blue occupant, he expects a welcoming gesture of some sort. They've danced together, after all. But he's greeted by the same reflexive recoil. He crouches, slides both arms under the seat cushion, watches wide-eyed as the radiance draws back along the tattered fabric like a retreating octopus. It's not shrinking, just gathering at the top of the seat, concentrating as far away from him as it can without leaving the fabric. Because it looks like it can't leave the seat—not its cushions or its bent metal struts. It's anchored to this material by a force Vernon doesn't understand.

Good, he thinks. *That'll make it easier to carry.*

He's right. He barks with laughter when he realizes how light it is. Hell, he could have carried it away from the crash site in both arms. The seat can't weigh more than ten or twelve pounds. It's the shape that makes it awkward. After a few minutes of struggle, he realizes the best way to transport it is to flip it upside down so that the cushion and legs are sticking into the air above his head as the rest of it sits against his back like a backpack. He half expects the radiance to lose its battle against gravity and pour down over him in a waterfall. It does nothing of the kind. It must be rising up off the back of the chair like smoke from a magical chimney, all to avoid contact with his skin.

He's a few paces from the cabin when he sees the same glowing blue particles tumbling through the air on either side of his face, bound for his exhales.

It's just like the first time. They seek out his breath, but they don't force their way into his nose and mouth. He has to invite them in with a long, deep inhale. Which he'll do again in time. But for now, he needs a break. Needs some time to sit with the gift and study it. His mother always told him the solution to his strangeness was clear, orderly directions. She wouldn't have sent him this gift if she didn't have some for him now.

His mother always told him that she loved him despite his limitations. But she also told him that anyone could overcome their limitations through discipline and effort. Both things became so hard with her gone; maybe she got tired of watching him struggle. And that's why she's sent him this gift. So he could overcome his limitations.

But *love* is a word he's never quite understood. It slaps the outsides of his mind like a raindrop hitting the windshield when the car's going fast, spreads out in all directions, slowly losing its center the more he tries to learn its shape. Love is something his mother said as she did things he liked, gave him things he wanted. And so in his mind, everything his mother did was love. And when she was gone, so was love.

He knows what the opposite of love is. It's what Uncle Johnny did to him in the yard that day when he was little, the way he made blackness and stars come. That was not love. That was why they never went back to Johnny's house after Vernon spent those days in the hospital, attached to beeping machines and smelling all sorts of plastic smells. He'd never known plastic could smell so many different ways until he went to the hospital. After they moved to Spurlock, Vernon learned another word. It was the word his mother used to describe what Uncle Johnny did to him; it's a word that makes tingles happen in his chest even now, makes him want to rub his hands together to burn off the excess energy that surges through him whenever he hears it.

That word is *torture*.

His mother didn't like the excitement some words brought forth in him. She explained again and again that what had been done to him sometimes made him put the wrong feelings to the wrong words, or no feeling to a word that needed one. This wasn't his fault, she'd explained. Things had been done to him, bad things—Vernon knew she meant torture but didn't want to say it around him because it got him excited—and this was the reason for his strangeness.

Was it love he saw in his mother's eyes the day everything changed?

Vernon's pretty sure it was terror.

One minute she was making them breakfast; then she turned to him as if he'd said or done something strange, but all he'd been doing was outlining a picture of politicians in the newspaper and filling in their faces with black ink because he liked the shapes of their heads better that way. He did it all the time, and she'd never said anything about it. Before he could defend himself, she hit the floor on one knee, and he realized then the blank expression on her face wasn't about him. It was about something happening inside her body, something so bad she couldn't say what it was. When she fell to her side, she didn't moan softly and scramble to her feet like she always did when she tripped. Didn't make some comment about how her knees were aging faster than the rest of her. Instead, she lay there like a fallen tree in the forest.

He crawled across the floor toward her, gathered her into his arms, and hoisted her head onto his lap. Expected her eyes to flutter open, expected a weak whisper explaining what she was feeling. But her lips stayed slightly parted, and when he placed his fingers there he couldn't feel a breath. But he wasn't seeing her face; he was seeing the terrible look she'd given him as she'd gone down. Over and over again, he was seeing it. He peeled back her eyelids, but her pupils stared. The lids didn't tug at his fingers. No blinks. No blinks at all. And that's when the true meaning of a word that has always seemed as sweeping, as vaporous and ill defined as love, filled Vernon.

Death.

I saw death.

Death is no blinks.

He was still thinking these words when there was an explosion just above his head. Something hot and sticky lashed the back of his neck. It had to have come from the pot his mother had set to boil on the stove right before she went down. The eggs in it were exploding. One after the other, like little mines.

And this seemed unfair, that he had to tend to breakfast when all he wanted was to hold on to his mother and see if there was still life stuffed down way deep inside her. He gently set her to the floor, rose to his feet, and turned off the stove. That's when he realized his breaths sounded strange. Like a tired dog that'd been out in the heat, and he thought, this was a moment when his mother would rush around in search of a solution. This was a moment like when the street flooded during the big storm and they had to put sandbags under the front doors of the shop, and she said, "Now, Vernon. We need to get to work *right now.*"

Her eyes, he thought. *The problem was in her eyes. I could see death in her eyes, and now there are no blinks. And that means her life was coming out of her eyes, and maybe I can stop it just like we stopped the flood from getting into the shop.*

After she'd discovered the aquamarine stones that had washed off Mount Antero into that creek, they made another, much longer hike up the mountain's peak to find more. Up high, where the slopes were windswept and free of trees, aquamarine might shimmer every few feet in the fine brown dirt. They'd both filled little pouches that day, and his mother had been happy. Proud of him for making the long and difficult hike without getting distracted. Once they got back to the car, she'd taken him for ice cream at Pelton's on Pine Street—strawberry, his favorite. He loved the ice cream parlor because when his mother took him there, when she looked at him as if he could do no wrong, the other people in town stopped looking at him as if they thought he'd try to stab them the second their backs were turned. When he and his mother got home, they spread their finds out on a blanket on the floor, and after studying them all with bright eyes, his mother had smiled at him and said, "You know, I'm not going to use these, Vernon. I'm going to save them so they always remind us of this special day. And this will be our color always. Our special color. The color of heaven."

Vernon did feel special that day, surrounded by what she called her love for him.

A stone lives longer than we do.

It's the most important thing she ever taught him.

So Vernon went to get the aquamarine. She kept the plastic containers in a special box on a shelf above her workstation. The stones were clean and polished, and he thought that was a good sign, a sign she knew this moment was coming.

He didn't move her off the kitchen floor because he feared that might waste valuable time, so with her favorite glue gun, he went to work. Doing it made him feel better, even though he knew the glue felt hotter than usual because the skin he was applying it to kept getting colder. It took one entire tub to cover her eyes, nose, and mouth. And he wanted to save some aquamarine for her when she came back. That seemed fine. He'd used it to cover the most important parts, the parts where life leaked free. To cover the rest of her face, he used her other stones, and by the time he was done, his mother was adorned with a glimmering, rainbow-hued mask made of the things she loved most. Vernon sank to the floor, rested his back against the cabinet under the sink, pulled her as far up onto his lap as he could so he could stare down at her new face as he ran his hands through her hair.

It didn't feel natural running his hands through her hair, but it's what she used to do to the dog before she gave it away because she was afraid Vernon might hurt it.

But when the heat didn't return to her body, when the face staring up at him started to look alien, he realized it wasn't working. The mask hadn't captured the last of her life inside her. The stones didn't capture death. After a while—he's not sure how long—he started shaking her, and when none of the stones came free, he heard a voice that sounded like his uncle Johnny's.

You only did it to make that look go away, the voice said. *All you did was try to cover up that look on her face as she went down, down, down, forever. You're a FREAK who can't save SHIT, kid.*

He made sounds he'd never made before, then sounds so loud they brought the Scuttlers from down the road. When his neighbors appeared in the doorway, wide-eyed at the sight that greeted them on the kitchen floor, he couldn't bring himself to explain. Couldn't bring himself to tell them he let the life leak out of his momma and there was nothing he could do to stop it.

Sheriff Jorgensen and the doctors came and, eventually, the men in hoods. They let him grab one little plastic tub full of the aquamarine, but when he went for the second, one of the men slapped him on the back of the head, causing Vernon to spill the stones to the floor. "The stuff you *need*, dipshit," he snarled behind the fabric covering his face.

He'd failed his mother, he thought as the men drove him far from home with a blindfold around his eyes. His mother had always understood his strangeness and protected him from what the world might do to him over it, and he'd failed her in her worst moment.

But wasn't it the stones that had failed him?

A branch snaps somewhere behind Vernon. He turns as quickly as he can with the chair on his back, half expecting to see the little boy in the orange jacket again. But Vernon hasn't felt his ghostly presence since leaving the crash site, so maybe that's where the boy stayed. And there's no ghost in the woods behind him, nothing but branches bathed in the magical glow from the chair.

But now that Vernon is alone with this incredible power . . .

That should feel good. But first, he has to make sure he'll be able to fill himself with it a second time.

———

Two Dog Flats Grill has an expansive view across the sparkling waters of Saint Mary Lake to the granite spires of some of the most dramatic peaks on the eastern edge of Glacier National Park. Randy Drummond knows the view well, but today it's a stunner. And there's barely anyone else around to see it. Bad for them, good for Randy. It means he and James McDermott have the place mostly to themselves, save for the family on the other side of the restaurant with a baby letting out opera-level shrieks.

The place should stay this empty until evening time. Unless an early snow blows in, Going-to-the-Sun Road won't close for another few weeks, so as soon as it starts to get a little dark, the restaurant will fill up with tourists who made the jaw-dropping trip earlier that day. A nice strong drink is the first thing most visitors need after driving the narrow two-lane road where the waist-high stone barrier between you and a ten-thousand-foot drop sometimes vanishes completely.

Randy welcomes the privacy for the last meal he'll have with James before the man's replacement takes over. The park ranger has served them well over the years, no doubt thanks to backpacks full of cash like the one Randy slid under the table when James arrived. This one's bigger than most. A goodbye gift, if you will. Randy's going to miss the old guy. He's been easy to understand. Easy to manipulate. He's divorced, but he's got a mother in South Dakota with chronic diabetes and lousy insurance, so the cash has been helpful, and the questions have been few. No vices that make him unstable. Or chatty. His replacement at the Park Service is a different story.

"Missed you at the retirement party," James says.

"Don't remember an invite."

"I texted you one, I think."

Randy grunts, eats one of James's french fries without asking for permission. They only communicate using prepaid cell phones

Randy replaces twice a year. He figures the disposable little things aren't good with attachments.

"Was it fun?" Randy asks.

"What do you think?"

"Take it the National Park Service didn't spring for a stripper."

"A stripper's your idea of fun, huh?"

Randy shrugs. Wonders if he'll miss James because he's used to Randy's injuries and no longer stares-without-staring at the way the facial reconstruction surgeries he underwent at Bethesda make it look as if his right eye sits too loose inside his skull.

"What do you do for fun, Randy Drummond?"

It's a good damn question and one he's not interested in answering. So he shrugs, as if the whole idea of fun is something nobody explained to him when he was a kid.

James's fingers caress the longneck he ordered after the food came. It's the first time the man's consumed alcohol in his presence, a little tribute to the fact that their professional relationship is coming to an end as of this meal.

"Did we ever get close?" he asks. "You know, with . . ."

James gestures to the window. He's gesturing to the park, to its vast expanse, to the mystery contained within. Contained by *them*.

"Three years ago," Randy says, "a couple of big lightning storms put us in the risk window for a few weeks. That was the closest we got. But we made it through. You did your end and I did mine, and we ran a tight ship. I'm going to miss working with you."

James nods, but it's clear he's not satisfied with the answer. Just like Randy is now inheriting James's replacement, James inherited Randy a few years back. James was there the night they flew Apollo and Artemis to the hospital, still talks about the glimpse he got of the little girl in her bed, arm in a cast and scratches latticing her pale face, expression so stunned it was like she'd been dropped in from another world and couldn't figure out this one. Working to avoid a repeat of a sight like that is probably part of what kept James so loyal over the years. The same won't be true of the little whippersnapper that's replacing him. Which means Randy will have to plop down more money, or just scare the shit out of the guy now and then to keep his mouth shut. He's not above doing either.

"Whatcha thinking, James?"

"You're never going to tell me what's out there, are you."

Randy could feel the question coming like a thunderstorm building over the park. But that doesn't mean he's got an answer for it. He breaks eye contact first, uncaps the bottle of ketchup, pours some onto the side of his bread plate. The waiter comes and asks them if they'd like anything else, and Randy shakes his head. For a long while neither man speaks. They listen to the clatter of dishes being carried to the kitchen.

Finally, Randy says, "The new guy bought a drone. Tell him to shelve it."

"Scott? The drone's for fun. He takes it out on his boat on Flathead."

"He's had the boat three years. He bought the drone three weeks ago. For cash. After my first meeting with him."

Over the years with James, Randy has dropped subtle hints about the extent of their surveillance. But he's never had to go full NSA on him. The same might not be true of his replacement, and Randy figures it's better to have James relay that message first, along with all the nervous fear the man might add to it.

"I'll say something to him," James says quietly.

"Appreciate that."

Randy would have preferred to end their last meal together on a more cheerful note. But his work will continue no matter who he's dealing with, and bringing the new guy into line is priority one. Randy stands, extends his hand. James does the same. For a second, he thinks they might be able to end this warmly, which would be nice.

"You ever killed anyone, Randy Drummond?"

"I'm not at liberty to discuss my operations overseas."

"I'm talking about Montana."

Randy's purposes are best served by not answering at all, so he smiles and bows his head, as if the question somehow flatters him. Then he releases James's grip, tips his Stetson, and heads for the door.

———

By the time Randy gets inside the Trailhawk, he's already seen the two missed calls from Benjamin Running Creek. They both came in during lunch, which he told the ranch crew about that morning, so whatever Ben's calling him about must be urgent.

He locks the doors against the bracing down-mountain wind, connects the phone to the SUV's Bluetooth speakers, and starts for the road.

Ben answers after the first ring. "Where you at?"

"Just leaving the diner. What's up?"

"Passenger jet went down in Colorado a little while ago," he says. "Apollo was on it."

It takes Randy a second or two to process what Ben's saying and what it really means. Like three cars slamming into each other at the same time, this feeling. And each one's full of literal bullshit and babies.

"You're kidding," he finally says.

"I'm not," Ben says.

It's chilly outside, but a thread of sweat travels Randy's spine. "Rupert?"

"He wasn't flying west with the kid. He tailed him to JFK; then he headed to the city so he could check on the bugs we got in the apartment. He's standing by, waiting for orders."

"Where's the crash site?" Randy asks.

"Remote. Mount Elbert, it looks like. They had to use military helicopters to reach it."

"And no word of . . . anything strange?"

"Other than the bodies and the wreckage? No, but it's soon."

"How's Papa Bear taking the news?" Randy asks.

"Yelling, pacing, drinking. But that's a regular day for him. If his walls could talk, they would tell him to shut the fuck up."

It's a sad statement on what's been done to the Huntley family that they've given the dad this shitty, childish moniker, but the kids are nicknamed after Greek gods.

"He just lost his kid. Maybe a little respect."

"Did he, though?" Ben asks.

"All right, all hands on deck," Randy says. "Full team meeting at the tech center in thirty. Conference Rupe in from New York. And Sean, he's still in LA?"

"Eagle Rock. Outside Artemis's house. The stepsister and her husband are with her. Says she's taking it badly, drove off the road on the way home."

"Conference him in too."

"We knew this day would come," Ben says.

"Yeah, but not with this many damn cameras aimed at it and military helicopters overhead. Jesus fucking Christ."

Randy hangs up and starts in the direction of Thunder Ranch.

5

It took Claire an hour to get Melissa to leave the bedroom, an hour of explaining that she'd taken too many of her little blue friends that morning when she was in shock and that's why she'd freaked out on the mirror. But as she'd collected the broken glass off the floor, first with a hand broom, then with bath towels to protect her skin from the larger shards, Melissa never let Claire out of her sight, as if she worried she might try to grab a shard and slash her wrists with it.

Finally, Melissa relented, but she insisted Claire leave the door open a crack, which has forced her to overhear little snippets of the phone calls her stepsister is having with airline representatives and the concerned friends and relatives who have started calling the house because Claire's not answering her cell phone. The rare exchanges between Melissa and Phil are sounding more and more tense. Phil's been pacing so badly Melissa asked him to sit down on more than one occasion. It's like the crash has hit him on a deep and personal level. Which makes no sense. He'd only met Poe once, at her mother's funeral.

Claire's biggest fear now is that her stepsister will take it upon herself to call Dr. Fitzsimmons, and then Claire will be obligated to tell her therapist how many pills she's swallowed since that morning. She dreads the prospect he might suggest some sort of a facility. On a temporary basis, of course. It's always been a point of pride for her that she's managed to hold her mental health issues in check while keeping terrifying terms like *suicidal ideation* and *seventy-two-hour hold* at bay.

Does Melissa have the man's number? To ask would be to raise the subject, and Claire doesn't want to do that at all.

She keeps telling herself she needs to grab a pen and paper and write out everything that's happened to her since that morning, even if it just ends up being a laundry list of crazy she reads to Dr. Fitzsimmons at some point. But she's paralyzed, sitting with her feet up on the bed as if a monster might grab her from underneath it if she lowers her legs to the floor. Rocking back and forth like someone already in the madhouse.

Still, she's got no choice. Even though it will bring back memories of her attack at the whiteboard that morning, she's got to get a pen in hand. Like her mother, she's a list maker, someone who draws comfort from seeing complicated issues shrunk down to the level of ink and paper and bullet points. And the situation in which she currently finds herself is beyond complicated.

It's crazy, and it has been since the crash. But that's not completely accurate, she realizes with a jolt.

The crazy started before then, in front of the whiteboard.

Even though she told herself she wouldn't—not today of all days—she opens the browser on her phone. Hunting for a specific piece of information gives her a sense of purpose that makes it easier to wade through headlines like ALL LIVES ABOARD ASCENT AIR FLIGHT 62 FEARED LOST and ENGINE BREAKUP OR SABOTAGE? SPECULATION ABOUNDS ABOUT CRASHED TRANSCON AIRLINER. She doesn't allow herself to look too long at the first images of the smoking crash site taken from high in the air above.

Finally, Claire finds what she's looking for. It confirms Melissa's account when she got home. The distress call from the cockpit came in at 12:40 p.m. Mountain time. An hour ahead of the West Coast. The same time as her attack at the whiteboard in front of her American history class. An attack during which she'd written something against her will for the first time. A message.

love you bear.

She didn't know a damn thing about the crash yet, so she can't blame it on some kind of stress reaction, the way she's been explaining the hallucinations she's suffered since.

Crazy, she thinks. *This is crazy.*

In the nightstand is a notepad she used briefly during a failed attempt at dream journaling after her mother died. As soon as she takes the pen in hand, she feels it. The dizziness, the hollow feeling in her chest, the sense that all the blood in her body is moving into her right arm, toward the fingers gripping the ballpoint. The same feeling she had at school. She swings her legs to the floor and starts across the room for her purse.

Four pills, she thinks. *Five, if you count the one from earlier, and it's about to hit again. This is insane.*

But before she can get to the purse or the pills inside, her arm rears up as if possessed, and suddenly the tip of the pen is wedged deep in the wall above the bed.

Jesus, she thinks, as if she's watching it happen to someone else.

The pen in her hand is moving again, only instead of the squeak of felt on whiteboard, the bedroom fills with menacing sounds of wallpaper tearing and scratching against drywall.

Then, just like this morning, she's instantly released from this unseen grip.

When Claire stumbles away from the wall, she's grateful there are no staring, stunned students behind her to read this.

STOP WITH THE PILLS UR NOT NUTS BEAR

Relief. Why does she feel relief? What's just happened is impossible, crazy. But it feels like these words didn't come *from* her; they came *through* her. And while she was perfectly ready to believe her hallucinations in the car were the result of some psychotic break, she's not willing to believe she has dissociative identity disorder.

The tension returns to her arm. This time it feels less like an assault and more like an inviting urge caressing her arm muscles. She doesn't fight it, brings the pen to the notepad she just tugged from the nightstand drawer. Gives it the paper like leading a horse to water. And when she doesn't fight the long, broad sweeps of her hand that follow, the breathlessness and the racing heart don't return, and the whole thing feels less terrifying all of a sudden. Like surfing a wave instead of drowning. The hollow feeling in her chest is there, but it's got a different quality now. Like excitement. Adrenaline. Like she's taking big gulps of needed air after starving herself of oxygen.

"Claire!"

Her stepsister is behind her, approaching, drawn by the scratching sounds in the wall, no doubt. But Claire's determined to push through, and when Melissa and Phil see what she's doing, they stop cold on either side of her.

She has just completed a beautiful impressionistic sketch of a place that lives forever in her memories, a place she glimpsed in the full-length mirror a little while ago. Pier 39 in San Francisco, where her family spent hours during that long-ago trip. The view looks down from the second level onto the carousel she and Poe rode a dozen times, and rising from the cityscape beyond are the unmistakable outlines of Coit Tower and the Transamerica Pyramid. During their breaks from arcade games and carousel rides, she and Poe would head up to the pier's second level and watch their parents talk on one of the benches below, seemingly happy and content in each other's presence for the first time in a while. Claire had always believed that if not for the camping trip that happened the following year, the happiness her mother and father found in San Francisco might have sustained their marriage.

"You're still connected."

It's Phil who says these words. Melissa looks as astonished by them as Claire feels.

Phil is a business school graduate and a real estate agent whose favorite movies all involve football underdogs, and who only reads books in which men in the military do consequential things. He's never expressed a modicum of belief in religion or the paranormal in Claire's presence, and now he's staring at the drawing on Claire's nightstand as if it's evidence of something he's secretly suspected for some time.

"Phil?" Melissa finally asks.

Phil looks at both of them, a deer caught in the headlights.

"He asked me to help him. Poe. He reached out after he got sober. He needed somebody to watch Claire."

"Watch Claire do what?" Melissa hasn't been this tightly coiled since Phil accidentally let the dog out during one of their movie nights and she didn't want to blow up at him in front of the guests.

"Anything. Everything. He was . . ."

"We're listening," Melissa snaps.

"OK, um. The night of your date, Claire, remember? The bad one. Where you had your stomach thing."

"It was nothing," Melissa says. "The tests all came back negative."

"Poe was stabbed. In the stomach. At that exact time. In New York. He almost died. It's why he got sober. It was some sort of drug deal gone wrong. After that is when he got in touch."

Claire stares at Phil, waiting for him to look to the floor or fidget uncomfortably or do any of a hundred things to suggest he's made this up. He remains perfectly still.

"Why?" Claire asks. "Why did he get in touch?"

"He said when he stopped drinking and using drugs he started drawing things he'd never seen. And when he looked them up online, they were all in LA. And he'd only been here once, for the funeral. He drew your school, Claire. Has he ever been to your school? Have you sent him pictures?"

Claire figures this is a rhetorical question, but she shakes her head anyway. Because the answer is no.

"He could find pictures of the school online," Melissa says.

"Yeah, but we started talking and that's when we figured out—"

"Just talking?" Melissa asks.

"I didn't have an affair with Poe. Come on."

Melissa holds up her hands as if her husband's secrecy has placed all options on the table.

"A few weeks after we started talking, he almost got hit by a cab as he was stepping off a curb, and at the same time, *here*, in LA, Claire had to pull over on the way to school because she had one of her attacks and she didn't want to take a pill right before first period—"

"I told you that," Melissa snaps. "You know these things because *I* told you these things. Because your wife confided these things in you and—"

"I know, I know. He was going to spell it all out tonight at dinner. But he asked me not to say anything before then because he wanted to make the case to you first. He had a notebook full of entries, and he was going to bring it with him and lay it all out."

"Lay what out?" Melissa asks.

"That he and Claire have been . . . *connected* ever since that night in Glacier, and they've both tried to drug it out of existence."

"Claire isn't a drug addict!" Melissa says, exasperated. "She's under medical treatment for a psychiatric condition—possibly a traumatic brain injury—and her behavior is nothing like what Poe has—"

"It's not about judgment, Melissa. But the effect is the same. He said the pills could be blotting out the connection on Claire's end and that if she would stop taking them, then maybe . . ."

Phil follows Claire's gaze and falls silent. Apparently he and Melissa both missed the sight of it as they barged into her bedroom, but now they're staring at the words Claire carved into the wall above her bed.

STOP WITH THE PILLS UR NOT NUTS BEAR

"Did you write that?" Melissa asks.

"Poe did," Phil answers.

"Goddammit, Phil!" Melissa roars. Her husband reaches for her as she tries to leave the room, but she whirls on him with such energy he backs away. "My father, her mother, all our lives we tried to protect her from this kind of crazy bullshit. And now you go and—*Jesus!*"

"Missy, please."

"I can't! I can't with you right now."

And then Claire and Phil are alone together. Claire finds herself more concerned for the state of his marriage than she does herself, figures it's just a coping skill she's always used to deflect. But once she's alone with Phil, his pain fills the room. Whatever relationship he developed with her brother, whatever information Poe shared with him, it has changed him irreparably.

"I would make him go first," he says. "You know, like, I wouldn't tell him about your attacks or whatever. I would make him tell me what had happened to him and give me the time; then if it matched up, I could make the determination without being prompted. Sometimes it would take us days to figure it out. But it just kept happening, Claire. Week after week, so many times over just the past year. It was usually big stuff that would light you both up. You know, primal stuff. Fear, sex, his withdrawals."

Sex. The word gives her a little jolt. It's been forever since she's had any, so Phil must be referring to Poe. The thought that her brother's sexual experiences might have resonated through her body makes her a little nauseated. She sinks to the edge of the bed. *Connected* could mean so many different things. But in this instance it means *invaded.*

Claire manages a nod, all she feels capable of. Phil, she realizes, needs more than that. He's been so convinced by what Poe shared with him that he risked his marriage over it. And thanks to him, Claire has gone from feeling like a lone lunatic shut up in her bedroom to realizing there was always something larger at work, something bigger than her. She doesn't want Phil and Melissa's marriage to be the price for that.

"Claire?" Phil asks.

"This is a lot to take in."

"Start slow. I did."

"A little late for that."

Phil nods, head bowed. "True," he mutters. "But just don't . . ."

"Don't what?" she asks.

"I'm not off my rocker here," he says. "And he wasn't either."

Believe me, he's saying.

"I can't draw," she finally says. As if the facts are clear now. As if she's got no choice but to believe him.

And then suddenly, the larger implications of Phil's earlier proclamation wash over her.

You're still connected.

Still connected even though Poe's plane smashed into a mountainside at hundreds of miles per hour.

Claire's trying to breathe this in when she suddenly hears familiar voices coming from somewhere else inside the house.

Her students.

And they're on television.

6

"Did we do this?"

Randy Drummond is standing at the head of what was once Thunder Ranch's dining room table when he asks the question. The varnished surface is sun bleached in the shape of the windows it sat next to before it was banished here to the guesthouse.

It's the first time he's assembled his full team in weeks, and even though two of the guys are joining via encrypted video uplink, the expressions before him are united by the same collective sense of restrained shock.

There's his answer, but he wants to let his guys twist a little bit. See if anyone averts their gaze or shifts in their seat.

All six of his men are former special operations. Some he served with on SEAL teams; others were recommended by his first hires. Dave Collins, the oldest guy out of the bunch, was actually one of his training instructors back on Coronado Island. The fact that he reports to Randy now is kind of a head trip. Like the other men, he's staring at Randy as if he's not sure what to make of his question.

Rupert Powell breaks the silence. His face is currently filling one of the iPads they've set up on the far end of the table. Rupert's a former city kid from Newark, so he signs up for Apollo duty every new quarter. He always jokes that it gives him a chance to visit his favorite barber so he can refresh his short Afro with a temple fade. But the truth is, he enjoys the travel part of working for Thunder Ranch more than he enjoys Montana. That's why he's in New York now.

"OK. Well, since I was the only one who was actually at JFK today, I can say, no, I did not bring down that plane." There's a slight pause. Then Rupert adds, "Was I supposed to?"

"We don't run secret ops around here," Dave says.

"Whole thing's a secret op," Zach Fisher grumbles. In the wake of his every wiseass comment, he studies Dave as if the older guy might pop him one. The relationship between the two has always seemed paternal; apparently the kid went to a dark place after he left the SEAL teams, and Dave was the one who brought him back. Zach's one of those tiny shitkickers who puts truth to the Hollywood lie that former SEALs are all seven-foot-tall gladiator types. A lot of big guys wash out during training because endurance is harder to maintain when your circulatory system's got to service a body over six feet tall.

"On each other, I mean," Dave says.

"We all knew he was bringing that notebook to his sister," Randy says.

"Well, he wasn't bringing it to the *New York Times*, for Christ's sake," Rupert says.

"And they're connected, so what?" Zach asks. "I mean, so what if Apollo figured it out, and so what if he was going to tell his sister. It doesn't draw a map to Thunder Ranch, does it?"

"That's a matter of opinion," Randy says. "I'm just saying, he's been a lot more curious about his past since he sobered up. That was making all of us nervous. Am I wrong?"

"You're not wrong, but a bomb didn't bring down that plane," Ben says. Out of all their team, Benjamin Running Creek is the one Randy calls a true friend. Maybe because they've been working together on the ranch the longest. Ben was one of his first hires, and as a result he's sometimes direct with Randy in ways that make the other guys go wide-eyed. They're both from the area: Randy from Columbia Falls, a scrappy little town at the gateway to Glacier National Park, while Benjamin's a child of the Blackfeet Reservation who returned

76

to it later in life after leaving the military. In Randy's experience, time in special operations often flattens previous political affiliations and identities out of a man. With Ben it's been the opposite. Whatever he went through on missions led him to spend his later years embracing an identity and a history he scoffed at and ran from as a young man. Given how seismically Randy's own views of life and death have been altered by what he experienced overseas, he understands.

"Why are you so sure about that, Ben?" Randy asks.

"Reports are all saying the distress call was about the right engine. Bomb's never going to be on an engine. It's going to be in the cargo hold or on a passenger in the main cabin."

Dave says, "You can put a bomb on an engine."

"How do you get it to stay there for three and a half hours of flight, and then why do you set it off at thirty-eight thousand feet over Colorado? A transcon flight's heavy as shit with fuel on takeoff. If you're going to bomb the thing, you blow it in the few first minutes and let the tanks do the work for you. You don't wait until they're half-empty." Benjamin shakes his head. "Severed hydraulics brought that plane down. Sad thing is, they could have landed with a crippled engine. It's what comes out of it when it blows that gets you. I'm telling you, this was an accident."

"For us, it's a lot more than an accident," Randy says.

"I've got an idea, but I don't like it," Sean Peck says. It makes Randy nervous that their man in LA is raising his voice to be heard on the video call, but Sean's assured them he's parked a safe distance from Artemis's house but still in eyesight. Artemis has always been sharper than her brother, so they make sure that her surveillance changes out on a regular basis. Also, Sean's got pretty-boy good looks and the vanity to match, and Randy's always been worried he might cross the line and assume his surveillance of Artemis includes trying to date her. Which it most certainly does not.

"Say it."

"What if it wasn't a bomb?" Sean asks. "What if it was him?"

"Apollo?" Randy asks. "You think he brought down his own plane?"

"Maybe he didn't mean to. Maybe he developed some new ability and it got out of control at thirty-eight thousand feet."

"I doubt that highly," Thomas Billings says, sitting up for the first time. He's their resident doctor, so his opinion carries weight. He can't stand it when Sean, who has no medical degree, starts speculating. Which Sean does often because he reads a lot of science fiction and enjoys the sound of his own voice.

"Maybe sobriety's having an effect beyond the mental, know what I mean?" Sean says. "Maybe he's changing."

"He doesn't have 'abilities,'" Thomas protests. "He has a limited psychic connection to his sister that's tied to extreme physical and emotional events, and he's been too drunk to realize it until now. He doesn't go from there to sending out some kind of pulse that can crash a plane. Even on Thunder Ranch."

"We don't know what's going to happen to them as they continue to age, though," Sean says.

"Randy," Thomas says to the man, "none of our test subjects have developed abilities over time, like Sean's suggesting. We've got to stay—"

Sean says, "I'm right here, thank you, and I'd just like to point out that all of our test subjects have four legs." Sean waggles four fingers in the air as if none of them can count.

"Thomas is right, Sean. I realize we deal in some crazy shit, but we need to keep our speculation in a reasonable lane here. That said, if Artemis starts levitating tables and throwing shit across the room with her mind, you let us know, OK."

"She's too busy chewing pills," Zach Fisher grumbles.

And that's been a big advantage to us, Randy thinks. But it's not the pills that have helped them. It's what they signify about her, about who she's tried to turn herself into. She's never wanted to believe that something unexplained happened to her that night in the park. What happens when that changes? They haven't seriously considered the question.

"So what do you say, Drummond?" Dave asks. "Operation Clean Sweep?"

No one speaks for a while. This time the silence is more patient than tense. It's a momentous decision, and he's not sure he's ready to make it.

"You want to talk to our boss about it first?" Ben asks.

There are a few stiff smiles in response to this, but they fade quickly when the others see Randy isn't smiling back.

"No," Randy says, "I don't want to bother her with it."

"Fair enough," Dave says, "but if we're going to do it, the window's short."

"We don't have any reports from the crash site?" Randy asks.

"Not the kind we'd be looking for," Ben answers. "They helo'd the first few rescue crews in, and nobody's leaking photos of anything bright and shiny."

"Maybe it's not going to go down like we think."

His men are silent again. Because they don't believe him.

Randy scans the table, wondering who's best suited for the job he's about to assign. His eyes land on Dave. Clothed, he looks like a reasonably fit, broad-shouldered guy who should be cruising toward retirement while punching the clock at a midwestern insurance agency. Get his shirt off and you'll find an eight-pack and a nest of knife scars. Like most of the team, his attachments are few, and he's brushed up against death in ways that opened his mind to the mysteries of Thunder Ranch. Then there's the tight leash he holds over Zach—just the kind of bond needed on a two-man op.

"Dave, Zach, gear up and load one of the Trailhawks and hit the road. I want you headed to the crash site ASAP. It sounds like it's going to be a hike, so learn the trails and then travel your own."

"It's at eight thousand feet, so yeah, copy that," Dave says.

With Operation Clean Sweep off the table for now, some of the guys are sitting back in their chairs, staring at their laps. Relaxing, but also pondering, which has always struck Randy as an ironic combo since the latter usually screws up the former.

"Rupe, I know you love the Big Apple, but I need you back. Catch the first flight."

"Copy that," the man says with a thumbs-up.

"And Sean, stay on—"

"Whoa," Sean says suddenly. He's looking past his phone and down the street outside his parked Jeep. "Artemis has company."

"What kind of company?"

"The kind with cameras," Sean says.

A couple of the men curse under their breath.

"She's a relative of a crash victim," Randy says. "She didn't go to the airport. Maybe they're trying to find out why."

"At her house?" Ben asks. "That's a lot of trouble for one family member."

Dave's standing now. "Still sure you don't want to do Clean Sweep?"

"Get going, both of you," Randy says. "And somebody pull up CNN on their laptop. Let's see what the hell this is about."

7

Claire figures it's Scottie Gregory who uploaded the footage to YouTube. She's busted him for cell phone use in class three times over the past month, and sometimes she worries she's too aggressive with him because he's one of those smug, swaggering teenage boys who talks to his female teachers like he thinks they all want to sleep with him. This was probably his way of getting back at her. Because that's how guys like Scottie Gregory think.

But the news story that drew her out of the bedroom and into the living room didn't turn out to be the sneering hatchet job she'd feared. The few students interviewed sounded earnest, genuinely concerned for her well-being. They spoke as if they'd been in the presence of something divine, important, something that gave an edge of the miraculous to the tragic events of the day. The reporter's tone mirrored their muted sense of wonder.

Watching it happen on camera, Claire is stunned by how organized her behavior looked compared to how it felt. From her torso up, at least. The disconnect was apparent between her upper body and her legs, which looked like they were trying to back her away from the board. But her arm kept writing. And it wasn't just writing. She retraced every line several times as she went, giving each finished letter the same impressionistic energy as the sketch of Pier 39.

The story and its assumptions hinged on the knowledge that Bear had been her brother's nickname for her. At first, she was terrified Leonard or Deanna had blabbed to the press. Then she remembered a conversation she'd had a few weeks back with Kim Johnson, who'd been struggling with the proper pronunciation of Francis Snarsbrough, one of the first Jamestown colonists. She'd tried to make her feel better by telling her how her little brother's mouth couldn't manage the hard consonants in her name when he was a child, but on her way home she'd worried she'd unintentionally insulted Kim by comparing her to a toddler. Apparently not, because she'd now gone on television to say, "Ms. Huntley is one of the calmest, most together, and best teachers I've ever had." In that moment, a few of Claire's tears slipped free.

The story ended up with a freeze frame of the words she'd written on the board.

love you bear.

Now, a secret she thought might never leave her bedroom has been broadcast to the world. Now, everyone who's seen the newscast is wondering if Claire experienced some moment of psychic connection to her brother at the time of the crash. It will only be a matter of minutes until someone churns up her connection to a strange incident in Glacier National Park when she was a kid. And when that happens, over two decades' worth of her mother's protectiveness will be gone in an instant, thanks to one student's phone.

Claire and Phil are seated in the kitchen, the sketch of Pier 39 resting on the little butcher-block table between them. Melissa stands at the sink rewashing dishes that don't need to be washed. Several reporters have knocked on the front door, but they mostly gave up after the first few tries. The chorus of low metallic hums coming from the television vans parked outside are audible from everywhere inside the little house.

"When did you guys go?" Phil asks.

It takes Claire a second to realize he's talking about San Francisco, the subject of her—*Poe's?*—sketch.

"I was eleven, so . . . a year before the divorce. It was one of our last happy memories together. Poe and I loved Pier 39 so much they brought us there every day of the trip. I remember my mother danced."

Phil's eyebrows arch. "Susan danced?"

"The carousel, it was playing that song 'Hooked on a Feeling.' It was one of her favorites. She actually got up off the bench and started busting a move."

"A lot of people think that song's about getting sober," Phil says.

"Really?"

"Yeah, B. J. Thomas, he didn't write it, but he made it famous, and he sang it a lot after he stopped drinking. Maybe that's why Poe's—"

"Let's make a statement," Melissa says, back still turned to them. The force with which she slaps the rag into the sink makes a strange accompaniment to her suddenly cheerful tone. Phil reacts to the sound as if his wife just slapped him.

"What kind?" Claire asks.

"I don't know. Something that says this is just teenagers getting worked up. You know, something that'll make them all go away. I'll go out there and read it myself. I don't care."

"I don't know if that's what this is," Claire says.

Melissa turns to face them, carefully avoiding her husband's expectant puppy-dog look. "OK, then. Walk me through it. Seriously. I'm trying to understand here. So at 11:40 or 12:40 or . . . whenever the plane has its . . . issue, you had this moment at the whiteboard where you saw—"

"No," Claire gently interjects. "No, I didn't *see* anything at the board. I wrote something. Against my will. And around the time of the actual crash, I hit the floor."

"Hit the floor," Melissa says, as if she thinks getting Claire to repeat the words will make her realize how ridiculous she sounds.

"Yeah, it was like the floor was ripped out from under me and I just face-planted. Later, on the ride home, that's when I started seeing things."

"Him," Phil adds.

"But now it's both," Melissa says. "You're writing things . . . from him, I guess. And you're seeing things. But you didn't see things before the crash."

"No."

"So whatever this is, it's never involved hallucinations before."

Phil says, "Honey, that's not exactly true—"

"Um, *honey*, why don't you let Claire and me—"

"Why don't you take me out of the doghouse so you can ask these questions of the guy who's actually been talking about this stuff for a year."

"OK. OK, fine, Psychic Detective Man. Has any of this involved hallucinations before now?"

"Like I said, Poe was drawing things he couldn't have possibly seen, so maybe that qualifies as—"

"Unless he went online and looked for them."

"And why the hell would he do that, Missy? Why would he try to perpetuate some fraud on—"

"Because he's been a drug addict since he was fifteen! Because he came to Susan's funeral and stood over her coffin and read a poem about his sex life that included the line 'my molten, serpentine penis always seeks the light.'"

Melissa's eyes go wide as she realizes that she's just spoken ill of the dead. And with incredible volume. And specificity.

"I'm sorry," she says. "It just . . . it was a very upsetting moment."

Nobody speaks for a while, but Claire can feel the morbid laughter building, threatening to erupt. "But you remembered it," she says, "so maybe that's the sign of a good poem?"

"No," Phil says, "it isn't."

"You're right," Claire says, "it was a horrible poem." She can't contain it any longer. She doesn't care if it means delirium is setting in. But suddenly she's laughing into her palms, and Phil's doing the same, and now it looks like Melissa's on the verge of giving in too.

Once she catches her breath, Claire says, "It was one of the worst I've ever heard. I mean, it was one of the worst *things* I've ever heard, not just one of the worst poems. Like one of the worst sounds. Or series of sounds."

Melissa's hands fly to her mouth, a sign that she, too, is laughing against her will.

"He apologized for it every time we talked," Phil says. "He said that was part of why he was coming home. To make it up to you, Claire."

A new silence falls. Melissa pulls back her chair and takes a seat.

"Where does this go?" she finally asks, sounding winded. "I mean, come on. We all know where this road'll take us. Right back to your dad and his 'theories,' and this whole thing about how it wasn't a bear that night and—"

"It *wasn't* a bear that night," Claire says.

Melissa is stone-still. Phil looks up at Claire as if she's just clapped her hands. For a while no one speaks.

"Claire," her stepsister finally says, "for as long as I have known you you've said it was—"

"Because it was the only answer my mother would accept, and I didn't want to lose her."

"So . . . aliens?" Melissa finally asks.

"I don't believe that either," Claire answers.

"What do you believe?" Phil asks.

"I think we don't know and that's worse. I think that's what drove my father crazy. The not knowing."

Another long silence falls.

Melissa says, "Your mom always said that when she and your dad decided to get divorced that they let you two—"

"*They* didn't decide," Claire says. "She told your father that story because she didn't want him to think she was impulsive and rash. The truth was, when she found out how far we were from a designated campsite that night, that Dad had to leave us alone and unconscious for hours to go get anyone who could even call for help, she picked up the phone and called a divorce lawyer. From the hospital. When she told Poe we were going to live with her, he lost his mind. They actually had to sedate him."

"He wanted to stay with your dad?" Phil asks.

"Because he didn't think it was a bear either?" Melissa asks.

"He was ten. He didn't want anything to change. He wanted us all to stay together forever."

"You were only twelve and you picked your mom," Phil says.

"Because she didn't leave the room," Claire says. "Dad kept leaving my hospital room to yell at people and fight with people, and Mom stayed. I thought that's what a real parent does no matter what the truth is."

"So she just let Poe go?" Melissa asks.

"She said it was worth it to get me. She said Poe was always a daddy's boy anyway. Poe told me later he thought that was code for she knew he was gay even then and didn't want him around. But she never said a bad thing about gay people her whole life. I think she said it because she knew it would make the custody dispute easier. You know, if they each got one kid."

Claire feels guilty about abandoning the most stable family she's known. Melissa's got a savior's spirit, and the discovery that her stepsister was concealing various wounds from her has got to sting. And Melissa's the last person she wants to hurt.

But Claire feels relaxed for the first time in hours. It's a little far outside the regular window for it to be caused by the pills. The delirious laughter, the unloading of secrets, it's calmed her, and as a result of her muscles loosening, she feels the call of nature.

"I need to use the bathroom."

"Yeah, um, alone?" Melissa rises to her feet as Claire does.

"I'll be fine, seriously. I'll use the guest bath, not the one in my room."

Melissa follows her down the hall, and when Claire goes to step inside, Melissa gently grips her shoulder. "OK," she says. "Just . . . if you're going to break a mirror, call us and we'll break it for you."

"Is that the plan?"

"I don't know. Just don't break another mirror. I don't want you getting hurt."

"I won't."

Suddenly Melissa hugs her with quick force. When she pulls away, Claire's stunned by the tears in her sister's eyes.

"Listen," Melissa whispers, "I just need to say something."

"I won't hurt myself. I promise."

"I know, it's just . . . I'm your sister no matter what you believe, OK? Don't you ever forget that."

Claire hugs her back. "Deal, but you have to do something too."

"Anything."

"Forgive your husband. Please."

"Fine, but he's not getting sex for a week."

"A *week*? You guys are doing better than I thought."

"Ten minutes and then I'm coming in after you."

She smiles, but keeps watching Claire until the door is closed.

Claire never thought she'd be so grateful to sit on the toilet and go to the bathroom. It's not like she's been holding it in for hours. But it's a relief to have something about her body work exactly as it should.

When she finishes, she finds herself staring at the perfect job Melissa did of covering the mirror above the sink. She used one of the spare flat sheets for Claire's bed, tucking it neatly around the mirror's

edges, primly draping the excess along the back of the basin and letting it spill over the edges in roughly equal amounts on each side.

She's touched by the attention Melissa gave the job. But the overall effect seems silly now. Was Claire's order about protecting herself,
or hiding her visions from Melissa and Phil? Now that TV viewers
all over LA are in on Claire's crazy, what's the point of hiding it? As
invasive as it felt at first, the news story has had a paradoxical effect.
She no longer feels alone.

No longer feels as alone as she felt for fourteen years, hiding the
truth of what she thought about that night.

Would her mother have sent her off to live with her father if
she'd expressed doubts about the bear attack theory? Maybe not, but
the trauma of seeing how quickly her mother cast Poe aside stuck
with Claire like a form of PTSD. During her mother's final days,
spent under hospice care in the living room of this very house, she'd
thought about raising the subject. Thought about telling her mother
about the shadows she saw that night in Glacier, the ones that suggested a light source of incredible size came roaring toward her and
Poe out of the dark. But every time, it had felt like an attempt to make
her mother's suffering about herself, and she resisted the urge. And
then her mother was gone.

Is Poe gone now too?

She tells herself she's got no choice but to take the sheet off the
mirror. Slowly, she untucks the top of the sheet from the mirror and
lowers it.

It begins to happen almost instantly, but with leisurely speed, like
it's been waiting for her.

First comes the fog, and then here comes little Poe, walking
toward her, small enough to fit inside her chest at first, then growing larger as he gets closer to the glass. Same orange jacket, same
wind-tousled hair. Behind him, a blur of golden light swirls through
the fog. She thinks it might be the old carousel at Pier 39, and she

can faintly hear the strains of the song that made her mother get up and dance.

Her heart races, and the scream that wants to rip from her is making her gut clench.

Don't fight it, she tells herself. *Do like you did with the sketch. Don't drown in it. Ride the wave.*

Poe's eyes are glowing. A fierce shade of blue she's rarely seen in nature. He's raising his hand, and for a second she thinks his palm might flatten against the other side of the glass. Instead, his fingers open. He's extending his hand to her and as she focuses on it, she feels the nerves on the back of her neck jangle, as if there's a presence behind her, feels the tension spread up the back of her neck, across the crown of her skull and down the sides of her face. Maybe it's a panic reaction, or maybe it's getting stronger because she's lifting her hand to the glass. Just to see. Just to see if something might happen if she tries to interact with this vision. Tries to touch it.

There's a pounding on the door so loud Claire cries out.

"It's your dad, Claire!" Phil shouts through the door.

She expects to see the mirror empty. It's not. Instead, little Poe is lowering his hand and backing away. The glow in his eyes is gone, and she wonders if it left the second she broke eye contact. Because that's what seemed to light up his ghostly eyes—eye contact. Her refusal to look away, her refusal to give in to fear. She sees him mouthing words as he backs into the fog. She can't hear them, but the movements of his lips are short and simple.

Get it, he's telling her.

And then she's staring at the reflection of the bathroom again. Of her. And she can see how much effort it's taken her not to lose her shit. Her eyes are wide and bulging, her nostrils flaring.

She didn't end the vision this time.

He did.

Phil knocks again.

"I'll be right there," she says. She's not sure why but she covers the mirror again. If whatever's in her head is capable of turning these visions on and off, then her only real power resides in keeping the glass covered.

She steps out into the hall and almost runs smack into Phil. Melissa's a few feet away, holding the portable phone in one hand.

"It's some woman," Melissa says. "But she says she's calling for him."

"Did she give a name?" Claire asks.

"Margot Hastings," Melissa says.

Claire takes the phone from Melissa.

"You know her?" Melissa asks. "She's not a crank?"

"I know her," Claire says.

8

Margot Hastings is the most recent in the long line of her father's indulgent girlfriends, and the only one who's ever tried to build a relationship with Claire. Abram Huntley has never suffered from a shortage of women willing to tolerate his imbalanced behavior. Probably because for most of his life he's looked like a cross between Brad Pitt and Sam Elliot, and, according to some comments Claire's mother made after too much wine—comments Claire wishes she could unhear—he's a dynamo in the sack.

"Smart women don't marry the one who blows their doors off," her mother used to warn her on a regular basis. "They marry the one they can count on, and they're almost never the same guy. Don't make the same mistake I did. You'll save yourself a lot of time."

Margot is also insanely rich, which Claire discovered when she Googled the woman's full name after her first email arrived. She's the sole heiress to a Pacific Northwest timber fortune, and she's dedicated her privileged life to studying the paranormal—which means funneling her money into the study of topics no university is willing to explore. It's not a mystery how she met Claire's dad. Over the course of her correspondence with Claire, Margot has made it gently clear that she thinks Abram's life would improve if he reconciled with his daughter. Claire doesn't agree, but she hasn't said so outright because she wants to keep the communication flowing. When Margot first wrote to her, the debacle of Claire's mother's funeral had banished Poe from her life, and Margot became Claire's only source of information about a father she barely knows.

Margot's references to their day-to-day life have made it sound like she and Abram are on a luxurious and protracted retreat together at her Mercer Island mansion. Apparently they spend hours in what Margot describes as "study," which is when Claire's father devotes himself to various hobbies: pottery classes, getting his pilot's license. Claire figures there's also a lot of weed involved, but she's never asked. It all seems like proof that with great money comes great boredom, and she would have picked a far different fate for her father's later life, one that involved lots of *I'm sorrys* and *thank yous* and hours spent volunteering at soup kitchens and pretty much anything else that might teach him to put other people's needs ahead of his personal obsessions.

When she answers the phone, Claire hears car sounds and the gentle ticking of a turn signal. "How are you holding up, sweetheart?" Margot asks. But the woman's crisp, businesslike tone doesn't match the term of endearment.

"Well, have you seen the news? About me, I mean."

"I have. And so has your father."

"Wow. So it's gone national."

"It has."

"Where are you guys?"

"We're not together, Claire."

"Like at all?"

"He moved out several months ago."

"Oh, OK."

"I'm in LA working on a documentary. That's why he called me. He wants us to go see him."

"Where?"

"Montana."

The state, which her family visited so many times by car that it started to feel more like a suburb of Spokane in their minds, used to invoke warm feelings of campfire smells and gorgeous vistas and clear, crisp mountain air. Every time she's heard the name since that night, it's felt like a slap across the back of the head, a reminder of all she lost and all she doesn't know.

"What is he doing in Montana?" Claire finally asks.

"I don't know exactly, but he's been there since he moved out of my place."

"Why? Why does he want me to go to Montana?"

"He says he's got some things he needs to tell you."

Margot's sense of detachment from Claire's father is jarring, a stark contrast to their previous emails, in which Margot spoke of Abram as if she were obtaining a doctorate in his moods.

"OK, well, no offense, but if my father has something he wants to tell me, he should really call himself."

"I'm not offended, and I understand, and that's exactly what I'll tell him."

Oof, Claire thinks, *this was a bad breakup.*

"Thank you."

"I'm so sorry, Claire."

"Thank you," she whispers.

Claire hangs up, turns to find Melissa and Phil watching her like cats watching the food can open.

The thought that her father might call sets her heart to racing. They've seen each other only once since the divorce. Claire was allowed to join him and Poe for a single meal at a restaurant of her mother's choosing—even though her mother refused to attend—a restaurant located almost exactly midway between the hotel where her dad and Poe were staying and her mom's new house in Eagle Rock. Her aunt Eileen drove them to the meal so her mother wouldn't have to lay eyes on Abram.

Poe, as always, played the clown to cut the tension—cracking crude jokes, spilling food on himself, whispering goofy nicknames for the other diners based on how they were dressed. Claire had only been in California a few months, but it felt like she was eating with strangers. Throughout the meal, her dad was a tightly coiled caricature of himself, still sporting the look of a manicured mountain man with his trimmed mustache and shoulder-length hair. But she could sense his desire to pelt her with questions about everything she could—and couldn't—remember about that night in Glacier. Knowing full well that if he did, her mother would go back to court to take away what little visitation rights he had.

During that awkward lunch, Claire had felt her father's silent gaze turn her into little more than a function of that awful night. She was a mystery for him to solve and nothing else, and so, if Claire's mother had forbidden her to discuss it, then his daughter was of little interest to him. Everything about the visit felt halting, so uncommitted—the restaurant in the middle of some LA neighborhood she didn't know, the city still so massive and unknowable, blocks and blocks of strip malls, every other one housing either a sushi restaurant or a yoga studio. It might have been a Denny's, but she's not sure.

The worst part had come at the end, standing outside the restaurant, after her father had given her a cold, perfunctory hug. For a second, it seemed like Poe would do the same, but as soon as he stepped back from her, he burst into miserable tears. Big wet sobs he did nothing to contain. He kept looking at her even as he swiped at his nose and eyes, openly grieving the departure of the sister he'd known all his life. Finally, his father steered Poe away with one hand on his shoulder, and Claire stared after him, her own tears a wet sheen in her eyes. But she'd managed to hold them back, and in that moment, it had seemed like a victory. Like an adult thing to do. She'd been angry with Poe then, as if he'd violated some secret code by letting his feelings show. But that's how it always was with her brother. His sensitivity, his thin-skinned nature, turned him into a tuning fork for all the emotions they were trying to silence in themselves. That's why, she'd decided then, he belonged with their father and she belonged with her mother, who made plans when she was in pain.

On the ride home, her chain-smoking aunt let slip they'd agreed on the place because her mother wasn't comfortable letting them eat at the hotel. And on the condition that her dad seat them right inside the front windows so Aunt Eileen could keep an eye on them from across the street. That's how afraid they'd been he'd try to make off with her. But there'd been no kidnapping attempt that day, quite the opposite.

Her father, it seemed, had let her go.

Then there was nothing, save for birthday cards, until she was seventeen. That's when he sent her an email that had her pacing for days on end. The question seemed simple enough—had Poe traveled to visit them in California? Once she read it several times, the real meaning of it sank in. At fifteen, her brother had either run away from home or disappeared. She'd been so frightened she told her dad everything, betrayed confidences Poe had made during their occasional emails. Poe had been cutting classes, sometimes making long drives from Spokane to Seattle to go to gay bars, drives with college-age guys he'd met on the internet. She even said Poe described some of the guys as being totally obsessed with him, sending him pictures that could land them in jail. When he'd first told her these things, they'd sounded mysterious and exciting, as if Poe were some powerful force capable of making grown men risk arrest. But when she repeated them to her father, all she could see was her brother chopped up in a ditch. Her father responded to these details with a single line that sounded like both an excuse and an admission of guilt.

Jesus. I just thought I was letting him find his own
way.

They agreed to get in touch immediately if either of them heard from Poe. But when Claire had told her mother, her eyes had glazed over and she'd quietly said, "Well, if he shows up here, he can't stay. That's not how it works." She'd left the room before Claire could say anything else, before she could ask, "How *what* works?" Life? Divorce? Parenting? You?

The first message from Poe came a few weeks later. A picture of him on some wild Pacific Northwest coast full of forested cliffs. He'd bleached his spiky hair and pierced his nose. Don't worry, sis. Just living.

Of course, she'd demanded some form of proof of life. Told him to write specific things on notecards and hold them up, which he did, but always with his own message added in. He'd write the time and date as she instructed and then below it, Calm down, Bear. And don't tell Crazypants. He's busy chasing little green men and I don't even tan. Beyond that, his photos never revealed anything else about his travels or the man he was probably with. Which, along with the fact that he wouldn't call her and risk divulging those details, were all signs he knew she'd probably share them with his father.

Which she did.

Once she told him Poe was alive, her father retreated again. Possibly into rejection, possibly into shame. The fact was, Poe had been his responsibility. Had he really just been giving him space, or had he let him wander off while he was visiting supposed interdimensional vortexes in Sedona or traveling halfway across the world to UFO conventions?

Finally, she says, "I haven't spoken to him in years. I mean, he can't just—"

The phone rings.

"You want us to answer?" Melissa asks, which seems silly since Claire's still holding the phone.

She checks the caller ID. It's the area code for Montana.

She answers before she can think twice.

"Claire." He says her name like someone who's not sure he should be allowed to speak it.

"I'm here," she says, because she's not sure what else to say.

"Come to Montana. I have some things to tell you."

"Why don't we just start with a phone call?" she asks.

"I did. I called you. Now come here."

Just like her father of years ago. All impulse, all action. A voice that always sounds hoarse from his last outburst.

"I'm not sure getting on a plane right now is the—"

"You can't stay in that house!" he barks. "You got reporters all over the place."

"I'm sure there are even more at the airport."

"Margot's got her own plane. That's why I called her."

"We haven't seen each other in years. And we're both kind of going through the same thing right now. I'm not sure how much help we're going to be to each other."

"You're talking about feelings. I'm talking about facts."

"*Facts?*" She's red-faced and breathless in an instant. "Was it facts when you lied to anyone who would listen and told them we saw strange lights in the sky that night before we all went to sleep? Was it facts when you made your own kids sound like liars? You put Poe under hypnosis to try to force him to—"

"I wasn't *forcing* anything on him. I was trying to help him. I was trying to see what he could remember."

She's stunned by how close to the surface her anger is. And his as well.

"Yell at me all you want, Claire. Just do it here. In Montana."

"I'm open to a visit at some point. Either me there, or you here. But right now, with everything that's happening, I just—"

"I have answers. Real answers. Proof."

When he doesn't continue, she says, "And you won't share them with me unless I come."

"I don't really want to give it out over the phone."

"That's a little tinfoil hat, don't you think?"

"Yeah, well, maybe if you'd been wearing a tinfoil hat in class today, things would've gone smoother."

"OK. You know what? I'm not going to—"

"Yes, you are. You're gonna get on a plane, Claire. It's real nice, not some junky little Cessna. It's got leather seats and everything. I'll see you when you land."

And then he hangs up on her.

She hands the portable back to Melissa. "He says he has answers."

"What are they?" Phil asks.

"He won't tell me unless I fly to Montana with his ex-girlfriend."

"Oh, for Christ's sake." Melissa heads for the fridge and pulls out a beer.

No one speaks for a while.

"He lost his son," Phil finally says. "Maybe he just wants his daughter."

"Then he should come here," Melissa says.

"And walk right past the media up the front porch?" Phil asks. "That'll lead them right to whatever happened in Glacier."

Melissa sags with defeat, takes a long, thirsty pull on her Corona.

Answers. Claire might be short on them, but she's got something else. Something Phil called a connection. If it's real, if what she's seeing in every reflective piece of glass isn't a hallucination but a vision—a *transmission*, she thinks against her will, then rushes to push the word away—can she keep that from her father and live with herself?

Melissa reads her expression, frowns at the floor, and takes another slug of beer.

Claire goes to her, slides her arms around her. "I'm going to call Margot," she says.

"You're going, aren't you," Melissa says.

When Claire nods, Melissa sets the beer bottle on the counter and slumps into her embrace. "I feel like we failed you," she whispers.

"How?"

"My dad and I, we were supposed to give you a normal life."

"You were supposed to give me a family. And you did. Every day."

Melissa wilts a little more. Phil, she sees out of the corner of her eye, is closing in.

"He loved her, you know," Melissa says. "He thought she hung the moon. But he always knew he wasn't the love of her life."

Before Claire can absorb this, Phil is reaching out to his wife, and Melissa relents and allows herself to touch her husband for the first time since their earlier blowup.

Claire is pleased by this. Maybe more than she should be, given her own life is still a complete mess.

———

As soon as she hears the clamor of the reporters out front rushing to intercept Melissa and Phil, Claire starts across the backyard, duffel bag slung over one shoulder, pulling one of her mother's rickety old wooden lawn chairs toward the fence. She's swung a leg over the top when her neighbor, Louisa Bailey, appears out of the darkness on the other side, two ghostly arms reaching for Claire's duffel bag.

As discussed, Louisa has killed all the security lights along her back porch, probably to give them cover, but it's also made it hard to see, and Claire realizes, almost too late, that her neighbor is standing on a stepladder, which wobbles under her feet when she takes Claire's weight in both arms. For a second, it feels like they both might fall; then Louisa, summoning some burst of core strength she's cultivated at her many yoga classes, hoists Claire to the dirt like she's a giant potted plant.

Claire tugs her phone from her pocket. She'd dimmed the screen so it wouldn't mark their furtive path through the shadows.

Close, reads the text from Margot.

Just then, a sleek black BMW SUV slows in front of Louisa's little house.

Claire steps up and into the front seat of what feels like a cosseted leather womb. She pulls the door closed behind her with a thunk, and suddenly they're moving forward.

And her little brother is staring back at her from the reflection on the windshield.

"Stop!" Claire barks.

Margot slams on the brakes.

"Sorry. Not you."

Little Poe glowers at her, fades into a wreath of fog, and then she's staring at the dark street ahead of them.

She turns and looks Margot Hastings in the eye and is relieved to see that the window beside her reflects only the dull glow of the dashboard lights. Margot is as pretty as her pictures online, but her flame-red hair is shorter, and her leather jacket and skinny jeans make for a fairly utilitarian outfit until you get to the jaunty red-and-white silk scarf at her neck.

"So," Claire says, "I hear you have a plane."

"I'm as startled by all of this as you are, to be frank." She returns her attention to the road, her manicured hands resting in a perfect ten and two o'clock position on the leather steering wheel. In person, she seems colder than her emails.

"It's been a pretty startling day."

"Obviously I'm not referring to what's happened to Poe. I would never be so callous." There's a hint of an accusation in her tone. If Claire made this assumption, her tone suggests, it's due to a weakness of Claire's, not Margot's own words.

"No, I understand."

"And if you'd like to wait before getting on a plane, all things considered, I'm happy to get us some hotel rooms and explain it to your father."

"No, I figure we should just pull the Band-Aid off all at once if we're going to do this."

Margot nods, focuses on the road. She seems comfortable with the sudden silence between them.

Claire is not.

"So I guess you don't have any idea what he wants to tell me," Claire says.

"None. But I can tell you he's never come up with any answers that satisfied *me*." And there it is. Claire can hear it. The woman's anger is with her father, who has apparently used tragedy to yank what little scab has managed to form over the wound left by their breakup.

"Really? I would have thought you'd been on board with his alien theory."

"Never. In fact, that's what ended our relationship."

"Seriously?"

Margot nods. "UFOs are becoming more mainstream with all these video releases from the Pentagon. Publishers started shaking the trees for new books. Mainstream publishers, not the small presses I usually deal with. A couple found him."

"Oh my God. Please tell me my father doesn't have a book deal."

"I don't know. I just told him I wouldn't support him while he wrote it. So he departed my lair, if you will."

"So you knew he made up a bunch of stuff about that night?"

Margot nods. "He said he was just trying to be heard. I told him eventually he needed to come clean. That lies like that hurt our work in the long run. But I didn't put a date on it. Until the publishers started calling."

"If my father is making me come to Montana so he can put all this in a book . . ."

"I don't know for sure, but I doubt that."

"Do you know what he's been doing there?"

"I do not. So, with that said, I can take us to Van Nuys Airport, or I can get us some rooms out at the Casa del Mar in Santa Monica. It's one of my favorites. The room service will be on me too. Diets are suspended today. And possibly for the next six months. But that should go without saying." Margot smiles for the first time since Claire stepped inside the SUV. She seems delighted by the prospect of the two of them spending time together in a nice hotel.

"That's very kind of you, but I don't have much of an appetite."

"I understand."

"And your plane sounds nice."

Margot shrugs, puts her turn signal on, and heads toward a freeway on-ramp.

"I hope my father didn't choose a book deal over you," Claire says.

"I can't say. What he did choose was not to have a woman in his life who told him the truth."

"Well, he's about to get two," Claire says.

Margot smiles, and for a while they drive in silence. There's something comforting about forward motion, Claire thinks, about not being behind the wheel. Or maybe it's the comfort of realizing she can stop the visions with a single word.

"Would you like to talk about why you shouted at the windshield back there?" Margot asks, indicating the subject's been circling in her mind since Claire stepped into the SUV.

"Not yet," Claire answers.

The surveillance center is an old bunkhouse for ranch hands tucked into the pines that form the eastern border of Thunder Ranch. The insides of the windows are boarded up. For the most part it looks more like a man cave than some high-tech facility designed to ensure one of the greatest discoveries in the course of human existence remains a secret.

It's where Randy reviews footage from Claire Huntley's kitchen up until the moment she ducked out the back door with her duffel bag and her stepsister and her husband went out the front to create a diversion for the press. Long ago, Randy made a strict rule against planting cameras in bathrooms or bedrooms, so he's been trying to piece together the origins of that damn sketch from the conversation the three of them had in the kitchen. The camera boundaries had been even tougher to implement with Poe over the years. His various living situations had tended toward the one-room kind, which gave a bunch of the guys a crash course in sexual possibilities they might not have been familiar with before Thunder Ranch.

Ben rolls his chair back from the table and removes one of the earbuds he's been using to listen to the microphones implanted in Abram Huntley's ceiling.

"He's renting a car," he says.

"Abram?"

Ben nods. "From Avis at Glacier Airport. Is the girlfriend landing them at Kalispell?"

"She's not his girlfriend anymore. What the hell does he need with a rental car?"

"I don't know, but he's asking for something with four-wheel drive."

"He's got four-wheel drive."

"Yeah, but what else has he got in his car?"

"Us. You think he's onto us?"

"I think he's switching cars right before his daughter gets here. It's kinda odd."

"I agree."

For a while, neither man says anything.

Ben breaks the silence first. "Randy, I wasn't kidding about what I said at the meeting."

"About it not being a bomb?"

"No. About our boss. I think you should talk to her."

"It's not as simple as just talking."

"I know, but she needs to be brought in. We've never been this close to Clean Sweep before. Maybe she's changed her mind about stuff."

"I'll take that under advisement," Randy says.

Ben nods and pops the earbud back in. He knows better than to press the point.

He also probably knows that despite pretending otherwise, Randy's about to do exactly what he suggested.

9

The woman did such a good job of sneaking up on his cabin Randy Drummond didn't notice her until she was a few paces from the front steps. The light rain that day made subtle music on the branches, and she walked with her head bowed and her slicker's hood pulled up. But there was a strain to her steps that marked her as someone older even before she looked up at him, revealing her deeply lined face.

By then, he'd unholstered the SIG at his waist. Her eyes were as blue as a glacial lake; the mop of snow-white bangs plastered under her hood suggested she'd once been shockingly blonde.

"You shouldn't sneak up on people, ma'am," he said.

"You should get a gate and a buzzer, then," she said, "and a phone."

The speed of her response, the lack of fear in her expression, impressed him. The truth was, he kept a sat phone and a radio for emergencies, but if he needed the internet, he drove down to the Flathead County Library in Kalispell and ordered things sent to his PO box from there. But how would this woman know that? How did this woman even know where he lived?

"I'm not doing interviews," he said.

"I'm not a reporter," she said, "and besides, you made that clear to all the other reporters." She did a slow survey of the cabin's porch, as if she found its emptiness and cleanliness suspicious. "Is it because of your face?" she asked.

No pity, no condescension. The absence of both was refreshing. The surgeries were considered a success in the eyes of those who'd performed them, but in crowds, the subtle not-rightness of the bone structure around his right eye had proven in some ways to be worse than a bad burn. It drew out the whole process by which people gradually noticed, stared in search of the wrongness, then quickly looked away. If he'd looked like Freddy Krueger, they'd wince and recoil in three seconds flat.

"I mean, do you not want to be on camera because of your—"

"I know what you meant, lady. Where's your vehicle?"

"Is that really a question you want to ask of a woman who came to visit you alone?"

"I'm asking if you came alone."

"Yeah, I got that, son. Why not just ask me where I want to be buried on your property?"

"What if I just asked you to leave?"

"I got dropped off. By someone who's expecting me. You know, in case you turned out to be nuts."

"Direct answers keep me sane. Promise."

"Sane? It's why you're living way the hell out here without a phone. So what's the deal? You just hide out in the woods and wait to save families from burning houses?"

"I was driving by at the right time, that's all."

"Most people would have called the fire department."

"They weren't exactly a hop and a skip down the road."

"You saved a mother and her two children and you're not taking any credit for it."

"And you're sounding more like the reporter you said you weren't," Randy said.

"You a man with enemies, Mr. Drummond?"

"I'm a man who knows anyone can become one."

"Says more about you than them."

The old woman stepped up onto the first step so she could get out of the light rain, a reminder to Randy that he hadn't invited her any closer, which would have felt rude if the woman had radiated anything that seemed like vulnerability. She reached into the flaps of her jacket and Randy stiffened, thought about raising his gun arm. But she was bending over, the top of her hood—and the crown of her skull under it—a soft target as she set a card on the porch.

She straightened and smiled. "I'm hiring. Humble heroes fit the bill."

"I'm not a hero."

"That family disagrees."

"I did what I was trained to do."

"You were a SEAL, not a fireman, Mr. Drummond. If you rise to every moment you were trained for, you're never going to be able to sit down and enjoy a good meal."

"I don't do mercenary work. You got some rival rancher disrespecting your property line, take 'em out the old-fashioned way. In court."

"It's not that kind of work."

Randy stared at her; she stared back. Eventually she'd get the idea that he wasn't going to take the bait and ask what kind of work it was. But apparently it was going to take a while.

A long while. He was tempted to go back inside, but something about the woman's fearlessness kept him from turning his back on her.

"I don't need work."

"You need something. Your dad left you with a ton of debt on this place. Might be nice to ensure one roof stays over your head, at least."

"Who are you, lady?"

"I've been around here awhile. I know who to talk to when I want to know something."

"I keep a low profile."

"Not when you've got the itch for some pretty little tourist you can have with no strings attached. You do know people work in all those places, right? Even the motels."

"I need you to leave, ma'am."

The faint smile left her face, but what replaced it was flinty. Not wary, not disappointed. So he'd take more recruitment than she'd planned, her look seemed to say, but that was fine because she had all the time in the world to complete it.

After a while of them listening to the drip drip drip of the rain on the roof, she said, "My name's Agatha Caldwell. And I know all about war too. In ways you don't."

Randy felt his eyebrows go up. Most people would be hard pressed to know war in all the ways he did. A Chinook crash in Afghanistan, thanks to a rocket-propelled grenade. Two members of his team dead, several of the others alive today because Randy had dragged them free. A host of capture-or-kill missions in Iraq to assist the so-called Anbar Awakening that was supposed to be a turning point in that raging, never-ending clusterfuck of a war, which ended for Randy when he took a bullet to his cheek that resulted in the rearrangement of part of his face. And if Agatha Caldwell was so damn smart, did she also know that a fair number of the pretty little tourists he tried to take home begged off as soon as they got a good look at his right eye in the sodium-vapor lights of the parking lot? Probably so.

She took a step back, pointed to the card, and said, "Talk to you soon, Mr. Drummond."

Then she was walking back up the dirt road through the dripping brush.

He called her two days later, figuring he'd be able to sleep again if he did.

She gave him directions to what had to be ranchland. It was so far east on US 2 it was almost clear of the mountains and on the Blackfeet Reservation.

The place had no signage. So it wasn't a resort, and probably wasn't much of a working ranch either. The high electrified fencing was unobtrusive, concealed by brush, but he noticed it right before he entered the code she'd given him. The giant gate swung open and he nosed his truck through. The road took a series of turns around a dense stand of lodgepole pine that concealed the property from the road. Later, he'd learn the place had a name, Thunder Ranch, but like her own, the woman had made sure nobody discussed it much in town.

A two-story Victorian house came into view off to his left, then farther away and to the right, a horse pasture and a giant barn. Something about the barn struck him as off, and later he realized it was the doors; they didn't look as scuffed or weathered as they should have been if they were being opened and closed every day in the course of regular ranch work. And the horses looked like they'd never been ridden hard. The place was a ranch, for sure, but he had no idea what she was ranching. By the time he'd parked and started for the house, he was worried he'd gotten himself into some bullshit security detail for some Hollywood celebrity he'd failed to recognize.

It was a clear big-sky day, the mountains sharply etched against a dome of blue. Agatha was waiting for him on the house's front porch, standing next to a row of empty rocking chairs occasionally jostled by the strong gusts. She'd laid her long white ponytail over one shoulder, and her lean, fit frame was hugged by jeans and a plaid shirt. She didn't bother with a formal greeting, just a small, satisfied smile and nod before she gestured for him to follow her inside.

Randy hesitated on the bottom step, told himself this was about more than curiosity. He had no choice but to find out all he could about a woman who'd gone to so much effort to learn so much about him. But maybe all this sparkly, clean, and seemingly unused land didn't say Hollywood as much as it said human trafficking or drug running or some other backwoods criminal enterprise struggling to look legit.

Inside, she offered him a cup of tea. He rejected it. When she invited him to sit, he refused the chair she offered him. Instead, he took the one with a solid wall behind it and the best vantage point of the room's two entrances.

"Why'd you quit?" she asked him.

"Quit putting you off, you mean?"

She smiled. "The SEALs."

"Bullet in the face'll do that to you."

"Will it?" She sipped tea. "Your mobility looks right as rain. You didn't have any trouble saving that family. Is your vision messed up?"

Nobody had been as direct with him about his injuries since the doctors at Bethesda, and he couldn't decide if it was a tactic meant to throw him off balance or if she was a woman without the time for pleasantries. The latter didn't seem right. There didn't seem to be another soul on the ranch, and she'd certainly had time to decorate the place and keep it up. It was a riot of old western knickknacks and big puddling draperies the color of pine needles.

"My vision's fine," Randy said. "It was my skull under it that got messed up. But a couple surgeries and it was back together."

And just like that, she had him selling his abilities as if this were a normal job interview.

"So what was it, then? Did you lose your nerve?"

"Nerve is what you need to clap back at the person at the dinner table talking politics you don't like. Being a SEAL takes more than nerve."

"OK, well, whatever it takes, did you lose it?"

"I didn't come here to be insulted."

"I'm interviewing you."

"For what?" he asked.

"We had a retirement on my staff. The job is twofold. Security and containment."

"Christ. How much are those horses worth?" Randy asked.

"It's not the horses."

"Well, what is it? They're the only damn things here."

When Agatha Caldwell met his eyes, he had trouble pinpointing the emotion in them—a sudden alertness, tinged with offense. But his offhand remark had struck her somehow; she seemed to be studying him now more intently than before.

"They are not the only things here," she said.

Suddenly, Randy was at a loss for words. Her intensity sent chills down his body, chills that seemed to ferret out every scar and lingering battle wound and caress them with too much lascivious intention. And suddenly the quiet of this ranch, its placid surface, seemed threatening, like a still ocean surface beneath which sharks circled.

"I'm not down for anything criminal," he said.

"Why'd you leave the SEALs?" she asked again.

"What's that got to do with anything?"

"I assume you've seen things that other people never have and never will. But where has that left you, Randy Drummond? Has it opened your mind or worn it out? Because I need to know if you're ready for an experience you might not understand."

His first instinct was that the woman across from him knew exactly what she was hunting for, exactly why he'd left the teams. But that was damn near impossible, because he'd never really told anyone. Not in anything that could be described as specific detail.

"I had an experience." It came out a little breathless, a little choked, the way he always sounded when he used somebody else's words to describe a topic that made him uncomfortable. But he'd put just enough emphasis into the word *experience* to indicate he wasn't just talking about the bullet and the surgeries that followed.

"When I got shot, I . . . I left my body."

Agatha Caldwell didn't flinch or raise her eyebrows or make any gesture of dismissal or disdain. He fell silent because he was trying to come up with a way to describe the color of the light that had embraced him during it, a blue unlike any shade he'd ever seen in nature. His first thought as he'd felt death's embrace was that he'd floated up into the sky itself. But he'd quickly realized that wasn't right. That it was as if whatever had given the sky its color had poured forth from some tear between this world and the next and enveloped him.

"You could see yourself," Agatha said quietly, "as if you were looking down on yourself."

"For a moment, yes. And then . . ."

What he'd seen next was something he'd never described to anyone, but it had looked just like the inside of the old revolving restaurant atop Reunion Tower in Dallas. He'd only eaten there once in his life, but his dad, who'd been from the area, had loved the place, and so they'd gone there for lunch one day when they were visiting his grandmother, and that was the lunch where he'd told his dad he was going for the SEALs. His father, who'd rung the bell twice on Coronado Island, who'd never made it past the first week and felt almost constant shame over it, had teared up with pride, and Randy had felt overwhelmed with gratitude, as if it had taken him that many years to realize he'd been blessed to have a dad who didn't see him as competition or a threat, a dad who could be brought to tears of joy by the prospect of his offspring finishing something he could not. That lunch had been one of the happiest moments of Randy's life, and so at first, he'd thought it was no surprise his brain would glom on to its memory as a comfort once death was near.

"You had an NDE."

"A what?" he asked.

"A near-death experience. Go on. I'm sorry for interrupting."

What he'd realized in that moment was that it was not a vision he was experiencing. He had gone somewhere; what he was seeing had substance, a reality that couldn't be blinked away. And even though the sunlight beyond the windows had been brighter than it had been during that long-ago lunch, even though the tables all around him were occupied by ghostly silhouettes, he had known where he was. He hadn't traveled through time. Rather, it felt as if he had traveled to a version of the memory that had always remained anchored somewhere in the universe.

"My father was there."

"And what did he do?"

"He asked me if I wanted to . . . continue."

"Into death?"

"That was one option."

"He gave you a choice. To live or to . . . continue on."

Maybe if she'd phrased it as a question, a quick, hot tear wouldn't have slid down Randy's right cheek. Or maybe it was the way she referred to death as continuing on. A road not taken. A road not taken because he had thought it meant quitting but which she'd just made sound like an opportunity, a new mission, a new world beyond this one. In the end, he decided it was her complete absence of skepticism, her complete understanding, that collapsed a wall inside himself he'd been holding up with both hands ever since he returned to his broken body on Iraqi soil. It was one thing to tell your truth; it was another to be so unreservedly believed by a stranger. Maybe that was the experience Agatha Caldwell thought he wouldn't understand.

For a while, neither of them spoke, as if she were allowing him to remember the way his father had smiled proudly and retreated into the brightening blue-tinged sunlight after Randy made his choice. But when he finally looked at her, he saw something warm and open. He saw something else too.

Relief.

"You chose to come back," she said. "To live."

Randy nodded.

"Do you regret it?" she asked.

"On some days."

"Is that why you left the military?"

"I left because I knew I wouldn't see it as taking life anymore. That I'd just see it as nudging someone into whatever comes next. And that meant I'd lost the discernment required to be a good operator."

"If death is just a doorway to something better, why think twice about mowing down anyone in your path?"

"That's one way of putting it," he said.

"Isn't that what most people think already?"

"Believing and experiencing are two very different things."

At these words, Agatha Caldwell's stare became as steady and intense as any he'd ever been subjected to.

"I'd like to show you what's in the barn," she said.

They crossed the grass between the main house and the shiny unused structure in question. She donned a jacket first, which struck him as odd. It wasn't cold out. She pulled both barn doors open without asking for his assistance, then shut them behind Randy once he stepped inside. Once they were enclosed by shadows and the smell of horse stalls, she dug into the pocket of her jacket and extended a pair of solid-black sunglasses that looked capable of shielding his eyes from a nuclear blast.

"Put these on. When we get down there, I mean."

"No hazmat suit?" he asked.

"Not here," she answered.

Which was not the answer he was expecting. Was there really a place on her ranch that required full-body protective gear? She stepped back, then kicked aside the dirt from a little metal plate set in the barn's floor. Crouching down, she removed a putty knife from her jacket pocket and pried up a little metal square in the plate's center, revealing a depressed door pull. Suddenly she was hoisting open a car-size metal door into the air. She walked it out until it flipped onto its top. Underneath was a set of double storm doors. While not as large, they looked twice as heavy as their protective covering. There was a keypad in the wood frame surrounding them.

Randy felt like it was rude not to help her, but it also felt like this process was about to become intricate and dangerous and he might screw it up if he intervened. So he watched her hoist the storm doors open, revealing a set of stairs. He neared the entrance so he could get a better look down, realized, with a knot in his gut, they went far deeper than your average storm cellar.

She gestured for him to go down first. He just stared at her.

"I'll give you a gun if it'll make you feel safer," she said.

"I'm carrying."

"And I haven't asked for it, so that should be a sign you're all right."

"Guns aren't much good against radiation," he said.

"There's no radiation on Thunder Ranch."

With a placid smile and a jerk of her head, she gestured for him to start moving.

He descended, hearing the well-oiled hinges of the doors being closed overhead. Then suddenly there was darkness, save for the glowing lights of another keypad on the wall in front of him.

"Put the glasses on," she said next to him.

"Lady, if this is some kinda—"

"I know it's dark now, but if you don't put the glasses on, you're not going to be able to see a damn thing when the door opens."

He consented. Saw her finger make shadows against the glowing keypad. There was a slight hiss. He realized it was an electronic lock opening, and then suddenly the woman was pushing open a door into a silent explosion of fierce light that quickly turned her into a black silhouette.

Caldwell gestured for him to step into the glow, and he did, feeling his mouth hang open at the dazzling sight before him. She was right—he would have been blinded without the glasses. He still felt blinded. After a few moments, he realized he was staring down a corridor lined with glass cells, similar in architecture to the one in that movie *Silence of the Lambs*, only from inside each one came a shimmering radiance.

He didn't even notice her close the door behind him because his feet had taken over and now he was walking down the length of the cells, staring within. Some of them looked like those silly terrariums you'd see at a natural history museum, the kind with stuffed animals positioned in vaguely lifelike-looking poses. But the closer he looked, the more he realized each cell only contained scattered elements of wilderness environments. Broken branches or stones, and their reason for being there was simple. They were either the source of the rising, pulsating blue radiance, or inextricably bonded to it.

His gut told him that if he peered too closely into the light, he'd lose either his mind or his lunch, so he tried to take in the other details first. Saw that on the outside of each cell was a photograph of a different animal. No explanation or text, just a picture. One cell showed a picture of a bear, the other a deer, the other birds.

Jesus, Mary, and Joseph, he thought. *That's what they used to be.* That's what these shimmering things used to be.

"The color," Agatha said. "Is it the same color, Randy? The same color you saw when you got shot?"

"Death," he said before he could stop himself. "It's the color of death."

"Oh, but see, Randy, that's just the problem."

She followed his gaze to what had once been a grizzly bear but was now a gentle, rolling storm of blue light rising toward the ceiling like smoke from a splintered section of tree trunk.

"What we're looking at," Agatha Caldwell said, "can't die."

II

The Park

Death is a word, and it is the word, the image, that creates fear.

—*Jiddu Krishnamurti*

10

When the first burst of turbulence hits, Claire raises the window shade next to her seat, braced for the sight of her little brother's face. But there are no serpentine trails of fog reflected in the glass, no glimpse of Poe's bright orange jacket. Just clouds ripping past, briefly glowing ivory in the plane's flashing wing light before vanishing into darkness. One admonishment has scared him off. If she wants him to reappear, will she have to invite him?

She feels a sense memory from that moment in the guest bathroom at her house, of the tingling that spread from the back of her neck across the crown of her skull as her little brother extended his hand to her from the other side of the glass. Feels a sudden burst of longing for the ghostly sight of him that's been stalking her ever since the crash. Is her mind opening, or is she losing it?

I can't draw, she hears herself saying again. Panic attacks and breakdowns are one thing. Manifesting an elaborate skill out of nowhere is quite another.

The plane bounces so hard Margot holds her iPad to her chest. She's warned Claire an early snowstorm's blowing into the Flathead Valley, the kind that might get them redirected if they were flying commercial.

Margot tucks her iPad into the big padded pocket on the side of her recliner-size chair. She didn't ask why Claire wanted all the shades down, even during flight. Hiding from reporters was a good excuse on the tarmac, but at cruising altitude? She's been exceedingly patient with Claire, and Claire appreciates it, even if she thinks it's a sign Margot knows the reunion awaiting them is going to be challenging.

As soon as the plane leveled off, Margot moved to the plush leather seat facing Claire across a table that could fit two formal place settings with room to spare. No doubt she's been reading everything she can find about Poe's crash and doesn't want to upset her with any of the accompanying images.

Claire's never been a nervous flyer, never hit a bout of turbulence strong enough to trigger memories of being knocked off her feet that night in Glacier. There was a car wreck with her aunt Eileen that did it when she was younger, left her shaking and dazed for hours, even though both of them walked away without a scratch. And contact sports were never her favorite thing. Another player slamming into her could trigger memories of that night and the way it had felt like someone had yanked her head to one side with vicious force.

Her dad's been right about one thing so far: The plane is nice, comfortable. Thick carpet, plush leather seats, lavender air freshener that smells like it costs more than a seat in coach does. There's even a sleeping compartment in the back Margot said she could use but which Claire hasn't set foot in.

"How come you didn't believe him?" Claire asks.

"Your father?"

"His alien theory."

Margot considers this, crosses her hands over one knee. "Not enough missing time, for one. Abductees sometimes report hours lost, half days. And there were other little things that didn't fit with what I've found in the literature. With abductions, there's often a sort of preparatory dance between a craft and an abductee, and maybe a searchlight of some sort that scans the area and the person. Almost like the human subject is being examined before they're taken up. There was none of that."

"You mean in the versions he didn't make up," Claire says.

"Correct."

"What do you think it was?"

Margot raises her eyebrows and clears her throat, as if she's accessing a mental file in her head that's within reach but hasn't been opened in a while. "Well, to *me* your father described something with defined borders. A quick, blinding pulse. He was a good distance away from you and your brother when it struck, so he could probably see the nature of it, the shape, pretty well. Better than either of you could."

"Why wasn't there more damage, then?" Claire asks.

"You and your brother had significant injuries."

"The trees, though."

"Didn't you tell the doctors that a bunch of branches broke and came down on you?"

"If it was a shock wave like he described, it would have been entire trees coming down."

"There was some damage, apparently, but the Park Service blamed downdraft from the helicopter that lifted you guys out of there. All I know is that I believe you experienced something powerful and unexplained. But *earthbound*. I don't think the three of you left the ground during the experience. And I wanted him to embrace that. That it could be unexplained and significant and life changing without being an abduction story."

"But then he'd have to cop to all the lies he told about it," Claire says.

Margot doesn't dispute this.

"How'd you get into all this?" Claire asks. "Not just my dad. I mean, this world of . . ."

"Nutjobs?" Margot smiles. Claire smiles back. "I experienced a sighting. When I was fourteen."

"Where?" Claire asks.

"My family's lodge in the Cascades. It was pretty typical of the stories you hear. A craft that moved too quickly through the sky, made maneuvers that weren't possible given the technology of the day. Or today, for that matter."

"And so from fourteen on you were just . . . devoted."

"Obsessed. And it was more like twenty-three on."

"Why twenty-three?" Claire asks.

"I dismissed the experience for years, and then one night several members of my family admitted they'd seen it too. And we'd all just never said anything about it. We'd gone . . . what? Nine years having witnessed something truly mind-boggling and none of us ever said a word. So I visited the towns nearby, started asking questions, and eventually I turned up more people who'd seen the exact same thing that night. I mean, they described it to a T. Without any prompting. Many of them didn't even know each other, and they all said they'd never discussed it with anyone."

"How many people did you find?" Claire asks.

"Fifteen," Margot says. "That's when I learned how powerful the fear of ridicule can be. It kept fifteen people silent about an experience they couldn't explain, an experience with incredible implications. And I thought, how many people are there like us the world over, shoving extraordinary experiences into the back of their minds because of this fear? Imagine all the discoveries that could lie behind that wall of shame."

Claire is thinking now of the hours she's spent on YouTube watching seemingly sane and ordinary people describe in vivid detail experiences that defy explanation. Encounters with crafts like the one Margot just described or big hairy monsters in the woods. One after the other, she'd watched them, hunting for the ones she could dismiss. The ones who seemed to hog the camera in some desperate bid for attention or whose stories spiraled ever outward into ridiculousness with each new, theatrical detail. But more often than not, she found herself sitting awestruck before the accounts of people whose tones didn't carry a whiff of ego or insanity, wondering if she could have become one of those people had she taken a different path.

"Claire."

"Yes?"

"May I ask what *you* think it was?"

"Military." Margot looks startled by the answer, so Claire gives her a second to process. "It was so quick. I thought maybe it was a downdraft from some kind of aircraft they were testing over the park. But then I'd think maybe I was just confusing my memory of being airlifted out with what happened before. So I don't know, is basically what I'm saying."

"And your mother?" she asks.

"We didn't talk about it."

"Poe?" Margot asks. "What did he believe?"

It comes out of Claire with ease, the story of the past twenty-four hours. Up until that moment, Margot, like most CNN viewers, has only known of the possibility that Claire received some sort of psychic message from her brother as the plane went down. The other details leave her wide-eyed and stricken, maybe because she has no fundamental resistance to them, no self-protective skepticism.

Then Claire feels it, the massaging of a muscle inside her arm.

"Paper," she says.

"What?"

"It's happening again," Claire says. "Give me paper."

Margot is scrambling for her carry-on bag suddenly, no small feat given the plane's rock-and-roll descent. Eventually she pulls out a leather portfolio, flips it open to reveal a legal pad. She manages to get a pen into Claire's hand before stumbling back into her seat and hurriedly buckling her seat belt.

It takes effort not to fight it this time, maybe because the transmission's exerting greater power to overcome the bouncing turbulence.

But a sketch is taking shape once more. Only it's not Pier 39. It's not anyplace familiar.

It's not anyone familiar, even though it's a person.

A man.

Perfectly balanced features, an angel's face, except for the frenzied markings indicating both filth and a heavy beard, and the thick hair so matted it looks like a broken helmet.

Claire thinks the whole thing might be over with. Then her hand starts to move again. Writing this time. Is she actually going to sign the damn thing like a professional artist?

HE KILLED SOMEONE

The second her arm goes lax, Margot's pen slips from her hand and drops to the thick carpet.

The engines groan, the plane rocks side to side as it battles crosswinds. She's not looking for it, so when she sees it, she lets out a startled cry. Little Poe is visible inside the plane's window now, and for the first time, his palm is pressed flat to the glass. His hair is being tousled by lazy winds completely out of sync with the ones ripping the clouds behind him. How is that possible? A hallucination, she figures, would steal from and twist what she's actually seeing, not add a completely separate layer over it. How could her mind create a completely different set of winds that only affect her brother's hair and nothing else?

"Claire?" Margot asks. "Are you seeing him?"

She nods. Poe lowers his palm and backs away into the dark, and she realizes the fear in his expression was enough to match her own.

"You didn't, I take it?" Claire tries to maintain calm, but she sounds as if she's breathing through a straw.

Margot shakes her head. When she sees the sketch, she falls silent, stares at it.

"Who is this?" she finally asks.

"I have no idea."

Margot is nodding as she studies it, but it looks reflexive, nervous, like she's trying to maintain her calm as well.

"Have you ever seen anything like this?" Claire asks.

"Automatic writing, yes. But a drawing this detailed . . ."

"Out of someone who can barely draw an orange."

Margot is silent for a while.

"Let's wait to tell your father all this," she finally says. "Let's . . . see what kind of condition he's in first."

Condition. The word doesn't seem to come easily to Margot, and it leaves Claire wondering if a potential book deal was the only reason for their breakup.

Finally, Claire nods and does nothing as Margot closes the leather portfolio and slides the sketch into her carry-on. And it takes Claire a moment to realize that Margot, who travels the world studying all manner of extraordinary events, is astonished by what she's just witnessed.

11

Twelve Years Ago

They didn't plan to stay the entire night, but they set up camp just in case. The temperature started falling the minute the sun went down, the valleys far below pooling with a darkness that felt alive. The storms that had thundered through the park over the past few days had left everything with a wet sheen that glistened in the moonlight, so they laid saddle blankets on the rocks that would offer them the best view. It had been almost a year since Agatha had first shown him her cellar and the miracles within, but in that time, she had shared the nightmare that gave birth to their source as well, and as a result, Randy's opinion of her had been forever changed.

She wasn't lying when she said she knew war in ways he didn't. She was being humble.

He'd also done the most sacred thing a combat veteran can do—he'd shared not just everything he experienced in combat, but almost everything he'd felt about it since. And she'd listened patiently, maybe because she felt it was the price she had to pay for ensuring he kept her secrets.

She'd assured him their current campsite would be the perfect vantage point to watch the display to come, if it did. All the atmospheric readings were lined up, placing them inside what she referred to as the "risk window." If the ranger had done what they paid him to do, the valley below was clear of life. He'd reported two families camping close to the edge of the danger zone, heedless of the rain, and had managed to encourage both of them to decamp with false reports of bear sightings. Just in case, Randy had swept the treetops with Agatha's little heat-seeking drones earlier that day. The scans turned up nothing human, but some animals always slipped through, Agatha assured him. Hence, the need for her cellar. The small creatures would be broken by the shock wave, their shimmering remains easy to collect. That was good because it meant the birds, the ones most likely to fly away before their team could capture them and hide their secrets from the world, would be instantly killed; the larger animals might be injured and have to be carted away, which would take more work. But never again, she'd told him with greater emphasis each time, could they let humans slip through their barriers.

"What would you have done?" Agatha asked him suddenly, as if picking up a conversation they'd been having all day, when the truth was they'd been all business for the past few weeks. "If I hadn't tracked you down, what would you have done?"

"With my life, you mean?" Randy asked.

She nodded.

"Fixing up my dad's house, probably," he said.

The house where she'd surprised him one rainy day with her business card and an enticing offer. He'd barely visited the place since and was considering putting it up for sale.

"Yeah, I would have just thrown myself into it, I guess."

She'd sat down on a large rock at the end of the little clearing. He took a seat next to her. His eyes adjusted to the darkness. The forested contours of the ridges below them gained resolution, but beyond, Lake Michele was lost to darkness.

"So many people think land will fix it, whatever it is," Agatha said.

"What do you mean?"

"I don't know. They just think if they finally get enough space around them, it'll clear their head. I don't think it works that way.

Plenty of people have been driven mad by open spaces, and too much land can become a prison."

"You talking about your ranch?" Randy asked.

She nodded.

"Who's the prisoner?" he asked. "You or the things in your cellar?"

"I have to choose?"

Even though he couldn't quite see her face, Randy could hear the smile in her voice. She wasn't in the habit of making a candid, raw admission like that without some truism attached to the end, something that kept her pain from hovering in the silence, unaddressed, something that made her sound like the tough, ranching mountain woman who thought it was an honor to carry a burden of secrets and grief.

"You sure we'll be all right up here?" he asked.

"We'll be fine. But would you care if we weren't?"

"Is that why you picked me? You thought I wouldn't care if I got exposed?"

"Maybe," she said.

She'd been exposed. She'd shared that with him early on. Whether she cared was a question she'd yet to answer in any detail, maybe because he hadn't asked it directly.

"I've got a sister," Agatha said after a while. "She was a baby when it all happened. I raised her myself in Whitefish. Kept her off the ranch."

Randy was stunned. She'd made no mention of a sister until that moment, which was a shock, given he knew horrifying details about the other members of her family. It was a reminder that even after a year of working together, lowering their guards, there were still details she'd kept from him. And if they were anything like the story she'd already shared, there would be no preparing himself for the revelations to come.

"She's got no idea?" he asked.

"When she started to get one, I made sure she stopped."

"How?"

"I let her think I was running something bad enough for her not to want to know, but not as bad as what it really is."

Randy remembered his own first impressions when he drove onto the ranch: thoughts of human trafficking and drug smuggling and other criminal conspiracies that might hide behind a facade of ranching props and set pieces that were too unused and clean.

"You guys ever talk?" Randy asked.

"She's got a family down in Wyoming now. Kids. Her husband's a state senator."

"So, no," he said. "Any men?"

"Men?"

"You know what I mean."

The minute the question was out of him, he felt his face get tingly and hot, as if he'd just revealed thoughts he'd hoped to keep hidden.

"A few," she answered. "I got serious with this guy in Bigfork who managed vacation rentals, but he kept wanting to come to the ranch, so . . ."

"So that was the end of it."

"Pretty much. You're the first man to ever cross my threshold and stay, Randy Drummond."

"What about the guy I replaced?"

"He didn't spend much time in the house," she said.

His heart was racing. He told himself it was the anxiety of waiting for the valley below to briefly ignite. But he knew that was bullshit. It was the flirtatiousness in her tone.

"You know . . ." He stopped suddenly, feeling like his breath had been stolen from him in an instant.

"Know what, Randy?"

"You didn't turn out to be who I thought you would," he said.

"Same here, Randy Drummond. Same here."

A little while later, it happened. First came a pop like thunder, then a sound like an engine revving deep within the valley. If they'd been closer, both sounds would have seemed ungodly and overwhelming. But from up high, they were like something you'd hear late at night from the high floor of a downtown hotel. Next came the shock wave—it sounded like wind-driven water rushing through the valley far below. Then, the pulse—fast as lightning and just as bright, but with a reach and radius that stunned him silent. In an instant, the entire valley, every ripple in the surface of Lake Michele, became visible and briefly frozen in its glare. He couldn't help but imagine those poor little Huntley kids—Artemis and Apollo, she called them—getting caught up in it and tossed like rag dolls.

Standing now, Agatha was briefly silhouetted by the flash, and her sacrifices, her secrets, her pain, and her grief were all made clear to him in an instant, leaving him awestruck by the quiet stoicism required to stand guardian like this for so long.

"And there it is," she whispered.

And for a while neither one of them spoke.

Randy moved to her and tenderly placed his hands on her waist, waiting for a flinch or a recoil that told him he needed to withdraw. Whether it was true or not, he'd told himself he'd reached that place men struggle to reach, where they can admit their desire without collapsing into anger and ego if their advance is rejected.

She didn't pull away. Agatha leaned into him and tilted her head gently, as if offering him the side of her neck, and when he kissed it tenderly, she reached down and gripped his hand. He stopped, preparing for her to draw it off her body. Instead, she clutched it between her breasts and stroked his fingers with hers. She was old enough to be his mother, and before she opened her ranch to him, that fact would have mattered in some instinctive, shallow way. But together they'd entered a world where age was irrelevant, where the once-immutable facts of the human body seemed to be perpetually in question, and the only intervals of time that mattered were the years that passed between eruptions like the one they'd just witnessed in the valley below.

"Let's go to the tent," she said.

And he obeyed. He had never made love to a woman of her age, and he wasn't prepared for the authority in her touch, the experience it radiated, how she smoothly directed him and guided him and how that confidence made what could sometimes seem like a shameful, fumbling, degrading act feel like something both inevitable and fundamentally correct.

It felt different than it had with any other woman, and Randy knew that could only mean one thing.

———

"How well do we think this is going to go?" Benjamin asks.

Randy's been so lost in thought he hasn't noticed the man's return to the tech center. Suddenly there's a big steaming mug of coffee on the table next to him, and Ben's taking his seat. Randy was watching the feed from the dash cam in Thomas Billings's Trailhawk, watching Abram Huntley steer his rented Jeep into the pick-up lane at Glacier Jet Center, before memory overtook him.

The snow's still dancing and bouncing on the wind, like flocks of moths trying and failing to fly a straight path.

"We're just watching for now," Randy says.

"No, I mean this little father-daughter reunion that's about to go down."

"Well, we're not going to be able to hear the first act since he switched cars."

Randy leans back in his chair, examines the feeds before him. The one that gets to him is the empty night-vision view of Poe's studio apartment in Queens. He'd expected a friend or someone else to make entry by now. That'll probably happen tomorrow, once the shock starts to wear off. For now, the place is quiet as a tomb. There's a little row of art books on the shelf affixed to the wall above the vintage metal school desk where Poe used to draw. They're still jostled from where he'd knocked his backpack against them in his rush to make his flight that morning. The fact that they're still holding the same tilted position makes it seem like they're paying tribute to their lost owner.

"If Papa Bear's onto us, maybe he's figured out more than we think," Benjamin says. "Maybe most of what we've been seeing from his house has been for show."

"A possibility," Randy says.

"And maybe now that he's got his daughter, he's going to try to get outside our surveillance network. Make a run for it."

"If so," Randy says, "we're more than ready."

12

Claire isn't prepared for the lancing cold that strikes her as soon as she and Margot step out of the terminal. This isn't the occasional damp chill that turns a Southern California evening into an excuse for cashmere. This is the type of Arctic blast that sweeps down over the Canadian border with little warning, bringing snowstorms to northern Montana as early as late summer. Cold like this is the reason their childhood camping trips were confined to the months of June and July, even if it meant being hemmed in by the frequent lightning storms that roared over the park.

She's also not prepared for the man standing next to the double-parked Jeep to be her father. He seems too frail and hunched over. Her last memories of Abram Huntley are of an imposing and powerfully built man who strode through life on the balls of his feet, shoving open doors with the palm of one hand as he went. But all that muscle hasn't sagged. Instead, it's withered away. He's wearing a dark green knit beanie that hides whatever's left of his once-long hair, and under the flaps of his waffle-print coat he's got a tattered V-neck fleece over a T-shirt. The light snow swirls through headlights he hasn't turned off, and he's bouncing from foot to foot, either because he's cold or because all the strength and determination with which he used to move through life has turned jittery and diffuse. Or maybe he's high. She hates the fact that her head goes to that place first, but given their family history, it's understandable.

Glacier Jet Center is Glacier Park International Airport's private plane terminal, and it strikes Claire as deeply ironic that on one of the worst days of her life she's arriving in Montana through the VIP entrance celebrities use to visit their multimillion-dollar mansions on Flathead Lake.

"What's up with your hair?" her father barks.

"Excuse me?"

"I just figured you'd grow up to be a short-hair person," he says.

"Why's that?"

"When you were little, you were always moaning about having your hair in your face. Thought you'd chop it all off as soon as you could. It was your mother who liked your hair long."

Maybe someone else would be startled by his boisterous tone. She's not. It's the same tone some of her male students use with her when disclosing that terrible things are happening to them at home. A defiant blend of stiff-upper-lip and performative amusement over life's darker twists and turns, like the trauma they're suffering is no big deal and their sudden, unprompted disclosure of it to an authority figure is something they've been compelled to do by a world determined to make them feel bad about what's ultimately no big deal. That's the kind of energy coming off her father now: *I look like a wreck, my son is dead, but we can still chat about your hair because I am just that strong. Got it, sweetheart?*

"That's not how I remember it, but OK," Claire says.

"Well, it wasn't me."

"I didn't say it was you. It's me, actually. I enjoy having long hair."

"OK. Well, you didn't always."

"Sure, all right."

"Everybody remembers things different, I guess."

Something tugs on Claire's right hand. It's Margot, taking her duffel bag from her. When she starts to carry it toward the parked car, Claire realizes the little display's meant to send Abram a message about his rudeness. Margot tries to open the cargo door, but it's locked. She says Abram's name once, with strained patience. He hits the remote without even looking at her.

"You look tired," he tells Claire.

"Do you have a book deal?" she asks.

"A what?"

"A book deal. Did you ask me to come here because you have some book deal about what happened?"

Abram rolls his eyes as if the question's beneath him, then turns to Margot. "Thanks a lot."

Margot closes the cargo door with a loud thud. "I'll just go ahead and assume you're thanking me for flying your daughter here on a moment's notice. Keys, please." She extends her hand.

"I'm driving."

"It's been a difficult day for both of you, and it's probably better if I—"

"I said I'm driving, Margot. Jesus Christ. Get one of those little rich-lady lapdogs so you can boss it around in your free time. Get in the car." He turns to Claire. "You too."

He's about to slide behind the wheel when he sees Claire hasn't moved an inch.

"Answer the question," Claire says.

He studies her. It's a long look and leaves her wondering if he truly did expect a submissive twelve-year-old version of his daughter to come toddling off the plane.

"No, I do not have a book deal."

"But you have answers?"

"Not out here," Abram says through gritted teeth. She follows his nervous glances in both directions. There are other cars parked nearby, but it's late. Still, he's probably right to consider that a reporter might have been able to trace her journey here, especially if her father's got a local footprint. They still share the same last name.

A second later, she's sliding into the front passenger seat, wondering what to make of the fact that Margot instinctively got into the back. Is she trying to keep her distance? Should Claire do the same?

On the ground, the winds aren't as fierce, but the flakes are fat and steady, and her father has to keep the wipers going as the little airport becomes a smear of light behind them.

"Is this your car?" Margot asks.

"Rental."

"What happened to the truck I gave you?"

"Listen, the hair thing," Abram says as if Margot hasn't spoken. "I didn't mean to say it because of your mother dying."

"I don't even know what you—"

"I didn't mean to say I'd expect you to chop it all off just because your mother was gone finally."

"Finally?"

"That's not what I—"

"Has everyone eaten?" Margot asks loudly. "How about a meal?"

"We're going to go for a drive," Abram says.

"In the snow?"

"Contrary to what you might want to believe, I actually do know how to do things without you."

Margot mutters something that involves taking the Lord's name in vain.

"What I said about your mother," Abram says to Claire, "I didn't mean it like that. I just . . . what I'm trying to say—"

"The reason you think I don't like having long hair is because the only time you spent with me when I was a kid was on camping trips where having long hair was often an issue. So what you were seeing was my problem with being on camping trips, not with long hair."

"Well, you sure grew up to be a schoolteacher."

"That's correct. I am a schoolteacher."

"You loved camping."

"No, I loved the library, and you told me I couldn't spend all my time there because I'd gain weight."

"I never said that!"

"You said it three times, and then the third time Mom threatened to throw a plate at your head."

"That part I believe."

"Well, they kind of go hand in hand."

"All right, well, it didn't take much for your mother to threaten physical violence against me. And just because I'm a man does not mean that I have to accept—"

"OK, you know what? I don't want to talk about Mom. I'm not here to talk about *Mom*."

Her father is studying the rearview mirror as he drives.

"You're afraid of reporters?" she finally asks.

"What did she tell you anyway? About the divorce."

Margot sat forward and placed one hand on the back of each headrest. "All right. Look, there's been a lot of years, so maybe catching up can come later, and right now we can focus on what's going on."

"Just tell me what she told you."

"For the last time, I am not here to talk about my mother."

Abram rolls his eyes, drums his fingers on the steering wheel.

"Perhaps a drive-through?" Margot whispers.

"I already ate," Abram says.

"Customarily, when one is hosting visitors, one allows for the possibility that they might have stomachs too."

The silence that follows gives Claire time to reflect on whether she's made a terrible mistake by coming here. More time than she'd like to devote to the topic.

"Where are you living?" Claire finally asks.

"Columbia Falls," he answers.

"Then why are we going to Whitefish?"

"Sharp. I wouldn't expect you to remember your way around."

"Yeah, well, the final chapter kinda seared it in my memory."

"Not really the final chapter since you're back now," Abram says.

"What are *you* doing here?" she asks.

"Still looking for answers."

"So that's what we're calling it."

"What is that supposed to mean?"

"You know *exactly* what it means."

He's been so barky and combative since getting in the car she expects him to start clapping back at her like a kid, but instead, he stares at the road.

They pass over a long river of railroad tracks, leaving the town center in their wake as they head in the general direction of the Lodge at Whitefish Lake. They'd stayed there once when rainstorms kept them out of the park, a magical night of room service and jumping on a big cushy bed and pay-per-view movies, only to have their mother flip her lid over the bill when they got back. She doubts her father got them rooms there now, and she doubts Margot would have done so without saying anything. Where she's sure they're *not* headed is Columbia Falls, which is behind them and a little way's east.

So far, Claire's awareness of her visions has felt like grief, a sudden shock that keeps returning to remind her that her life has been forever altered. It feels just like those first waking moments when she thought her mother was still clinging to life in the hospital bed they'd moved into the living room, and then a little voice would say, *Mom's gone. The living room's empty.* And it stayed that way for months as old likes, hobbies, and obsessions all tried to captivate her the way they used to, only to be chased off by that crushing reminder. The same thing is happening to her now. Her anger toward her father, one of her frequent pastimes, barely has time to consume her before a little voice in her head says, *Sure, but you're going nuts.*

This time, she talks back to it. *Since when is suddenly being able to draw like you went to art school evidence of going nuts?*

"I did what I thought I had to do to rattle the right cages," her father finally says, jerking her back to the present.

"Who would those cages be? The government? The Pentagon?"

"If you don't want to talk about her, stop sounding like her."

"Meaning?"

"Stop talking to me like I'm bonkers."

"I never said you were *bonkers*. I said you lied."

"Everyone was lying about *me!*" He slams the steering wheel with one fist, causing Margot to jump in the back seat. "Everyone was saying I got shit-faced and let my own kids almost get eaten by a bear."

"They were speculating on the most probable theory based on the evidence. You, on the other hand, made up things—"

"What evidence? Not a single claw mark on either one of you. Not a single bite! There was no damn evidence of what they were saying, but they ran with it and made me sound like I was some fuckup—"

"We were miles from where we should have been," Claire says, "and you had to leave us for hours to get help! You had broken every promise you made to my mother. We weren't at a designated campsite. You didn't check in with anybody. And you were drinking. Nobody had to invent that story, Dad. You did all of that on your own."

They're traveling uphill. The woods close in around them; the snow's lighter now but still pelts the windshield every now and then. For some reason, her father has chosen to enter a twisty mountain road in the middle of the night, far from where he supposedly lives. Are they headed to some secret commune of fellow cranks living off the grid somewhere above? Should she jump out of the car now?

"She knew," Abram finally says.

"Knew what?"

"She knew you were connected."

Claire wants to interrogate him, demand to know exactly what he means. But she knows, and it feels like a crushing defeat. Her dad contacted her the minute her classroom incident made the national news, because it revealed a secret he'd been keeping most of his life. And now he's telling her that her mother had kept that secret as well.

"When?" she asks.

"She figured it out when I did. In the hospital."

"The hospital. You mean the night it happened—"

"Well, she didn't get there the night it happened. It took her another day before she—"

"You know what I mean."

"We figured it out while you were both in the hospital. It was your arms, at first. You'd each broken one, but you were both complaining about how both your arms hurt. They were worried about how much pain meds they were giving you both for it. Then when she went to tell Poe that she was going to try to take you both away from me and he lost it, *your* heart started racing so fast the nurses came in. You were twitching. You even started to cry. We kept testing it. Your mother didn't want to believe it at first. But you remember how you asked to be put in the same room as Poe and she wouldn't even ask the hospital? It's because she was seeing it and it scared the shit out of her and she thought it would get worse if you guys were closer together. So we decided to separate you."

"Separate us? By getting divorced?"

"The divorce was going to happen no matter what. You two were another matter."

"You agreed to this?" she asks.

"I thought once we did it, she'd realize she was wrong and the connection wasn't going to go away no matter what we did, and then she'd come back. You'd both come back. And we'd all be together again. Instead, you all found your own ways to suppress it."

Now Claire sees that long-ago lunch, the last time she saw her father, in a new light. Had he really been letting her go that day? Or had he been staying quiet, biding his time before a reunion that never came? And her mother's words upon learning that Poe had run away. *He can't come here. That's not how it works.* Had the *it* in that sentence been her plan to keep Claire from her brother? And over the years, had her plan gone from trying to sever a psychic connection between them . . . to hiding it?

But these are distractions, Claire knows. Distractions from the sense of bone-deep betrayal she feels.

She knew. Her mother, who'd forbidden all talk of that night, who'd talked about her father like he was some backwoods lunatic, had known all along that something unexplained connected her children, and she'd swept it under the rug. And in response, Claire had stuffed her real suspicions about that night down deep, not even sharing them with her many therapists over the years. Focusing instead on a minute analysis of the maybe-not-panic-attacks that had consumed her, obsessed her the way that night had obsessed her father. And her mother had let it happen.

"Guess she never told you any of this?" Abram asks. "Too busy trashing me, I guess."

"And you asked me to fly here just so you could trash her memory. Today of all days."

"And there's my answer."

"And you never told Poe."

Now it's her father's turn to stay silent.

"He figured it out, you know," she says. "The connection thing. Once he got sober, he could feel it more. That's what he told Phil, at least. He started spying on me using my brother-in-law to see if he was right."

"Your *step*brother-in-law," he grumbles.

141

"Whatever. Poe had a whole notebook full of events. Big things happened to one of us, and the other one felt it too. It's why he was flying to LA. To tell me everything. So, you know, good move keeping it a secret and all."

The silence in the car is electric, and Claire can feel Margot tense up. Too late, she realizes what she's just said. Shame blooms inside her, but she can't find her voice through it. Feels herself rationalizing the accusation even as its poisonous burn moves through her: Poe never would have been on that plane if her father hadn't kept all this to himself. She feels like a hypocrite. How many times has she lectured her students on the difference between taking accountability for one's actions and trying to shoulder the blame for a chaotic universe?

"You think I got your brother killed?" He sounds calm, but it's the false calm produced by someone rushing to speak before all the breath leaves their lungs. She's not sure, but she thinks she sees the glisten of tears in his eyes.

"Well, you're wrong," he says. Then he taps the rearview mirror. "*They* did."

She's afraid to look up at first, afraid some new vision will assault her. Instead, she sees what he means. Yards behind them, following them up the twisty, ice-flecked mountain road, is a giant SUV. With its headlights off.

"I think it's time to ask them some questions, don't you?"

The next thing Claire hears is squealing tires, and suddenly her entire world is tilting sideways. A turnout, she realizes. Her father must have been waiting for one to appear before he made his move. As the Jeep spins, its headlights stab across the ghostly SUV that's been following them, like lights from a submersible suddenly falling across a shipwreck under the sea. Only the shipwreck's coming straight for them. When she realizes they're suddenly in a game of chicken, Margot starts shouting Abram's name.

A gun is on Abram's lap. A gun he must have pulled from one of the pockets on the inside of the driver's door. It all makes sense suddenly. His jittery nature, his insistence on driving, his deflective talk—it was all designed to distract them as he landed them on an isolated road late at night.

Suddenly the inside of the Jeep is a blaze of white light, fierce and unrelenting, terribly familiar. She tastes dirt, feels memories of broken bones. But she can make out the outline of rack lights along the top of the approaching SUV. A cold blast hits her, and she realizes her father has rolled the window down, and that's when she and Margot start screaming.

The approaching SUV swerves out of their way. Suddenly her father is speeding downhill in the opposite direction and the SUV that was tailing them a moment before is flying past her father's open window, its own windows ink black and still rolled up. The gunshot is a thunderous boom accompanied by a muzzle flash. By the time Claire realizes her father's just taken a shot at a car driven by strangers who may or may not be following them, her world is upended. The windshield is flying toward her in a shower of broken glass, and when her stomach rises up into her throat, she realizes the Jeep is somersaulting downhill.

Her father is bellowing, as if years of rage and frustration have been loosed from him by their glass-shattering plummet. And then the spinning comes to a sudden stop and the seat belt is like a river of fire across her chest, exerting terrible pressure on her right breast. Her head feels like it's full of water. She is hanging upside down in her seat.

This time when she sees Poe, she doesn't tell him to go away. The passenger window is shattered, but he's leaning down, peering through one of the intact sections, and the juxtaposition between his orange jacket and the dark, snowy woods is stark, like a drive-in movie screen still showing its film despite being gnawed on by a tornado.

But she is doing what she was too afraid to do before, because she's exhausted. Because she is desperate to escape the biting pain in her chest and the spinning in her head. She is gazing into her little brother's eyes, watching them turn a bright shade of blue that starts to coat his entire face. It's coming from his little hand too as he reaches out for her. There's still a part of her mind that tells her not to reach for him. But she can't resist. Anything other than this, anything other than this ruined car and the terrible sense that her accusation made her father do something fatally reckless.

Claire reaches for her brother's fingers. The glass seems to vanish, as if they are truly about to touch across some great divide. But at the precise second when their fingertips should brush past each other, the blue light swallows her and all she hears is music. Cheerful, melodic music that once made her mother get up off a bench and dance.

———

"Bear?"

She's moving. She fears the Jeep's started tumbling downhill again, but she's flat now, not dangling or somersaulting, and the motion is smooth, easy and regular. And there's something under her. Arms. Small arms. She's being held. Claire opens her eyes, stares up into her little brother's face. Only now, no glass separates them. A sob wells inside her chest. But something is missing. Her brother's face is only inches from hers, but his breaths don't tickle her nose and mouth.

They are lying on the floor of a carousel, surrounded by a controlled stampede of brightly painted horses, as "Hooked on a Feeling" pours from the speakers all around them. The horses are riderless, but they rise and fall with a lazy rhythm.

"It's real. Promise."

"Can't be," she says.

The carousel starts to slow down. As Poe helps her sit up, she takes in more and more of the world beyond the carousel's edge. There are the weathered boards she'd glimpsed in her full-length mirror. The wooden staircase to Pier 39's second level. She sees patches of the sky, thick blankets of fog that part in places to reveal a sky of such universally bright brilliance it seems to have no single, remote sun. And this brilliance is blue, as blue as the light that came from her brother's eyes when she reached for his hand.

Finally she stands, reaches for a horse's head to bring herself to her feet, realizes it's higher than it should be. In one of its large reflective eyes, she sees she's the same age she was during their trip, bundled in the 49ers jacket their dad bought her. Her straw-colored hair is in the french braid her mother made before they left the hotel because she insisted that if Claire was going to wear a man's jacket, then she would have to sport a hairstyle that was suitably feminine.

There is a low clamor of warm conversation, but it sounds distant, like background noise in a movie, something weakly remembered. It has to be coming from the silhouettes that move leisurely throughout the pier. They sit on benches; they stroll around the carousel. Their details are a blur of shadow, fringed in places by glittering traces of blue light. She can't help but look toward the bench where her mother and father sat while she and Poe rode the carousel and explored the shops. When she sees them, she goes still—two silhouettes posed just like her parents that day, her father leaning forward with his elbows on his knees, her mother's arm braced behind him and on the back of the bench, as if she were constantly fighting the urge to pull him into an embrace. But like the other circling shadows, whose feet, she sees now, do not touch the ground, they are featureless and vague. She's reminded of the shadows of people that were burned onto walls when Hiroshima was bombed. Only these versions move and chatter.

"It's not them; I checked," Poe says quietly.

"*Because it's not real,*" she says against her will. "*None of this is real.*"

"*No.*" Poe turns her to face him. "*We're real, and we're here. Both of us now. It's all memories, Claire. Our memories.*"

"*My memories.*"

"*All right, fine, then. Whatever! I picked Traffic Cone Poe because you always thought he was cute, so I figured he wouldn't freak you out. Lot of damn good that did. How's this?*"

A new version of her brother stands next to her. He looks around thirteen. That would put him at an age when they barely spoke and traded no pictures. His hair is shorn into a sidewall like a junior ROTC recruit. His face looks long, his features slightly misaligned by a sudden growth spurt. He's wearing a T-shirt she's never seen him in. The word AC/DC is divided by an illustrated tear in the fabric that reveals the words The Razor's Edge *against a blood-red background.*

"*Yeah, sorry. There was a whole retro metal period after you left,*" Poe says. "*It was kinda loud. Be glad you were spared. But Dad said it was too pricey for me to be into bands whose only souvenirs were collector's items, so he told me to either become one of Lady Gaga's little monsters or get a job.*"

She can't take her eyes off the shirt. Were its little snags and stains put there by her brother after she and her mother moved away? She has never seen this version of Poe, and if she made him up, the detail is extraordinary.

"*What's it going to take, Claire? I mean, I know you organize your pencil drawer by color and size and all, but what's it going to take for you to let go and admit this is really happening?*"

He turns her by her shoulders. She looks at herself in the horse's mirrored eye again. She sees herself at fifteen, sees she's changed in tandem with her brother. The french braid and football jacket are gone, replaced by the Jennifer Aniston–style shoulder-length hairdo she thought made her seem so sophisticated and mature when she was a teenager, and one of the polo shirts she used to favor because the other girls her age were going for halter tops that made her feel naked.

"See?" he says. "Here, we can be whoever we've been."

It's the clarity of it all that convinces her. Claire has never dreamed like people in movies do, mistaking her dreams for reality until she sits up in bed. Her dreams have always had a stark unreality to them—halting, surrealistic montages that seem to fall apart and fade the minute she wakes. Everything about this experience is clear. Vivid. Her brother's voice ringing in her head. The acrid smell of San Francisco Bay wafting up through the boards, blowing in on the wind she saw tousle her brother's hair in hallucination after hallucination.

Vision after vision, she realizes.

"Poe . . ."

"It's me, Bear."

Then she's sobbing and his arms are around her. There's the clarity of everything around him, but there's also the sense that she is the same person, that her emotions have traveled with her from the overturned Jeep to this place. And the grief she's been holding in for hours comes pouring out of her as Poe embraces her. Some of it feels like relief over being reunited with him again, but they have not been reunited in a place she understands, so the relief comes weighted with a stronger version of the sadness she's been battling since the plane crash. They have been reunited in a version of the past.

Their past.

She feels the shift instantly. Realizes the carousel horses around them are lower because they're both taller. When she pulls back, Poe has the face of the man she kicked out of their mother's funeral, only he seems healthier and more radiant, and his outfit's clean and neat. Is it what he was wearing when the plane went down? She places her hands on his cheeks, feels a warmth there. Not the sweaty heat of flesh. It's the warmth of a campfire, the warmth of a pure spirit. In his eyes there's a subtle blue glow, a muted, almost hidden version of the radiance that

147

spread across his face when she raised her hand toward the window of the tumbled Jeep. She raises her fingers in front of his face, testing a suspicion from before. No breaths come from his nostrils, and as she studies him, she sees the subtle signs. His chest doesn't rise and fall, his nostrils don't flare.

She places her hand against her face. The same isn't true of her. She can still feel breath filling her lungs. Her heart races in her chest. Or this otherworldly version of it anyway.

She is still connected to some sort of physical body.

But her brother is not.

"I'm not . . ." he says. He hesitates, reaches up, and takes her hand in his. His touch is more pure warmth, similar to the massaging sensation she felt inside her arm before he made her write and draw. "I'm not in my body, Claire. I'm somewhere else."

Up until this moment, she would have assumed there was only one place you could be if you weren't inside your body. It was called death. The fact that her brother doesn't call it that means she's wrong. Or she's right and he doesn't want to confirm it.

"How were you seeing me?" she finally asks.

Poe raises a hand and points, and as she follows the direction of his finger, she realizes it's moving, sweeping across the perimeter. "The glass, just like you. The storefronts. All of them. They're like windows into your world."

But the minute he says it, he sees what she's seeing, and his expression darkens. The windows display nothing now.

"Did you see me, or were you just seeing everything I was seeing?" she asks.

"It was all through your eyes. I could only get you to look back when you saw your reflection in something. I wasn't trying to freak you out. Promise. But seriously, I mean, I didn't know what else to do. I was yelling like crazy, but you couldn't hear me."

He takes her hand, leads them past the silhouettes of an entire family gathered outside a sweet shop with a sign featuring an intricate and colorful painting of a dripping candy apple. Only the family has no faces, and their laughter and chatter sound like they're coming from down a long, empty corridor. The shop looks closed. The glass is dark. So dark her own reflection doesn't appear in it as she approaches.

Poe places his hand flat against the glass. But it's dark on the other side, and nothing seems to happen on the glass or beyond it. He lowers his hand and backs away, the joy of their reunion fading from his expression, replaced by fright.

"Were all these windows ever dark like this when you were watching me?" Claire asks.

He shakes his head.

For a while, they don't speak.

"So they're dark because I'm here," she finally says.

"Maybe," he whispers.

"Does it mean I'm dead?" she finally asks. "Does it mean I died in the car?"

"I don't even know if I'm dead. Just . . . here."

Neither one of them can speak for what feels like an eternity. Either whatever lies beyond the glass is so dark it drowns everything inside the store, or there's nothing inside it. Just a void. She reaches for the door's knob.

"Don't!" Poe cries. He's right next to her suddenly.

"Did you try to open it?"

"Yes, and it hurt. I put my hand on the knob and it was weird. Nothing else here hurts. And I was worried . . . Well, when I could see you through them I was worried if I opened the door and went inside I might fall into your head or something and make you worse. But it didn't matter, because none of the doors would open."

"But you tried, even though it hurt?"

"Yeah, and it hurt bad."

149

Only one thing will help her manage this flood of information. A narrative, a chronology.

"Tell me everything that happened," she finally manages.

"The engine blew up and pieces of it flew into the cabin and we started losing pressure and everyone panicked. It was clear the pilot didn't have control of the plane, and it was stupid, but I wouldn't put my mask on. Like I thought I could fight it or something. And I just remember thinking that I loved you and that I was never going to see you again. Then the ceiling started coming apart. The holes, they were getting bigger. A bunch of pieces flew toward me and the people close to me started screaming and then . . ."

"What, Poe? What came next?"

"I wasn't in my body anymore. I was seeing what was left of me in my seat, and there was no body, Claire. There was just blue. There was just . . . this light. And everyone who could see it was stunned and they'd stopped screaming and . . . it didn't look like death, Claire. It didn't look like I died. It looked like I changed, and the way they were looking at what I had turned into . . . I don't know, it was like they'd seen an angel or something. And I remember thinking 'OK, well good.' Good. Something to distract them from what was happening because it was so horrible, and I was leaving them and it didn't seem fair, and then I could smell the bay and I could hear a foghorn and . . . I was here."

The story seems to have exhausted him, as if telling it for the first time has forced him to accept the surrealism of it.

Claire holds him close. Over his shoulder she sees the glowing spires of the Transamerica Pyramid and Coit Tower rising above the pier. The light coming through the skyscrapers' windows is an even shade of blue that suggests there might be nothing within except for that glow. These versions of the landmarks are more slender, their lines more severe, than they are in real life—altered, interpreted, adjusted to fit whatever this realm is. The idea that there might be a whole city like this, a whole

version of San Francisco built entirely of their warped and uneven
memories of it, stuns her.

"Have you tried to get out?" she asks.

"I can't get farther than behind the carousel, and I tried to jump
into the water. Both times I just ended up back on the carousel. But . . ."

"But what?"

"There was another way, but it's gone."

"Where did it lead?"

"A bad place. And he was there."

"Who?"

"The man I made you draw," he says.

———

Vernon finds it easier to think when moving, so he paces the cabin,
whittling away at the hand-size wooden spear he's been carving since
he got back. The comfort of having his mother's gift safely inside has
long worn off, leaving him with the challenge of figuring out why she
sent it to him in the first place. Its light fills the cabin he's struggled to
make a home. For almost six months, he's endured each night with
gas lanterns and fire flicker from the cast-iron stove. The shack has no
electricity, so it's miraculous to see the interior of this place bathed in
bright blue. It makes Vernon's carvings look alive.

The tall figure he's been working on for weeks now, the one whose
spindly legs terminate in a thick block of wood and whose arms are
raised like those of the men who drove him from town, casts a long
shadow across the wall behind him. The little animals he's carved,
the birds with round, fat bodies and skinny necks and jagged wings,
the ones with holes along their stomachs from where he's driven his
little spears deeper and deeper into them to make the bad thoughts
go away, seem to dance along the ledges of the boarded-up windows.
Many of them are carved from aspen wood, which makes them bone

white. The light makes ripples across the little twin mattress he stole from a cabin down mountain and the backpack of belongings the hooded men allowed him to take.

He's been walking in circles around the airline chair, studying the borders and outlines of the shimmer, the way its tendrils kiss and then spread briefly across the cabin's ceiling before disappearing. He sets his little spear and blade aside; then, from the woodstove, he removes a burning log, brings the flames to the edge of the radiance to see how it reacts. It retreats from fire the way it retreats from flesh. Vernon thinks of that movie with the alien that shoots lasers everywhere and sees the world in heat signatures, and wonders if this substance is the same. But the word *alien* turns his stomach sour. It's not what he wants this to be.

He returns the log and approaches it, and the blue pollen, as he thinks of it now, floats toward his lips, toward his breath, asking to be invited in. And so Vernon does. He's prepared for the pain this time, for the cold shock firing up both nostrils, and when he tells himself the pain in his skull is required to make amazing things happen, it's easier to endure.

The vision from the last time comes back, even though he doesn't want it to: twisted storefronts with frames that look carved, like the tall man in the corner of his cabin, carved by Vernon's hand but bigger than anything he's ever carved in real life. He sees more of Spurlock now, recognizes the spire of the Lutheran church on the corner of Pine and Alexander Streets, only it's so twisted he's not sure how it stays standing, how the bells stay inside the tower. But its structure is bright white, like the aspen wood he's been carving for months.

Sometimes, when he'd say the wrong thing in public, his mom would call it a brain hiccup, and he figures that's what this is. A brain hiccup. But he doesn't like it. It feels real. Feels like a space that might actually exist somewhere outside his head.

———

A jarring new sound drowns out her mother's favorite song.

Is it coming from the carousel's speakers too, or is its source some-where else?

The glass storefronts all around them are lighting up suddenly, but the light isn't coming from inside; it's a reflection of some new source that's sprung to life behind her.

Claire turns. The entire facade of the two-story structure behind her has changed. A giant vertical sign fringed in bright blue light bulbs now proclaims TRAVEL UNDER THE SEA. *Paralleling its words on a downward arc is a school of brightly colored fish studded with fat gray sharks. The fish all look like they've been drawn by her brother's hand. They point the way to a set of double doors that are slowly drifting open.*

When she asked Poe if he'd opened any of the doors, his answer had been no.

As the doors open farther, the sound gets louder. It's scratchy but rhythmic. Like subtle little hammer strikes leveled by the same careful hand. She's heard the sound before. In school, whenever she walked past the woodworking shop. The sound always seemed like a comfort, a nostalgic tribute to a simpler time amid a curriculum that was all about preparing kids for the split-second ferocities of the digital age.

Here, it feels different, menacing. Too loud, and getting louder.

"This is wrong," Claire says. "The aquarium was at the entrance to the pier, not behind us. And it was called something else. There was some kind of restaurant here."

"This is the aquarium we made up," Poe replies. "Remember how I was all excited because I thought the real one had tunnels that went under the bay? Then when we got here we saw they were just tanks that filtered bay water. And I was so disappointed because I thought we were going to walk all the way out to Alcatraz and see fish swimming all around us the whole time. So Mom started lecturing me how the

water would be too murky, and then you started talking about how there might be sharks. And I told you it would be cool if the aquarium was right there . . ."

The double doors have opened all the way. The light coming from inside isn't blue. It's the deep green of the bay, and it ripples with refracted light. The color frightens Claire, suggests something that might consume her. Drown her. But why should she be afraid of anything now?

She starts for the doors. Poe grabs her hand. "No!" he cries. "Just wait and it'll close."

"I don't want it to close. It's a way out."

"It's not. It's a way to him!"

"The man you made me draw?"

"I don't know. It leads to his version of this, and it works the same. There's glass there on the other side too, and I can see what he's doing."

"Who is he?"

"I don't know. I couldn't read his mind or anything. I couldn't read your mind either. I could just see."

"What is he doing here, then? If this place is just our memories, what is some stranger doing here?"

"I think he has me."

"Has you?"

"What I turned into. On the plane. I think he has it now, and it's letting him do things. Bad things."

"What kind of things?"

"He can move things with his mind. He's hurting people. I saw him kill someone, Claire. A passenger was still alive, and he killed him just to make him be quiet. I wanted to think it wasn't real, but when I got back here I realized everything that was happening with you was real, and if I was seeing it in the same way, through the glass, that meant he was real too."

She starts for the doors.

"Claire, stop!"

She whirls. "We're already dead! What are you afraid of?"

Poe recoils as if she's slapped him, and for a while he can't speak and there's just the grating battle between the whittling sounds drifting out through the open doors and the continual loop of their mother's favorite pop song.

"We're not dead," he finally manages. "We're just somewhere else."

There is no sun here, she realizes. There's no denying it now. The quality of the light is unlike anything she's ever seen. Wherever the fog parts, it reveals a sky of the exact same blue luminescence. And it makes her realize how much she took the sun for granted, how much it shaded and gave texture to the days, even by its absence at night. But this universal light, obstructed only by the shifting patterns of fog and wind, makes this realm appear limitless, despite her brother's promise that there's no way to leave it.

Or only one way, and it's bad.

She starts for him. "You used to be our little explorer. That's what Dad called you, remember? Come on, that's what we're going to do. Explore."

"You want to go over there because you think it's a way out, but I'm telling you it's not—"

"I'm the worrywart, remember? You're the one with all the courage. Come on. We have to—"

"Courage?" Suddenly Poe changes form before her eyes, as if the sheer force of his despair has made him ten years old. He is the Poe of that night, the night they were knocked off their feet. His bright Gore-Tex jacket with the rubber hood bunched up and resting on one shoulder, his face dirt splotched. He's the Poe she followed into the woods. "My courage destroyed our family. My courage is the reason we almost died that night. If I'd stayed in the damn tent, none of that ever would have happened."

Her brother is sobbing, she realizes, but he sheds no tears. Just little blue pulses that rim his eyes in brief flashes, effervescing out from his face in little bursts. It's so painful—the terrible guilt in his words, matched with this dazzling display—she wants to look away.

"You're not asking for some brave little kid, Claire. You want the guy who ruined everything! You want the guy who couldn't sit still, who couldn't stop scratching every itch and taking every drug so he didn't have to feel anything. You want the guy I've been trying not to be for a year. That guy isn't courageous, Claire. That guy was terrified to be alone with himself, and that's why he was always racing into the dark in search of something new. And I don't want to go back over there. It's not our space. This is. Stay with me. Here. Please."

She thinks of her father all of a sudden, wondering if the painful guilt trembling inside Poe's words is proof he feels the same way her father did when she pretty much accused him of getting Poe killed. The clarity of this connection to the physical realm she left behind convinces her again that this is a real place. That all the essential parts of her have arrived here intact, save for whatever bodily functions the universe has decided are not essential to the ongoing journey of her spirit.

If she can get them back to the real world, she has to try.

"I'm just going to look," Claire says. "Just one look."

She takes off. She's through the aquarium's double doors by the time she hears Poe's footsteps pounding the boards behind her. By the time he calls her name, she's descending a set of steps into deep green darkness. She tells herself if she slows down, Poe will catch up with her and try to stop her, but the sight that greets her terrifies her. The giant tank below offers a massive window under the surface not of San Francisco Bay but of a child's nightmare version of it. The water is clearer than it should be, revealing the dark shadows swirling through the depths with fluid, searching motions. A mad gallery of shipwrecks litters the bay's rocky, uneven floor, and among them, she sees sections of passenger planes. The Spanish galleons and battleships are in similar states of decay, jumbled across the bay's floor without any kind of historical accuracy. The shadows have sensed her presence. They surge toward her.

One rises up from under the tank, giant teeth bared as it swims upward, flashing her its massive white chest as if to show off its size. The size of a Greyhound bus, with fins like small airplane wings. Its dark eyes taper at the top, giving them a menacing expression no real shark would ever possess. It crests the top of a tunnel that's somehow formed through the water itself. A tunnel all the way to Alcatraz, she thinks. Just like Poe wanted as a boy. The opening is in the center of the tank, and as she nears it she sees the length isn't contained by a polymer tube but by some kind of energy that has turned the deep green water into a mad but consistent swirl. If she runs down the tunnel in search of the light at the other end, the only barrier between her and these nightmare sharks will be some sort of energy she does not understand.

She is lower to the ground suddenly. She lifts her hand, sees she's wearing the football jacket again. She turns. Poe is next to her, but his despair has turned him into the version of himself he was that night in Glacier, and her fear has made her twelve years old again.

"Claire."

Poe's close. Traffic Cone Poe, hair tousled, puffy orange jacket making swishing sounds as he approaches. Again, they've changed form in tandem.

"Claire, I'm sorry. I'll go with—"

And then she's ripped backward into a blaze of blinding light, and she hears her brother screaming.

Vernon's not sure where the mirror is, but he knows there's one wedged among the stuff he's stolen. He'd swiped it a few months back, figuring that eventually he might have to go to a store and he should probably shave beforehand so he doesn't draw too much attention, but he's never used it. It's the only piece of intact glass he owns, and the only way for him to see if the little ghost boy from the crash site is back.

But he doesn't want to. He doesn't want to know.

Just a brain hiccup, he says. It'll go away, just like it did last time.

The quiet of the forest outside, the quiet he's lived with now for months, calms him as he studies the brilliant blue display before him. The color feels more and more like a taunt with each passing hour. The blue, a reminder of the mask he made of his mother's face, the one that failed to hold her life inside.

It can't just be a taunt. If his mother sent it, she wouldn't want to remind him of how he failed.

It occurs to him suddenly that she might want to remind him for a very different reason.

The little tub of aquamarine, the one Vernon managed to snag before the hooded men blindfolded him and forced him into the car, is sitting on the shelf where he's kept it since his arrival here. When he gestures in that direction with his glowing hands, the lid comes off the little tub and the stones float into the air. He guides them toward the light streaming off the mangled airplane seat. The tendrils recoil, as they do from anything that's not his breath. But when the stones pass in front of the light, it looks like they've been consumed by it— that's what a perfect match the color is. He is rocking back and forth, which he's allowed to do now when he gets excited because there's no one around to see. *To judge,* his mother would have added quickly.

It hits him suddenly. The gift is not supposed to remind him of his failure.

It's supposed to undo it.

And for the first time in months, Vernon has a plan for something beyond his next meal.

He floats the little stones back into the tub. He told himself he wouldn't work out his strangeness on the tall man until he was finished carving him, but Vernon has done good work and he deserves a reward. He imagines the little spear he was just carving flying across the room, and it does. He imagines it piercing the center of the carved man's chest, and it does.

He imagines it spinning like the bit of a drill, and it does, shedding sawdust as it bores deeper and deeper into the wood. And as Vernon laughs and clasps his hands together, it's as if the energy he's been forced to keep locked inside all his life is suddenly allowed to roar free.

He is something he has not been in a very long time.

He is happy.

13

She's torn backward by a force as powerful as a tornado. Then she's hurtling upward out of a dark void.

Claire's heart roars back to life inside her chest, sounding mad as hell about it. Her stomach, which she couldn't feel seconds before, cramps like it's primed to burst. The bed beneath her has a metal frame that creaks and bends under her wild thrashing. As her arms flail, multiple sets of hands grab her at once, forcing her to the mattress. Her fist connects with something hard and solid, something that lets out an *oompf* and recoils. Just this glancing touch of flesh and bone under her knuckles feels sharp and hot.

Now she's lying as still as she can, trying to contain the worst nausea she's ever felt. She's returned to the world she knows too well, the world of sweat, skin, breath, and pumping blood. And her body's reacting as if she's been poisoned.

"Sit her up," someone says quickly. "Sit her up now."

Strong arms pitch her forward. When vomit doesn't splash to her jeans, Claire realizes whoever these people are have shoved some kind of gleaming metal bowl onto her lap.

But the hands holding it aren't gloved. The bed she's lying on looks like a gurney. The blinding light is more suited for a surgical suite than an emergency room. Compared to the strange diffuse glow that filled the place from which she's just come, it makes for a more vicious assault than her stomach's rageful awakening. It's shrunk a limitless, magical world to a single unforgiving halo. She can't see the faces of the three people standing close to her bed. But she sees blue jeans, shirt sleeves with plaid patterns, cuffs rolled up over hairy, tattooed forearms. No scrubs.

If they're doctors, they're not inside a hospital.

Which means she doesn't know where the hell she is. Again.

"Fifty micrograms of adrenaline," a man's voice says. "Most we could give you without blowing out your heart. But it brought you back, so that's good."

His voice sounds nothing like her brother's did moments before, not rich and full inside her head, but strained and echoing in a way that suggests this room is mostly bare. Tears come. Real tears, hot and wet, streaming down her cheeks that are once more flesh and blood. She's back in the world of the living, and from what she can see, her brother is not. Once again, he's been ripped from her in a cruel instant. She wants to ask where he is, but that would reveal information to people she doesn't know, people she can't trust.

"How about some water?" the same man asks. "You think you can keep it down?"

"Where am I?"

"Someplace safe."

That remains to be seen, she thinks.

There's a screech of chair legs on a hard stone floor. The next thing she knows, a man in a cowboy hat is sitting next to the bed. There's something slightly wrong with his face—old injuries that have long healed over but left his right eye out of whack.

"Who are you?" she asks.

"My name's Randy Drummond. This here's Thomas Billings, our resident medical professional." He gestures to the scruffy, milky-skinned guy next to him. He's short and wiry, with a sharp nose and small eyes that crowd its narrow bridge and make him seem constantly suspicious. The forest of tattoos on his muscular arms looks criminal until she recognizes American military iconography laced through them. "And this here's Benjamin Running Creek, basically my number two, but don't let the other guys hear it."

Other guys, she thinks. *So it's not just the three of them.*

Benjamin is brown skinned with jet-black hair, movie-star handsome. Like the other men, he has a rigid bearing, along with a thick beard and a piercing look in his eyes that suggests a train would have to be speeding right for him to make him blink.

"Ben's the one you punched, by the way," Randy says.

He doesn't look like he's expecting an apology, so Claire doesn't give him one.

Special forces, she thinks. Just the type of guys to be following her dad if he was really being followed.

"Margot? My father?" Claire asks.

"They're fine. The roll could have been a lot worse."

"I need a mirror."

Randy studies her face. "Somebody wipe her mouth, please."

She's about to use the sleeve of her own shirt when Thomas, the doctor, hands her a little towel. She's not sure where to clean, and she doesn't feel like asking, so she wipes the entire lower part of her face. When she's done, she says, "That's not why I need it."

"Margot told us what you did in the car," Randy says. "How you reached for something in the window and then it was like you were dead to the world. But what she doesn't know is that basically you were dead. For forty-five minutes. And when we peeled your eyelids back, your pupils were doing a dance that would have made a regular doctor mess their shorts."

Claire looks to the man they introduced as Thomas. "How are your shorts, Thomas?"

"I'm not a regular doctor," he answers. "And in my book, shorts are a young man's game, to be frank."

"If I can't have a mirror," Claire says, "can I have a pen and paper, please?"

"Where'd you go, Claire?" Randy asks.

"Down a mountain, it sounds like."

"More like an incline. In another fifty feet it would have been a cliff. You're lucky."

"That's not really how I've been feeling."

"I understand."

"Do you? Is that why you drove us off the road?"

"All due respect, I'm not the one who pulled a one-eighty on an icy mountain road and then started firing a gun unprovoked out my window at a moving target. While driving. You call it driving you off the road. We call it watching the driver ahead of us lose his mind and go over the side all on his own while we scrambled to save your lives."

"Is that why you took us straight to a hospital? 'Cause you're so interested in saving our lives?"

Randy nods, as if to say *touché*. But he doesn't answer.

"My father thinks you killed my brother," she says.

Randy's jaw goes rigid, which she figures is the man's way of trying to keep his eyes blank and steady.

"We had nothing to do with what happened on that plane," he says.

"How about what happened to us in Glacier? Was that you?"

Randy raises his eyebrows, looks to his lap, where, she notices for the first time, his fingers are interlaced in an uneasy and shifting steeple. "My boss would like to meet with you," he finally says.

"Bring me a pen and paper first, please."

"It's kind of a big deal. My boss doesn't meet with a lot of people."

"And he's not going to meet with me until you bring me a pen and paper."

"Later," he says.

"If you're afraid I'm going to try to stab someone, then bring me a crayon or something. Just give me something to write with and *on*. Please."

Randy looks at Thomas. "We don't have a day care here, so crayons are out, I'm afraid." At Randy's gesture, Thomas pulls a tiny notepad and ballpoint pen from his shirt pocket.

Steeling herself for the silence she feels is to come, Claire places the pad on her lap and writes, Please tell me you're still there.

A feeling that terrified her only hours earlier—the sense of some force blossoming inside her arm, massaging her muscles in what now feels like gentle encouragement—brings tears of relief to her eyes. When her hand starts to move, her sob rips from her with embarrassing, stuttering force.

adrenaline did that.itwas like you were a comet in reverse Claire's comet.like Halley's only more whacked haahah

She writes again. Prove it's really you.

A second later, the response. lord how many bitchy voices do you have in your head bear

She laughs. Indulge me.

Silence. Her arm feels empty and still. She looks up and sees none of this has frightened the three men. Their expressions remain stoic as they watch the conversation on the notepad unfold.

Her hand moves. ask the ben guy if he's into dudes because OMG what a snack.

She writes back. Behave.

A brief second, and then another burst. you said really be me though. She's about to write back with more specific instructions when the massaging sensation returns. you took me to see brokeback mountain when we were kids even though mom said no rrated movies because you knew what I was even then and the ticket taker let us in because she was totally queer and had a rainbow pin and everything and after I asked you if you thought it always had to be sad when a boy loved another boy and you said no I think that moment might have changed my life don't cry it's not sad it's a good memory Claire stop cry—

If it's true that Poe can see only what she sees, then he must know she's crying, because her tears are staining the ink and wetting the paper even as he compels her hand to move.

It's the confirmation she needs that the thread remains between her and that dreamlike realm even after this baffling return trip. The journey felt so physical she's trying to trace the shape of it in her mind, the way she'd map a plane flight in her head. Are there maps for where she's just been? Do these men have them?

Randy is staring at her. There's a new emotion in his eyes, and it startles her.

"It'll get easier," he says quietly.

"What will?"

"Being back here."

"How would you know?"

He breaks eye contact with telling speed.

"We call it a memory deck," he finally says.

The men on either side of him both tense up. Either they feel Randy's revealed too much, or the name alone frightens them.

"We've all got one," he continues. "Most of us only go there once or twice in our lives, and if we manage to come back, which is rare, we usually don't remember much of it."

"And if we don't come back, where did we go?" Claire asks.

"It means we completed the dying process. The memory deck is the first place we go when our bodies experience a physical death. It's like a waiting room."

"For death?"

"For the loved ones who guide us into the next stage of death."

"And what's the next stage like?"

"I wouldn't know. I haven't been."

"But you've been to the memory deck. Excuse me. *Your* memory deck."

"Many times. And I have some very important advice. Can your brother see and hear everything we're saying?"

She nods.

"Don't try to open the doors."

Her hand moves so quickly she barely feels it coming. A second later, Poe's written a check mark on the tablet. He gave her the same warning.

"What if some of the doors open by themselves?" Claire asks.

Randy looks up as if a gun's gone off. "Did that happen? While you were there?"

Claire nods. Randy rises, moves off into the glare, returns unfolding the drawing Poe made her do on the plane.

"Did this man come through?" he asks.

Claire's hand starts moving. didn't come through he was on the other side saw him in the glass there made things fly through the air and killed someone from the plane at the crash site to make them be quiet.

The fear that moves through all three of the men standing over her is so powerful she feels it like a pressure against her chest. "Jesus," Thomas Billings whispers. "Jesus Christ, Randy."

Randy lifts one hand to silence his compatriot. She expects the gesture to also be a prelude to some further explanation, but Randy—who has described completely bonkers concepts with the same ease as when Heidi Stockman, the biology teacher at Arcadia Heights, explained to Claire how kidneys work—is suddenly at a loss for words.

"Did we manage to get the guy's name?" Randy asks.

Claire's hand writes, no.

"Maybe time to revisit the 'Don't open the doors' rule?" Ben asks under his breath.

Randy is silent, staring at Poe's last message as if it's upended his world. To which, Claire thinks, *Join the club, my new cowboy hat–wearing friend.* She keeps waiting for Randy to break the silence. And he doesn't.

She flips the notepad closed. Since they've all been staring at it intently, maybe this will get their attention.

"What in the name of God happened to us in Glacier National Park?" she asks.

Randy swallows, looks her in the eye. "Like I said, it's time for you to meet with my boss. Let's go."

The men don't draw guns or pull out handcuffs, but when they all move forward to help her off the gurney, she can't help but think it's a subtle form of restraint. Maybe they just doubt her footing. She can walk just fine, it turns out, and she figures the wobbliness in her legs is caused by the adrenaline. Outside the light's blinding glare, she discovers basic hospital equipment and bare stone walls.

Ben holds the room's metal door open, revealing a stone corridor outside. Following Randy and Thomas into it, she sees more heavy metal doors. They're all closed.

As if reading her mind, Randy says, "Your father's relaxing. He was very distressed when we brought him in."

"You going to wake him up with adrenaline too?" she asks.

"It wasn't our first choice. You had all the physical signs of someone on their memory deck, but we had no idea how you got there. Thirty minutes is the longest someone can stay, and we were starting to get past that. We brought you back because we were worried. I apologize if it was unpleasant, but we didn't know what else to do."

"Brought me back? Was I dead?"

"No," Randy answers.

"I thought you said we only went there when our bodies died. What do you mean thirty minutes is the longest you can stay?"

"Claire?" Margot is calling her. Claire moves toward one of the metal doors. Only it's shut. And locked. The men close in, but no one tries to restrain her.

"Claire, are you all right?" Margot calls.

"I think so. Are you?"

"Cuts and bruises. Just do what they say. For now. OK?"

Randy clears his throat. "You're not hostages."

"Oh, OK," Margot says from behind the door. "Drop us at a nice hotel, then, sweetie? A room with a nice big tub. Maybe heated floors."

The men are silent.

"Exactly," Margot says.

Randy says, "We'll reassess our current arrangement after the meeting. Come on."

Ben appears to be staying behind—guarding the hostages who aren't hostages, apparently. But they've let her keep the paper and pen, essentially a phone she can call her brother on. This calms her some.

"And if anyone's hungry after, I'll make us some food," Randy adds.

"Well, so far, you've only made me throw up, so that'll be a nice change of pace," Claire says.

Ben sputters with laughter. Thomas looks to the floor to hide his smile.

Randy's smile looks strained. "After you, Ms. Huntley." He gestures to the door Thomas has just opened. The steep cement stairs leading up suggest they're in some sort of basement.

Thomas goes first. She follows. They emerge into what looks like a break room for a staff of men with no design sense. A coffee station, a humming refrigerator, two muted TVs turned to sports stations. Messy bookshelves with used paperbacks—mostly old westerns and science fiction novels, sprinkled with some hardbound history books about the area. Then they exit onto the broad front porch of what appears to be a small guesthouse.

The snow has stopped, but it's left icy fingers across the grass outside, and white clouds are threaded across the night sky. Stars are visible now, clear and bright, unobscured by urban glare. The kind of stars Claire and Poe used to gaze up at during camping trips, lying flat on their backs, hands linked, like they were about to make snow angels in the leaves and twigs.

There's a large, elegant Victorian on the near horizon; its facade and upper floors sport pinpoint lighting that makes it look ready for an HGTV shoot. She stops in her tracks.

"Not what you were expecting?" Randy asks.

It wasn't, but she doesn't say so. She was expecting stark military barracks in the middle of nowhere, low-slung concrete buildings with no sign of help or civilization for miles. But the glow coming from inside the main house is inviting; the windows contain the silhouettes of curving, lush draperies. She tells herself not to be deceived by a design scheme. Most cold-blooded killers don't have a charnel house for a living room.

But Randy starts in a different direction. "This way," he says. "We're going to the barn."

14

The first snow was still weeks away, but the temperatures at night had started to fall, so Randy was following a new recipe for steaks he could cook without heading outside to the grill. A good ten minutes of iron-skillet roasting on high heat after pan-searing them on both sides. Agatha was a fan, and this little nightly ritual, moving about her kitchen as dusk painted the ranch in spreading rivers of pink and deep orange, had long ago become his favorite time of day. It focused him the way prepping his gear used to focus him before an operation.

Her kitchen had always been blessedly free of those KISS THE COOK or IT'S ALWAYS WINE O'CLOCK signs that made him want to punch a wall, but the Wild West accents intruded here too. Even the ceramic utensil holders and spoon rests were decorated with imagery of mountains or ranchland or cowboys. In the beginning, he'd thought it all a display for outsiders. But she never welcomed outsiders, so he came to realize she hugged the trappings of the Wild West close for her own benefit so she could bury her family's actual roots even deeper. Just like the cowboys of old, she had remade herself on the frontier.

He'd just set the meat out to reach room temperature when he saw Agatha's walkie-talkie resting on the kitchen counter.

Chocolate and Rodeo were both loose inside the horse pen, but there was no sign of her favorite, Wind. No sign of him inside the barn either.

Her truck was still parked in the driveway.

He called the monitoring center. Ben said he'd spotted her heading out earlier on her favorite stallion, but there was no sign of a return.

It was rare for Agatha to ride late in the day like this, especially without her walkie-talkie. The older she got, the more he nagged her to carry something strong enough to stop a bear, especially when she was riding alone, but she shrugged him off. As he started for the ATV, he wondered if leaving the radio behind was her way of pushing back against his protectiveness.

The ATV was single passenger, but it was still too wide for the narrow trail that led to the gravesite for Agatha's mother. The aspen branches were also too low to allow for an approach on horseback, which was how Agatha had designed it. Wind wasn't tied up at the trail's entrance, and that discovery quickened his pulse.

The sight of the gravesite at the top of the grassy swell left him as speechless as it always did. Surrounding the plain, squared-off grave marker, a giant stone doorframe rose fifteen feet into the air, capturing the vista of alpine mountains. It faced west, and so at this time of day, the slanting sun set the rustling aspen leaves aflame, as if the trees were gently ushering the spirit of Agatha's mother through the open doorway and into the mysterious expanse beyond. The door was carved with the shapes of clouds, but the carvings were subtle, almost like etchings. They all but disappeared except when the sun was directly overhead. The beauty of this place always gave him a strange longing to let other people see it, but this hidden grove was a secret gift a grieving daughter had made to her ruined mother.

When he saw the fresh flowers resting in the holder atop the headstone, his reverence was replaced by anxiety. The penstemon's dark blue petals were thick and healthy as they rustled in the breeze. Their stems green and freshly shorn. They'd been picked just hours before, he could tell.

Heart racing, Randy rounded the grassy mound, entered the open space beyond. There, gently rolling grasslands traveled all the way to the electrified fence that marked a sudden drop into the creek bed on the neighbor's property.

That's when the walkie-talkie at his hip crackled. It was Ben. Wind had just showed up at the barn. Without Agatha.

Randy was heading back toward the gravesite when he saw her. His first thought was that she was lying down on her back to take in the expansive mountain view. She was yards north from the aspen grove, not too far from where a horse trail emerged from the pines.

The closer he got, the better he saw she was staring skyward with glazed eyes. And her lips were turning blue.

The last thing he noticed was the bloody tree stump. When he saw it, he let out a sound like he'd been kicked in the gut and started running faster. He kept wondering how the thing could have ended up on top of her chest that way; then he realized it had been driven straight through from her back when she'd fallen on it. A week before, one of the guys had been clearing pines infested with bark beetle when dusk snuck up on him, so they'd left behind the jagged stumps with plans to smooth them down later.

He hit his knees next to her.

She tried to form words, but only rasping breaths came out. She returned his grip with one hand, but her strength flickered, and it was like she was seeing only glimpses of him.

"A bear," Agatha whispered, "bear spooked the horse and . . ."

"We'll get you—"

"No. No, Randy."

And that's when he understood her fear, her hesitation. Blood was already pouring from underneath her in a thick tide; an artery had been speared and she was bleeding out. And she knew.

No hospital. No help. No letting anyone see what might become of her the minute death tried to claim her body. He had never anticipated this, but there it was, the worst cost of the secrets Agatha had sworn to protect. She would be forced to face a death like this—a remote, accidental one—without intervention.

If he honored her request.

Randy was on his feet, voice going hoarse from everything he was shouting into his walkie-talkie. Thomas was in the park checking monitoring devices and out of range. But it was almost dark, so maybe he was back now, and if he was, then he needed to get out here now, now, now.

"Randy," Agatha whispered.

There was resignation in her tone. If she'd had a different history, if she had not been exposed to a force that still lay beyond their understanding, this would have been the moment when she might have welcomed the great beyond with peace and courage, when she would have prepared to leave her body the way he had when the bullet pierced his skull back in Iraq, only never to return. But the fate awaiting her could be very different, they both knew; as strange and tangled as the secrets housed inside the cellar below the barn.

"Keep me here, OK," she whispered. "Whatever happens, keep me here with you."

When he nodded furiously, it only made the tears come harder and faster.

He held her as best he could, the cold in her body seeping into his bones.

And then her body ceased to exist.

There was no other word for it. He was blinded by light, and suddenly it felt as if his arms were wrapped around water, and then the water emptied from between his arms and he had no choice but to rock backward onto his haunches and watch. He had thought, hoped, even, that he'd have a moment to watch the contours of her face fade, or even collapse. But it happened almost instantly. The shimmering radiance that had been Agatha was repelled by his touch, curling away from him and then skyward like a smoke cloud drawn by an air vent. It was as if everything fundamental to the woman he loved had suddenly revealed itself to be an indifferent and inhuman force, repelled from his touch like a frightened dog. Then it tried to spread in all directions, but its upper edges contracted while the bottom remained tethered to the trunk. It was being stopped, arrested. Trapped, just like the animals in the cellar. And it was silent, this process, leaving him with only the sounds of his own gasping breaths and the rustling of the breezes in the tall grass around them.

This is not death, he realized. *It is not even half of death.*

After a while, what had once been Agatha settled into a familiar serpentine pulse. The shades and hues of the blue within were deeper and more complex than anything housed under the barn, and as he stood and moved closer to them, he wondered if they were a siren song, inviting him to madness or physical destruction. Wondered too if he was drawn by them because he'd been wrapped in these very same colors when he'd left his body in Iraq.

Something emerged from them now. Particles tiny and blue that reminded him of dandelion pollen blown into a wind. He'd seen a similar substance emerge from the animals, but they'd been recoiled by his breaths. These little particles went for his exhalations like they thirsted for them.

Life seeks life, he thought.

Distantly, he heard the chugging of one of the ATVs heading up the horse trail Agatha had been riding toward before Wind threw her. The particles were riding his exhales, in and out. He told himself he had no choice. Told himself he was on the verge of reconnecting with the love of his life, the woman who'd melted his heart, the woman whose loneliness matched his own, who'd allowed them both to become survivors of a shipwreck together on this, her ranch, her island of secrets and shame.

Even as he heard Ben running toward him and shouting his name, Randy inhaled.

15

Claire wants to call them ghosts, but they have no faces, and they don't reach for her with smoking arms as she walks past their glass cells. Instead, they shift like kelp in gentle ocean currents, the same shade of blue as the accent color threaded throughout her memory deck's version of Pier 39.

What, she wonders, do these men call what she's seeing now?

Before they descended the stairs on this side of the storm doors set in the barn's floor, Randy insisted she don a chunky pair of black sunglasses. She's grateful she did. She'd be blind now without them.

"All of these were created by exposure to the pulse," Randy says. "Figure I don't have to explain why we call it that. Especially to you. Some of these got hit on purpose. For research. Others because they didn't get out of the way in time."

There are photographs taped to the glass of each cell. Bears, mountain lions, deer. An eagle or two. No sign of any such creature inside the cells. That she can recognize anyway.

She opens the pad, starts to write.

Is this like what you turned into on theyesyesyesyes.

It's the first time he's taken over midsentence, and she's surprised how effortless it felt.

"Animals," she says to the men, mostly to distract from closing the notepad to hide Poe's response. "These were animals. And then they got hit with what my brother and I were hit with that night."

Randy nods. "In some cases, the shift was simultaneous. If the pulse broke their necks, for instance. In others, they were exposed, and we were able to capture them alive and bring them here. When they died, the shift happened. This was the result. We call it bloom."

They pass a section where the walls start to look newer, the paint fresher, and she realizes the corridor has been added to recently. More cells have been put in, and at the corridor's end, a keypad and a heavy metal door.

Randy punches in a code. The locks buried inside the frame hiss.

Claire expects them to step into some office, his boss's office. Instead, they enter a room with only one glass cell, the largest they've seen. But unlike the ones they passed on the way in, there is furniture beyond the glass. A four-poster bed carved from dark wood, its columns spiraling to a square wood-framed canopy fringed with dark green ruffle. On the mahogany end tables are two porcelain lamps with swollen bases of frosted glass emblazoned with patterns of rose petals and fiercely green leaves. Landscape paintings hang on the wall in gilt frames; the walls are painted dark green.

At the room's center is a rotten tree stump, its tangles of roots spread out on all sides of it, splintered into formations so they can lie flat with the floor, then held together with wire. Rising from the stump, tendrils of blue radiance.

My boss doesn't meet with just anyone.

"Meet my boss," Randy says.

For a while, no one speaks.

Maybe they're waiting for Claire to lose her mind.

Maybe she would be if she hadn't just entered an alternate dimension by way of her little brother's glowing fingers.

Randy approaches a keypad in the center of the glass wall. "Everyone stay back."

He pushes open the door and steps inside the cell, approaches the glow, extends one finger. It recoils from him like an octopus. But then, almost too small to see, tiny little particles emerge from the tendrils. Suddenly, they're riding Randy's breath. Claire cries out like she's just noticed a toddler stumble too close to the edge of a cliff. But Randy seems calm and poised, as if he's deciding whether to ingest them like he'd decide whether to have a snack on his way through the kitchen. Instead, he steps back. One step, then another, and eventually he's placed enough distance between himself and the little grains of blue that they withdraw and vanish into the radiance once more.

"If I'd breathed that in just now, I'd have been able to move objects with my mind for about thirty minutes."

The simple statement lances through her.

Her brother's words come back to her.

He can move things with his mind. He's hurting people. I saw him kill someone, Claire.

Because the bad man has her brother, and this, before her, is what her brother's turned into.

"What?" Randy asks, approaching her.

"You're saying your boss's body gave this off when she died?"

"No," he answers. "I'm saying this is what *became* of my boss's body when she died. This is what became of my boss."

The word *boss* slides awkwardly off his tongue, and the boss in question is apparently a *she*. He wets his bottom lip. Everything inside this subterranean bedroom is immaculate, well cared for; the bedside lamps are gleaming. So are the gilt frames on the walls. This woman was more than just an employer to him, Claire realizes, and if their eyes weren't hidden behind glasses, she might have noticed this sooner.

"Bloom is a fusion of human flesh and quantum material we can't normally see." Randy walks toward her, turning his back on the cell's extraordinary inhabitant. "Most folks would call it a soul, but that's not quite right. It's a death that can't finish, basically. A soul that can't leave. Our theory is that it sheds the stuff that allows someone to move objects with their mind because that's the fuel we all use to dematerialize and detach from our bodies before we pass into the memory deck. Into death."

"Telekinesis," Claire says. "You believe the telekinesis is a by-product of the dying process."

"Yes, but exposure to the pulse literally screws up the dying process. What should happen in an instant when you experience physical death gets stuck, entangled. The fuel used to decouple our spirits from our bodies starts to shed into this dimension, and our consciousness gets trapped on the memory deck. It's like one split second of the dying process, a process we can't normally see, has been frozen in time."

Randy's next to her now. Together, they look back inside the cell. "That," Claire says, tapping the plexiglass, "is *not* frozen."

"Fair," he answers.

"And that happened to my brother. And that's going to happen to me."

"We believe so."

"How can you be sure?"

"Because I was there when it happened to her," he says.

"When she shifted, or when she was exposed?" Claire asks.

"When she shifted."

"Then it's time to talk about what we were exposed *to*."

Randy gestures to the luminescent presence filling this haunted, elegant bedroom under the earth. "Hence, the meeting."

"I see. So I'm going to get answers. All I have to do is inhale a woman's half-formed soul. And oh, by the way, when I do, I'll be given a little burst of telekinetic power I can use to vent my frustration on the men who abducted me, my father, and his ex-girlfriend, and who kept secrets about the event that destroyed my family for . . . how long? I mean, how long have you guys worked for her?" She's started pacing without meaning to, and when she finishes, she sees the men haven't moved an inch.

Randy seems unfazed. Maybe he was expecting this speech. "I was the replacement for the guy who screwed up and let you and your brother get exposed. Atmospheric conditions can usually tell us if a pulse is imminent. Some pivotal monitoring instruments were broken that night, and he didn't notice it until it was too late. He never got over it, and he drank himself to death. I'm sorry about what happened to you and Poe, but I'm not to blame for it."

"Is she?" Claire asks, gesturing.

"That's for her to say."

"Can she hear us now?"

"No."

"I have to breathe her in first?" she asks.

"Correct."

"And then what happens?"

"How did it go with your brother? After you touched the window in the Jeep, I mean."

"I woke up in his arms. On the memory deck, as you call it," she says.

"This is going to be like that. Only more complicated. The doors I told your brother not to open?"

"Yes."

"She's going to open one of them," Randy says.

"How?"

"There's a key. We just need to tell her where it is."

"And how are we going to do that?"

"It's there, on the memory deck. Maybe you saw it during your last visit. If Poe's there, maybe he can find it for us. It's an item of incredible value to you, something you lost in life."

"Before we talk about opening doors in my mind, maybe you can give me more of the big picture here."

Claire feels the massaging sensation in her right arm, but she ignores it. For now.

Randy takes a deep breath, looking annoyed for the first time since she met him. "I'm offering you the big picture on a level no one's ever been offered it. *She* is making you that offer, and you are standing here wasting my time."

Claire enters the cell for the first time, trying to keep her face blank as she approaches the thing they call bloom. Trying to signal to these men that she's not afraid of it or them or anything about this place. "How were you going to contain all this if Poe and I got hit by a car on a street corner? What were you going to do if everyone in the East Village on a Sunday afternoon suddenly got a look at Poe's *bloom*? Is she going to tell me that?"

"Look, the meeting is her idea, not mine. My priority right now? Dealing with the fact that your brother's bloom is in the custody of someone who murdered a plane-crash survivor to make them be quiet. Someone who now has the power to move anything he damn well pleases with his mind. Someone who got to that crash site before anyone else did. And my job is to find that man before he unleashes hell on earth. And the longer you subject me to this interrogation, the less I'm able to do that."

"We were about to introduce ourselves to him when you brought me back," she says.

Both of the men are stunned. The massaging sensation inside her arm gets stronger, insistent. Her brother is begging to be heard.

"There's a set of doors that opens. Apparently the man is on the other side of it. Or his memory deck is."

"It's not that simple," Randy says, "and you're not qualified. Neither of you. You might have been about to cross a bloom bridge into this guy's memory deck that opens when he inhales Poe, but you wouldn't have had the first idea what to do once you got there."

She opens the notepad anyway and starts writing. Is the aquarium still there?

gone only stays a little while then doors close and go dark but I think I see the key they're talking about and I can—

As Randy starts toward her, she snaps it shut.

"If you're keeping information from me about this—"

"You'll what?" Claire says. "Ruin our lives some more? Yeah, I'm shaking, dude. OK. I'll do this, but tell me something else first. If we each have our own memory deck, why is my brother on mine? What about what my brother and I did in the Jeep?"

"That," Randy says quietly, "is something we've never seen before. It has to be because of the connection between you two. It followed him into death. We're limited in what we know about joint exposure. With humans. We've only done it to animals, and it's re-created some of the same aspects of what happens between you and Poe. When you're not both jacked up on powerful drugs."

She glares at him. He glares back.

"Because your job is containment," she finally says.

"Yeah, and if I'd taken it too seriously, you and your brother would have been down here with the animals from the moment I was hired. But we let you have your lives. Because you're not the only person on this ranch who had to find a way to deal with something they didn't expect and couldn't explain."

He's talking about the woman behind him, she's sure. Or what's left of her.

Or what she's turned into.

182

Shifted into.

And Claire doesn't care.

"I remain unmoved, cowboy," she whispers.

Randy throws up his hands, gives Thomas a look, which the man returns with an icy stare.

Claire says, "You've done it before? Breathed in this . . . bloom."

"Hundreds of times."

"*Hundreds*. She's more than your boss, isn't she?" Claire asks.

"Like I said, she'll tell you what she wants you to know."

She steps closer to the pulsing tree of blue light rising from the desiccated stump.

"All right," she says, "tell me how this is going to work."

Randy is right next to her now, following her gaze into the hypnotic, otherworldly swirls of light. "The bloom will seek out your breath, just like it did mine. Especially your exhales. It seems to get a kick out of carbon dioxide. All it'll need from you is a short, sharp inhale to take it in. And then it'll hurt like hell for about thirty seconds. And I'm serious. Like hell. Like your skull's going to explode."

"Great," Claire whispers.

"And then you'll get a glimpse of your memory deck."

"Pier 39 in San Francisco."

"OK. Mine's the old revolving restaurant atop Reunion Tower in Dallas."

"Then what?"

"It'll probably be the hardest part, and it'll feel like time travel. First you'll get a glimpse of your memory deck. Then you'll be completely immersed in one of your memories."

"From the memory deck?"

"From the vault. Which is on your memory deck. Everything that's behind the doors, that's your vault."

"Except for the aquarium doors. The ones that come and go."

"Correct. The doors that come and go, that open by themselves, don't go to your vault. They go to a bloom bridge. The doors that are always present on your memory deck—everything behind those is your vault. Agatha's going to open one of those, and when she does, it'll be like time travel for you. I'd say brace yourself, but it happens so quickly you won't have time. You'll just be in it suddenly, and it'll be *very*, very real. Go with it. Don't fight it. Bad things happen when we fight what's in the vault."

"Do I get a say in which memory I have to go through?" she asks.

"Nope. The factors that influence what comes out of the vault when a door is opened are numerous. We think they have to do with your emotional state at the time. What you've been through over the past few days. The moments that have been triggered, stirred up. That sort of thing."

"Oh, this should be really pleasant, then."

"It will not be. Trust me. Let the memory play out. Surrender to it; it will guide your actions, your words. You'll feel helpless inside, but it will happen as it should. Then the two of you will be face-to-face on your memory deck, and then you can talk."

"Me and your boss?"

Randy nods. "Yes."

"Can I take the glasses off?"

"Sure."

Randy extends his hand. She hands him the glasses. The glow before her isn't blindingly bright; it was the profusion of them on the walk here she needed to be shielded from.

Claire's heart races as the little blue particles tumble toward her nose and mouth.

A dozen more questions fly through her mind, but there's something more powerful in her heart. The desire she's buried for years because pursuing it seemed to drive her father mad.

She wants to know.

And so she breathes in, a short, sharp inhale.

The pain is even worse than Randy described. And then through it, she sees the glimpse of Pier 39 Randy promised her. The carousel glows, but it doesn't spin, and she sees Poe, the grown-up version, backing away from the glass, turning to study the arrival of something she can't see. Weightlessness sweeps her body, as if her muscles have turned to velvet cords and her bones to cotton.

The vision fades, and suddenly she's back in the cellar, realizing the blue light dancing off the walls isn't just coming from the desiccated tree stump before her. She lifts one hand and studies her glowing fingers, sees Randy watching her from several paces away, tense as a coiled snake. Wondering, perhaps, if she's going to make good on her jokey threat to vent her frustrations.

She's wondering whether or not to assure him she won't when he's replaced by a strange, shadowy darkness. But the smells that assault her next are familiar in a way that brings layers of dread to this otherwise-magical experience. They're the noxious blend of scents that had overtaken the living room of her home after her mother decided to die at home without a fight, the strawberry-meets-lime-meets-pine-tree blend of medical ointments and the eye-watering rubbing alcohol smell of everything the hospice nurses constantly sterilized.

No, she thinks, *please not here.*

"Yes, here," a woman's voice responds. Not her mother's voice, even though Claire can feel her mother close, across the shadowed room, in the hospital bed they set up where her TV chair used to be. "But not for too long. I'm sorry."

Realizing her thoughts are now audible to the woman who's entered her mind, Claire tries to surrender with silence, which results in a falling feeling, followed by the touch of both men catching her and lowering her to the floor. But the feel of their touch grows distant.

"I'm sorry, Claire Huntley. Sorry for everything."

There's a glimpse of fog-shrouded Pier 39, just as it appeared before, and then the only reality Claire knows is the living room at her house, when it was still her mother's house, the place where her mother had chosen to die.

16

"Claire?"

"Yes, Momma," Claire answers.

It's 9:00 p.m., the time when her mother usually starts to fade thanks to the morphine, and Claire, having graded papers in the kitchen for most of the evening, gives the hospice nurse a short break while she turns out the lights in the front room so her mother can sleep more soundly.

The nurse on duty is in the backyard, making a quiet call on her cell. Claire always feels strangely guilty at this time of day because she's about to be released from her duties, and this gives her a little burst of elation, the kind she gets before a three-day weekend. She's already taken a glass of wine into her room, where she'll slide into bed and read a chapter or two from a novel in which the men are both handsome heroes and werewolves, their miraculous physical nature a universe away from the oppressive mortality that has descended over their home.

"I take back what I said. About him."

Claire turns. "About who?"

"Your father."

Despite her drugged haze, her mother can read the confusion on Claire's face. There's so much she's said about her father over the years, most of it in anger, it's hard to know which statement she wants to retract.

"If you want him there," her mother says, "at the funeral, that's your call. I just figured he might pitch some kind of scene. Make it all about him. And I didn't want you to have to go through that."

At the edge of the bed, Claire places her hands on the plastic barrier, the one with the keypad in the side that adjusts the recline. The glowing buttons seem like more of an intrusion when the room is dark, a violation of the place where they once laughed at *The Big Bang Theory* together on the sofa.

"But, you know, the truth is," her mother continues, "the funeral's really for you."

Claire feels a stronger version of what she's been feeling since her mother's diagnosis. The sense of having swallowed a sword until the tip of its blade is sitting right above her stomach, and the fear that if she shows too much emotion it will slip deep and do lasting damage.

"I want it to be what you want too," Claire says.

"It'll have to be one or the other, sweetheart. And since you'll still be around, it's up to you, really."

Once again, she's astonished by how small the disease has made her mother. Not by shrinking her height, but by eating away at the ample weight she carried for most of her adult life. But her mother's brittle sarcasm has also withered away, and with it her quick shifts to glowering, teeth-clenched anger. Claire would be lying if she didn't admit she welcomed the departure of these things. It's as if dying has taught her mother how to smile without fearing ridicule, and that's what she's doing now. Smiling with the innocence of a baby.

"OK, well, the music's going to be all your favorites," Claire says.

"And nothing with spinach at the reception because it's an evil vegetable."

"Absolutely."

Her mother places her quaking hand on Claire's. She has never been affectionate. Her love came in the form of verbal approval and tangible rewards for goals achieved. A supersize jar of Nutella to celebrate a good grade on a final, a fancy dinner at Mastro's Steakhouse to celebrate her admission to UCLA. And regular visits to the Santa Monica Pier because its frenetic energy and postcard-ready vistas made her feel like both a local and a tourist. And because, in no small part, it reminded her of those visits to Pier 39 in San Francisco she loved when she was a girl. Tangible rewards, not hugs, are the currency of her mother's love.

"Claire," her mother whispers.

"Yeah?"

"Will you sleep in here tonight?"

She tries to keep her breath from leaving her in a loud rush. Tears will follow if she doesn't.

For most of their lives, her mother never showed weakness, never asked for help. A few years after her sister, Eileen, died, the one who'd put them up for almost a year after their move to Southern California, they'd driven up to San Luis Obispo to visit Eileen's husband, Cal, who'd retired there after his wife's death. A pleasant afternoon of walking around the quaint downtown, buoyed by the ever-present youthful enthusiasm of the town's many college kids. An outdoor lunch, her mother and uncle sharing fond memories about her departed aunt. It had seemed to Claire like the perfect day. And then, that night, after they returned to their motel, as they were both walking silently to their rooms, her mother had exploded into hard, bitter tears, as if hours spent discussing her sister in pleasant tones had suddenly made her absence real. And when Claire had offered to sit with her for a while in her room, her mother shook her head, offered the best smile she could through her tears, and told her she'd be fine, closing the door behind her quickly before Claire could do anything further. Claire had gone to her room alone, feeling hollowed out, useless.

So if her mother's making this request of her now, if she's exhausted her own stoicism, it means the end must be near.

"Of course, Momma," Claire whispers, hoping these simple words don't unleash the flood of tears. "Just let me change and set up the sofa."

She leans over, kisses her mother on the forehead, expecting to feel a recoil; instead, her mother reaches up and gently caresses the side of her face.

Claire's hands tremble as she changes into her nightclothes. As she makes her way back to the living room, with a blanket under her arm, the hospice nurse gives her a sympathetic smile from the kitchen. When Claire returns to the living room, her mother is in a fetal position, arm across the pillow over her head so as not to tangle her morphine drip. The pose allows just enough room for Claire to slide into bed with her, so she lowers the barrier on one side and takes the space next to her mother. Her tears come quickly. Pent up and relentless, as raw and full of pain as her mother's tears over her sister all those years ago. Only instead of sending her away this time, her mother reaches up and brings Claire's hand to her bony chest. And Claire realizes it's not just the funeral her mother wants to be for her; it's this too. This last connection.

Eventually Claire's tears subside, and she's startled by the emotion that comes next. Forgiveness—a forgiveness so vast and deep it makes clear for the first time the depth of unaddressed anger she's harbored toward her mother over the years. And at the same time, it makes it all seem childish and pointless. Because all the slights, all the wrongs, all the offenses in our lives, she realizes, are leveled against us by those who have this potential frailty lurking somewhere in their bones. And it makes their cruel words and their attacks feel less like thunderbolts from above and more like the lashing out of a child driven slightly mad by the constant awareness of their own imminent death. Most of us, she thinks, go through life expecting others to save us from what afflicts us all—the knowledge that it will all end in a moment of total physical collapse. And maybe we place this burden more heavily on our parents because we cannot bring ourselves to accept that the ones who gave us life can't save us from our own deaths.

Claire drifts on this realization, savoring the sense of release it has brought her.

———

Her mother goes cold in her arms. The sheets collapse, and then they are gone, and when Claire opens her eyes, the streetlight-latticed tree branches that were just rustling outside the window have been replaced by total dark.

There is no bed. Claire is lying on the bare floor. A stranger is standing in the dark corner of the room, next to a door outlined in vague blue light. The stranger has a long cascade of white hair and a face she can't see.

"How dare you," Claire whispers to the woman. "How dare you."

"I'm sorry." It's the same voice she'd heard when she glimpsed the memory deck. The voice of Randy Drummond's boss. "I'm sorry I had to do it this way."

Claire says, "You did this on purpose. You want us to forgive you for whatever you did to us, and so you made me remember how I—"

"That's not how the vault works, Claire."

"Who are you?"

Claire sits up, looks behind her. Darkness. Not shadows, not a lightless room, but a black void that seems so deep it makes her feel as if one wrong move might get her sucked into it.

"My name is Agatha Caldwell."

The stranger steps forward. Her eyes are big and blue, and her face is deeply lined in a way that makes her small mouth look perpetually poised to speak. There is a wall of glass next to her that looks like it could be the inside of one of the storefronts Claire saw earlier. But from this perspective, the glass is translucent, except for the gray-blue glow pressing against it from the outside.

"If this worked the way it should," the woman says, "if this were a normal death, I'd be someone you knew, someone you loved and trusted, and I'd guide you through a life review. If your body was struggling to hold on in the physical realm, this review, the memories in your vault, would be used so you could make a choice about whether or not to go back. Or to continue on. That's my theory anyway."

"Based on what?"

"My research into near-death experiences reported the world over, and our experiences since I got here. Thank you for letting me in. It was the right thing to do."

"For who?"

"Take a moment if you need to, but we don't have a ton of time. I've got a lot to show you."

Agatha Caldwell pushes the door partly open. Claire glimpses the carousel beyond, her brother rushing Agatha like a patient trying to get news from their loved one's surgeon. This slender glimpse into her memory deck somehow makes it feel even more real and fully realized.

She searches the room again. It's embarrassing, but she knows what she's doing. Searching for any trace of her mother and the living room of their house as it once was. And there is nothing. Just the lure of cheerful music outside.

She rises, opens the door, and when she steps outside, Poe's arms are around her instantly. Grown-up Poe, in tattered designer jeans and a formfitting T-shirt. The warmth she lost when the sheets sagged under her arms is replaced by the feel of her brother's spirit. She leans into it, but when she closes her eyes, she's back there, arms wrapped around her dying mother.

"You wanted me to give her the key, right?" Poe says. "I didn't do the wrong thing, did I?"

"No, you didn't. What was it?"

Claire pulls back, looks down into his open hand. A silver necklace with a little pendant on it, emblazoned with a trio of powerful-looking redwood trees that soar into wide Vs at the top. A gift from their father to their mother, and she remembers now how her mother lost it at Pier 39 during that trip and didn't realize it until they were on their way to the airport to head home. They'd been so afraid she'd get upset, but instead, she'd gotten a distant look in her eyes and said, "Well, I guess that's the price to pay for all the fun we had." And for a second they couldn't tell if she was saying they'd been punished for having such a good time on their trip or if the lost necklace constituted an acceptable sacrifice. With their mother, it could have been either sentiment.

"I found it on the bench," he says.

She takes it from his hand and places it in her pocket.

"There's no taking it with you," Agatha says. "It'll just end up right back where it was."

"Thanks for all your help, ghost ma'am," Poe says. "You're, like, fourteen years too late, but whatever."

Ignoring Poe's dig, Agatha asks, "Do you have anything on you right now that came from here? Any objects? Anything?"

Claire and Poe both shake their heads.

"Good," Agatha says, "because they won't make the trip. Come with me."

For the first time, Claire sees the new addition to the pier. The spot where the aquarium doors opened earlier is gone, returned to black storefronts and glass panes with fathomless dark on the other side. But opposite from where it appeared, just beyond the carousel and in the direction of where the city should be, another set of double doors has opened, topped by a brand-new sign decorated with snowcapped mountains. Climb The Heights, it proclaims, and the light coming from within is bright blue and flickering. Will there be ocean depths beyond, filled with nightmare sharks?

"How about you just give us some answers right here?" Poe asks.

"I'm going to give you more than answers. I'm going to give you memories."

"Oh, I'm sure Claire wants to sign up for that again," Poe says. "No, thanks."

"My vault is more stable and easier to manipulate."

"Why?" Claire asks.

They both seem surprised she's found her voice. She's still holding on to her brother for support.

"I'm not making any new memories," Agatha says. "I think it's more stable because I'm not adding anything to it."

"Randy Drummond says he's met with you on your memory deck hundreds of times," Claire says.

"He has. But those memories don't get stored," Agatha says. "The vault's designed to receive memories from our physical bodies. At least that's what I think. Nothing here works exactly the way it should. In us."

"Because we were all exposed to the pulse," Claire says.

Agatha nods grimly and starts for the double doors behind her.

"Stop!" Poe cries. "Look, I'm down with the whole near-death thing. But just tell me if it was friggin' aliens or not, because in every movie I've ever seen about aliens, they looked like giant bugs and I hate bugs and I don't want to meet one over on your memory deck, or whatever."

"Do you also have a problem with wolves?" Agatha asks.

Poe stares at her blankly. "You know, given what's already on my plate, I hadn't given them much thought today."

Agatha says, "They're going to be all around the bloom bridge as we cross over. Don't look them in the eye and they won't be able to make any trouble."

"I guess that's the same deal with the sharks," Poe says.

"Sharks?" Agatha asks.

The woman's ignorance of the aquarium doors and everything that lies beyond is a reminder that even though they're moving through impossible realms, they've yet to encounter something omniscient and all-seeing. This world they've entered has its own structure and divisions, and even though they're roaming its byways, they're limited in what they can see and hear.

"Bloom bridge?" Poe gestures to the double doors. "That's what you call that thing? I mean, could you guys have spent any time on these nicknames? It sounds like something you'd buy at Home Depot after you've fucked up all your floors."

"A simple naming system is a defense mechanism against things that feel overwhelming," Agatha said. "Same as your sarcasm. We should get going. We have thirty minutes until my bridge to you collapses."

"And then what happens?" Poe asks. "What happens if we're not back here?"

"Randy compares it to flying backward on a roller coaster and then shooting fifty feet up in the air in about ten seconds. He says it's hard not to throw up."

"He's right," Claire says. "I failed that particular test."

"Yeah, what about me? I don't have a body to go back to. What happens to me if I get stuck on your side after thirty minutes?" Poe asks.

"I don't know. Everyone I've interacted with here has been a living person who inhaled my bloom by choice and then let me into their vault so that they could cross the bridge to my memory deck with me."

"How many people have done this?" Claire asks.

"Three of them. Randy and two others."

Claire figures that includes Benjamin Running Creek and Thomas Billings, the doctor.

"But I died and somehow ended up on Claire's deck?" Poe asks. "Which shouldn't have happened?"

"Or," Agatha says, "you share a memory deck, and you just got here first. Because of the connection between you two. That's my theory, at least."

"Yeah, you've got a lot of theories, lady, and maybe it's—"

"Hence my offer," Agatha says, voice tightening as she closes the distance between them. "Look, I'm responsible for what happened to you two. And I don't expect kindness or even respect. But I've got things to offer, and you'd be fools to turn them down. I can teach you how to navigate this place so it feels less like a prison, and Claire can use my bloom to come back here anytime she wants. That said, the return trip is a bear, so she's going to want to space out her visits so that—"

"She's been here already," Poe says.

Agatha looks shocked. "When?"

"We've got our own back and forth going," Poe says, "and it doesn't involve this bloom stuff. It's more like a mirror-and-finger thing."

"Gross," Claire whispers.

"What?" Poe whines.

"It just sounds gross when you say it like that," she says. "We're connected in a different way is what he means. We used it earlier, and I was here longer than thirty minutes. Randy shot me full of adrenaline to bring me back because he was afraid of how long I'd been under. Or over. Or however you want to put it."

There's a long silence. "Well," she finally says, "like I said, uncharted waters. But your connection to me has thirty minutes, so we better cross."

Agatha starts for the double doors.

"Are you an alien?" Poe calls after her.

Her brother's pissed, Claire can tell. The woman who ruined their lives is bossing them around like they're lazy tourists, and it's probably another minute or two before a full-on argument breaks out. Claire takes Poe's hand and guides him toward the doors. The impossible sights surrounding them on the bridge aren't as frightening as the ones that awaited her in the aquarium's tank earlier, but the same cycling energy tunnels throughout a landscape of ferocious white. Snow, she realizes, and moving through the ice-fringed tree trunks on all sides of them, *four-legged shadows the size of bears, but moving with the slow, stalking grace of wolves.*

"Just don't look them in the eye," Agatha calls back.

"Or else what?" Poe asks.

"They'll get aggressive," Agatha says. "Ultimately, my consciousness doesn't like what we're doing right now, but it doesn't have a good way to stop it."

"I don't know. Wolves the size of trucks seems like it might work on most people," Poe says.

They keep walking.

"Jesus," Poe finally says. "If I'd have known it was going to be all walking, maybe I wouldn't have run my mouth. I mean, isn't this like heaven adjacent? How come we can't fly or float or something?"

"There's a lot you can't do, but there's a lot you can do," Agatha says.

"Give me some of the cans," Poe says.

"You can imagine certain things into being. Nothing too complex, and it has to be something you were familiar with during your physical life. Mostly objects, mementos. This entire place is designed to facilitate a life review for the dying or the newly dead. So everything I've found here suits that purpose in some way. But the force that's supposed to power it all on never shows up."

"You mean death never shows up?" Claire asks.

"Death comes for the dead," Agatha says, "and technically, we aren't dead. Which means the loved ones, presumably deceased, that are meant to guide you into death can't enter here."

Poe says, "So it's like an amusement park, but nobody knows how to turn on the rides."

"More like a car lot and you have to hot-wire all the cars," Agatha says.

"And you can only drive in circles," Poe adds.

"You're getting it," Agatha says. "Good."

"How long have you been here?" Claire asks. "I mean, maybe death just takes longer with us."

"Then with me it's three years and counting," Agatha says.

"Fuck me," Poe whispers.

Up ahead, the tunnel opens. The music pouring from it sounds classical, a string quartet. A song Claire doesn't recognize, but it's pleasant and inviting. And they're suddenly on a set of wide carpeted steps rising up into some sort of atrium with soaring cathedral-like windows and a vaulted ceiling with thick, exposed rafters. Instead of stained glass, the windows offer stunning views down onto a bright blue river that rushes past. Behind it, a backdrop of jagged snow-covered mountains. And above it, the same universally blue sky divided by thick gray clouds that look pregnant with more of the snow dusting the pine-shrouded slopes.

The string quartet of faceless shadows plays in one corner of the room. More shadows waltz on the bright red carpet before them. Overhead, the round metal chandelier is the kind in which Claire would expect to see imitation candle-flame bulbs. Instead, its bulbs are starkly round, a design feature of a bygone era, she thinks. Off to their left is a dining area positioned to take advantage of the river view. A smattering of shadows dine and laugh together.

Claire looks back. There's a sign over the opening through which they just came. The bright red script is stylized, some sort of font meant to evoke medieval times. BAYVIEW ROOM. Just as on their deck, the sign is vague but congruent with the overall setting. This is the basic signage you'd expect to label the conference areas of a high-end resort. Decades ago, if the font is any indication.

Now that they've crossed the bridge, Agatha seems less pressed for time. But Claire sees she's riveted by the sight of two shadowy diners next to the window. The candle flickering on the table reflects along the edges of the massive gaps in their forms in a way that turns Claire's stomach.

"Who are they?" Claire asks.

Without answering, Agatha crosses to the table. The shadows continue with their strange pantomime of a romantic dinner. If this place is as she described it, perpetually awaiting the arrival of a deceased loved one to usher you to the other side, Claire wonders if their arrival would bring these shadows to life, or at least fill in some of their details and make the illusion more complete.

Resting next to one of the china plates is a bright diamond ring. Agatha takes it.

The key to her vault, *Claire thinks.*

Then Agatha turns and starts for a double staircase that plunges into the lobby from a loftlike second floor. "This was a luxury resort in the Canadian Rockies. It burned down twenty years ago. We visited when I was a freshman in high school, before my sister was born." *She's mounting the steps when she adds,* "It was a good trip."

"So you've just been hanging out here in the lobby for three years?" *Poe asks.*

"No," *she answers.* "I spend most of my time in the vault. Like I said, it's become easy to manipulate."

"You relive your memories?" *Claire asks.*

"I've figured out how to sample the good ones. And I don't always have to do it alone."

Randy, *Claire thinks. Definitely not just an employee.*

They mount the stairs, come out onto a carpeted landing where bright, neon-colored 1960s carpeting extends to the railing, and the furniture is sparer and starker than it might be today. But they're moving past it, toward the entrance to a corridor. A corridor lined with guest rooms. Rooms with dark, heavy doors, all of them closed tight.

"One question, sort of a technicality here," *Poe says.* "If I imagine a whole bunch of cocaine into being and I snort it here, is it technically a relapse?"

Agatha turns, stares at him. Despite her charitable poise earlier, her patience is clearly wearing thin.

"*Is it possible for you to be more serious about all this?*" *Agatha asks.*

"*OK,*" *he finally says.* "*Let me be serious, ma'am. I'll get super serious. Just 'cause you asked. You ruined our fucking lives, lady. If you know what's behind all this and you didn't tell us, then you ruined our fucking lives. Our family. Our everything. So pardon me if I'm not exactly jumping at the chance to take a deep dive into your memory vault. There! I said it! Serious enough for you? I mean, Jesus Christ. You've ruined death too! Who the fuck ruins death? It's, like, already the worst thing ever.*"

"*Poe, come on,*" *Claire whispers, taking his hand.*

He falls silent. Maybe he feels betrayed that she isn't joining him in his anger. And maybe she's chiding him because the memory from her own vault has staying power. It's probably preemptive, she figures, to extend the same forgiveness she felt toward her mother in her final hours to the woman standing in front of them now. But the memory's too powerful for her not to.

"*Claire can go alone if you'd like,*" *Agatha says.*

"*No,*" *Poe barks.* "*No. That's not going to happen.*" *He tightens his grip on Claire's hand.* "*She only got exposed to your little pulse thing because she followed me into the woods that night. Where she goes, I go.*"

"*Admirable.*"

Agatha starts for the nearest door.

"*How is this going to work?*" *Claire asks.*

"*You'll see it as I did. You'll feel it as I did.*"

"*And we'll forgive you, is that the point?*" *Poe asks.*

"*Your choice, once it's over,*" *Agatha says.*

No one speaks for a while.

"*Are we doing this?*" *Poe asks Claire.*

"*I have to know,*" *she says.* "*And you do too; you just won't admit it.*"

"*Know it all,*" *Poe mutters.*

"*It's a curse.*"

200

She tightens her grip on his hand. Together they approach the door.

Agatha opens her palm and the diamond ring floats out of it and into the keyhole on the heavy wooden door. The ring vanishes, as if the lock has devoured it, and a thread of bright blue light spills through the hole. The door opens ahead of Agatha's outstretched fingers.

She gestures for them to step through, and when they do, the feeling of the ground underfoot seems to disappear, but Claire doesn't feel like she's falling. Instead, she's surrounded by darkness, and somewhere close by, a woman is screaming.

The Pulse

Only the dead have seen the end of war.

—*George Santayana*

17

Fifty Years Ago

Her mother's voice awakened her in the hours before dawn. But there was a force and a madness to it Agatha had never heard before. It had to be her mother, though. Who else would feel free to scream gibberish with such abandon on their ranch in the middle of the night? Not Hilde, for sure. Their housekeeper and nanny never spoke above a stern monotone, and they were miles from any town and whatever lunatics might call it home.

Just shy of her seventeenth birthday and still blinking back sleep, Agatha stumbled to her bedroom window and saw that, yes, it was her mother far beyond the glass, bent-kneed and writhing as her father held her firmly by both shoulders. They stood outside the stab of headlights their truck made across the gravel driveway as Maryanne Caldwell, who always spoke perfect English lightly accented by her time in Swiss boarding schools, erupted again and again in a guttural opera that made Agatha's stomach churn.

There was a pattern to the nonsense, Agatha realized, and if she tried to write it down, she might capture it. She went for a pen and paper on her desk.

Die jooden warden oons am indie alle beganen . . .

Am induh sind weir alle eins und dies . . .

She was still scribbling when her baby sister began wailing down the hall.

Then, a hard, echoing slap ended her mother's screams.

In response, Banjo, their Australian cattle dog, began barking up a storm inside the barn.

Dr. Theodore Caldwell had never raised a hand to anyone in Agatha's presence, and now he'd struck her mother with such precise force it was as if he'd been practicing for the blow all his life. Pen forgotten, she watched him lead her mother toward the faraway guesthouse, as if she were infected by something that could not be allowed within range of her daughters.

Her mother didn't fight him. That single blow had driven the strength from her bones.

But when they passed under the guesthouse's porch light, Agatha saw the man wasn't her father at all.

It was the junior partner in his medical practice, Dr. Hall.

She did not like Dr. Hall. His attempts to engage her in political discussions—Did she think Nixon was getting a fair shake in the press? Did she find the bombing of Cambodia justified?—always seemed vaguely bullying and inappropriate coming from an adult. And now he'd slapped her mother.

She scanned the shadows, looked back to the truck. There was no sign of her father at all.

In the nursery, Agatha collected Catherine from her crib, held her close. She bounced the baby against her chest, stunned by the nation of distance that seemed to lie between the mother who'd left the evening before and the one who'd just returned. Her parents had planned to spend a long weekend away at one of their favorite inns in Sandpoint, Idaho, and here it was, early Friday morning, and her mother was already back and in a state of hysterical nervous collapse. She'd sat with Agatha for an hour the night before, as she always did before their weekends away, as if she worried her daughter might feel excluded from the getaways and wanted to make her feel recognized. But she'd been calm and controlled, as always. A picture of poise, the other mothers called her. Who despite her lack of pretension always wore her wealthy background and her European education like fine but understated outer garments.

Now she was undone.

The door to the nursery opened, and Hilde entered, fastening the tie of her robe around her ample frame, her gray hair piled atop her head and speared with wooden pins.

"German," Agatha said before she could stop herself.

The word seemed to root Hilde in place. It was too dark to see her expression, but their maid and nanny reacted as if it were a slur. She was the only German in their house.

"Did you hear her?"

"Who?" Hilde asked brusquely.

"My mother. She was yelling. It was German, wasn't it?"

"Of course not." Hilde crossed the room and tugged Catherine from Agatha's arms.

"What's going on?"

"Some sort of quarrel. Your father will handle her."

"It's not him."

Hilde froze next to Catherine's crib. "What?"

"Dr. Hall's with her. Dad didn't come back."

For what felt like a full minute, Hilde was silent. Then she moved to the window and stared out into the dark. Finally, she muttered, "You go rest. I'll see to it."

Agatha wanted to argue, but with Hilde, it was no use.

Once she'd returned to her bedroom, she pulled a chair close to the window, waiting for a sign of anyone from the guesthouse, but it was quiet. A little while later, Hilde's shadow started for it, and when she finally passed under the porch light, Agatha saw she carried baby Catherine in her arms. Maybe she thought Agatha's mother would be calmed by the presence of her younger child. Agatha waited for someone to emerge, but no one did. After a while, she nodded off in her reading chair, the echoes of her mother's incoherent screams piercing her fitful dreams.

When her alarm clock went off at six, she dressed hurriedly, found her parents' bedroom empty, and rushed downstairs. Hilde was waiting for her in the front room. She was a stout woman whose pale cheeks blushed easily, but this morning she was milk white, and her hair was still as tangled as it had been the night before.

"Your mother has had an accident," she said. "She takes medicine for her nerves, especially for long car rides. Before they left yesterday, she took too much and had a reaction. That's why your father brought her back to Dr. Hall's. And Dr. Hall thought she'd be more comfortable here."

"Where's Dad?" Agatha asked.

"He has meetings scheduled in Sandpoint he must attend to. Dr. Hall will stay with your mother now."

Nothing about this story made sense. Sandpoint was an isolated lake town. The nearest city to it was Spokane, and her father never did business there. He was a doctor with a small family practice. Most medical-supply folks came to him while making a circuit through the more populated parts of Montana. Her parents crossed the border into Idaho to escape, not work; it's why they never brought her along. Who could her father possibly be meeting with there? And how could the meeting be so important he'd abandon his wife in the midst of an emotional crisis so wildly out of character for her as to seem like a possession?

And nerve medicine? The idea seemed absurd. Her mother had taught her how to fire guns and ride horses with icy calm. Agatha had never seen her take so much as an aspirin.

"She needs to be watched, is all," Hilde said.

"I didn't know she took medicine for her nerves," Agatha said.

"She didn't want you to know. I'm sorry you found out this way."

"I want to see her."

"Not right now. You go on to school. All should be right by the time you're home."

"And I can see her then?"

"You'll see her when I say."

There was a flash of anger in Hilde's eyes. This was not the matronly aggression with which their housekeeper usually sought to bend Agatha to her will. This was the ego of someone who had either forgotten her station or come into some knowledge that made the limitations of her station irrelevant.

Agatha knew better than to ask again about the German. In light of the lies she'd just been presented with, and there was no other way to think of them, the paper containing her hurried transcription had become an object of immense and secret value.

Driving to school took all her focus. Occasionally she would stay up too late reading, and the long, winding drive to Whitefish the next morning would test her sleep-deprived reflexes. To keep herself focused, every few seconds she had to squeeze the steering wheel until her hands hurt.

She knew who she should talk to next, but she wasn't sure of the right approach.

An idea came to her during lunchtime, thanks to the chatty complaints of her good friend Lucy Merriweather, who was going on about another one of her nerdy little brother's obsessions. Agatha suspected Lucy was mostly jealous of the attention these fixations, the latest of which was shortwave radio, earned from their father. Their father had been hiking with him into the park at night so he could test a theory. "The little dweeb thinks he'll hear the Soviets if he goes up high enough."

"How's he going to do that?" Patricia Collins asked. "They're all the way east, not on Mars."

"I don't know. Something like how the shortwaves bounce off the sky and then back down, but the Soviets aren't broadcasting a damn thing they'll let us hear. Hey, Aggie, you going to eat that potato salad?"

Agatha pushed the little Styrofoam bowl toward her friend without another word, fighting the urge to kiss Lucy on the cheek for giving her something that felt like hope.

Mrs. Deville taught French but was quick to tell anyone who'd listen that she was proficient in multiple languages, many of which she'd be able to teach as soon as the school decided the students were worthy. Agatha wasn't sure if German was among the languages, but if anyone at their school spoke it, Mrs. Deville would know. She was a tiny woman whose flowing brown hair brought a little eruption of hippie mystery to their otherwise-staid high school, but she tempered her hints of wildness with outfits of muted floral prints and tweeds. When Agatha caught up with her in the hallway between classes, the older woman seemed overjoyed to encounter a student genuinely curious about something besides their sports teams' scores or the mysteries of the opposite sex. Agatha's heart raced as she turned over the paper she'd written on that morning.

"I can certainly give it a go," Mrs. Deville said. "German's not exactly my forte, but I'm reasonably proficient, and I have a few friends I might call. Where did you hear all this, Agatha?"

At the prospect of her mother's words spreading out beyond the radius of Whitefish High School, her heart started to race. Whatever story she gave now might be repeated, which is why she'd practiced it several times since lunch.

"Shortwave radio," she said, as if she'd been saying the term all her life. "My dad's got one and we take it into the park. Sometimes we go up as high as we can to see what we can pick up. A couple nights we kept hearing this . . . and well, I wasn't even sure it was German, so I just started writing it down."

"Well, it certainly looks like an approximation of German. Phonetically, I mean. You did your best, I'm sure."

She smiled and Agatha returned it.

"I've got some time this afternoon," the teacher said. "Stop by after the end of last period and we'll see what I have."

Mrs. Deville departed. Agatha stayed rooted in place, waiting to see if there was anything close to suspicion on her face. But the teacher was so busy reading Agatha's scribbles she almost collided with a knot of students heading in the opposite direction. By the time she rounded the nearest corner of the hallway, she'd barely looked up from the paper once.

Agatha sleepwalked through her afternoon classes. With the paper out of her hands now, she was without an action plan, and if Mrs. Deville hadn't pulled something together by final bell, there'd be nothing to do but return to the ranch, where she'd no doubt be subjected to more of Hilde's lies.

Mrs. Deville rose from behind her desk as soon as she saw Agatha standing in the doorway to her classroom. She approached with a look of muted concern. The paper was still folded as it had been when Agatha had handed it over, and she thought for a moment that might mean the teacher hadn't managed to translate anything. Then Agatha noticed fresh red ink bleeding through the paper and realized the woman had done plenty of work on the assignment but was afraid of exposing any of it to passing eyes.

"Shortwave radio, you say?"

Agatha nodded, afraid that if she repeated the answer aloud it would start to sound like the lie it was.

"I imagine it was some sort of play," the teacher said. "Radio plays were a big deal when I was a girl, not so much anymore. *The Green Hornet*. Did you ever hear of it?"

"Is that what it was?" Agatha asked. "*The Green Hornet*?"

"God, no," Mrs. Deville muttered, shaking her head. "*The Green Hornet* was a great deal of fun. And I'm not sure they ever did a German version. Certainly not back then. Whatever this is . . . well, it's quite dark, I'm afraid. Perhaps it's religious . . . I don't know. They're talking about the war. That much is clear."

The word *war* curled something in Agatha's gut.

"Vietnam." Agatha was deliberately playing dumb in hopes her teacher would speak more.

"World War II, I'm afraid. I asked for some help from Mr. Clark. He wrote his master's in college on Goethe and knew more German than I realized." She handed over the paper and then fell silent, as if she were expecting Agatha to read it in front of her. But reading the translation here, with school not yet entirely drained of students, would be akin to exposing her mother's fresh madness to all of Whitefish High.

"Thank you, Mrs. Deville. I owe you one."

"Let's not go spreading this around, Agatha. I'm not sure the administration would be pleased should they . . . Well, let's just say the contents were not what I expected. Not obscene, exactly. But disturbing. Quite disturbing."

"I won't tell anyone. And maybe Mr. Clark shouldn't either."

"No, no. He won't. I'm sure. He was very rattled."

"I'm so sorry. I didn't know . . ."

"There's nothing to apologize for. But if this is what you're picking up on your radio, perhaps you'd benefit from a less distressing hobby."

She nodded, tucked the paper inside her bag, tried not to break into a run as she reached the Pinto. Once she was inside the car with the doors locked, she unfolded the paper. At first it was soothing to see how the teacher's block printing had turned Agatha's scrawl into a clean paragraph of highly legible text. Then she began to read the translated words.

She felt like her breath was a thread being pulled quickly away from her and she'd better grab at it before it was out of reach, but she couldn't move.

The Jews will meet us at the end and they will take our bodies. We will become them and they will become us. All become one, and no God waits for us. In the end, there are no bodies but what we have done with our bodies in life will be visited upon us. . . . I blinded her. I blinded her and so she was waiting to show me what I had done, and I could feel the blindness I had inflicted upon her inside of myself, and the wound became ours. We shared the wound because we are one. In the end, we are all one and this will be our punishment before it is our reward.

Agatha lost track of time in the parking lot, read and reread the translation so many times the sun had started to sink behind the mountains by the time she felt as if she were back inside her skin. On the way home, she pulled over and read the paper again.

Her mother was not German. Her mother was an American whose wealthy parents had died while she was away at European boarding schools. She was brought home just before Hitler's invasions rocked Europe, where she met Agatha's father while he was putting himself through medical school.

They'd worked for the government.

The US government.

They lived on a ranch in Montana because they loved the mountains, and the government had paid them well for their services, and their families were all dead. And they did not put their families' pictures out for others to see because their deaths had been premature, and this made them sad. And her parents did not like to be sad. It was a wasted emotion, they said.

Instead of driving through the gate to the ranch, Agatha drove past it, then onto the shoulder, parking as far into the brush as she could.

On foot, she hurried to the ranch's pedestrian gate, unlocked it with her key, then slipped into the dense pines that traveled along the property's southern border all the way to the guesthouse where she'd seen Dr. Hall take her mother in the hours before dawn. She was surprised when Banjo didn't rush to meet her. Was he still locked up inside the barn? He was an Australian cattle dog, which meant he was a runner and roamer and would probably drive the horses insane if they'd been let out into the pasture.

She was sneaking around the back, paces from the bedroom's window, when she heard Hilde and her mother speaking to each other. This time she was certain the language was German. But it was the tones that struck her. Hilde did not sound submissive or deferential. She did not sound like the woman who was able to scrub their kitchen without making a single sound that disturbed them at the breakfast table. It sounded like she was giving Agatha's mother orders, and her mother had no interest in complying.

The drapes were drawn, so there was no peering inside. As Agatha pressed herself against the wall, she closed her eyes, used sound to build a mental picture of the scene.

Her mother's words were suddenly muffled, as if she'd swallowed her own tongue midsentence. Then came several metallic clangs. Small sounds, but made by something pulling against the bed's metal frame. Footsteps followed, along with an eruption of wails from Catherine as Hilde carried the baby into the front room of the house. The choking sounds continued, then stopped, followed by more metallic jerks.

She could envision it all as if she'd seen it with her own two eyes.

Her mother had been gagged and tied to the bed.

Heart racing, she moved around the side of the house, waited for the sounds of Hilde crossing the front porch, her shoes crunching twigs. They never came. Hilde was standing guard, and now, Agatha couldn't tell if the old woman was keeping Catherine in the guesthouse to comfort her mother or if the presence of the baby was meant to ensure her compliance.

Agatha snuck back out to the road, drove through the front gate as if she'd just arrived home.

It would be dark soon. When she entered the main house, she saw the dining table had been formally set, but with a single place setting. There were even long white candles in the silver candelabras her mother loved. There was a note on the counter, written in Hilde's spiking, rigid cursive, alerting Agatha to the plate of food in the oven that she'd only need to heat for ten minutes.

There was an eruption of screams from the guesthouse, so eerily similar to the night before Agatha's first thought was that she'd been seized by a flashback. But it was two women this time, and one was attempting to shout English to drown out the other's German.

Hilde and her mother, and it was coming from the guesthouse. And then a third voice, baby Catherine, crying in response.

Agatha shot to her feet and ran.

The guesthouse's front door was cracked, and as soon as Agatha threw it open, she saw Hilde and her mother wrestling in the front room. A plate of food had overturned and smashed to the floor. It was impossible at first to see whose raised arm formed the center of their strange dance, because there was so much blood on their hands. But as they stumbled together, it became clear Hilde was gripping one of her mother's wrists, and in her mother's hand was one of the wooden pins Hilde often used to spear her great pile of hair. Hilde must have removed Maryanne's restraints in order to feed her, and her mother had then managed to yank out one of Hilde's hairpins.

But the blood wasn't Hilde's. It was pouring down her mother's face from the grotesque sockets where her eyes had been. Agatha could only think of the words of the translation she'd read earlier: *I blinded her, and so she was waiting to show me what I'd done.*

Just then her mother gave up the fight. She slid down the wall, laughing hysterically and clapping her hands together. And Agatha couldn't help but believe she was expressing satisfaction over having just gouged out her own eyes with a sharp piece of wood.

She ran back to the house and called an ambulance.

And she did not return to the guesthouse until she heard its siren approaching and saw its lights splash the ranch's front gate. Then she ran to the gate and pulled it open, shouted to the men behind the wheel to follow her. As she ran toward the guesthouse, she saw Hilde, her face blood-spotted and her hair a tangled mess, emerge onto the front porch. When she saw what Agatha had done, her expression went cold as ice, as if Agatha had brought the long hand of the outside world into the most private of places.

Which had been her intention precisely.

18

Randy had figured the presence of a medical cart and a pallet would have frightened Claire if she'd seen them upon entering Agatha's cell. So he kept them in the corridor outside, then went to get them the minute Claire inhaled. The first time Agatha managed to cross from the common area of his memory deck into his vault, his physical body had collapsed to the floor of her chamber so hard he'd ended up with a lump on his head. They've managed to avoid a repeat with Claire.

Now, Thomas kneels next to Claire's prone and seemingly lifeless body, checking her vitals, making sure the frenzied movements of her pupils aren't even more out of whack than they should be.

Footsteps approach down the corridor's metal floor. It's Ben. "Sean's back from LA. He's in the infirmary with our other guests."

Randy thought he heard the Kodiak come in for a landing earlier, but he was too distracted monitoring Claire's vitals, and sounds from above sometimes have trouble making it all the way down to the cellar, which is as it should be.

"So what's the plan here?" Ben asks.

"Agatha's giving away the game, it sounds like," Thomas says.

"It's not a game. It's her story. And it's hers to tell if she wants."

Thomas nods. "Sorry."

"It's been a day," Randy says. "I get it."

"Almost morning," Ben says. "Papa Bear's stirring."

"Is he complaining about the service?" Randy asks.

"Doesn't sound like he's got the energy to complain about much," Ben says. "Yet."

"I'll go check on him. Radio me if anything goes wrong. And if her vitals go nuts, shoot her up again and bring her back. Don't give it a second thought. She's not like us. She's been exposed, so everything with her will be harder to predict. I'll explain it to Agatha if I have to."

Thomas nods, and then Randy's out the door, up through the floor of the barn, and crossing the icy lawn back to the guesthouse and its subterranean infirmary.

Sean's standing guard outside the door to Abram's cell. Whenever he returns to the ranch, Randy's always a little shocked by his appearance. It's Sean's job to blend in with LA crowds, so he always looks like some vaguely stylish corporate supervisor dropping in for a visit from the head office. Formfitting designer jeans, a solid-color dress shirt with some shine to it, tailored to his V-shaped form. Today's color is dark purple.

"Good flight?" Randy asks.

"Better than some."

"Hilarious."

"Sorry. Gallows humor," Sean says.

"How's our guest?"

Sean waggles his hand.

"Watch the door," Randy says. "I'm going in."

Sean takes a step back. Randy opens the door with his key, pulls it firmly shut behind him.

The room's much like the one in which they kept Claire, previously used for monitoring their return trips from Agatha's memory deck. It's not meant to hold captives, and the sight of Abram Huntley sitting on the edge of the gurney, bent forward with his elbows on his knees, looking like someone's just whacked him across the back of the head so hard he can't stand up straight, twists Randy's gut a little.

"Mr. Huntley, my name's Randy Drummond."

"Am I dead?"

"No. But you're a terrible shot. And a worse driver."

"Yeah, well, I was drinking, so . . ."

"You were drinking before you picked up your daughter from the airport and took her up an icy road?"

"Oh Jesus. Just waterboard me or something. Don't do the family-therapy routine. And you know good and well I was drinking. You've had me under surveillance since I moved here. If you were concerned about the other cars on the road, you could have stopped me sooner."

"So *we* were your big reveal to your daughter, huh? That's why you had her fly to Montana?"

Abram shrugs, but it looks like he still can't sit up all the way. "What the hell did you give me?" he asks.

"It'll wear off. So here's what I'm thinking. You know you're under surveillance. You figure she is too. You get her to fly here on a moment's notice, figuring you'll pull her away from whatever eyes we've got on her in LA. Then you get a rental car we don't have time to bug, and as soon as you got her in it, you drive hell for leather and figure we'll spring into action and expose ourselves."

"Something like that."

"So you used your daughter as bait?" Randy asks.

"Did you kill my son?"

"We did not. We had nothing to do with what happened on that plane. You have my word on that."

"OK. Can I have your gun too?"

Randy laughs before he can stop himself.

"Was I getting close at least?" Abram asks.

"No."

"I found a cave I thought was something, or the ghost of one anyway," Abram says. "Down at the library, I found some old journals from hikers from the sixties. Mostly self-published stuff, but it's on file under local interest down there. They said there was a cave right next to Lake Michele that folks used to explore. I went looking myself, and it's gone. Just a big pile of granite. Must have been some sort of cave-in around the late sixties, early seventies."

"Is that so?"

"Half the trees around that lake were carted in and replanted. They don't belong there. Now, either you're replacing ones that get knocked down by whatever happens out there, or you're trying to make sure the woods stay nice and dense so folks don't start trying to kayak nearby."

"I see," Randy says.

"Where's my daughter?"

"Hearing the story I'm about to tell you now."

Randy unholsters his gun, sets it on the rolling metal cart against the wall, having been recently cleared of anything Abram might use as a weapon. Abram's eyes light up at the sight of the oily, black SIG, but he doesn't make a move for it, even as Randy backs up and takes a seat in the chair against the wall.

"And if I don't like it," Abram says, "I can vote with your gun?"

"I'd rather you didn't. Kick back, though. It's a long one."

Then Randy started to speak, summoning every detail Agatha's memories had imparted into his consciousness after she welcomed him into her vault.

19

Fifty Years Ago

Even though Agatha's father was not present, his reputation had followed them to Kalispell General Hospital, where the ER doctors came to visit Agatha and Hilde in the waiting room more than they did the relatives of the other patients who'd been wheeled in that evening. It was not a shock to learn her mother would be permanently blind. Agatha wanted to grieve for her mother's eyesight, for her big, beautiful blue eyes, but her mother had surrendered these things willingly, it seemed. So it was her mother's sanity she had to grieve for instead, and that felt impossible. Like swallowing a whale.

Hilde looked as if her entire world had crashed in on her. This woman, who moved through the world like the prow of a Viking longboat, was hunched over in her chair, rocking back and forth, clutching Catherine to her chest as if she needed the baby's warmth more than the child needed her. The rickety confidence she'd displayed that morning as she'd lied Agatha out the door had been cracked down the middle.

Each time she told the doctors that Agatha's father was unreachable, more of her confidence seemed to leave her. The lie was so shoddy, so hastily assembled, that it had not been designed to hold up under the scrutiny of medical professionals. The doctors returned to tell them that her mother had been stabilized and that she was being transferred to the ICU, where her wounds would need to be constantly treated and re-dressed, and that there would be a chance for Agatha to see her, but only briefly.

> *I could feel the blindness I had inflicted upon her inside of myself, and the wound become ours. We shared the wound because we are one.*

A little while later, the doctor came to escort them to the intensive care unit. And when the nurse who greeted them said it was family only, Agatha turned to Hilde and said, "That would be me."

"I will go too," Hilde said. "I've been with her all day."

"And look how that turned out," Agatha said.

She'd never talked back to Hilde with that much venom, and the woman recoiled as if she'd been slapped.

"And you're not family," Agatha said.

Something moved beneath the angry mask that had captured Hilde's expression, something deeper and darker and harder to name.

Then the nurse was urging Agatha forward with a hand against the small of her back. When Agatha looked over her shoulder, Hilde was glaring at her from behind swinging doors, the baby held to her chest like a prized possession.

The sight of her mother leveled a blow against the center of Agatha's chest. Bandages wrapped the entire crown of her head, covering her eyes and half of the bridge of her nose. But it comforted her to have her mother surrounded by nurses and sharing space with other patients whose areas were cordoned off mostly with curtains and walls. This horror that had befallen her had happened in isolation. And now that others were around, perhaps her mother was safer. Her hands, she saw, had been cuffed to the sides of the bed with leather straps. Agatha gripped as much as she could of the one closest to her.

"Mother, it's me."

There was no response. She pressed harder. Several loud huffs puffed her mother's nostrils, and she coughed.

"Mother."

"You have to stop him."

There was no madness in her mother's tone. Just a raw exhaustion, possibly dulled by whatever drugs they'd given her for the pain.

"The key is in a lockbox in his nightstand drawer. Remember this number. Are you listening?"

Agatha nodded before realizing her mother couldn't see her, would never see her again.

"I'll remember."

"Eight . . . three . . . two . . . one . . . five . . . four . . . nine . . . six."

Agatha repeated it back until she was confident she had it memorized.

"What's it to, Mom? What's the key to?"

"The basement of the guesthouse, there's a door."

"To what?"

Her mother didn't answer, but the calm and focus with which she'd said these words somehow made her act of self-mutilation seem all the more horrific.

"You will never forgive me," her mother finally said. "But you will never stop him unless you know. And you have to stop him."

Her mother relaxed her grip inside the leather cuff, and when Agatha said her name again, there was no response. She knew deep down her mother's silence was an act, a pose, a trick to get her to leave.

When Agatha stepped through the doors to the ICU, there was no sign of Hilde.

And no sign of baby Catherine either.

———

The ranch house was dark when she returned, but the truck Hilde had followed the ambulance in was there, and as Agatha crept through the shadowed house, no one came to greet her, and no footsteps creaked in nearby rooms.

The lockbox was where her mother said it would be.

The key was inside.

The basement of the guesthouse was another matter. It was stuffed with outdated equipment from her father's old medical offices, back when he used to practice out of his home in downtown Whitefish, years before Agatha was born.

Concealed behind two gurneys that had been folded up and stored parallel to the wall was the vague outline of a door. With her flashlight, Agatha searched the floor beneath the gurneys, saw their bottom wheels resting in grooves on each side of a metal rolling platform. The platform would have been easy to miss if she'd been standing and scanning the room, but it was also easy to move if you knew it was there.

A visual obstruction, but not a real one.

She rolled the gurneys away from the wall, opened the door with the key.

In the darkness, she groped for a wall switch and found one.

Braced for a flood of harsh overhead light, she was surprised when two soft golden table lamps clicked on. They sat on either side of a massive mahogany desk. Most of its surface was covered with a black leather pad intended to make an accommodating writing surface, and there were elaborate carvings down both sides of the desk. They were too intricate to see in the dim light. The walls were painted black, which seemed like an effort to make them disappear, or give the illusion of hardwood. A more formidable desk lamp was controlled by an individual switch, and when she turned it on, light fell across wooden carvings hanging on the walls. They were by her father's hand. Woodwork was his hobby. But these pieces she'd never seen before. They were not the wolves and wolf heads he'd fashioned for years and decorated their property with, although they had the same blocky, squared-off style. These large panels each depicted a giant, muscular man, nude save for a cape tossed over one shoulder and a sword held back and resting atop the other. Beneath each of the man's feet were carved the words *Furs Vaterland*.

As soon as she whispered the words aloud to herself, she backed away from the wall.

Fatherland . . .

There were file cabinets pushed against the wall. Each folder inside bulged, but the first few she extracted didn't spill their contents to the floor.

All of the writing was in German, but certain words drifted out to her, easily translatable thanks to history classes and television specials. One, a name she'd heard again and again.

Dachau.

When she came across the first photo, she wasn't sure what she was looking at. At first, Agatha thought the person in the bathtub had been burned to death. But while that might have explained the grotesque discoloration, it didn't explain the strange spotting of its pattern or the swollen sections of the body. In the same file, with shaking fingers, she found two similar photographs that had slid free of the paper clip they once shared. The body was in different conditions in each one, and she realized they were a sequence that had fallen out of order. There were notes written in German on the back of each photograph, but two words appeared again and again: *Höhenprüfung* and *Todes Puls*. The latter was easy to remember, but the first was more complex, so she grabbed a pen and wrote it on the palm of her hand. The words also appeared on the title of the attached report. Because by then, it was becoming clear what she was looking at. Three photographs of the same bathtub, the same man, but in the first, he was an emaciated concentration-camp prisoner. And by the third, he had been exploded. She regretted lining them up in sequence, because now their full horror was threatening to overwhelm her.

Her mother's words returned to her. *The Jews will meet us at the end and they will take our bodies. We will become them and they will become us.*

But here was a man—most likely a Jewish prisoner—whose life had been taken from him in a manner so grotesque it defied understanding. And the more she was able to look, the more she saw little reflections the camera flashes had made that suggested the bathtub and the prisoner had been placed inside some sort of transparent chamber, some sort of chamber that had subjected him to terrible forces.

Agatha told herself she had to keep looking. That this was what her mother had asked of her and she had to be strong. To fight back the tears and the nausea and the pounding in her temples, and so she did. And then she came to a photograph of her father holding up the sides of a woman's head. The top of the woman's skull had been removed, but her hooded eyes suggested she was still alive, if narcotized, and there were various pins driven into the exposed brain matter, but her face was as shrunken and malnourished as that of the man in the bathtub.

But it was the expression on her father's face she could not look away from. His slight, polite smile, his raised eyebrow, as if he were presenting to the camera an image as innocuous as a butterfly he'd managed to cup in both hands during a walk through the woods. And then she saw the insignia on the shoulder of his lab coat, and the bile she'd been holding back started to rise, and she ran from the office. She hit the steep basement stairs so fast she lost her balance. Her forehead slammed into one step hard enough to cause ringing pain in her ears, but she got right up and kept running. She made it as far as the steps to the guesthouse before she collapsed to her knees and vomited. Grateful, on some level, that her body had commanded her into a grotesque ballet because it felt preferable to being paralyzed with shock inside that office of horrors.

As her breath returned, she thought suddenly she'd made a terrible mistake running from the office, leaving it open, exposing herself like this. But when she lifted her head, she saw the ranch was empty. If anyone was watching her, they were watching her from the dark.

She returned to the basement, to the soft glow of golden light spilling across evidence of the abominable. She locked everything away without looking at the photos again. Once she'd slid the gurneys back into place, she checked her palm to make sure she hadn't smeared the word. *Höhenprüfung.*

Her sister's helpless cries drifted toward her through the night, and Agatha found herself running in response. It was a strange urge, the desire to protect an infant with a barely formed brain from all she'd just seen in the basement of the guesthouse. But it was more than that, she realized. Her sister was alone with Hilde, alone with a housekeeper who spoke a language her mother had secretly spoken for years. A housekeeper who'd reacted with barely restrained fury at the suggestion she was not family.

Inside the house, she heard Hilde's footsteps upstairs, creaking the floorboards as she hurried toward Catherine's nursery. Before Agatha could stop herself, she went to the gun case in her father's library and removed the brand-new Ruger Security-Six he'd proudly displayed to her when it arrived. She was a child of the mountains and had been taught to use guns from an early age. Their cowgirl daughter, they'd always called her, no matter how much she hated it. It always sounded like a joke about her weight, even though they meant it quite differently. Her parents wanted to believe their decision to raise her in Montana had turned her into something admirably unique, and different from them. Heartier stock compared to their privileged upbringings.

Now she feared everything they'd told her about their upbringings had been a lie.

The nursery door was halfway open. Light spilled from a porcelain lamp close to the window. Agatha pushed the door open the rest of the way with her foot, the Ruger raised and shaking slightly in her grip. Catherine was in Hilde's arms. She'd stopped crying, and her big blue eyes gazed up at the old woman as she gripped one of her fingers with several of her tiny ones.

"Are you mad, girl?" Hilde whispered.

"Put her down."

Hilde didn't comply.

"Put my sister down. Now."

Without taking her eyes off Agatha, Hilde set the tiny baby into the crib. Agatha took another few steps forward and opened her other palm, revealing the word she'd written there earlier.

"What does this mean?" Agatha asked.

The old woman's lower lip trembled. Her breath left her in a long, stuttering exhale. She was trying to be strong, Agatha could tell. She didn't answer, but she couldn't take her eyes off the ink across Agatha's palm.

"Tell me what it means," Agatha repeated.

"High-altitude testing."

"And that's what he did?" Agatha asked. "At Dachau?"

Hilde stumbled to the windowsill, gripped it with both hands, her back heaving as if the mere mention of the concentration camp's name had sent fire coursing through her veins.

"What did she tell you?" she finally whispered through stuttering tears. "What has she told you?"

"Who are you?" Agatha asked.

Hilde whirled. "They will kill her, do you understand? They will kill her if she does not stay silent."

"Who?"

"You must stop, Agatha. You must stop this."

"She said I have to stop him, but that I'll never forgive her. Why? Did she work at the camps?"

"No! She worked for the party in Berlin."

"The Nazi Party."

"We were Germans," she whispered miserably. "We were Germans in a time of war."

"He was doing experiments on prisoners at Dachau. He wasn't just a German. He was a Nazi."

"He was to find ways to keep pilots alive. In the sea. High in the air. In the cold. They told him to use whatever means necessary."

"Who are you?" Agatha asked again.

"I am your grandmother." Hilde's eyes filled with tears.

"Who's . . ." Agatha's words were stolen from her, as if she tried to form a sentence while diving face-first into cold water. "Who's . . ." She could hear her breaths whistling in her nostrils, but she couldn't feel them. Her lungs felt both empty and small.

"Your mother," Hilde said. "Your mother is my daughter."

Agatha shook her head. The revelations in the basement should have prepared her for this, but those were revelations about abominable crimes in a country far away. This was a crime—a deception—that had unfolded day in and day out, and an arm length's away, in the years since.

"All of this was for you. All of it, so you and your sister could have a life. So you'd never know what it meant to live on the losing side of a war. Your father was not supposed to be brought over; he was too close to the Führer. After the war, the scientists who had been close to Hitler were to stay in Germany and do their work on behalf of the Americans there. But your father told the Americans he'd discovered something tremendous, and they feared he'd give it to the Soviets if they did not bring him and his family here."

"What? What did he discover?"

"It didn't matter. He couldn't re-create it once they brought him here. They let him go. Him and your mother. And they let him bring me over then."

"*Todes Puls*," Agatha said.

Hilde's breath left her in a defeated groan. "She is mad. She is *mad* to tell you all these things."

But in the hospital her mother hadn't sounded mad at all. She'd sounded focused and clear. As if gouging out her own eyes had given her a newfound clarity. And if Hilde assumed Agatha's mother had shared this word with her, then it was possible the old woman knew nothing about her father's secret office, and Agatha wanted to keep it that way.

"What does it mean?" Agatha asked.

"Death pulse," Hilde answered.

"What is it?"

"He found a moment in the dying process, a second, where the body gave off a form of energy that had never been documented before. But he said it was like a door that opened an inch which he had to hold open so he could capture it."

"How did he capture it?"

"Don't ask questions you don't—"

"How did he capture it?" Agatha bellowed.

"He could do anything he wanted to any of the prisoners. His lab was designed to keep people alive under terrible stresses. He said the pulse was stronger when the body was subjected to certain forces. Drowning. Suffocation. Strangulation. When the struggle was greater, when the pain was greater, there was more *Todes Puls*. But when they brought him to America . . ."

"They wouldn't let him torture people and kill them."

Hilde's answer was in how heavily she looked to the floor.

"They let him go," Hilde finally said. "They gave him a new name and they paid for all this."

"Why didn't they send him back to Germany?"

"He'd have told everyone how they broke their own rule bringing him here in the first place."

"And my mother?"

"Your mother was a German in a time of war."

She knew, Agatha thought, her heartbeat aflutter. *She was part of it.*

"But now she says I have to stop him," Agatha said. "What does that mean?"

"I don't know."

"You're lying. You were with her all day. She told you everything. You gagged her to keep her quiet."

"He made it work."

"Made what work?"

"The capture device, he calls it. It took him years, but he finally found the moment, the precise second, when the death pulse is strongest across all forms of death. And he didn't need to torture anyone to do it. She wouldn't let him. But it is a millisecond from the time of death itself. And your mother . . . she offered up herself as his test subject. She let him bring her closer and closer to the end. Last night he went too far. He had to bring her back. But it worked. The capture device is still charged. It's working."

"What does *working* mean?" Agatha asked.

Hilde just shook her head.

"What do you mean, it's working?"

"It means your father will have an incredible power."

The man in the photos would have that power, the man who tortured and butchered prisoners of war, treated them as pin cushions and lab rats.

"Why does he want it?" Agatha asked.

"I don't know."

"You don't want to know."

Hilde met her gaze. "Neither do you, girl."

"Tell me what she did. Tell me what my mother did."

"She's lost her mind. You saw yourself."

"Over there! What did she do over there?"

"Nothing. She obeyed her party. She filed things. She was a secretary."

"She blinded someone."

"This is nonsense! She threw gravel into the eyes of a Jew who grabbed at her dress as the Gestapo took her away. She did not blind the woman."

In the silence that washed over the nursery, it seemed as if Hilde herself heard the ludicrousness of what she'd just said, presenting her mother's assault on a woman doomed to die in a death camp as if it were no more than a brief tussle.

"Your mother has lost her mind and her reason. And now she hurls the truth upon her daughter with no thought of the consequences. You will be mad to do her bidding in this moment, Agatha."

"She died. She died and she saw what was waiting for her. She saw what she'd done. She felt it. She felt the hurt she caused, and it changed her."

"Her brain is damaged, nothing more. And now her eyes."

When Agatha started for the crib, Hilde stood up straight and stumbled back a few steps; then, when she realized Agatha only meant to collect Catherine into one arm, she went still.

"Where are you taking her?" Hilde asked.

"Where is he?" Agatha asked.

"I don't know."

"You're lying. Where is my father?"

"You cannot take Catherine to him now. Leave her here with me. She's safe with me."

"I don't know you! Where is he?"

"He's not alone."

"Dr. Hall's with him?"

"And others."

"How many others?"

"Agatha, this is madness. You cannot."

"Where are they?"

Finally Hilde gave up their location. She was weeping by then because Agatha had closed the distance between them and placed the muzzle of the Ruger against her sweating forehead.

She was still weeping when Agatha took to the stairs, realizing that it was the feel of her baby sister's warmth in her arms that turned her into someone willing to threaten another's life.

Her grandmother's life.

───

When Lucy Merriweather saw Agatha standing on the other side of the glass holding her bawling baby sister in her arms, she raced for the front door, hurriedly tying her bathrobe closed as she went.

The story came tumbling out of Agatha with tearful ease. Her mother had been rushed to the hospital. Hilde had a fever and shouldn't be near the baby. Could they just watch Catherine for a few hours while Agatha went back to the hospital to check on her mom? They didn't question her. Ethel Merriweather took the baby, and suddenly Lucy, one of Agatha's closest friends in the world, threw her arms around her. The embrace, rather than a comfort, felt like a hot, sweaty prison. She was the daughter of a death doctor, and if Lucy held her too long, she would feel this poison in her blood.

Hilde had given her the location of an old ranger station. Agatha and her father had hiked to it years ago, right after it was abandoned by the construction crew that had taken it over from the Park Service.

She could go to the hospital. She could sob her way into the ICU, demand more answers from her mother. But the fact was, she could not face her mother yet.

Was Hilde right? Was Agatha mad to follow the commands of a woman who'd gouged out her eyes, who'd concealed her true identity from her own daughter, from the world, for years? In the end, she drove into the mountainous dark not because she thought a resolution might await, but because everything behind her had been ripped from its foundations. With each passing minute, there was nothing to go back to.

Her father was not some small-town doctor; her mother was not an heiress. Their ranch hid subterranean secrets that could destroy all their lives if made public.

Her father was still the man who'd put her on his lap when she was a girl and read children's stories to her. But now she remembered his insistence that he would only read to her from those books with illustrations that were tasteful and beautiful. Now she realized what those two words really meant. No fairy tales unless all the characters therein were porcelainlike children with cornsilk blond hair and pale, white skin. This little flash of memory made her stop on the side of the road.

Sobs ripped from her with humiliating force. And with them, withering self-judgment. Had she been a fool not to sense these secrets writhing beneath the surface of her life? She was barely seventeen. Did all adults eventually suffer some moment like this? Would the other juniors at Whitefish High have a night where their innocence was stomped underfoot like twigs beneath horse hooves? Or was she doomed to enter a special class of people, an exile class?

The answer terrified her, so she started driving again.

As the world lost its sharp edges beneath a star-crazed sky, Agatha felt the comfort of numbness. Then she reached the turnoff she knew would take her to the old ranger station, and her heart started to pound with enough force to make her fingertips pulse.

On that long-ago hike with her father, they'd nosed through its three empty buildings, widely spaced across an open meadow fringed with tall pine. And he'd wondered aloud then if the sockets were still wired for power or if the construction crews had severed the lines after they'd left.

Power, she thought. He'd been looking for a power source. An abandoned one.

She killed her headlights, rolled slowly down the gravel road. It was so overgrown in places that branches played a chalkboard song along the Pinto's roof. Then she came to the opening of the meadow. It took her several minutes to adjust to the darkness because not a single light came from any of the three buildings. Their exteriors, she knew from her previous visit, were weak attempts at an imitation Swiss chalet, but at night they looked like lava domes of dark earth.

Ruger raised, she started for the main building.

When she stepped inside, a breeze hit her that told her all the building's doors were open. She wondered if this was a deliberate act to get rid of the scorched rubber smell that filled the interior.

When her foot caught on something, she almost fell, managed to right herself. Her flashlight had landed on a thick black snake of cable that ran across the hardwood floor to an outlet nearby. From the outlet a black scorch mark traveled at least three feet up the wall. She figured the same ignition event had seared through the cable where it had once been plugged into the wall. She turned slowly, following the cable's serpentine path across the floor, found the other end close by, also seared through, and a similar black burn covering the floor underfoot. She took several steps back, held the flashlight's beam in place. After a few seconds, she found three other matching cables, also sheared through from similar ignition events. The quartet of scorch marks on the floor outlined part of what must have been the base of something that had protected the floor from the little explosions.

The words *capture device* thundered through her memory, blended with the sounds of Hilde's wretched tears.

Whatever the case, it was gone, moved. This entire place had been abandoned. Recently and with haste.

A force struck her from behind. Her feet went out from under her, and she slammed into the floor face-first. Involuntary screams tore from her, a combination of rage and terror brought forth by the entire night. She was trying to organize them into cries for help, when suddenly her attacker stopped trying to pin her facedown and rolled her onto her back.

Not her father, not Dr. Hall, but Edward Proctor, the nurse from their office, the one who always gave her appraising looks, as if he thought he might have a right to her body if her father approved of his job performance. Her mother and father joked that she should marry him someday, even though fifteen years separated them. His severe handsomeness had never enticed her because it was always offset by his icy nature. Discovering herself alone with Edward in any other circumstance would have disturbed her. Now it terrified her.

As if he'd done nothing more than tug on her shoulder, he said, "You can't be here."

He was about to speak again when Agatha pressed the muzzle of her gun into the center of his chest. Edward's full-lipped mouth became a silent O. Crouched down, he backed away from her as she got to her feet. And he kept backing away, despite the gun.

She had, in a second, crossed the threshold from self-protection to threatening his life, and Edward's wide-eyed glare seemed to indicate he was just as astonished by this choice as she was.

"We're working on something very important. But it's not ready, Agatha. You need to—"

"Where is he?"

"They left." Realizing he'd just given her too much information, he winced, but he didn't stop backing up.

"Who is he with?"

"Agatha, there's no need for this. Put the gun down and let me—"

Suddenly he turned and grabbed for the shadows behind him. For the first time, Agatha saw a table there. But before he could grasp whatever weapon he'd gone for, a dark silhouette rose up from the doorway next to him, and Edward let out a desperate-sounding wheeze, sustained by pure pain as he hit the floor. Then Hilde was lowering the shovel she'd struck him with.

"Cunt," Edward hissed through gritted teeth. "You fucking cunts. What are you—Jesus!" The young man erupted into a chorus of agonized groans. He was down on all fours now, trying to crawl forward, but the blow from the shovel had both stunned and injured him.

"Where is the capture device?" Agatha asked.

The words silenced Edward immediately. Head hanging so heavily she wondered if some part of his spine had been damaged, he said nothing.

Hilde tossed the shovel aside, and its metal blade thunked hard against the floor. Edward jerked but didn't try to get up. She drew a gun, not as new as the Ruger Agatha had stolen from the case.

"Answer her question," Hilde said.

"You can't stop him. Nothing can. What he has now is brighter than heaven itself, and more powerful." He laughed hysterically. "If you shoot me, he'll tear you apart," Edward hissed. "In ways you can't even imagine."

"You?" Hilde growled. "Some impertinent little errand boy? You think he cares for you? Do you know how many he's used and thrown away? You know nothing of what he's been."

"Yes, I do, bitch."

It wasn't *Sieg Heil*, but it was damn close.

"He can't go far," Agatha said. "He needs a power source to use this thing."

"Not anymore he doesn't," Edward whispered.

Agatha thought of the words Hilde had used earlier that night, the words her mother had shared with her. The device was working. The device was charged. Charged by the energy thrown off by her mother's death. Brighter than heaven. Her father was not in search of a power source. He wanted secrecy, but also shelter. Concealment.

Edward sank to a seated position, and for the first time, she saw the shovel blow had cut the back of his neck. Blood painted the side of his throat and face.

"You'll never stop him," he said.

"From doing what?" Agatha asked. Even the question made her stomach turn.

"From breaking every dam on the Blackfeet Reservation and flooding the brown scum from the earth. From walking the streets of the Negro ghettos and setting their buildings aflame. He will win the war of which he has already fought one battle, and with the power in his hands he will wipe the *undermenschen* from the earth."

"Shut up, boy!" Hilde roared.

Teeth bared, Edward turned to her, the German ripping from him with hateful force. "*Reinige die arische Rasse! Reinige die—*"

A muzzle flash lit up the vast space. Half of Edward's head was replaced with a burst of gore. His lifeless body hit the wood floor.

Hilde did not lower the gun. Rage still held her every muscle in its grip. Had she killed the man because his hate had exposed the hatred in her heart as well, or had he made the mistake of dragging her back to a hellish time with his words?

Either way, her grandmother could not bring herself to look away from the man's fallen body.

And she had not turned the gun on Agatha despite the fact that Agatha had placed her Ruger to the old woman's forehead an hour before.

Her ears were ringing. There was heat on the bridge of her nose that must have been Edward's blood. It was the first time she'd seen a man killed, and the speed and suddenness of it made it seem unreal, as if the shot had yanked the life from his body the way you'd yank the last of a dead tree stump from the earth. But all she could think of was her mother's breakdown the night before. Was Edward now plummeting into some moment of reckoning similar to the one her mother had faced the few feet beyond death's door? Or was Agatha using a fevered delusion on her mother's part to blot out the horror of his deformed head and lifeless tangle of limbs?

Hilde didn't move as Agatha slowly backed away, and out the nearest door and toward her car. Her ears were still ringing when she got behind the wheel, but she had the focusing momentum of a destination.

If it was isolation and concealment her father was after, she knew exactly where he'd go.

Lake Michele was protected from hikers and tourists by the fact that it had almost no beaches to speak of. Its eastern shore was taken up by a sheer rock face that rose straight out of the crystal-blue waters. On its other banks, pines intruded right up to the waterline. Only the most intrepid hikers were willing to carry their kayaks and canoes through the dense forest to reach the water, and so at any time of day or night, its placid surface was an almost perfect mirror for the sky.

The only good nearby trails came up behind the mound of granite on the eastern shore, and in their race to reach the top and its view of the gorgeous lake hundreds of feet below, most hikers sped past the openings to the knotted cave system hidden underneath. She and her father had almost missed it themselves. It was Banjo, their intrepid explorer of a dog, who'd first found an entrance. He'd burrowed into a hole too small for a human to do anything but crawl through, but their attempts to lure him out had inspired them to look for other breaks in the granite. Eventually they'd found a different opening tall enough to get through without crouching.

At the first glint of metal in the Pinto's headlights, she turned them off and slowed to a stop. Her father had parked the truck in the same spot where they'd started their hikes. She gave her eyes a minute to adjust to the darkness, then headed for the vehicle. Its cooling engine still ticked, but she was more interested in the temperature of the open cargo bay. Its canvas covering was hot, and as she searched the bay, she found scorch marks similar to the ones she'd seen on the ranger station's floor. The metal floor of the truck bed was as hot as if it had been baking in the sun all day. The words *brighter than heaven* pulsed through her mind, but they were drowned out by the memory of Hilde's gunshot, which played on a tape loop in her brain.

Agatha told herself she just needed to see it. Whatever the damn thing was, she just needed to lay eyes on it, and maybe then she could tell someone who mattered, describe it in some kind of meaningful detail.

Who would she tell? She had no idea. Not yet. Someone more important than a girl with a gun and parents she'd never really known. But when she came to the person-size entrance to the caves, the one she and her father had found that day, she couldn't understand what she was seeing. She listened carefully to the sounds of the quiet wilderness to make sure she was really alone. Then she pulled the flashlight out and raked the fresh wall of tumbled stone before her.

Something of incredible power had widened the opening by several feet overhead; then, a few feet later, a wall of jagged pieces of granite blocked the entrance. At first sight, it looked as if the transformation of the entrance was the result of a cave-in, but the closer she looked, she saw evidence of two separate events. Something or someone had first widened the entrance with a force beyond her understanding; then, after passing through it, they'd caused some sort of cave-in behind them. And it was recent. She ran her fingers along one of the jagged boulders. Fresh dust came away on her fingertips. Breath threading out, fingers trembling, she thought of dams being broken on the Blackfeet Reservation, of neighborhoods aflame.

Then she thought of the first, narrow cave entrance Banjo had found that day, the one that prompted her and her father to search for this one, and she went for it.

The fact that she had to squeeze herself into an inching crouch to fit inside it felt like a comfort. For most of the night she'd felt exposed and vulnerable, racing through dark expanses with only the Ruger as her protection. Now, at least she felt sheltered and hidden. Then the space became so cramped she had to push herself along like an inchworm. This gave her no choice but to place the gun an arm's length ahead of her while she moved.

Agatha crested what turned out to be a subtle rise inside the narrow cave, and blue light bathed the walls all around her. She froze, thinking she'd been spotted by someone at the other end, but this was no flashlight. It pulsed and danced along the walls with a pattern that didn't seem mechanical. Shadows moved across it, shadows with human shapes. She inched forward and heard voices.

Her father's voice. Her father and Dr. Hall.

Another few feet and she saw it. The wormlike cave opened about six feet above a central chamber she and her father had explored years before. As her line of sight widened to take in more of the space, she realized the blue light was emanating from what looked like a large metal chair. But the closer she got to the opening, the more she realized the chair was about twice the size of any you'd find in an office, or even a medical practice, and on either side, concave steel walls enclosed the seat almost entirely. Luminescent blue waves pulsed up their surfaces, then met at the top. The parabolic cap that crowned the device looked designed to capture the waves, but instead they traveled across the cap's surface and up into the air for several feet before they faded to nothing. If it weren't for the pulses of blue light, the device itself would have looked crushingly ordinary. Goofy, even. And yet it played host to a light show that seemed to be coming from another world.

It was not brighter than heaven, as Edward described. But it had been at some point, and that explained why it had burned through its electrical cables at the ranger station, and why the men had been so desperate to move it here. It was raging with energy it looked barely suited to contain, and the light show might have drawn someone's attention from the air if they'd left it at the ranger station. But now its charge was fading, and when she saw the person tied up in the corner with a black sack over their head, she realized with a jolt why that might be. Her father and whoever he was working with had abducted a new test subject.

A new power source for the capture device.

A fresh *Todes Puls*.

Someone they wouldn't have to bring back to life as they had her mother.

Scrabbling another few inches forward, she saw Dr. Hall crouched over some sort of instrument panel connected to the base of the capture device. He didn't like what he was seeing, and he and her father were speaking to each other urgently. What they didn't see was that their captive, sitting with their back pressed against a rock wall, was jerking with small movements that could only mean one thing.

It happened in the blink of an eye. First, Dr. Hall cried out. Then the person in the hood shot to their feet, having freed their wrist restraints by rubbing them against the rocks. The next thing Agatha knew, the person's desperate flight had been arrested and they were flying backward through the air, their feet jerked clean up off the ground. The hooded person slammed right back to earth, inches from where they'd first made a run for it. It was all so impossible and had happened so fast, it was like her mind was assembling puzzle pieces out of sequence.

Too late, she realized she'd screamed.

And now her father was staring at her. He stood next to the capture device, one hand pressed to the metal exterior of its curving back. The pulses of energy it gave off now moved through his body like a redirected current. They'd shot through his hand and his fingers and given him the power to immobilize his prisoner in an instant.

As he glared at her, she saw the whites of his eyes had turned blue.

Later, Agatha would realize it would have been harder to do what she did next if he hadn't been so transformed. If he'd looked more like the man who'd helped her complete her schoolwork at the kitchen table when she was a little girl. Who'd taken her on so many hikes through the park and explained the natural world to her with a reverential tone that suggested he preferred its movements and secrets to those of human beings.

But he didn't look like that man. He looked like an angel that had brushed up against hell.

She fired.

Her father's eyes went wide, and he looked down at where the bullet had struck him. There was no blood, just a bright shock of blue that was already three times the size a normal bullet hole should have been. His wound expanded outward like the widening flare of a cigarette fringed with blue instead of glowing embers. Then suddenly the energy that had been coursing through him shot out on all sides of him like a starburst, drawing and quartering him in an instant. His blood, which should have geysered, was pulled apart into a fine black mist that remained suspended in the air for an instant before the spreading halos of blue flame shot it in all directions across the interior of the cave.

She had not just shot a man, she realized. She'd shot a force. And it had just exploded, unleashing a type of hell the world had never seen.

The capture device's parabolic cap shot upward, trailing blue fire. Dr. Hall was bellowing at the sight of the bloody stump where his right arm used to be. There was no trace left of her father.

A second shock wave blew Dr. Hall off his feet. Screaming, he vanished inside a wall of bright blue.

The sound that came next was like a giant guitar string being drawn back and released by God's index finger.

Light and heat rushed toward her.

The walls of the narrow tunnel began to crack and shift.

Agatha let out a piercing scream drowned by the roar of great, grinding rocks.

20

"Go," a voice says behind them.

Claire feels Poe's hand take shape inside hers. They're both pressed to the floor, and the walls of the cave retreat like puffs of smoke. When Claire looks behind her, blue light spills through the door and she can hear the string quartet again, and there's the older Agatha with her long white braid and deeply lined face, gesturing to the half-open door.

"Go! We're almost out of time. Cross the bridge now!"

Poe is gasping for breath, and when Claire pulls him to his feet, he resists at first, then struggles to get his balance. She sees he's been stricken by the same thing that terrified her back in her own vault—the sense that the memory's retreat has left behind a great yawning void behind them.

She tugs hard on his hand.

They take off, following Agatha across the loft and toward the staircase, then down into the lobby, where everything is as it was before.

"Tell Randy I want him to finish, that we took all the time we had," she says.

Claire feels like she's been pulled out of bed in the middle of the night and yanked into the outer bands of a hurricane. Given his veering path next to her, Poe must feel the same. They're running across the bridge, besieged by the huffs and growls of nightmare wolves when Agatha calls, "You can come back. You can always come back!"

The piercing loneliness in the woman's voice makes Claire want to look over one shoulder, but the prospect of what might happen if the doors to the pier ahead close, choking off the milky-gray light of their memory deck, terrifies her, so they keep running. And when they make it through the doors, it feels like a relief.

How could this place, which seemed so alien and impossible just a short while ago, feel like a familiar home?

Poe is still holding her hand, but he's frowning. Wincing. This time he's prepared for what's to come, and she almost reaches out to put her arm around him, but she's afraid of dragging him along for some rocketing ride she still doesn't fully understand.

Before she has time to reconsider her decision, she's ripped backward. This time, however, she doesn't scream.

———

The return trip is as awful as it was before, but Claire manages not to throw up this time. Maybe because she braced for it with every muscle in her body.

There's a welcome presence next to her where she lies on the floor of Agatha's cell, and she smells nice—Margot. Her sweet floral perfume is more suited to a stroll through a high-end department store than a violent awakening in a subterranean chamber of dark secrets.

If these guys have let her change or freshen up, that's a good sign, Claire thinks.

And if Claire is desperate for anything right now, it's a sign of something, anything good.

"Hey," Margot says softly, looking down at her.

Benjamin Running Creek and Thomas Billings are backing away, maybe because they're confident her stomach will stay settled.

"They're offering us food. Steaks, I think, but to be honest, it's almost time for breakfast."

"Steak and eggs, then," Ben says.

Claire shakes her head, gestures that she needs a minute. Margot nods, gently smooths Claire's sweat-matted bangs from her forehead.

"Do you understand how dreams work?" Thomas asks. "Like at the level of neuroscience, I mean?"

"Some," Margot says.

Claire figures the question's for her, but she's glad Margot answered. Holding the nausea at bay means lying stone-still and keeping her eyes closed. For now.

"OK, so when you're sleeping," Thomas says, "your brain's deprived of all the sensory input it uses to establish a sense of linear time. Sight, touch, smell, taste—even if it's just the subtly changing taste inside your mouth from what you last ate—these are all things your brain uses to establish a clock. So while you're asleep, there's no clock. Your brain's just firing images, but they're circulating there in a kind of haze. They don't have a storyline because you've lost the ability to understand one. Temporarily, at least. Until you wake up. That's when your sense of linear time is restored and your brain automatically turns all that haze into a comic strip. With a narrative.

"We think a trip into the vault is similar. In the moment, it's a cascade of images and memories and emotions that don't employ language, but it's so powerful it separates you from your physical body and your brain's clock. So you need some time to absorb it all, then process it into a coherent narrative as you regain consciousness."

"Nazis," Claire whispers.

A silence falls.

"Sounds like she's putting it together right quick," Ben mutters.

"Why is there time over there?" Claire asks.

"What do you mean?" Thomas says.

"If we need physical sensations to establish a body clock, like you said, why does time unfold on the memory deck the way it does here?"

"Well, I'm not sure that's an accurate—"

"An inhale lasts for thirty minutes here," Claire says, "and a bloom bridge stays open for thirty minutes there. I'm not a physicist, but that's the same clock operating in two different dimensions."

"Correct," Ben says. "It's the bloom's clock, because the bloom is still here. Your brother is still here. We just don't have him."

Another minute passes, and then Ben asks, "Are we ready for some food?"

"I don't know," Claire says.

"I get it," Ben says, "but you're also going to feel depleted as hell, so we should get you close to some nutrients so you can scarf 'em down the minute you're ready."

Margot whispers, "Something tells me they're getting us together for more than a meal."

"To shoot us?" Claire asks.

"If that's all we wanted, you'd be dead already," Thomas says.

"That's some wicked bedside manner you got there, Thomas," Ben mumbles.

Margot helps Claire to her feet, slides Claire's tinted glasses back on. Margot, she sees, has a pair for herself too, and suddenly they're walking past the cells full of animal bloom with the speed of bored tourists departing a zoo they tired of hours ago.

An ATV is parked inside the barn. Margot guides Claire onto the bench seat, Ben gets behind the wheel, and a second later they're chugging across the grass toward the main house as Thomas walks behind them. Dawn's first light gives a faint eggshell glow to the main house's second-floor windows.

As she mounts the front steps, Claire wonders if they're showing her the house to prove everything she saw in Agatha's vault was true. The house's details match up almost exactly.

Inside, the newel post at the base of the staircase is the same; the walls are the same off-white wallpaper with columns of little green designs so small she can barely tell what they are. The same cherry-wood crown molding and baseboards. The art is different, more jumbled, but like the scenes hanging on the wall of Agatha's cell, they're mostly pastoral images of the Old West. The old Oriental rugs are gone, replaced with newer, more monochromatic patterns. But for a second, she feels as if she's stepped right back into Agatha Caldwell's memories again.

Then they enter a formal dining room with a long hardwood table and mahogany dining chairs with open backs and leafy detailing carved along the shoulders. The puddling draperies are hunter green with a big valance that blocks out too much of the mountain view, suggesting the people who eat here have long since tired of it. A man she doesn't recognize is setting out a giant bowl of salad. He seems too fit and poised to be a domestic, and he's dressed more stylishly than the rest of them. Another man she hasn't met yet, this one about six feet tall, is seated in the corner of the room. He's got an Afro top fade and a closely shorn beard. He looks up from his phone as Claire enters, eyes widening before he nods curtly and looks back to his phone, like she's a celebrity and he's been told to keep his cool.

Her father's seated at one head of the table, hunched over, nervously rubbing his hands together on his lap. In the spreading light of early morning, he looks like an exhausted and ruined man. There's a bruise on his forehead and a spiderweb of angry red scratches above his right eye, probably from their car wreck. He swallows nervously as she enters. Despite almost getting them killed a few hours before, in this moment he seems capable of neither an apology nor a deflection.

Ben guides Claire to the head of the table opposite her dad; then Randy enters carrying a platter full of steaks and a ceramic bowl of scrambled eggs with a giant silver serving spoon stuck in it.

Benjamin and Thomas both take chairs against the walls. Randy sits in the middle of the table, across from Margot.

Normality, Claire thinks, *that's what this is all about. They know what I just did, where I went, and they're trying to give me something normal to come back to.*

When Ben sets something on the table next to her plate, she jumps, sees it's the notepad and pen she was using to communicate with Poe. And when she looks up, her father is staring at it with pain and longing on his face.

But when he catches her looking at him, he focuses on his lap again.

As the mercenaries ringing the room stare at Randy as if his cheerful-host routine is proof he's lost his mind, Randy casually spoons eggs onto Margot's plate. When he offers some to Claire, she holds up a hand. "Just another few minutes until . . ." She gestures to her stomach. Randy nods as if it's normal. Like it's all normal. Like they're dining together at a country inn. It's strategy, no doubt. An attempt to win her over. And his men clearly have their doubts about its chance of success.

Good, she thinks.

"So, Rupert, why don't you introduce yourself," Randy says.

The man she'd first spotted upon entering the room looks at Randy like he's gone nuts, but then he composes himself and says, "I'm Rupert."

"Rupert was in charge of following Poe," Randy says. "Sean here mostly handled you, Claire, although we rotated that duty some. The whole team's fonder of the LA weather, I guess."

"Just putting all the cards on the table, aren't we?" Rupert mutters.

"You got a better suggestion?" Randy asks.

"If you didn't ask earlier, why are you asking now?" Rupert says.

To Claire, Randy says, "We had a strict no bathrooms or bedrooms rule."

"For what?" Claire asks.

"The cameras," her father grumbles.

Nobody says anything for a while.

"Where did you all leave off?" Randy asks. "You and Agatha?"

Margot raises one hand. "I'm sorry, a moment here, if I may." She focuses her gaze on Claire. "So Agatha got into your head because you inhaled her bloom, is that right?" When Claire nods, Margot continues, "And then you crossed over into her head and—"

"Head's not exactly how I'd describe it," Randy interjected. "Think of it as a movie theater in your brain, but it looks like someplace you remember very clearly. Someplace you loved. Behind every door in that place is a unified realm we call the vault. It's full of your memories. So if we go with the movie-theater analogy, the doors are like the curtain, the vault is like the screen, and the ticket to the movie is something we call the key. An item of sentimental value you lost during your life. When you bring it close to a vault door, it literally enters the lock and opens the door. We believe that in a person who's experienced a normal death, the opening of the vault triggers something near-deathers call a life review. The whole 'life flashing before your eyes' thing. The problem is, no one here, Agatha included, has visited the memory deck of someone who's died a normal death, so our experience of this realm is limited. We're dealing with a half-cocked version."

"A movie theater without a projector, essentially," Margot says.

"I'll go with that," Randy says, "but even without the projector, this half-cocked movie theater can open up a circuit to another one. If someone in this room inhales the bloom of someone who's been exposed to the pulse and shifted—"

"Someone like Poe," Claire says.

"Or Agatha," Randy adds. "Something we call a bloom bridge opens between their memory deck and yours. They can enter the common area of your memory deck, and if they can find the key, they can open your vault and take over your consciousness."

Everyone was silent for a while. Her father looked like he wanted a very stiff drink.

Memory deck, key, vault.

Movie theater, ticket, screen.

It all sounded neat and tidy until you remembered it was possible to teleport from one movie theater to an adjacent one.

Randy broke the silence. "We think this process is pivotal to whether or not someone truly passes into the afterlife or returns to their body. But we've never visited a memory deck in the presence of an actual dead person, so the version we know of it is . . . limited."

"And we've all got a memory deck?" Margot asks.

There were enough nods around the room to indicate most of the team had inhaled some of Agatha's bloom and let her open their vaults.

Evidence of the afterlife. And they'd all kept it a secret for . . . how many years?

"All right," Randy says. "So, you and Agatha."

"The cave," Claire says. "It was coming down. She'd just shot her father."

If they do all know the story, they bristle at hearing one of its bigger moments stated so plainly.

"All right, well," Randy says, "guess I need to wrap things up, then."

21

Fifty Years Ago

Agatha ducked her head, felt the heat of the blast rake her back, sending jagged little pieces of rock down the length of her body, tearing open her clothes in little strips that exposed her flesh to more and greater heat.

She started crawling backward. What at first seemed like a mercy, the womb-like shelter of the tunnel was now a prison. An oven. The granite walls around her groaned and protested.

Suddenly the cave floor beneath her gave way, as if she were crawling on a balance beam someone had dropped at one end. What had become of the entrance she'd crawled through?

She pushed herself backward with greater speed, then crawled forward again, using gravity to her advantage now that she was on a freshly made downward slope. When one of her hands touched dirt, when she felt cool night air on her arms, she realized she'd made it to what remained of the entrance and was now crawling out a newly formed opening. She almost wept with relief.

Solid ground had never felt so welcoming. When she hit it, she took off running into the trees. She was almost as far as her Pinto when she got the courage to look back.

Silence had fallen over the woods, and through the shadowy pine trunks she could see the vague outline of the granite mound on the lakeshore was now misshapen. Hikers would no longer be able to ascend cleanly to its crown, once smooth and rounded by years of exposure to snow and shaping winds. The collapse, it seemed, had happened primarily inside its central chamber, and everything above had settled down into a new formation. Now the crown actually looked more like a crown—a decayed and weathered one—with the lumpy remnants of jeweled spikes.

But it was the quiet that calmed her.

It also made her keenly aware of how badly her clothes were shredded, of the coppery taste of blood and granite dust coating the back of her throat. She blinked, became aware of the dust in her eyes. With all her strength, Agatha walked back to the mound, saw, as she got closer, that a dust cloud still hung over it, barely visible in the weak moonlight and a pale suggestion of the true violence she'd witnessed within. There were no flickers of the blue light that had turned her father into an alien being. No sense that something that had torn a hole in the fabric of reality had just operated within. Once she reached the section of cave she'd backed out of, she saw how close she'd been to being crushed.

She walked toward the other, larger entrance and saw it was now crushed like an aluminum can.

She stumbled through the trees and found the water's edge.

The shock of the freezing water chased all feeling from her body. At first, she'd meant to walk in up to her knees, maybe clean her face and eyes of the dust that coated every inch of her. But when the water rose up around her body, she gave herself to it. Let it close over her scalp and push the sounds of the night farther away.

Then, beneath the surface, she heard a rumble.

Agatha rose, walked back toward the shore, and realized, to her sudden terror, that the sound was even louder above the surface. And it was coming from the pile of granite on the lake's shore. The sound that split the air next was familiar. The same snap of a giant guitar string that had preceded the last and most significant blast inside the cave's central chamber.

The entire lake lit up with a brilliant flash of white. For an instant she could see straight down into its vast glacier-carved depths. Then she was thrown backward by a single wave of force that seemed almost elegant in comparison to the riotous chaos of the cave-in. The branches above her snapped and rained down all around her. She slammed into the earth.

And it was impossible not to think that it might be his revenge, this blast. Her father's final attempt to lash out at her from his new granite prison. But after a few minutes, she realized she was alive, bruised and even more battered, but alive. And when she got to her feet, the night was quiet again.

Agatha thought maybe what she'd witnessed had been the last gasp of something beyond comprehension puttering out and leaving this realm of existence.

But even in that moment, she suspected she was wrong.

Suspected, on some level, that what had happened that night would never be truly over.

That she had not killed her father's invention after all.

———

Shock, when it came, took the form of a low and constant tremor in her bones, a sense the world she moved through now was paper thin, and one tear might release monsters beyond imagining.

Some instinctive, self-protective part of her brain had decided whatever flash of light she'd been exposed to on the lakeshore would eventually kill her. Maybe before the night was over, maybe within days. Either way, this knee-jerk assumption made the consequences of all that had unfolded in such a short span of time seem easier to deal with.

Dawn's first light was pushing against the sky behind the mountains when Agatha drove back to the ranch.

Hilde stood on the front porch, dressed exactly as she'd been at the abandoned ranger station. She did not flinch or even widen her eyes at the mutilated state of Agatha's clothes or her matted hair or the bright red scrapes and bruises that lashed her face and arms. Hilde, Agatha saw, had failed to wipe several spots of Edward's blood from her face, and they'd dried across her right cheek.

Finally, the old woman descended the steps, took Agatha gently by one elbow, and steered her into the house. On the stairs, she paused for a second, noticing the constant tremor in Agatha's bones, but she said nothing, just kept directing her up the stairs, then into her bathroom, where she sat Agatha down on the toilet lid while she drew a bath. She did not turn on any of the lights, but by then the vague predawn glow through the frosted window above the tub cast a milky pall across the porcelain surfaces.

Once the bath was halfway full, the water temperature to Hilde's liking, she tapped the edge of the tub three times. What would have seemed like a petty gesture a day before seemed suddenly momentous. An invitation to cross some line into whatever awaited them now that they'd both taken life. It seemed as if their separate acts of violence that night had placed them in a precarious balance that might swing out of alignment at any second.

What would it take for one of them to drown the other in the bathtub and make sure the secrets of this night were kept forever? Strength, Agatha realized. It would take strength neither of them had left.

Agatha stripped, sank into the water. Its warmth only served to remind her of the lake's freezing wash. The tremor in her bones intensified. She drew her knees up to her breasts, held them there. Sitting on the toilet, Hilde shook a cigarette from her pack and lit it. She extended the pack. Before, the woman had rarely smoked in her presence, much less offered her a cigarette. It was a gesture that said everything had changed, that Agatha, in the course of one night, was no longer a young girl.

"What did you do with him?" Agatha finally asked.

"Better you not know."

They fell silent. Her scrapes were bleeding gently into the water, making little red swirls just under the surface.

"And you?" Hilde asked.

Agatha stared at her.

"Did you do what your mother asked? Did you stop it?"

"I stopped him. Not it."

Hilde flinched, brow furrowed. She took a long, careful drag from the cigarette, as if she was desperate to know what this meant but couldn't stomach any of the possible answers.

"We'll figure out what to do next, then," Hilde said. "Together."

So she wanted an agreement. A peace treaty between them. Maybe she thought killing Edward had earned her the right. The cigarette was an inch from Hilde's mouth, like she'd meant to take a drag but forgotten about it.

"It won't be easy for you," Hilde finally said. "You will have to learn things."

"What things?"

"How to live with those you've beaten. It's what all victors must learn. Unless they plan to kill them. Or put them all in camps."

Hilde rose and went for the door. Her hand was on the knob when Agatha said, "What's your name?"

Hilde turned, studied her. "Gertrude," she finally said.

"What's hers?"

The old woman's eyes filled with tears over the thought of her blinded daughter. Her jaw trembled. Was it grief for their old lives, their lives before this night, before the war? Perhaps if you had her history there was no difference.

"Greta," she whispered, then left the room before the tears slipped free.

Once Agatha was alone with her own body, she studied her hands, her arms, looked for evidence of what had been inflicted on her aside from the scrapes and bruises. Looked for burn marks or lesions or anything else that might suggest something toxic and poisonous in that bright white flash of light that had illuminated Lake Michele down to its depths.

But the only wounds she could find were shallow and on the surface.

———

Agatha did not go with Hilde to pick up her mother from the hospital. A week had gone by, and she and Hilde had disposed of the truck her father had driven to the caves. A week had gone by, and Agatha had suffered no nausea or hair loss or anything else to suggest the pulse had been toxic.

On the day of her mother's release, Agatha fought the selfish urge to remove all evidence of her father from the master bedroom. Her mother wouldn't be able to see any of it, and if the police came around asking questions, it would look suspicious. Hilde had already gone to file the police report, and thanks to multiple canceled appointments for both Drs. Caldwell and Hall, word of their disappearances had spread through town.

When she heard the Pinto's engine, her stomach clenched.

Then came the careful footsteps of both women on the stairs. She left Catherine's nursery and moved into the hallway. Her mother's eyes were still bandaged. Most of her golden hair was gone. It would have been easy for a stranger to assume she'd cut her locks so they wouldn't get tangled in the head dressing she'd be wearing for some time, but Agatha was sure the severe haircut had been spawned by the same violent urge that had led her mother to gouge out her own eyes.

When they reached the top of the stairs, Hilde went still.

Her mother had come to a sudden stop.

Agatha, expecting not to be noticed, had been felt. But her mother did not call out to her, just stared at the floor in the general direction of where she sensed her daughter's presence. Now, laying eyes on her mother for the first time since obliterating her father, the sum total of all she'd done made Agatha feel like a stranger inside her skin.

Then her mother started forward again. Hilde matched her step for step.

When the door to the master bedroom shut, it felt suddenly as if her mother was the one who'd ignored her presence and not the other way around. Agatha blinked back her first tears in days.

A little while later, she entered the master bedroom and found her mother alone, sitting at the picture window that offered a view across the property to the barn and guesthouse. Was she seeing the landscape in her mind, or was she just cherishing the warmth of the sunlight streaming through the glass?

Her mother finally broke the silence. "I meant what I said."

"About what?"

"I do not expect you to forgive me."

"Do you want me to?" Agatha asked.

"I believe so, yes."

Her mother's accent was stronger than it had ever been. Had trauma resurrected it? Or did she no longer feel the need to hide it? Agatha's parents, according to Hilde, had spoken excellent English upon their arrival in America, and they'd gone to numerous speech therapists to get rid of their accents. There'd always been a trace with her father, but he'd claimed to have picked it up from her mother.

Now Agatha knew there'd never been any Swiss boarding schools. Just Germany, followed by countless attempts to Americanize themselves as deeply as possible, going so far as to move to what was once the frontier and raise their very own cowboy daughter in a house filled with paintings of the Wild West. But in the end, it was the alpine mountains that drew them, the American Alps, jagged, snow-blanketed reminders of their European home.

"I wish I could describe it to you, what I saw. It was as if I went to a place. The very street where I . . ."

"Threw rocks at a woman doomed to die," Agatha said.

Her mother nodded, and for a while neither one of them spoke.

"It's why it was easy," her mother finally said.

"Why what was easy?" Agatha asked.

"To remove my eyes," her mother answered. "Because now I know what they offer is but a drop in the bucket of what we are capable of feeling and seeing."

"When we die, you mean."

She nodded. Agatha needed a moment to digest her mother's choice of words. *Remove my eyes* . . . She'd not witnessed the actual event, only the gory aftermath, so she'd assumed her mother had done it in a violent, screaming burst. But maybe that wasn't the case. Maybe she'd done it as easily as she'd open a can of tuna. Hilde had been the only witness, and so far she and Agatha had only been able to discuss the mechanics of the cover-up they'd planned.

"What did you think would happen?" Agatha finally asked. "You must have known he could go too far, that you could die. What did you think would happen to you if you did?"

"Are you asking if I believe in God, my girl?"

"I'm asking if you believe in hell," Agatha said.

Her mother was silent for a while. Agatha had not meant it as an insult, but she realized this would be their curse for the time being. Her mother had kept so many secrets from her, every question of Agatha's would seem like an insult whether she wanted it to or not.

"I'd always believed that the moment of death would come with an understanding, a revelation of some sort. If not to the nature of the universe, then the nature of suffering. Of war."

"But you let him bring you to death's door again and again anyway."

"What are you asking me, Agatha? Be clear. There are no more secrets between us."

"I'm asking if you thought you were right. I'm asking if you weren't afraid of what might be waiting for you because you thought what you did over there was right."

"I thought I would be forgiven."

"For what?" Agatha asked.

"For making hard choices, difficult choices others were afraid to make. Choices that went wrong in the end but which were born of just causes."

"Just causes?" Agatha whispered. "Dachau. His experiments. These were *just causes*? Is that really what you think?"

In the silence that followed, Agatha realized her mother's eyes might have betrayed the emotions roiling behind her silence in this moment. But they were gone, and that access would be sealed off to Agatha, and to the world, forever. And she wondered suddenly if that's why her mother had truly mutilated her own windows onto the world. To mask her soul forever.

"Not anymore," she said. "I felt in the very center of my being how a handful of rocks can break a person's spirit, destroying their life and unleashing a flood of terror that filled me with the knowledge of what it is to be one woman trapped within the maw of a country gone mad with hate. I felt in my bones how a life is a history in and of itself, and when it is crushed, so many other things die with it, and I felt these things as I might feel a terrible pain deep in the gut or the center of my chest, a pain that has no language and cannot be argued with. It was as if my past became a place that exists outside myself, and then it became a river that flowed back into me, bringing with it tides of pain from all I'd hurt. And so I gave back the eyes that had been given to me in some small attempt to square the debt and prove to you, my daughter, that I know now what I have done. This is what death has given me."

Agatha was grateful her mother couldn't see her tears. Grateful that she couldn't see the evidence of her struggle. That this story, sincere as it was, might be enough for Agatha to forgive her.

After a while, her mother asked, "His office . . ."

"Moved," she answered.

"Where?"

Agatha didn't answer.

"That is fair, I guess," her mother whispered. "In this, you should have some power."

Power. She couldn't wrap her head around the word. Not in this moment. Nothing she had, nothing she'd done, felt like power. A single gunshot, fired in rage and hate, had triggered a mini apocalypse that had spilled beyond the borders of the rational world. The parents she had known were but shadows of their true selves.

"Hilde went to Edward's house," Agatha said. "She found pictures under his bed. There were only men in them, doing violent things to each other. Naked. She left them out where they can be found if anyone goes looking. The story will be that you walked in on all three of them doing things to each other, sexual things, and that's why they ran away. And that's why you gouged out your eyes. Because you were in shock and you lost your mind. But we're only going to say this if the police start thinking there's some kind of cover-up. And maybe they won't. Men leave all the time. But three men, at once. Who worked together. We might have to try to explain that somehow. So that's how. Hilde and I decided."

"You are an angel to do this for me."

"I'm not doing it for you."

"For you, then," her mother whispered.

"For Catherine."

When the hinges on the bedroom door creaked, her mother called out to her, turning slightly in her chair.

Agatha stopped.

"If I ever want to leave this world again," her mother said, "but I'm too afraid, will you help me?"

"No," Agatha said, then closed the door behind her.

She hadn't meant it to sound like a punishment, but she realized, as she stepped out into the hallway, that's exactly how it had sounded. But she didn't turn around and go back into her mother's bedroom to correct this impression.

She never did.

22

The rocking chair outside the window behind Randy throws a length-ening shadow across the porch's floor. The sun has crested the eastern horizon, and the song of waking birds makes for an ironic, mocking counterpoint to the terrible tale they've just been told. In a way, it's helped Claire to have Randy deliver the final chapter in his steady, affect-free voice. The process drove tent stakes through the mad swirl of sensory experiences that consumed her inside Agatha's vault, anchoring them to something that feels more like solid ground. Like history.

"Nazis," her father finally whispers. "Fucking Nazis."

"I would have preferred aliens, to be frank," Margot says.

"Me too," Randy says. "But look at it this way. Like all the best Nazis, they're dead."

He shovels a bite of steak into this mouth, even though it looks like his food went cold while he was storytelling.

"Three women built this place?" Claire finally asks. "The cellar?"

"Two, really," Randy answers. "Doesn't sound like Agatha's mother was much of a help. She lived for another three years before a heart attack took her. Physically she never recovered. The experiments might have played a role. Or . . ."

"The guilt of visiting her own memory deck," Margot says. "Seeing what was waiting for her in the end."

"But Agatha's mother wasn't exposed?" Claire asks.

"No," Randy says. "Experimented on, but not exposed. The charge her death pulse gave to the capture device was a different animal from the pulse. She died a natural death. No shift. They hired a ranch hand of sorts, a guy they brought in on it. I was his replacement after he died."

The guy who let us get exposed that night, Claire thinks. But saying this out loud would feel spiteful and petty, given the man destroyed himself out of guilt.

"And the sister?" Margot asks. "What happened to Catherine?"

At first, Claire thinks Randy's chewing a big bite; then she sees he's just hesitating. "She's down in Wyoming."

"Does she know about any of this?" Margot asks.

He lowers his fork to the side of his plate as if ten pounds have been added to it. Odd, considering how much he's already revealed. The men seated around the edges of the room are either shifting uncomfortably or averting their eyes from the table. A passing mention of Agatha's sister has them more disturbed than Randy's account of Nazi secrets.

Randy says, "Agatha's father kept an old house in Whitefish where he used to see patients when he was just getting started out here. He'd been renting it out. When Catherine got older, Agatha moved into town with her to keep her off the ranch and away from all the work they were doing."

"What kind of work?" Margot asks.

"Containment. Like I said. She went to the cave every day. Three weeks in she found the first shifted animal and knew it had to be connected. From then on it became her life."

"Where do you get your funding?" Margot asks.

"I'm not sure I'd call it funding. It's more like hush money."

"From the government?" Margot asks.

"Once it was clear the esteemed Dr. Caldwell wasn't coming back from wherever he'd gone, the government agent in charge of keeping tabs on him dropped by the ranch. He said the checks they'd always sent for Dr. Caldwell's past work weren't transferable to his children or spouse. Thank you for your service, and all that. That's when Agatha diplomatically let the guy know she had files proving exactly what her father's past work had been on behalf of our government and the Nazi Party and that she'd moved them to a location only she was aware of. So he could keep those checks coming, thank you very much. They've never stopped."

"So the government knows about the pulse?" Margot asks.

"Aw, hell no," Randy says. "They know one of their old Operation Paperclip scientists went missing under mysterious circumstances after they set him free in the US. They don't know he ever made any progress with the death pulse, and their MO was to cover up any evidence that they believed his damn theories to begin with and broke their own rules over it. As long as he didn't resurface, case closed. In my experience, the government wants to know a lot less than people think it does. The ones they pay are the ones who keep the secrets. Plausible deniability and all that."

Operation Paperclip. Claire's heard the name before: a government project that brought former Nazi scientists into alliance with the United States government after World War II. Mostly in the area of rocket technology. And most of it centered on a scientist named Wernher von Braun, who claimed to have barely known Hitler and helped the US develop one of its first space satellites. But the story of the Caldwell family and their ranch suggests there are dimensions to Operation Paperclip that are barely known to the public, despite its recognizable name.

"So a teenager blackmailed the federal government into paying for all this?" Margot asks.

"Blackmail's a little extreme. It's more a mutually beneficial arrangement than that. Besides, Agatha stopped being a teenager the night her mother made her do her bidding."

No one spoke for a while.

"Why'd you tell us all this?" Abram finally asks.

"Wasn't my decision," Randy says.

"It was hers," Claire says.

Randy glares at her suddenly. She sees jealousy there, protectiveness. Anger that someone other than him or one of his trusted men was allowed to commune with Agatha. He gestures to Ben, and Ben steps forward with a piece of paper. Randy unfolds it on the table, then weights down one corner of it with his plate. It's the now-familiar drawing of the man Poe saw on the other side of the shark-infested bloom bridge, the one whose face he made Claire draw on Margot's plane.

"We need a name and location for this guy," Randy says.

They're all looking at her now. She realizes then what they're expecting. The notepad's right next to her, the one with Poe's last messages scrawled on it. She picks up the pen. R u hearing this?

yes, comes the response, but didn't get name could only see what he was doing wasn't inside his head his vault I mean.

"So," Claire says, "you want us to get inside this guy's vault the next time the bridge opens?"

"Christ on his throne, no," Randy snaps. "No way. I want a name and a location. That's all."

"We're not going to get one unless someone says it out loud or writes it down in front of our eyes. Isn't that how the memory deck works?"

"Ask your brother about this guy's memory deck, the common area. What did he see when he was over there?"

The response comes fast, quickened, she thinks, by fear. small town main street but everything twisted weird way weirder than ours nothing shaped right church steeple tall and weird just weird sorry no music crazy loud sound like carving or something.

"Any street signs? Landmarks?"

didn't stay long enough scared.

"All right," Randy says. "Well, next time the bridge opens, go across it, see what else you can see through windows without getting too close, then cross back."

"Jesus Christ," Margot whispers. "Really?"

"I'm sorry?" Randy asks.

"You're just being a little cavalier about all of this, is all. I mean, asking a man who's been through this kind of trauma to just do a hop and a skip into some madman's consciousness using some construct we barely understand. I deal in the paranormal every day, and that's a bit much, to be frank."

"We understand the construct just fine," Randy says.

"Really? Do you? And you've shared your findings with MIT, no doubt."

"What's your point, lady?" Randy asks.

"My point, *sir*, is that over the past fourteen years this family turned into a circular firing squad as they tried to find ways to blame each other for what happened that night. Meanwhile, you and your girlfriend had all the answers and you kept them to yourselves. So why don't you start with an apology before you start giving orders."

"My job is containment and security." Randy taps the tabletop with one flexed finger. "My job is to make sure nobody else goes through what this family has gone through, and in that, I and my team here have been a hundred percent successful from the day I was hired."

"And I guess it was just an added perk that all the secrecy around here ensures you and your girlfriend will never be separated," Margot says.

"OK, you know what—"

"Enough!" Claire snaps. "Enough." When she sees she has their full attention, she continues. "Opening this guy's vault will not only tell us who he is, it'll have the added effect of knocking him flat for at least thirty minutes and then some, which is exactly what we should do if he tries to kill somebody else. When he inhales Poe's bloom again, one of us should do to him what Agatha did to me after I inhaled hers. On top of that, we'll walk away with all the information his memory provides. It's that simple. Why are you against it?"

"Opening another person's vault is incredibly dangerous," Randy says. "Everything Agatha just did took years of practice, and she got lost several times along the way."

"Lost?" Abram asks. "What do you mean, lost?"

"Did you turn around while you were in the vault, Claire?" Randy asks. "Did you look behind you?"

Claire nods.

"What did you see?" Randy asks.

"Nothing," Claire whispers.

"Exactly. No walls, no limits, no anything. You're not opening any damn vaults. That goes for you and your brother. We don't know what they are. We just know what's in them."

"And Agatha?" Claire asks.

Randy sits back in his chair, nostrils flaring.

"You're proposing a conference call of sorts?" Margot finally asks. "You inhale Agatha's bloom and the three of you wait on your memory deck for the bridge to this . . . *man* to open, and then you all go over together and break down his vault?"

"Not a chance in hell," Randy growls.

"Why not?" Margot asks.

"We have no experience opening vaults in unwilling subjects. But I'll tell you this. When one of us resisted the process during testing, the results got really freakin' ugly. Also, our memory decks—the three of us who've gone over—none of them are as weird as what Poe just described. Your brother has been inside the mind of a living nightmare, a man who somehow got to this crash site before anyone else and then made off with his bloom before anyone saw. Anyone who lived anyway. Whoever he is, this guy isn't just a passing motorist, OK? We don't know what we're dealing with. That means I want the basics we need to catch this fucker, not some deep dive into his crazy." Randy studies the room in turn, then adds, "Nobody, I repeat, *nobody* is going inside this guy's vault. The next time that bridge opens, I need your brother to get on his memory deck and explore the common area without trying to open any doors or drawing attention through the glass."

"I'm going with him," Claire says.

"No, you're not," Randy says.

"Who are you to tell me I—"

"If you go, there's more of a delay in when we get the information. We'll have to wait for you and Poe to come back from this guy's deck, then for you to recover from the return trip back here. During that time, we won't know anything about the guy's movements or location. Who knows how many people he'll hurt by then? Or worse, neither one of you comes back at all, and then we've got squat. And this guy just keeps at it until we can catch up with him on foot."

"Catching up with him on foot should be your responsibility since you're the reason he's got Poe to begin with," Margot says.

"Hence, my insistence that my team take him down using information Claire gets while she is sitting safely right here on this ranch."

"How do we know Poe will stay connected to me when he's over on this guy's memory deck?"

"We don't," Randy says. "We're going to find out."

"But we already know Poe sees and hears me through the storefronts on our memory deck. If he's not there, I can't talk to him."

"A one-way connection is better than no connection at all," Randy says.

"Well, aren't you a regular Cowboy Socrates," Abram grumbles.

"So he's going to be over there alone, is what you're saying."

"If he can communicate with us in any way, he's not alone," Randy says.

A silence falls. When Claire picks up the pen, she feels everyone's intense stares.

What do you think? she writes.

you'd just slow me down anyway i mean im just supposed to look right how bad can it be i spoke at an AA meeting in a prison last month I'm super tough promise.

She's sure it's a joke, remembers clearly the terror in his eyes when she threatened to cross the bridge herself. And now, after being reunited in some version of death she's just beginning to understand, she has to abandon him to that fear.

"Fine," Claire says.

"You're a direct line to Poe's brain. We need to keep it that way."

"Poe still has a *brain*?" Abram asks.

"Part of one, yes," Randy says. "The bloom's got these little blue particles in it, these things that look like pollen. In the presence of a living human, they come out of the bloom and go for your breath like it's candy. We call them ghost cells. That's what's left of Poe's brain and Agatha's brain."

And my brain, Claire thinks, *eventually.*

"If they're her brain, why do you call them ghost cells?" Abram asks.

"I said they're what's *left* of their brains. After a shift. And they were put there by exposure to the pulse."

Abram sits forward. "When my kids were in the hospital, they had, I don't know, three or four MRIs. All sorts of X-rays. If there were strange cells in their bodies, we would have seen—"

"The only way you would have found these is if they'd done an invasive biopsy of their brain matter, and no doctor under the sun would have done it unless there was a tumor or a growth they could see on a scan. And even then, they wouldn't have been visible to the naked eye or a microscope. Do you know how they trace magma cones in volcanoes?"

"They don't actually find the magma," Margot answers. "They find the outline of the magma. They map the earthquakes that happen above and on either side of it as it rises, and that gives them the shape of the cone."

"Exactly," Randy says. "You can do a similar thing in the brain matter of animals that have been exposed to the pulse. There's a . . . Thomas?"

Thomas clears his throat. "We call it a 'subtle crowding' of branches and cells inside the brain that suggests the presence of something that can't be seen by the naked eye. Until the subject shifts and the rest of the body dematerializes. Then they take the form you saw, Claire, and they're the only part of the bloom that doesn't recoil from a person. In fact, they seek it out. Like they're looking for a new home."

"How did you figure all this out?" Claire asks.

"Not all of the shifted animals in our cellar just didn't get out of the way fast enough," Thomas says. "We exposed some of them on purpose. For some of our tests, we *did* try to re-create what happened with Claire and Poe. We exposed animals both genetically related and not to the pulse at the same time, right next to each other. Both sets walked away with similar disruptions in their brain matter. But only the genetically related set experienced a psychic connection that was triggered by extreme emotional or physical trauma in the other."

"Until one of them shifts," Margot says.

Abram clears his throat. "All right, um. So it feels like there's two agendas here, maybe. There's what you guys want to do, which is get Poe back from this psycho, or whatever. Which, you know, I'm all for. And then there's what I'm thinking about the whole time we're sitting here talking, and I don't think it's off base to say my daughter's probably thinking about it too."

"What?" Claire asks.

"What happens to Poe if we get him back? I mean, call me crazy. Apparently I've given folks plenty of reason to. But if there was a way to bring your girlfriend back from her memory deck, or whatever, I figure you'd have done it by now. So should we get our hopes up or not? Or the next time I see my son, am I going to have to breathe in his bloom or something?"

Nobody speaks for what feels like an eternity. After just a few seconds of this awful silence, Claire realizes the answer is something none of these men want to share.

Finally, Randy looks at Benjamin Running Creek. "Get me the video."

Ben rises to his feet. "Which one?"

"Catherine's visit."

Ben makes a low, disapproving sound in his throat. The seated men lower their gazes to the floor.

Catherine, Claire thinks. *Agatha's sister.*

They sit in awful silence until Ben returns, carrying a laptop computer, which he hands to Randy. He sets a little portable hard drive on the table next to it. Once Randy's prepped everything, he pushes his chair back from the table and gestures for them to move so they can close in and watch what he's cued up on screen. Claire does, followed by Margot and her father.

The men stay where they are. Whatever it is, they've probably seen it before. Or they've lived it.

The screen shows a split camera feed.

On the left side, a pair of headlights pulls up to the ranch's front gate.

On the right, Agatha's bloom does its typical languid dance in the center of her chamber.

"The woman driving is Catherine, Agatha's sister. Agatha never let her on the property. Made her think she was up to something criminal that Catherine wouldn't want anything to do with. They rarely spoke, but every now and then Agatha would wire her some cash, shoot her an email. I kept it up after Agatha's shift, but apparently I didn't do a good enough job."

As Catherine Caldwell steps from her Volvo station wagon on the left side of the screen, Agatha's bloom starts to change shape on the right. It brightens, losing its various shades, and what previously looked like tendrils of sea life thickens into a single bright column that fills the chamber with a near-blinding wash of white light.

"She got suspicious because she thought the emails didn't sound like Agatha. So she decided to pay a visit. A surprise one."

Randy's headlights roar up to the gate, and then he pops out from behind the wheel of his black SUV. Clearly unaware of what's happening down in the cellar, he opens the pedestrian gate, thinking he'll step out and have a talk with Catherine. Then she angrily pushes her way through, and he grabs her wrists to keep her from going farther.

On the right side of the screen, all semblance of the bloom as some celestial, heavenly body has been lost. It's a shade of pewter now, and it's risen by several feet. The top of it has spread across every inch of the ceiling, and still it presses against the surrounding walls. The blue light is gone. In a few seconds' time, it went from being a writhing mushroom cloud to a geyser that looks like it's going to coat the entire chamber, top down.

The glass wall containing Agatha's chamber shatters outward as if from a percussive blast.

The images on the right-hand side of the screen are edited together from several cameras to chart the progression of what happens next. Here comes Ben, running like hell past the animals' cells, when the door to Agatha's area comes flying toward him off its hinges. He hurls himself to the floor. A thunderhead of matter from beyond this world roars over him and down the corridor. It's left the desiccated tree stump behind completely as it goes airborne. Several of the glass walls crack as it passes.

And then, on the left side of the screen, there's Randy at the front gate answering a call on his earpiece. Clearly he's being told about the hell that's breaking loose down in the cellar, the storm that coincided with Catherine Caldwell's arrival.

"Well, Agatha's pissed," Abram says.

"It's not that simple."

On the left side of the screen, Randy pulls his gun on Catherine. The shock on her face replaces her desperate anger. Was he really going this far? Forcing her off her own family's property with a gun in her face?

Then they both hear something, the double doors in the barn's floor flying off their hinges with a sound like a tornado tearing a storm door free.

Randy fires, high and over Catherine's head. It looks like he's trying to drive her away. It works. Catherine scrambles for her car.

And on the right side of the screen, the rest of the bloom has become a single snake of unstoppable force capable of blowing through metal doors and shattering glass and expanding outward from its source with a determination that can only be described in one word: hunger. It's rising from the double cellar doors it just blew open and into the harsh glare of the barn's overhead lights. And there is no mistaking its color now.

Not blue. Not pewter.

The color of flesh.

Then Catherine's taillights whip out of frame on the left side of the screen.

On the right, the snake's head loses shape, form, and momentum, like the air's being sucked out of it. Growing more vaporous with every foot of retreat, it floats backward, passing Ben, who's still gasping and flattened to the floor. Then, despite the destruction and havoc it's just wrought, the bloom falls back into its previous balletic form, only now its blue light reflects off the jagged pieces of shattered glass strewn all over the chamber floor.

"Agatha . . . ," Abram finally says.

"She didn't know what was happening, but she said her vault went nuts. The doors all started rattling in their frames, and she thought they were going to blow open one after the other."

"She didn't stop it?" Abram asks.

"She couldn't. She had no idea what was happening. It stopped when Catherine drove away."

"And if she hadn't?" Abram asks.

"Bloom seeks out the breath of anything that's the same species. What we just saw, I think that's what it does when it senses someone with its genetic material. I think it was looking for a new home. *Her.* And God only knows what would have happened if it had made it to her. Look, I know you were probably hoping that when we got Poe back, you'd be able to connect with him again, but—"

Abram's barreling out of the dining room before anyone can stop him.

Randy gestures for two of the guys to follow him. Rupert and Sean comply.

"Maybe I said more than I should have," Randy says.

Nobody speaks for a while.

"You could have lied to us," Claire answers. "Kept our hopes up that there was some way to bring Poe back, just to get us all to go along with all this. But you didn't."

"Thanks, I guess," Randy says.

"I'm going to go talk to my father," Claire says.

"Claire, if the bridge opens, you gotta come right—"

"Yeah, yeah. I'm on board, cowboy. Slow your roll."

She picks up the notepad and pen off the table. The other men bow their heads as she passes. She can't tell if it's deference or shame.

23

Her father made it no farther than one of the many rocking chairs that line the house's wraparound front porch, maybe because Rupert told him to stop, or maybe because he ran out of energy. Strange that there are so many chairs out here: she doubts this place hosts many guests. Like the decor inside the house, maybe it's a design scheme to keep Nazi ghosts at bay.

He's smoking, which Claire can't remember him doing when she was a girl. She's got no idea when he picked up the habit, but the slow curl rising into the cold morning air drives home the years of distance between them.

"Can you give us some space?" she says to Rupert. "We're not going anywhere."

Rupert nods, moves off. Sean, the guy who used to follow her in LA, stands out in the grass like he's watching the house from a distance. She figures he's monitoring Abram's possible escape routes.

When she takes a seat in the rocking chair next to his, her father gives her a startled look. Tears glisten in his eyes. His cigarette hand trembles. A snaking white scar wraps around his forearm, the evidence of a vine he struggled through as he ran for help the night of the pulse. She's heard Poe describe it, but she's never seen it in the flesh. The wound was still raw and healing over by the time she and her mother moved.

"I didn't bring you here as bait," he finally says. "For them. So whatever he's told you—"

"You didn't bring me here. You asked me to come. And I did."

"I was just trying to draw them out is what I mean. I knew they were watching me, and I figured they were watching you too, and I thought if I got us all together we could outrun them. And having Margot and her resources on hand, I figured that was a good deal for all of us. And I did believe they'd crashed that plane."

"Do you still believe that?"

"No. If everything they've told us is true, why would they create this mess? Poe lived on his own miles away from us. If they'd wanted to silence him, they could have just yanked him off a street corner and into a van or something. But I'm not talking about them. I'm talking about me. I'm talking about why I—"

"I get it," she says.

"Do you? Do you really?"

In the morning sun, her father's face looks gaunt and emaciated, his stubble patchy, and she's not sure if the cuts and little red lumps on his jaw are from their crash or a bad shave job the day before. Maybe due to hangovers. He's got a drinker's plump, swollen nose. The breakup with Margot could have hit him hard, or a lifetime of going his own way has finally caught up with him.

Claire sets the notepad on the arm of the rocking chair where her father can see it.

"I figured we could all have a talk," she says.

"I see," he whispers. "Well . . ."

His words seem to leave him. He sucks in a long drag, and then it's just the sounds of the birds and the morning sun. A morning like the ones they used to wake up to on their camping trips all those years ago, only a lot colder.

She feels a massaging sensation inside her arm, and her pen starts to move.

if I can quit cocaine and toxic men he should be able to quit smoking.

Abram looks over, sees the message taking shape. The last of his drag puffs from his nostrils dragon-style. She can't tell if he's laughing or about to cry.

"Tell him," Abram finally says, "that, um, when he emailed a couple months ago and asked if he could visit, I didn't put him off because I didn't want to see him. I put him off because I . . . because he said he was sober, and I was drinking a lot and I didn't want to throw him off his game. Can you tell him that?"

"He can hear you," Claire says. "He can see you too."

"Right. Lot of windows on the memory deck, or whatever."

Abram looks into her eyes. For a second, it's like he's looking through her and into where he thinks Poe might be.

"You believe what Margot said in there?" Abram asks. "That we turned into a circular firing squad?"

yes, comes Poe's answer.

Abram looks at the pad and nods.

Sean's got his back to them now, and he's probably too far away to hear anything they're saying.

"I let you both go," he says. "I knew how bad I fucked up that night. I thought I didn't have a right to be your dad anymore until I found the truth. But I thought the only way to get at the truth was to tell a story big enough to scare someone into telling the real story. Then years go by and suddenly I'm so far out on a limb I can't see my way back. I mean, a lifetime of being the alien guy and then I turn around and I realize, How much time have I actually spent here, where it happened? The minute I show up, people are following me like I'm onto something for the first time. Something that didn't fly off into the stars, something that's still somewhere here and has been the whole time. How could I be that stupid?"

"You were getting something out of it, though. The conferences, the YouTubes. The Margots. You liked the attention, Dad."

easy bear, her hand writes.

"It's how you dealt with losing Mom," she adds. "And I don't blame you."

"Why's that?" Abram asks.

"Because I lied to keep her."

"What do you mean?" he asks.

"I knew it wasn't a bear. I saw shadows that night. Some kind of light coming toward us after we got knocked down. And it was big. And I never said anything because I thought I'd lose her if I did. And I picked her over you because I thought she was the reliable one."

"She was."

"Still. I lied."

"You didn't lie. You protected yourself. You did what I failed to do. Twice. Once, when I dragged you kids out into the middle of nowhere, and then again when I made you a spectacle. You didn't lie, Claire. Your parents failed you. Both of you."

Her hand writes. nobody failed cant you see sometimes things are too big for one family to hold.

"Maybe," Abram says, "and maybe we would have been able to hold it if we'd found a way to stick together. The point is, it was my job to find that way. Not yours."

The little bit of distance separating their hands feels like an ocean. When she crosses it, his fingers slide easily into hers. And then it's like a dam bursting. In her arms, his bones feel as fragile as her mother's felt that last night they spent together in the hospital bed. And after a while, she loses track of time, realizes he's shaking against her because he's sobbing. And so when the massaging sensation starts up again in her arm, she figures it's just Poe trying to add his own thoughts. She'll let him join in a second. Then the sensation becomes painful, and this pain, she realizes, must be his way of expressing panic.

When she manages to get her pen to paper again, the words roar from her hand.

travelunderthesea

———

"She needs something bigger," Margot says.

Claire doesn't understand what she means. Figures she's just nervously filling the silence that's settled over the dining room. Poe stopped responding to their questions as soon as he entered the bridge, confirming their worst suspicions. The connection died the minute he left their memory deck. His last words stare up from the notepad.

imagining objects works just like agatha said ive got my old watch from high school back.

"Bigger?" Randy echoes.

"More paper. Bigger sheets. If he makes her draw, the notepad won't be big enough. I've seen how this works."

Randy nods at one of the men, and Ben hurries off.

"Poe?" Claire asks again. She's already said it aloud twice since her brother started crossing the bridge.

Her arm tingles, and when she brings it to the notepad, everyone in the dining room seems to lean forward. cant hear you anymore so not sure if you can still hear me so going to keep sending stuff im almost there.

"OK, then," Randy says, as if it's all settled. "Looks like it's one way."

"Let's hope it holds," one of the men says. She's not sure which. Maybe Rupert.

Her hand starts to move.

tunnel comes out of bus stop i think but bus stop enclosure is white wood like everything else very white wood twisted like everything else cant read sign letters messed up letters everywhere messed up

"Shit," Randy whispers.

Ben returns with a handful of printer paper, sets the stack next to her notepad.

mountains on all sides close burning wildfires sound everywhere is like stonework or something.

"No, it's woodwork," Claire says. "Carving. I heard it myself when the bridge opened. It sounds just like the woodshop at my school."

Need to draw now.

Claire moves her hand to the pile of printer paper.

———

Vernon is proud of himself. And he's sure his mother would be too.

He's found his way to the same trailhead where he robbed a car the month before, and he's happy to see it's more crowded than it was during his last visit. The twisty mountain road lies between the slope where he's hiding and the trailhead's little dirt parking lot. There, the handful of parked cars are angled nose-in toward a wooden guardrail that marks a steep drop down the mountainside.

He figures the crash has closed trails on the north slope of the mountain, so people are starting their camping trips from here instead. Or some folks are leaving the woods early because they're creeped out by the prospect of stumbling across plane parts or a severed foot. This thought makes him feel strong and brave. He was able to enter the worst of the crash site and ended up rewarded for his courage.

A large family's packing a minivan decked out in bright bumper stickers featuring touchy-feely sayings. Nearby, an apple-cheeked little girl with golden pigtails hovers, as if she's considering lending a hand once she finishes the goofy little dance she keeps doing to a song only she can hear.

No one seems to notice him looking down on them from the slope across the road. No one's looking in the direction of the airplane seat several feet behind him. He was right. By daylight, his mother's gift is harder to detect. If he'd approached after dark, he and the seat would be lit up like blue torches, and folks would probably be either running like hell or coming toward him with flashlights and guns by now.

But nobody notices him, and that gives him time to plan his next move.

———

A church steeple, but it's twisted and malformed, and still her hand draws it with complete confidence, following its abstracted lines as if they are roads on an old and familiar map. It tapers to such a slender point in the middle, the cupola above shouldn't be able to stay upright, but it does. On all four sides of the elongated cupola, the windows are so severely arched at the top they look like giant spades. These distortions are more severe than the slender versions of San Francisco skyscrapers visible from her memory deck, another chilling suggestion that this particular mind perceives the world in its own contorted way.

"There's no real church like that anywhere," Ben says.

"Maybe Spain? That Gaudí guy?" Thomas suggests.

"It's probably a *version* of a real one," Randy says. "It's information. That's what we need. This is all good. This is all good."

Claire's arm thrums with energy that feels electric. Now she's able to recognize this particular burst of sensation as the prelude to a drawing and not just a written message.

She transfers her hand to a new sheet. What she draws next looks like a jagged row of teeth at first. Then an enclosure starts to take shape around it.

"The bus stop," Randy says. "That must be where the bridge comes out on this guy's side."

The half cubicle is twisted like it's been held at one top corner and pulled like taffy until its other walls are stretched almost to the limit.

A new drawing begins. This one pours from her hand. Maybe because it takes a familiar shape. It's the shape of a man with one arm raised over his shoulder, only the man's face is all black except for a little slash where round eyes stare back from beneath a hood. And in the man's raised hand is some sort of weapon, a nightstick, it looks like. It reminds her of old police sketches of rapists and serial killers who wore hoods to disguise themselves.

"What on earth?" Margot whispers. "Is that guy there?"

thats on the sidewalls of the bus stop where the ads are should be dozens of them everywhere wait theyre all over.

———

There are a lot of cars at the trailhead, but not the type Vernon needs. He needs a van or a truck with no windows in the back so his mother's gift doesn't shine all over the place while he drives where he needs to go next.

Right now, the station wagon the little girl is dancing next to is the biggest in the lot. Should he go for it, or should he wait? What he needs is a delivery truck, and he's probably not going to find one way up here. The road to the trailhead is full of hairpin turns, and nobody, expect for him these past six months, lives up here. Not full-time anyway.

But whatever he does, he's going to have to move some people around when he finally does make his move. He wonders if using his mother's gift on something that's living flesh and blood will be like pinching a grape between your thumb and forefinger while trying not to crush it. And the challenge of this is exciting. Like waiting to scratch an itch that's just gone from irritating to burning.

Maybe he should start by practicing on something small.

Something like the little girl.

---

some kind of logo looks normal.

Margot whispers. "How much time do we have?"

"Twenty minutes," Randy says. "He crossed the bridge real fast."

"He wants to get this over with," Claire says. "And I don't blame him."

Claire starts to draw again. At first, it feels like a giant *P* with a thick, frenzied spine and big swooping upper chamber. Then she realizes the spine is actually an ice cream cone.

"Note to file. Our target likes ice cream," Ben says.

"That looks like a standard logo to me," Margot says. "It has to mean something that it's one of the only normal things there, right?"

in the glass I can see him looking at cars and people.

"Shit," Abram whispers.

trailhead hes looking for something.

"A vehicle, probably," Ben says quietly.
"Tell him not to get too close to the glass," Randy says.
"I can't. Remember?" Claire says.
kids, Claire's hand writes. Little girl.

———

He's thinking maybe he'll just make the little girl's feet leave the ground. Have her do a little jump. Maybe she won't even notice. But if she cries out for her parents, someone might look up to the trees where he's hiding, and then he'd have to start hurting people for real.

Then he sees it. A big utility van painted with a bright logo. A glistening black motorcycle that looks larger than the jagged mountains painted behind it. The rider wears a leather jacket but has the smiling pink head of a pig—MILE HIGH ON THE HOG BIKE SHOP, the letters read, followed by a phone number and a Boulder address. The van rolls past the parked cars, headed for the big open space at the lot's far end.

The engine dies. The driver steps out, long ponytail threaded through his baseball cap, dressed in water-resistant hiking pants and a fleecy V-neck pullover. He walks around to the back of the van, pops open the cargo doors, and pulls out a loaded-to-the-gills backpack that probably has a week's worth of supplies inside. But it's the inside of the van Vernon cares about. He sees tool racks off to one side, but mostly empty space and bare floor.

Perfect.

Then the guy closes the doors and goes very still, and that's when Vernon realizes some of his blue shimmer is reflected in the door's windows.

Vernon's been spotted, and he has to act now.

Before the guy turns around, Vernon slams him to the dirt with such force the air goes out of him in a sound like a dog's yip. But it's too quick for anyone else in the parking lot to notice, and he's left too winded to follow it up with a scream. He'd only managed to get one arm through a backpack strap before noticing Vernon's glow, so the pack tumbles off the side as Vernon drags him across the asphalt with his mind. He's moving fast, much faster than Vernon expected. And this fills Vernon with elation, and this elation gives him courage. He imagines the man flying backward up into the air, and the man does, rising up above the road and then speeding backward, like a fatal plummet in reverse. Branches snap as he flies into the brush above Vernon's head. Vernon turns, following him, thinking, *So easy! So easy, even with people!*

And then the man's back slams into a tree trunk, and Vernon's not sure if the snapping he hears is wood or the man's bones.

Maybe too fast, he thinks. He holds the man pinned to the tree trunk, ten feet up off the ground.

Vernon approaches, studying his handiwork. Awed by his new power over human flesh.

Blood pours from the side of the man's mouth, staining his beard black. He blinks, his eyes glassy. But he's seeing Vernon, and if he's seeing Vernon, he can probably hear Vernon.

"I need your car keys," Vernon says.

The man jerks, coughs. Blood dribbles from his mouth. Something the man needs to speak might have broken inside him.

Oh well.

What he does next causes a light shredding sound. Two little seams tear up both legs of the man's hiking pants, exposing hairy pale skin underneath. Finally, there's a jangly plop. From the shredded right pocket, a key chain falls to the dirt at the base of the tree.

Vernon feels an excited gnawing in his gut. There's so much to try. He has the man all to himself. But he knows he should go.

So he starts doing the same thing he did to the man's pants to the man's right leg. Just to see what happens.

Blood bubbles from the skin on his right shin, traveling upward in a bright red line. Pain gives the man his voice back, and he lets out a startled cry.

That won't do.

Before Vernon realizes what he's done, the man's cry is choked off. The guy tumbles to the base of the tree like a puppet with cut strings, landing in a lifeless tangle. Vernon can see the shape of his throat's all pressed in. He choked the guy without touching him.

Oops, he thinks.

He probably should have tested this on the little girl before he got started. He's not prepared for how sensitive his mother's gift is proving to be when he has skin and bone under his control.

Slowly, Vernon approaches his former hiding spot, gets the trailhead in view. It doesn't look like anyone's noticed the backpacker's abduction and brief flight. And the utility van's rear doors are still open by an inch.

Vernon imagines the doors opening all the way. They do, slowly, and with a little creak that begs for some WD-40. The family with the little girl is still loading their minivan. A man and a woman are taking selfies at the guardrail. He thinks they own the red Nissan Sentra parked close to the van, but their car could be the green pickup truck no one's bothered with since he showed up.

He turns, traces the path between where he stashed the airplane seat and the rear of the van. Then he retraces it, making the bigger branches that cross the path snap like kindling, letting them tumble to the earth one after the other, until he's cleared what looks like enough passage.

He snatches the man's car keys from where they landed and pockets them.

He'll have to act quickly. There's no guarantee he won't be noticed. But given how brightly his mother's gift shimmers, that's a possibility no matter how well he performs this next move.

Claire's hand is shaking worse than it's ever been when she starts writing again. She doesn't want to ponder why, doesn't want to assume it's fear coursing from her brother's consciousness and onto the page.

sqmk134

"License plate number," Randy says. "Excellent work, Mr. Huntley."

Randy gestures and Rupert closes in, jots the number down on a notepad, then leaves the room. Probably bound for the nearest laptop.

A silence passes before Abram says what they're all thinking. "What happened to the little girl, though?"

Vernon makes the chair rocket sideways through the air, arcing over the roadway before it vanishes through the van's open doors. But stopping the chair requires a separate mental flex than sending it flying through the air, and he waits a second too long. The eruption inside the van is like giant pots and pans falling down stairs. The airplane's seat crashes into the back of the driver and passenger seats. He slams the rear cargo doors shut with his mind.

It's too late.

Everyone on the trailhead is frozen and staring at the van.

The father who's been loading the minivan starts for it.

"Everything all right over there, pal?" he calls out.

For a second, Vernon's afraid the man's talking to him, that he's spotted him on the slope. But the man's eyes are on the big, brightly painted van. He's headed straight for it. Blue light fills its two rear windows. From the way the selfie takers are now staring toward the van's windshield, Vernon figures the light's visible there too.

This won't do. This is all wrong.

He imagines the father landing flat on his ass, and the man does. Then he sends him sliding backward across the dirt, past the nose of his minivan and under the guardrail. Too late, he realizes he can't control what he can't see. The man's out of sight, and the next thing he hears are the piercing wails of the man's family members.

Did he sweep him off the side of the mountain without meaning to? It doesn't matter. He's done what he really needed to do. He's created a distraction. The family and the happy couple are all racing in the direction of where the nosy dad vanished.

Vernon runs, then leaps. It's a fifteen-foot drop to the road below, but he imagines himself stopping several feet short of the asphalt, and he does, his power acting like a little cushion. He sets himself down easily, then runs for the van, jams the keys into the ignition. He revs the engine, backs out, spins into a hard turn.

He's just hit the accelerator when he sees the little girl standing right in front of him.

She rockets straight up into the air before he realizes what he's done.

He slams on the brakes, sees her floating above the nose of the van, eyes saucer-wide.

She's wailing hysterically. She should stop. He just saved her life. She should be laughing, or at least giggling. Maybe thanking him.

He could be doing so many other things to her, bad things like he did to the backpacker, but he stopped and he saved her and she's OK because of him. Instead, she's crying, which is making him feel like he did something wrong. She's crying so loud he can hear it inside the van like she's inside it with him.

Stop crying, he thinks, which he knows is a dangerous thing. Because sometimes when he has the same thought over and over again, his mother's gift turns it into action before he can stop it. Like it did with the backpacker's throat, and the passenger at the crash site.

Then he sees someone staring at him. There are eyes in the rear-view mirror, and they're not the little girl's. They're not Vernon's either. A stranger's eyes. Vernon whirls, looks behind him, sees the airplane seat on its side, its blue tendrils rising as high as the ceiling and kissing its length, like compressed smoke. There's no one in the van.

He turns back to the mirror, thinking the eyes will be gone. Just a brain hiccup, like he had at the crash site. Instead, he sees a man's face now, and the man is staring at him with rage in his big blue eyes. And it looks like the sides of his fists are pressed against glass. Not the mirror's glass, but something that's inside the mirror. Something that's not behind him in the van, something that shouldn't be there. The man has bright blond hair and a nose ring.

When he sees Vernon staring back at him, he mouths three words. Vernon can't hear his voice, but it's easy to read his lips.

Put. Her. Down.

"Get out of my head or I'll crush her."

The man flinches. Vernon can't hear him, but it looks like he can hear Vernon just fine.

Now it's like he's searching Vernon's face, trying to see how serious he is.

"Get out of my head or I'll kill them all. I'll crush them like grapes."

The man's anger is giving way to something weaker, something with more fear than anger in it.

Vernon is proud of himself. Knows his mother would be proud of him too. His mother taught him that when crazy thoughts came, it was important to act decisively. To do the opposite of what the thoughts told you to do. *Right action,* she'd taught him, *can save us from wrong thinking.*

He turns the wheel, drives around the ungrateful little girl. Her sobs follow him as he leaves, and they make him angry. If it wasn't for the ghost in the mirror, he probably would have taught her a lesson. Then he remembers how scared she was when he lifted her off the ground and realizes he probably did.

———

back.

Can you see me? Claire writes.

yes.

Margot lets out a breath and sinks more deeply into her chair. Seated next to her, her father rolls his head back, closing his eyes, like a dog stretching in the sun.

You OK? she writes.

no he threatened me and told me hed crush them all if I didn't go away and he killed someone.

The little girl?

When there's no answer, Margot whispers, "Oh no," under her breath.

Finally, Claire's hand moves. not sure about her maybe not since I did what he said.

Some of the tension leaves the room, but not enough.

"Claire, look at me," Randy says.

She does.

"Poe," Randy says, "you did excellent work over there. We're going to work with what you gave us. If the bridge opens again, don't cross again unless you hear from us first."

There's no answer at first, and then Claire feels the first surge of a drawing. It's a van, and on its side, a logo her hand reveals in detail. A pig in a leather jacket astride a motorcycle, and then, down at the bottom, an address and a phone number. Then, a brief signature: van he took.

Randy nods excitedly, slides the drawing across the table, and hands it to Ben.

Claire's hand starts moving again. Furiously, this time.

wehavetostophimnow

24

Claire's been awake for thirty hours straight, but when Randy suggested a nap, she had to fight the urge to knee him in the groin.

You try taking a nap when your concept of physical reality has been upended and your brother's talking to you from a realm between life and death, jerk.

A shower. That's the only nod to normality she can make right now.

Ben and Sean are leading her upstairs to the second floor of the main house while Margot and Abram follow her. The bedroom looks like nobody's stayed in it for years. There, she finds her duffel bag resting on the pink carpet next to a four-poster bed with a fluffy pink-and-white comforter and lace-trimmed pillow shams. It's the old nursery, she realizes, the one where Agatha held a gun to Hilde's head and pried baby Catherine from her arms.

Very relaxing, guys, she thinks.

Her bag looks chewed on, no doubt thanks to the car crash.

"Shower," she says.

Margot and Abram nod. Standing just outside the bedroom door, Sean starts to say something that sounds vaguely helpful. Margot closes the door in his face.

"Have I ever told you that you hate men, Margot?" Abram asks.

"You have, and it was absurd then too. Pardon me if my distaste for soldiers of fortune playing games with other people's lives comes across as misandry. But if there were any women on staff here, I'd probably be just as disrespectful to them as well."

"Shower," Claire says again, as if she's reminding herself.

"Go ahead, sweetheart. Your father and I will bicker in here."

She shuts the bathroom door, tugs her clothes halfway off before she sees what's missing.

There's no mirror over the sink. Just a big expanse of plain white wall dotted with paint stains a mirror concealed up until recently. Maybe just moments before. She's gone from dreading the visions her reflection offers to mourning the loss of her access to them.

Her access to Poe.

She showers in a daze, half expecting to feel her brother tugging at the inside of her arm. He's either letting her rest or still processing his shock over witnessing a gruesome murder.

When she emerges from the bathroom, her dad is studying the blank section of wall above the dresser.

"I think there was a mirror here," he says, tapping the wall.

"They took the one out of the bathroom too."

Margot has set Claire's notepad on a little round table next to the curtained window.

How you doing? Claire writes.

the imagining thing is still working i made myself something new.

What?

gun dad gave me one when i was sixteen.

Claire glares at him.

"It was for hunting," her dad says. "We lived in Spokane, not Vegan Creek, or wherever the hell your mother moved you guys."

"Eagle Rock," Claire mutters.

What's the gun for? Claire asks.

if we cant find the key.

"The vault," Abram says.

Nobody says anything else.

She's doubtful the gun would have any effect on something as mysterious as the vault. What concerns her is her brother's desire for one.

Through the door, Sean asks, "Everything all right in there?"

"Peachy," Margot says. "But do you think we could get some semiautomatic weapons and a side of mirrors, please?"

"Stop flirting," Abram mumbles.

"Blow me," Margot whispers.

This isn't going to work, she thinks. *Poe can't do this alone. And he shouldn't have to.*

———

Randy calls Dave from his satellite phone, gives him a download of everything they've learned.

A van. A license plate their guy will probably ditch in no time. A logo he'll be able to strip away with his mind. It doesn't seem like much when he rattles it off, and apparently Dave agrees because when Randy finishes, he says, "How the hell did Apollo miss the name of the trailhead?"

"He didn't miss it. Our creep didn't look at it, so Poe didn't get to see it."

"Too busy looking at other shit," Dave mutters. "Crazy shit. Why'd it have to end up with somebody crazy?"

"Who else would go near it?" Randy says. "Near enough to breathe it in anyway."

"Good point," Dave says.

"All the rescue crews in that area probably have Twitter accounts where they put out public alerts about accidents. When word of this gets out, it'll light those up, maybe the news too. Keep your eye on everything as you get close. How far are you from Mount Elbert?"

"Forty-five minutes, but all due respect, it's a pretty big mountain with a lot of trailheads."

"I'm hoping we can give you a better sense of direction when you're close."

"But he was going downhill, you said."

"Correct."

"So he's coming down off the mountain?"

Or he already has, Randy thinks. He's confident Dave's thinking it too. But by the time Randy's hung up, neither of them has said it.

In the tech center, Rupert is having a cheerful conversation on his burner phone. His playful banter with whoever's on the other end makes a jarring counterpoint to the grim business at hand.

Community relations has always been Rupert's skill, and he keeps it sharp by interacting with the outside world more than anyone else on the team does. When Randy hired the guy on Thomas's recommendation, he'd just lost a gig playing Ed McMahon to a fellow SEAL turned guru whose podcast empire went down in flames after the vitamin supplements he was hawking sent people to the hospital. Rupert's story, like so many of their own, has illustrated the limited options awaiting the country's most skilled military operators after they aged out of deployments. Politics, Hollywood consultant, private security. CrossFit trainer. Or self-styled guru preaching the SEAL doctrines of fortitude and self-discipline to a population primarily invested in losing weight and not storming out on their spouse. Rupert thought Thunder Ranch would be a step down until he visited the cellar. And it had pleased Randy to give another guy like him a sense of purpose. A purpose that now seems to be unspooling.

"That's great," Rupert says. "Thank you, ma'am. I appreciate it . . . Yes, I'm sure. I'll tell him. I'll tell him to check in, yeah." Rupert hangs up, then stares at the burner phone in his hand, drained by the cheerfulness the call required. "Long Tooth Trailhead. That's the name."

"You sure?"

Rupert nods. "The logo on the van, the number for the bike shop. I called it and told them I'd passed the van on the way up the mountain and I might have some business for them and I wanted to catch up with the guy driving. She said his name is Lonny Peterson and he was heading out on a solo camping trip from Long Tooth." Rupert writes the name down on a piece of paper and hands it to Randy. "She's his wife."

Who has no idea she's a widow now, Randy thinks.

"Get the name to Dave and Zach," he says. "I just got off the phone with them. They've got the plate number and a description of the van."

Thomas has been listening to them intently. He sits at the one table that isn't taken up by flat-screen monitors offering various angles of the cellar and the shores of Lake Michele, Poe's drawings spread out before him. As he studies them, his tongue makes a lump under his upper lip.

"So we've got a plate number and the cops don't?" Thomas asks.

"Yeah, 'cause what we want right now is a bunch of cops taking shots at someone who's inhaled a bunch of bloom. You guys want to put a *second* pulse out into the world?"

Both men hang their heads, remembering, he hopes, his previous descriptions of what happened to the body of Dr. Caldwell when his daughter shot him in the chest. Imagining how that event might unfold outside of a cave. On a crowded highway, perhaps.

"Rupert, after you talk to Dave and Zach, I want both of you on memory deck analysis. Get whatever you can from these drawings. Focus on that ice cream logo. I hate to admit it, but I think Queen Margot's right. It's one of the only real things Poe saw over there."

"You sure you want both of us on this?" Thomas asks. "I mean, a memory deck might not be a map to where he's headed. Mine's the old creek in Ohio where I fell in love with Suzy Potthurst, and I haven't been there in twenty-five years, Randy. And Apollo and Artemis haven't been to Pier 39 since they were kids."

"They're Poe and Claire now," Randy says. "A memory deck is a map to who someone is. That's the info we need. If this is someplace this guy's been a bunch of times before, we've got a drawing of his face we can send to somebody there once we get the location. Maybe that'll give us an actual ID."

"What's a bus stop doing in some little rinky-dink mountain town?" Rupert asks, holding up the drawing of the twisted enclosure and tooth-studded bench.

"Could be Boulder or Denver," Randy says.

"Not with mountains on all sides, the way he described," Rupert says. "Is there some massive bus system that connects every little mountain town in Colorado? I'm from Jersey."

"Find out," Randy says.

"Maybe it's a trolley stop?" Thomas says. "Something that goes just through town."

"Or like the Snow Bus here in Whitefish," Rupert says. "The one that runs people up the mountain during ski season. They've got their own stops."

"So we're looking for a tourist place. That's good. This is all good. Keep at it. Rupert, call Dave and—"

The door flies open and Sean bursts in, looking breathless.

"She's going to the barn," he says.

"Who?"

"Claire. She wants to talk to our boss."

"No," Randy barks.

"OK. Then you tell her. Because she's not listening to me, and I figured you didn't want me to shoot her in the leg."

The tech center's normally a ten-minute walk from the barn, but Randy runs it in record time, and by the time he gets there, Margot and Abram are hovering nervously outside its open doors while Ben and Claire are locked in what looks like angry conversation inside. When Claire sees Randy approaching, she whirls.

"May I have the code, please?" she asks, as if all she wants to do is use a restroom.

Her hair is damp, but her eyes are bloodshot and she's paler than she should be for someone who was just standing under a rush of hot water. To his relief, Randy sees the key-coded doors to the cellar are closed. But the double doors that are supposed to cover them were left open by the last person out.

"I thought we agreed you'd get some rest," Randy said.

"After I talk to Agatha."

"About what?" Randy asks.

"Strategy."

"We have a strategy."

"It's not working. People are dying."

"Your strategy's worse, Claire. Nobody's opening that guy's vault."

"Let her say that. She's the expert."

"So am I."

"You said you and two of the other guys here have visited with her, right? That means she's opened three different vaults on three different memory decks. There's no reason she can't open this one."

"Yes, there is."

"What is it?"

"Because that guy's deck isn't normal. You're right. We've studied three of them. Four, if you count hers, and in not a one did we see the kind of distortions and images of violence your brother is describing. Not one, Claire. So I don't know how many of the rules even apply over there, and I don't want any of you going for longer than absolutely necessary."

"Just my brother."

"Your brother doesn't have a body anymore."

"Neither does your girlfriend, you prick!"

She flinches from her own anger. Tears spill from her eyes. She brings her hand to her mouth as if she thinks it will stop them, but it's too late.

Ben stares shamefully at the floor, pondering the secrets beneath.

"I get it," Randy finally says. "I get you, OK. You're the best version of what you could be given everything that happened. You go above and beyond for your students because you couldn't save your family."

Claire rolls her eyes. "Oh, for Christ's sake," she whispers.

"But this guy, whoever he is, he's not just some shitty student. You're not just going to be able to sit him down and have a talk with him about why he's crazy. This is way more complicated than that."

Claire starts moving, and for a second, Randy thinks she's going to blow past him and out of the barn. Instead, she stops right next to him. The look in her eyes will stay with him always, he's sure.

"Most of my job isn't about shitty students. It's about shitty parents. And you want to know what the worst ones all have in common? They think they're too 'complicated' to parent their kids."

"Get some rest," he says.

She stalks off toward the main house. After a tense silence, Abram and Margot follow her. And then Sean, but slowly, as if he's keeping his distance from her now to avoid being struck.

"We hid all the mirrors, right?" Randy finally asks.

"Yep," Ben says.

"You think I'm off base?"

"I think you've got a plan, but I think you should put a clock on it. Or a maximum body count."

"I'll make a note of that," Randy says.

"This has already been out in the world too long, Randy. If a lot of people see this, there's going to be no putting the lid back on."

"There's always Operation Clean Sweep."

"Moment for that's come and gone and you know it. Pumping the cellar full of wet concrete and moving Agatha to Canada isn't going to be enough by then. We've got other folks involved. And I don't mean to be insubordinate, but I'm not going to be part of anything that adds those three to the 'sweep,' if you get my meaning, friend."

Ben claps him on the shoulder, heads for the barn doors. "I'll go help with nap enforcement," he says, and then he's out the doors.

This time, Randy locks the barn up tight.

He figures he's cutting himself off from temptation too.

Agatha would have her own opinions about all this, he's sure, and he'd love nothing more than to lay his stress at her feet. But he knows what she'd do. She'd propose going over to this guy's deck herself and opening the vault, damn the danger. Damn the fact that the vault doesn't look like any other they've explored. She never would have shared her past with Claire if she didn't feel responsible for all this. And that makes him responsible too. But he'll be damned if she thrusts herself inside the head of a murderous psychopath. That's the least he can do for all of them.

He's wandering, losing track of time, telling himself he's just trying to make himself visible between the main house and the barn in case Claire tries to slip out again.

But the truth is, he's paralyzed.

Waiting.

Boots crunch icy grass in his direction. It's Rupert. He's got several pieces of paper in his hand, and his eyes are wide and alert.

"I think we got something," he says. "This look familiar?"

He hands him a printout of a church steeple, a picture from some photo-sharing site. It's similar to the steeple Poe drew if you subjected it to the laws of Newtonian physics. "Where is this?"

"Little town called Spurlock. It's definitely a tourist destination, so I had no trouble finding a bunch of pictures online. And they've got this." Another sheet of paper, this one showing a shuttle stop of some kind that could reasonably be the one Poe drew, only the bench is flat and the enclosure's covered with ads for a ski resort. "But Margot was right. Pelton's Ice Cream shop. Right on Pine Street. Here's the logo."

Randy's not prepared for the shock of seeing how close to reality Poe's drawing of the logo is. "Holy shit," he whispers.

"Yeah," Rupert says. "And it gets better. Or worse, depending on your point of view."

The third sheet of paper is a news article from the *Mountain Spectator*. The photograph above the headline forces a bark of surprise from Randy.

It's their creep. It's gotta be. The same evenly spaced eyes and rounded, cherubic nose and baby-fat cheeks. Only the filth and grime Poe's drawing depicted isn't there. Yet. The headline screams: Spurlock Resident Faces Charges of Interfering with Mother's Corpse.

"That's gotta be the guy, right?" Rupert asks.

"Has to be," Randy answers, but he's busy reading the article. The details are crazy pants. Something about the kid hot-gluing gemstones to his mother's face after she dropped dead in the kitchen one morning. Speculation from unnamed neighbors that he might have killed her, but a coroner calling it a normal heart attack. Reports of the kid acting strange around town throughout his life. The statement from the sheriff, Dean Jorgensen, sounds diplomatic, urging calm and an end to baseless speculations about a local resident with "special issues" suffering a tragic loss.

"Vernon Starnes," Rupert says.

"This article's seven months old. Poe's drawing is maybe what the guy looks like after that long living on the run. Did they charge him?"

"No. There's a follow-up piece, but it's short and there are no photos. They let him go. I printed it out anyway. It's in the tech center. Spurlock's about two hours northeast of the eastern base of Mount Elbert. You want me to redirect Dave and Zach? I'm sure they're close by now."

"No. We still don't know if this guy's headed to town. Cut the picture out, see if we can get an ID from Claire and Poe. But don't share anything else with them yet. They're jumpy as hell and they're making me nuts. Get back to the tech center after you talk to them. And tell Sean and Ben to stay in the house with our guests."

"Who are you calling?" Rupert asks.

"Sheriff Dean Jorgensen." Randy is already striding toward the tech center. "I want to see what he remembers about his old friend Vernon."

By the time he makes it to the tech center, there's a spring in his step. A sense of accomplishment, a little nudge from the universe telling him he's on the right track. Then he sees the drawing of the man with the hood over his head, his raised arm holding some sort of blurred weapon, and wonders, *What's the explanation for that?*

He's seeing it for the first time.

The distortions—the bus bench lined with teeth, the flaming mountainsides on all sides—it's not just the product of a broken mind. It's hate.

25

Twice now, Dean Jorgensen has tried reading one of those military thrillers Deputy Zander recommended, but the cold medicine he took this morning has him so fogged he found himself reading the same paragraph over and over again. And daytime television wasn't invented for guys like Dean. The talk-show laughter filling his living room seems channeled from some bright, sunny world he stopped being a member of years ago. When he first started in law enforcement, he didn't think he'd turn into the kind of bitter broken-down cop he'd seen in movies and TV shows, as long as he stuck to small-town life. Meth and opioids changed all that. Brought a kind of deranged criminal chaos to their corner of the woods that made for calls you couldn't get out of your head. He'd seen stuff done to kids by tweakers that would traumatize a Denver cop down to their bones.

Maybe that's why he lost Jill after fifteen years of marriage. He'd gone to that dark place they both thought small-town cops couldn't go. But there's a more likely explanation—her bitch sister, who'd always resented Dean for making more money. Maribelle's touchy-feely figures of speech were all over the goodbye letter Susan had left for him on the kitchen table a few months ago. Phrases like "not feeling seen" and "rediscovering my authentic self." He'd never heard that kind of shit out of his wife's mouth, but it sounded exactly like some hippie-dippie nonsense her sister put in her head during one of those book club meetings they'd always used as an excuse to run him out of his house for an afternoon.

Now he's realizing how much he used work as a distraction since the divorce. One bad cold and a sick day encouraged by his germophobic dispatcher and suddenly Dean's swimming in bad memories. And on TV, the interview with a new Latin pop star conducted by an aging, bubbly actress he feels like he should recognize isn't making him feel any better.

When his phone buzzes on the side table, he's relieved. Anything to take his mind off his life.

"I'm sorry, Sheriff. We've got a man on the phone says he's got to talk to you right now."

"About what?"

"Vernon Starnes."

The tightness in her voice tells Dean she knows what the name means. They all do. They've all heard the rumors.

For a while, Dean Jorgensen doesn't say anything. He's too busy seeing the kid sitting quietly in his cell, looking at the floor whenever Dean asked him a question about why he'd done his mother up like some Egyptian sarcophagus instead of calling 911. The kid had one of those perfectly balanced faces that reminded him of children in those illustrated soap ads from the 1920s his mother used to collect and frame. He's always wondered if that's why Julia Starnes cut the boy so much slack. Because he looked so damn innocent on the outside, she was sure there was some innocence inside somewhere.

Did she ever find it? He's got no idea. There's been no sign of the kid in town for months.

"Sheriff?"

"What's the guy's name?" Dean asks.

"Ben Griffin."

"Don't know it."

"He says he's not local. He's working private security for a client who says he had some kind of run-in with Vernon out in the woods on Mount Elbert. They recognized him from the papers, and apparently Vernon made threats about coming back to Spurlock."

Dean stops himself from whispering a string of profanities into the phone. Mercedes Anderson's a churchgoing woman who doesn't allow any crass talk within five feet of her desk. Dean jots down this Ben Griffin's number. But one detail Mercedes just gave him doesn't wash. Papers, plural? Vernon's story didn't go that wide. Also, the name *Mount Elbert* nags at him. Takes him a second to remember it's where that big plane went down yesterday afternoon.

Something's off, and he's only going to figure out what if he takes the call.

"I hope this is for real, Mr. Griffin," Dean says into the phone. "I'm trying to have a sick day here."

"Apologies. But it's very real."

"Private security, huh? What's your client do?"

"Manages his investments, mostly."

"I see. Tell me more about this run-in."

"My clients were hiking, and they came across this guy's hideout. He started talking about how he was planning to head back to wherever he was from. Maybe settle some scores. He mentioned some weapons."

"What kind of weapons?" Dean asks. He has to swallow because his throat's gone dry.

"Didn't give specifics, and honestly my clients were so freaked out they didn't hang around long after that."

Dean's tempted to pretend Vernon never would have spilled his guts like that to some strangers, but the kid's so crackers, there's no telling what he might do. He doesn't have anything Dean would call a filter, and before he went missing, he'd been banned from most of the stores in town. Lucy Lowe's gift shop was first, after she caught him twisting all the heads off the Kewpie dolls in the ninety-nine-cents tub at the register. Then the owner of the Sunny Side Up Grill lost his shit and banned Vernon after the kid developed a fixation with the guy's daughter and started leaving his weird little carved birds on all the tables in her section. If they'd been cute little stuffed animals, it would have been one thing, but Vernon's carvings were like something out of *The Nightmare Before Christmas*. The only exception in town was Pelton's Ice Cream, and that's because Vernon's mother always made good on her promise to Arnie and Kate Pelton that he'd never visit without her.

"Your clients were hiking where a plane just crashed?" Dean asks.

"They headed out yesterday. Didn't even know about the crash till they called in to tell me about their encounter."

"And they recognized Vernon from the papers, you say? I don't remember him getting covered in the *New York Times*."

"They gave me all the details he shared with them, and I put two and two together here at the University of Google."

"I see."

"So, what happened to this kid anyway?" the man asks.

If this guy's name's really Ben Griffin, Dean's George Clooney.

"You a reporter, sir?"

"Far from it. Private security. Like I said."

"That can mean a lot of things."

"It can. Look, it's weapons the kid talked about, so if you want me to call the ATF or the FBI, I can—"

"No, no. Don't bring that into my day. Please. I appreciate the warning. Thank you."

"He said something about men in hoods. Did somebody beat on this guy?"

A chill runs straight down Dean's spine, then makes his legs go tense. Maybe he's just getting a fever. Maybe talk of Vernon Starnes is giving him one. "I'll have my deputies be on guard."

"Did your *deputies* beat on this guy?" the man asks.

"They most certainly did not. Look, we held Vernon for as long as it took the county DA to decide whether or not she was going to charge him with interfering with a corpse. He was not charged. We let him go. End of story."

"Apparently not, if he's got a beef with your town."

"All right, which paper do you work for?"

"None of 'em. Look, I work for a very rich man who's used to getting his own way, and he's going to be breathing down my neck about what I did about the crazy guy he ran into in the woods. Also, my boss tilts a little to the left, so he's a little skittish about police-brutality stuff, if you catch my drift. So don't make me tell him this crazy guy's beef is with your department—"

"All right, all right, Jesus. OK. There were rumors. We asked around about them, we couldn't find anything concrete."

"What kind of rumors?"

"The mom didn't see to her will right. The bank got the house when she died. Vernon was squatting in it. The bank was trying to get him out, it was taking a while, and the kid's a lurker and nobody's ever much liked him, to be frank. Rumor is, the neighbors got together and took it on themselves."

"Took what on themselves?"

"Drove Vernon out of town. Literally. In a car. Now the guy was twenty-three last time I checked. He never showed up to make a complaint. There was nothing I could do. He was just here one day, gone the next. Look, Vernon's got real problems, OK? Some kind of mental health thing that never got diagnosed because the mother was so protective."

"Well, that fits with what my boss saw."

But just saying the words *mental health thing* brings back memories of the kid so vivid, Dean can't speak. He's seeing the shattered look on the boy's angelic face when Dean had to break the news about what his uncle had done while he was locked in a cell. It was the only time he'd ever seen the kid show an emotion that seemed close to human. Most of the time he went around as if he were seeing the world through a foggy pane of glass. And when Dean had seen that look, he'd hurt for the kid, but he'd also thought, *Good. Maybe the pain of all this will make him more human, and that's what he'll need since his mom's not around anymore to protect him from the world.*

"Sheriff?"

"Yeah."

"Just a thought, but, you know, *you* may not know who these neighbors are that took things into their own hands . . . but does Vernon?"

Dean doesn't believe a word of this guy's story. Private security, maybe. But the story about the rich client coming across Vernon during a hike sounds like a lot of bunk. In his experience, rich folks are more than eager to lecture local police themselves so they can show off what big deals and upstanding citizens they are. They don't have their minions do it for them. Unless it's a lawyer who's trying to get them out of something.

Given how little he knows about the man on the other end of the phone, what he's about to do could be considered a bad thing, maybe even unethical. But in the months since, he's always wanted someone to pay for putting that awful hurt look on Vernon's face, for forcing Dean to break that shattering news.

"You should warn his uncle. Johnny Starnes. They had a beef. He lives about two hours south of here in Leadville. I'll put in a call to him, but he's not great with cops and, uh . . . he might believe it more if it's coming from you."

"Absolutely. What's the beef?"

"While we were holding the kid, Johnny buried his mother. We begged him not to, told him it wouldn't be that long. But he went ahead and did it anyway. And he wouldn't tell Vernon where."

"Jesus," the guy whispers.

"Who are you really, pal?"

"Someone who might be able to take care of all this before it comes to your door."

"I'll believe that when I see it."

"Or don't see it. Stay sharp in the meantime."

Then the man hangs up and leaves Dean Jorgensen wondering what the hell he just got Johnny Starnes involved in.

Then he realizes he doesn't care, because Johnny Starnes is a son of a bitch who deserves every bad thing that comes to him.

26

If Johnny Starnes hadn't been on his way to take a piss, he never would have answered the front door. But whoever's standing on the porch now can see him through one of the side panes.

Busted.

Worse, the guy's rigid bearing suggests he's a cop.

When he gets closer, he sees it's not one but two tough-looking guys standing on his front porch like someone's run steel rods through their spines.

Johnny's not used to having cops at his house. Not since he and Bette had that big screaming fight about the pool and the neighbors dialed 911 after he used the kind of language with her that always turns women into screaming harpies. They'd been dating for a few months when he'd told her he was thinking of getting rid of the aboveground pool that took up half the length of his side fence, and she'd started going on and on about how much her kids loved swimming in it. And she got all emotional too. In a way that made it sound like the damn pool was the best thing about their relationship. There'd been a few texts since then, mostly bullshit about scheduling a time to "talk things through," and Johnny kept not having the time because he knew it was over. Like most women, she'd doled out grade-A blow jobs to seal the deal, then turned into a mess of needs and wants and who gives a fuck the minute he started paying for things.

And the truth was, he didn't want to talk about his real reason for getting rid of the pool. How every time he sees it sparkling in the sun, he sees the creepy way his sister's kid used to look at him. A look too smug and knowing for some little kid. Like he was possessed or something. And now that Julia's in the ground and her twisted little spawn's been run out of the state, he doesn't want any more reminders of the few awful years when they all had to live together because his sister decided to get knocked up and broke while planning some bullshit career selling healing crystals or some such nonsense.

Did the neighbors call the cops on him again? He doubts it. He gave them all a piece of his mind after they ratted him out over his fight with Bette. Almost gave that old witch Larissa Pierce a heart attack when he chewed her out on her front porch about minding her own fucking business when it came to other people's relationships. But a man's got to defend his home. Especially from nosy neighbors. And sometimes from cops, apparently.

And why the cops are at his place now, he's got no idea. He's home from work earlier than usual. The log loader was busted when they all showed up to the job site that morning, and after a few hours of the guys trying to fix it, their supervisor had called the day a wash and sent them all home early.

He doesn't get as many nudes from girls on the internet anymore, but he's trying to think of the most recent ones, and which of them might be underage. Then it hits him. *Freak Show's dead,* he thinks, and his heart skips a beat and suddenly he's hurrying toward the front door like a man who thinks he's about to be declared the winner of the Publishers Clearing House Sweepstakes.

But when he opens it and lays eyes on the two men outside, he thinks, *These guys aren't cops. They're way more serious.* Both of them are on the shorter side, but they're stout enough to hold off Mack trucks. One's got a lantern jaw and big unblinking eyes and a serious expression that makes Johnny feel like a pipsqueak, even though he's about twice the guy's height.

"Are you Johnny Starnes?" the older of the two men asks.

314

"Who are you?"

"I'm Jason Phillips and this is my partner, Scott Josephson. Can we come in?"

"No."

"OK. We can talk out here, then. We're investigating a tip about your nephew, Vernon Starnes."

"Is he dead?"

"Is that what you've heard?" the older guy asks. Johnny's already forgotten their names.

"I haven't heard shit about him since he killed my sister."

"What makes you think he killed your sister?" the younger one asks.

"Well, let's see. She drops dead in the kitchen one morning, and what does he do? Dresses her up like it's fucking Mardi Gras instead of calling an ambulance. What do you call that?"

"Mental health issues," the older one says.

"Yeah, OK, pal. We should give him some Paxil and some finger paints and he'll be fine, right? Maybe some therapy too. Who's gonna pay for it? You?"

"Were you and your sister close?" the man asks.

"Not with that freak show around. Where are you guys from again?"

"ATF. Sure we can't come in?"

"How about some badges?"

They each hold one out, and only once he's looking from one to the other does he realize he doesn't have the first damn clue what an ATF badge looks like. Isn't really all that sure what ATF stands for either and figures he'll have to look it up on the internet. But asking will make him look stupid. And they look legit enough and the photos match, so whatever.

"Out here's fine," he says. "So what's this tip?"

"We've heard he's stockpiling weapons in the mountains near here. We figured maybe you could use a warning."

"A warning. You think *I* should be afraid of Vernon? What's he going to do? Shit in the street and make animal sounds?"

"The weapons don't scare you?" the older guy says.

"He'd blow off his own foot before he shot me."

"Not a good relationship between you two, I take it," the younger guy says.

"He ruined my sister's life. She got knocked up by a rando, then out comes a weirdo. My parents didn't want either of them around. It tore the family in half. She couldn't accept it. Maybe if she'd kept her legs closed."

"Did he ever have a diagnosis of any kind?" the old guy asks.

"Freak show. That was the diagnosis."

"From a doctor?" the younger guy asks.

"She never let him see a doctor. Not for his head anyway. She never let him get close to anyone who'd tell him how crazy he was."

"And he was born that way? Was there some kind of injury or accident when he was a kid? Like he hit his head? Sometimes a really high fever when a kid's young will—"

"Vernon was born a freak. Trust me."

But there's gooseflesh on the back of his neck, and he's hearing his sister's high, piercing screams in the backyard that long-ago afternoon. And he's starting to think these men are here about a lot more than some random tip about a weapons stockpile somewhere in the mountains. And he wants them off his damn porch. Now.

"No offense, gentlemen, but I just downloaded some porn, and talking about my nephew doesn't exactly put me in the mood."

"Sure we can't come in first?" the older guy says.

"Yeah, I'm a solo masturbator. Thanks."

"Just to talk a bit more?" the younger guy says.

"People like you never just talk. Come back when you got a warrant."

He closes the door before he can say another word. Does his best to affect a nonchalant walk as he moves down the front hall, because he knows they can still see him. But the question about whether Vernon had an incident when he was a kid was too spot-on. And he could see judgment in their eyes when he told them the truth about what a sloppy slut his sister had been.

He's still got the text thread for all the buddies who helped that night, even though he's long deleted the messages in which they planned it. No way could Vernon know who they were. Most of them had never met the kid or even laid eyes on him before their little op, and Johnny was sure not to say a damn word or even touch him that whole night. Flip Morrison, Buddy Packer, and George Russell did the heavy lifting, and they'd all piled into George's old Suburban so Johnny could drive the freak all the way into Wyoming. They'd had some weird feelings about what they'd done, maybe because they'd expected the kid to put up more of a fight based on the horror stories Johnny had told about him. And yeah, Johnny had embellished some of those stories a bit. But the situation was serious. His sister was dead, and nobody would believe the kid had probably done it even though he'd always been crazy as a shithouse rat. And just as it always went in his family, it had fallen to Johnny to fix it.

He taps out a text.

> Possible Freak Show sighting. Everyone look sharp.
> Maybe a meet up later.

He wants to tell them to watch out for ATF agents, but that would be the same as saying the guys who just visited know all their names and what they've done. And that'll make it look like he didn't keep the promises he made to the crew when he asked for their help.

He wasn't lying about the porn, but it'll have to wait. Instead, he goes up and takes the shotgun out of its case in his bedroom closet, loads it, then brings it down to the closet on the first floor. Just to be safe. He's still sure Vernon's no more able to fire a gun than he is to win a Scrabble game. But if he tries and gives Johnny a reason to pop him one once and for all, so much the better.

———

"Jesus Christ," Dave tells Randy. "I'd call him a piece of shit, but he's way more than just one."

"But you didn't get inside, so no bugs," Randy says, pacing the tech center.

"No. We can wait and try for later, though."

In the background, Zach Fisher says something Randy can barely make out. A second later, Dave translates: "Fisher says he saw a service alley that runs behind the house, so if we stake it out, we're going to have to split up. One in front, one in back."

"You guys think this is where Vernon's headed?" Randy asks.

"Your guess is as good as mine, but our cover story notwithstanding, he's got a new weapon at his disposal and he's coming down off that mountain with a helluva sense of purpose. I mean, if you had something like bloom, wouldn't you use it to settle old scores?"

"I do have it. We all do. And that's not how we use it."

"OK. Well, then, pretend you're a guy who's been shit on most of his life, cast out by his own family. Maybe run out of town by his uncle, which is what my money's on, to be frank. Oh, and to top it off, that same uncle won't tell you where he buried your mother."

Zach says something else that makes Dave pause.

Dave says, "Zach says the guy turned white when we asked if anything might have happened in Vernon's childhood that messed with his head. I'm ninety percent sure he's going to show up here. I mean, Jesus Christ. Five minutes with the guy and *I* wanted to kill him."

"So no chance our pal Johnny's going to help us set a trap?" Randy asks.

"We could force his compliance. But we would have to force it, I guarantee you."

"No hostages."

"Yeah, you've already got too many, I hear."

"They're not hostages."

"Just your eyes and ears, it sounds like."

"That's you now. Stay on the house. Drive time from the Long Tooth Trailhead to your location's about an hour. If he doesn't show up in two hours, we'll reassess."

"Two hours from now? It'll still be light out."

"And if he waits until after dark, he'll be lit up like a blue torch and lose the element of surprise."

"You think he's smart enough to think that through?"

"He attacked the trailhead in broad daylight, didn't he?" Randy asks.

"True," Dave says. "And our orders if he shows up?"

"If he's not in the firing window, shoot on sight, get Poe's bloom, then bring me Starnes's body."

"And if he is?"

"Hold your fire. Prioritize separating him from the bloom if you can and getting it the hell out of there."

"And what about his last thirty minutes of glory?" Dave asks.

"He gets to do whatever he wants, and then he has to be himself again and deal with the consequences. But we'll have done our job."

Ben's comment about setting a maximum allowable body count for this operation comes back to him. He hasn't done it yet. Maybe he won't have to.

"All right, then. Over and out."

Dave hangs up before Randy can say the same.

Thomas and Rupert are at their stations, monitoring news and social media feeds on their laptops. When Randy looks up, he sees they're both looking back at him, expressions grim.

"Oh Jesus. What?"

———

"Nobody wants anything to drink?" Ben asks.

They're sitting in the living room because it feels like a change of pace. No way was Claire going to allow herself to be held prisoner in a fluffy pink bedroom where she saw a baby's life hang in the balance fifty years before.

Margot's sitting next to Claire on the floral-print sofa; Abram's across from them in one of the wing chairs. Ben and Sean are both hovering in different doorways, occasionally making attempts at chit-chat that land like sheets of plywood on bare floor.

"Is this her art?" Margot asks.

It takes Ben a second to realize she's talking about the framed oil paintings all over the walls. Landscape scenes of the mountain west. Some of them look old, valuable.

"Agatha didn't paint any of it, but she bought it all," Ben says. "She got rid of some of the more problematic indigenous stuff after I started working here."

"You'd think having Nazis for parents might have opened her eyes to that kinda stuff sooner," Abram grumbles.

Ben looks to the floor quickly, but Claire can tell he's trying not to laugh.

Claire breaks the silence. "I know you probably don't want us asking a lot of questions, but what's the plan when you catch up with this guy? Can someone else inhale Poe's bloom at the same time?

Would that diminish the man's power or at least ensure he was evenly matched?"

"Neither," Ben says. "The circuit closes once it's made."

"Meaning?"

"Meaning the power can't spread to a second or third person once the first person huffs it. We're dealing with a single consciousness here, and it can only enter one memory deck at a time."

"OK. What about the dead animals you have here?" Margot asks. "Can you use those to give yourself similar abilities to what he'll have?"

"Shifted animals, you mean. No, you can't inhale their ghost cells. It's got to be a species-to-species match. They won't even go up your nose."

"Can anything block this guy after he's inhaled?" Margot asks.

"Range. That's the only advantage we can use."

"You mean if you separate the guy from Poe's bloom, the power fades?" she asks.

"No, unfortunately. Not when he's in the firing window."

Margot furrows her brow. "Firing window?"

"What happens after an inhale, basically. For the thirty minutes when he'll have telekinesis. What I mean is, he can't manipulate objects if they're not within about three hundred feet of him and within sight."

"That's practically a football field," Abram mutters. "Christ."

"He could do anything he wants to anything within three hundred feet of him?" Claire asks.

"Not anything," Ben says. "He can move things without regard for weight. He can break things that have incredible mass. Up to a certain point. He can speed things to about seventy miles an hour. But beyond that, limitations start to set in. He can't just start a fire; he has to visualize the friction required to start one, and there have to be raw materials for that. And there're other limitations."

"What kind?" Margot asks.

"In a nutshell, he can't make things grow," Ben answers. "And it's difficult to cause substances to fuse or repair unless you've got a sophisticated understanding of the underlying processes required. The substance is designed to dismantle, to uncouple. To separate. And that's what someone who's inhaled it can do. Bloom is death, essentially."

Claire says, "So it can't make things grow or get bigger?"

"We've not been sitting on the solution to world hunger, no," Ben says.

"There's got to be something that can disable him," Claire says. "Something besides range. And a clock."

"There isn't. Trust me."

"Actually, there is," Claire says, "and it's here."

It gets so quiet, Claire can hear the appliances ticking in the kitchen nearby and the gentle howl of a strong wind pushing through the cracks under the windows. She's missed Randy's approach, maybe because he kept his footsteps quiet on purpose. But Ben's just moved out of his way, and now Randy's glaring at Claire from the doorway to the dining room. No doubt he heard what she'd just proposed.

"Agatha Caldwell is not a weapon," Randy says. "A bloom battle, or whatever it is you're suggesting, is not going to work. And it's not needed. Looks like we might have a lock on this guy's next location. Team's in place. I'm optimistic. Also, good news. It looks like the little girl from the trailhead is going to be OK. Just wanted you guys to know."

Claire feels more relief than she wants to, given Randy's rebuff. And Randy's smile looks uncomfortably stiff.

"What about everybody else from the trailhead?" Abram asks.

Randy hesitates long enough to let them know the answer's not good.

"Two of them didn't make it," he finally says.

Claire feels the now-familiar tug in her arm, brings her pen to the notepad.

tunnel open.

They're all staring at Randy now. His last order was for Poe not to cross over without permission.

"He has a gun," Claire says quickly.

There's a rush of needlelike pain up her arm. Poe, it's clear, thinks this is a betrayal and wants to give her a piece of his mind over it.

"Who has a gun? Vernon?" Randy asks.

"Poe. He imagined one into being. Agatha told him he could."

"A gun's not going to work over there."

In the silence that follows, Randy seems to realize his mistake.

"Vernon?" Margot finally asks. "Is that this guy's name?"

"How long have you known his name?" Abram asks, anger rising.

"For five minutes. Relax. My point is, I don't want Poe crossing over if he's going to try to mess with the vault doors."

"Yeah, well, it sounds like *Vernon* is doing just fine killing people all on his own," Abram says.

"If he's going to cross over, I need him to promise me first. No messing with the vault," Randy says.

Claire's hand is practically on fire from Poe's transmission, and as soon as she puts pen to paper, a mad scrawl starts—godammitwhydidutellhimIwasjust

KNOCK IT OFF.

It's the first time she's managed to interrupt him, and given her brother's still a breathless nonstop talker even in his shifted form, she figures this skill will come in handy.

Do you agree to Randy's terms?

Silence. More silence.
"The clock is ticking," Randy says, "obviously."

fine ill just look and come back.

"All right, then," Randy says with a sigh.

———

The longer Vernon works, the more quickly he's able to peel the long strips of paint off the van's shell without lifting a finger. Once removed, the paint flakes, then flutters to the dirt at his feet like ashes. He stands a few feet away, hands resting at his sides. All that's required of him is his concentration and his focus and his ability to see the task to its completion. Soon he's lost himself in the meditative nature of the work, and by the time he's exposed the van's raw metal shell, he feels a sense of pleasant satisfaction. But he's still lit up like heaven, so he'll have to wait until the power fades before hitting the road again. What was the point of installing the divider between the passenger seats and the van's cargo bay if he's going to throw off a traveling light show behind the wheel?

The trouble he caused at the trailhead will have people looking for the van, he's sure, so he crushes all the electronics inside that might give off a trace, tugs the license plate off without lifting a finger.

He heads deeper into the woods.

It's time to practice.

At first, he sends his will into the earth until he feels a clicking sensation inside his chest that makes him feel as if he's locked in on something. He imagines a ball of dirt rising into the air, and it does. It's much bigger than he expected. It crumbles as it floats, leaving behind a healthy-size crater. When he deposits it off to one side, just like a gravedigger might, he's so excited he finds himself bouncing at the knees.

Several minutes later, he's dug a hole at least seven feet deep, all without moving a step. Which he figures is exactly how far down he'll have to go when he finally gets to his destination.

The only thing that stops him is the sudden fading of his power that tells him it's time to hit the road.

———

"Burying?" Randy finally asks once they've read back through all of Poe's descriptions. "He's practicing burying something?"

no, Poe answers, not burying digging up.

Claire's surprised to see Randy's eyes light up. But when he catches her studying him, he doesn't look ashamed.

"That's good," he says. "That means we're on the right track. Ben, tell Rupert and Thomas to come in. Let's move everyone back into the dining room. Let's get ready to roll."

———

Vernon hasn't been to Leadville since they let him out of jail and he showed up at Uncle Johnny's house, banging on the front door and demanding to know where the man buried his mother. Uncle Johnny didn't answer that day or any other.

He'll have no choice but to answer now.

The mountains here are farther from the edges of town than they are in Spurlock, where the whole place feels cradled in pine-shrouded folds. Leadville's flatter, more exposed. It's a name that's always made his stomach feel cold, brought the memory of a sharp and terrible pain to both his temples even though he hasn't felt it since he was little.

A few drivers have checked out the van's exposed, metal exterior, but no one seems to have glimpsed his incredible cargo, so the plywood he's put over the rear windows must be working just fine, along with the divider between him and the back. The glow of his mother's gift is sufficiently contained.

No one seems to be following him either.

All Vernon's life, Uncle Johnny's lived in the same house, just a few blocks from what they call the historic downtown. Vernon likes the words *historic downtown* because his mother used to say them with something that sounded like satisfaction in her tone. She worked at a gift shop there when Vernon was a boy and they were living with Uncle Johnny because money was tight. Leadville is where she got the idea to get into what she called "the stones business." Some of his happiest memories are of waiting for her to walk home from work each day. When she rounded the corner onto their street and saw him running toward her, she'd get a big smile on her face and throw her arms out big and wide.

Johnny's house is a canary-yellow split-level with a sloping roof, a short set of stone front steps, and a big, sloping cement driveway where Johnny parks his battered old Land Cruiser. The alley behind the house is clear of other cars. And that's good. Because that's where he's going to park.

The back gate's over six feet high and solid wood like the rest of the fence, with a shiny lock that looks designed to keep out more than Vernon.

It's almost dusk, but the sky's still clear and a deep blue. A big evergreen sprouts from the dirt curb, sending its branches over Johnny's backyard. Vernon remembers playing in the shade when he was a little boy, while Johnny occasionally studied him from the porch as if he thought Vernon might be the source of a bad smell.

He's not prepared for what he sees next. Johnny should have gotten rid of the thing by now. It was proof he did a bad thing that day. But Vernon still got hurt, had ended up in the hospital afterward. Vernon assumed his uncle wouldn't want the aboveground pool around to remind him of all the screaming and his mother's accusations and the ambulance and the neighbors watching from their driveways. But it's still there, winds rippling its green leaf-covered surface.

The windshield in front of Vernon cracks. He's thrown backward against the seat with so much force he thinks an invisible hand is pressing against his chest. There's no hand. Just broken glass all over his lap. And blood, red and hot and pumping down one side of his chest.

Shot, he thinks. *Someone shot me.*

27

"Got him," Zach whispers.

Randy gives a thumbs-up to the assembly in the dining room, tries not to beam with pride.

Through his earbuds, both of Zach's shots sounded clean and smooth, thanks to the silencer.

In one corner of the room, Thomas bows his head, closes his eyes, and exhales. But from her seat at the head of the table, Claire Huntley's watching him like a hawk, waiting, it seems, for any tic in his expression that might suggest things have gone off the rails.

"Looks like a head shot, but I'm not sure. Going in for another just to be safe."

"Roger that," Randy says.

———

The sounds Vernon is making should only be made by little boys and babies, and as his mother would often remind him, Vernon is neither. But it feels like his left shoulder has been ripped off his body. The pain's so bad he can't move. He heard two muffled shots but felt only one terrible jerk backward. Did they hit in the same place?

Then he sees it—sees his mother's gift tumbling through the air in front of him. The second bullet went somewhere else entirely. Through the plywood divider behind him.

———

"I'm coming around the back," Dave says into Randy's ear.

"Wait till I confirm the kill, please," Zach responds.

"Those shots were quiet, but they weren't silent," Dave says. "We're gonna have company if we don't evac soon."

"Stay back, Dave," Randy says. "Wait till Zach gives the word."

"Fine, but—"

"Bridge!" a new voice screams, and it takes Randy a shocked second to realize it's Claire. Then he sees the new message from her brother. bridgeisopen.

"Clear out!" Randy screams. "He's in the firing window. Clear out—"

Before he can finish the sentence, he hears a sound that rattles his bones from miles away. It's the sound of something heavy and substantial slamming into a metal surface. And it's followed by miserable wheezes that remind him of that viral video of the newscaster falling off the platform where she was crushing grapes with her feet, the one everyone thought was so damn funny because she was wheezing like a cartoon, folks who'd probably never suffered having the wind and the sense being knocked out of them in the same instant. That's what he's hearing now, and it's coming from Zach Fisher.

Again and again and again.

"Motherfuck!" Dave roars in his ear. "Mother*fuck*, he's slamming Zach up against the front of the van. Like a fucking doll, man. Jesus. *Jesus!*"

"Get out of there, Dave. Get out of there now!"

———

So easy with people, Vernon thinks again. He's still in the driver's seat, hasn't even taken his seat belt off, and he's beating the bad man with the gun to a bloody pulp against the van's hood.

At first he did it just to knock the gun out of the bad man's hand, but now he's doing it because it makes him happy. Because this is the man who shot him, and it feels good to watch him hurt like Vernon was just hurting. He moves like someone's holding him by the back of his neck and bashing his head over and over again.

The blood's stopped pumping from Vernon's shoulder. The explosive pain of the gunshot was washed away by his first inhale of his mother's gift. But it feels as if the joy he gets from hurting the bad man is also stopping the blood and helping the pain go away. So he does it some more.

Then he hears two more shots, and the van lurches. He looks around, realizes the van's lurch came from the very back. The tires. Someone shot the tires. He looks in the rearview mirror and sees a flash of pumping legs as the guy tries to run away.

If I can see him, I can stop him, Vernon thinks.

"Randy?"

Ben's the only one with the courage to speak.

In Randy's ear, Dave grunts like he's been kicked in the stomach; then there's a terrible scraping punctuated by little crunches of broken glass, and he realizes one of the strongest men he knows is being dragged across the pavement against his will.

When the second shooter's lying next to the van's driver's side door, Vernon pops him up and off the ground, forces his back against the wooden fence. The man's hands are gnarled and bloody from where he grabbed the pavement along the way.

"Are you his friend?" Vernon asks the man.

The man tries to speak and coughs instead, spitting up blood. At first, Vernon thinks the guy was going to spit it on him, and maybe he wanted to but he doesn't have the energy.

"You don't know what you're messing with, kid," the man growls.

It's a strange thing for the man to say. It says he knows what's in the van. And that's not possible because it's a gift from his mom, and if she'd sent these men, they wouldn't have tried to hurt him.

"Was he your friend? The man who shot me?"

The man's eyes widen as he studies Vernon through the window. "Oh, look at that. What's that—a fucking inch from your heart? He really was our best shot. God bless 'em. You can beat him to death, but you can't beat that bullet, son."

"I don't feel anything."

"Soon as that wears off you're going to bleed out like a stuck pig."

"I'm not a pig!"

But Vernon's hearing the echo of the man's words. *Wears off.* How does he know it wears off? How does he know anything about why Vernon's glowing or what he can do?

"You're playing with something you don't understand."

"I understand!" Vernon whines. "It's for me. It's mine. It's from my mom!"

"Your mom doesn't have shit to do with any of this."

"You need to be nicer to me."

"I'd tell you to go to hell, but you'll be there in thirty minutes."

The man's brow furrows; then his lips go kissy-faced. Ropes of blood spit from between them, and that's when Vernon realizes he crushed the front of the man's skull. He didn't mean to, but he's glad the man's dead because he wasn't a nice person.

———

> Dude WTF. Can't just send a text like that w no info!!

Johnny Starnes is about to respond to the message from Buddy Packer when he hears the sounds of fighting coming from the alley behind his house, checks the Ring Cam on his back porch, and sees the van's roof. It barely crests the top of his fence, and it's not moving. He's pretty sure he heard something else too, something higher and sharper, but not quite loud enough to be gunshots.

The van changes shape in back, and he realizes someone, someone he can't see because they're below the top of the fence, has just opened the cargo doors, and the van emits a strange blue light. If it's Vernon, maybe he's fallen in with some weirdo potheads who are driving around in their own magical mystery bus.

Johnny turns off the motion detection on his Ring Cam so nothing that follows will be recorded; then he walks out onto the back porch, shotgun raised. When the gate to his backyard swings open, he's relieved. He'll finally have cause to blow a hole in his nephew the minute he steps through.

Two bodies come floating through the gate instead, and it takes a couple of seconds of them coming toward him across the yard for Johnny to realize they're not walking. Their dangling feet don't touch the grass. They're like puppets with invisible strings, their bloodied heads lolling on their necks. It's the ATF agents from earlier that day. The younger one's face is pure hamburger. The older one looks like a giant hand grabbed the front of his skull and pressed hard enough to cave in his brow. They part like a curtain and there's Freak Show, glowing like he's been doused in some kind of cartoon radiation, the whites of his eyes bright blue.

The bodies float higher and higher before they splash one after the other into the pool.

Decimate

The gate slams shut behind Vernon.

"Uh-oh," Vernon says. "Uncle Johnny had an accident."

That's when Johnny Starnes realizes he's pissed down one leg.

The hands gripping his shotgun are so sweat slick he's in danger of losing his hold on the thing. He's making sounds like the one that came from his old heat pump before it died.

"Back the fuck up!" he shouts. "Whatever you're doing, back the fuck up, kid!"

Vernon keeps coming. When Johnny raises the shotgun, it jerks forward and out of his hands. Did his sweaty palms do him in? No. The shotgun's floating in the air in front of him just like the bodies did. Now it's turning around.

Once the gun's pointed at his chest, Vernon says, "Don't run now," in that strange singsong way that makes it sound like he's imitating people he saw in TV commercials.

Johnny backs up, terror moving his muscles on its own. His back hits the edge of the door he left open, and he jumps, falls to his ass. The shotgun rises into the air, angling down.

Vernon mounts the back steps slowly. There's a damn hole in his chest, right above his heart. It should be bloody, but the blue light coursing through him rings it with sparkles that make the wound look like rock sugar.

And then Johnny sees something trailing in the air just behind Vernon, almost like a floating tail. Is it a goddamn airplane seat?

They drugged him. Those fucking ATF agents drugged him. Put something on those badges that he absorbed into his skin, and now he's gone full LSD or something, and this is all some twisted government plot.

"Where is my mother?" Vernon asks.

"Dead."

"Where did you bury her?"

333

"Evervale Cemetery, with our mom and dad."

"No, you didn't. I went there after you wouldn't tell me where, and she's not there. I went to a bunch of cemeteries after they let me out of jail, Uncle Johnny. A whole bunch. And she wasn't in any of them. So tell me where you buried her or I'm going to get really angry, Uncle Johnny."

Johnny's lips are wet. Is he bleeding? No, it's tears spitting from him as involuntarily as his piss did.

"Do you not want to tell me because the answer's bad, Uncle Johnny?"

"She's gone, kid. She's just gone. Let it go. Christ, please."

"She's not gone, though, see. She sent me this gift." The kid spreads his arms out like Jesus trying to embrace his flock. "And she wants me to do something with it, but I need her, and I need the stones I used to save her."

"They didn't save her!"

"But they will now! Now that I have *this*!"

"No," Johnny wails. "No, no, kid. You don't see things right. There's no gift. The stones aren't anything. You've never seen things right!"

"Look at me now and tell me what you see," Vernon whispers. "Maybe *you* don't see things right and that's why you just peed. It's blue, see? It's blue just like her favorite stones. Because it's from her. It came down out of the sky and it found me in the woods. 'Cause it's from her." When he sees the disbelief on Johnny's face, the kid grits his teeth and leans in. *"It's from her!"*

There's desperation in his voice, a desperation to believe this crazy story. *This is some kind of nuclear shit,* Johnny thinks, *some kind of radiation. Maybe connected to that big plane crash.* Julia did not send any fucking gift down from heaven for her freak kid. But if he rips the kid's delusion away, he'll die right here on his back porch.

And if you don't, you'll die five minutes from now, maybe inside, he thinks. He seizes with laughter that turns into a wet sob.

"You don't have to believe me, Uncle Johnny. You just have to give me what I want."

"I'm sorry." It sounds like someone else is speaking, some voice that's been waiting for this moment all his life, some voice that can only draw its breath from the small space inside the last seconds of a man's life. "I fucked up your head when you were little, and I'm sorry. I thought I would help you. I thought I would teach you things. How to toughen up. Be a little man. I . . ."

The blue filling Vernon's eyes makes them impossible to read. But Vernon's eyes have always seemed strange. Like he's either looking through you or not seeing you at all. And Johnny's suddenly terrified that whatever's happened to the kid hasn't changed him on the inside, it's just made him more of what he's always been.

"What did you do to my mother, Uncle Johnny?"

No lie will save him now, he realizes. Nothing will save him.

"I cremated her."

"Cremated," Vernon says slowly. "Burned. You burned her. Where are the ashes?"

"The mountains."

"Where in the mountains?"

"I don't remember."

And it's sort of true, because the real answer is he pulled over and dumped them off the side of the road so he could be done with her. Done with them both—she and her fucked-up kid who'd jacked up their family, turned his sister's slutty shame into a constant lurking weirdness on the edges of their lives.

"Vernon, we can—"

He sees the edge of the aboveground pool flying toward him suddenly. Realizes he's actually flying toward it. And that's fitting, he thinks, then feels blinding, thundering pain. Water crashes down on him and roars past him in the same instant, and right before he dies he realizes his entire body has speared the side of the pool headfirst.

————

"What's happening?" Claire asks for the third time.

On their orders, Poe has stayed on his side of the tunnel.

But Randy's ignoring her now. He's walked into the adjacent living room, back to them, one hand pressed to the side of his head as if he's fighting a migraine.

"Randy!"

She's sprung to her feet without planning to. Her shout turns every head in the dining room. But Randy's taking his time, as if he's moving through molasses. Finally he's facing her, but there's no anger or offense in his expression. He looks numb.

"We lost them," he says. "We lost our guys."

No one speaks. Randy turns, heads for the front door. In his wake, the men look stunned. This, most of all, sends Claire sinking back into her chair. Morbidly reminds her of the piece of advice Leonard, her old mentor at Arcadia Heights, used to give kids who were nervous flyers. *Look to the flight attendants and if they're not nervous, you're fine.*

Here, the flight attendants look devastated.

She feels tugging on her arm, returns to the notepad.

going over.

She wants to tell him to stop.

this isn't working going over.

Gun won't work, she writes back.

i know but we need to see men are dead.

How much time on the clock?

Poe doesn't answer, which could mean he's already crossing the bridge and can't hear her.

28

Ashes. His mother is ashes somewhere in the mountains.

His mountain? Did he walk through a cloud of her without realizing it? Did birds eat her? Did rain wash her away?

Ashes like the flaking paint he tore off the van.

Ashes like the ones that would drift onto Spurlock's streets whenever there was a wildfire in the mountains nearby.

His mother and the stones are ashes.

The smile she'd greet him with when he was a little boy, ashes.

And this means those things were never much to begin with, and so maybe it's dumb to be sad over them now. Vernon's memory of those things is not something he can wrap his arms around, but that also means it can never be burned. Does this mean it's worth less or more than his mother's body? He doesn't know. Sometimes he feels confused because it feels like he's thinking of everything at once.

And maybe he thought the gift from the sky was from his mother because he never saw things in the right way. But Uncle Johnny is dead now, and that feels right.

He was sure he'd draw her up out of the ground, that the stones, charged full of her gift, would bring her back to life and they would be together again, even if they had to live deep in the woods. And he would teach her how to steal so they could live in the woods the way she taught him to hunt and dress animals and find stones.

He can't bring back ashes, can he? It doesn't matter, because there's no finding them now. They've been blown all over the mountains. Eaten by animals and soil.

But taking care of himself is something different. Taking care of himself means keeping the chair close, remembering what the man whose skull he crushed said. When the gift wears off next time, he'll start to bleed again and he'll have to suck in real quick. He'll have to take care of himself.

Inside the house, the lights are still on and the TV is muted and playing some kind of sports game, and there's a chiming sound coming from the kitchen counter next to a stack of mail. It's a phone. His uncle's phone. When he picks it up, he sees alerts for seven text messages, but he can't unlock the screen.

Phone in hand, he walks to the pool. His uncle's body is soaked, his head vanished through the hole in the side. Vernon dries off one of Johnny's limp hands, presses his thumb to the little button at the bottom of the phone. Sure enough, it works just like his mother's used to, and now he can read the messages.

> Stop speaking in f-ing code and tell us what's up. We can always delete this.

> Johnny, srsly, dude, wut???

> I've got the kids tonight but shuld we meet?

> Freak Show is never coming back to Colorado. He was practically pissing himself by the time we dropped him in Wyoming.

His uncle.

His uncle was one of the hooded men, and these are the other hooded men. But they're listed by initials, and he doesn't know any of his uncle's friends so he can't figure out their names.

He remembers it all clearly. They kicked in the back door; then, once he'd stuffed one of his mother's backpacks full of clothes and things, they blindfolded him, stuffed something that smelled like socks in his mouth, and put tape over it and around his wrists. The next thing he knew he was in the back of a car, and they drove and drove with old-timey music turned up real loud on the radio. Eventually, they walked him out into frigid wind, and suddenly he was sitting on a cold metal bench. There was a tug at his wrists, then a ripping sound.

When he realized he could take the blindfold off, he saw the taillights of a big SUV driving away. There were no mountains for miles, none that he could see at night anyway. Just eighteen-wheelers roaring past, pulling in and out of the nearby service station that sat at the spot where several interstates met in a spiderweb of lanes and strobing headlights. It felt like Colorado, the state he'd always called home, had somehow coughed him up and dropped him on another planet, a cold and empty one.

He knew the hooded men wanted him to keep going like the cars were going. There was money in the bag. Not money from the house because there hadn't been any, but money they'd put there. And a note that said, COME BACK TO SPURLOCK AND YOU WILL DIE HERE. So he didn't go back to Spurlock. Instead, he went to the mountains he'd hiked with his mother for years as she searched for stones. Found the abandoned cabin they'd once passed, the one she'd told him not to go near because scary people might live inside. And she'd said the word *scary* with emphasis, the way she always said words she thought he didn't understand as well as he should.

But he knew deep down he was one of the scary people, so maybe it was the right place for him.

And his uncle did all of that, his uncle and these men he was texting with before he told Vernon the terrible truth.

Vernon brings one glowing finger to the screen.

> Bad things are happening. No one is safe. Meet me at Big Timber Brewpub in Spurlock in 2 hours please.

He has never been inside Big Timber Brewpub, but he knows the outside well, and his mother used to say it was the type of place his Uncle Johnny would like. She didn't mean it as a compliment. The men start texting back, some with complaints but most of them agreeing, so Vernon feels good. Because Vernon is taking care of himself like his mother would have wanted him to.

———

"Randy?"

Rupert sounds as if he's miles away and at the bottom of a canyon. The icy grass crunching under Randy's boots sounds louder. In the barn, he enters the code on the keypad to the first cellar door; then he's descending the steps, two pairs of footsteps behind him. If he's making a hurried walk to see Agatha, he's long stopped bothering with the glasses, just throws one arm over his eyes until he reaches the next keypad.

"Randy, man. Talk to me." Rupert again, closer now. Less concerned, it seems, for their slain teammates than for Randy's sanity.

Randy stops at the sight of Agatha's sinuous, predictable dance. He wants to go to her, breathe her in, come to on his memory deck, cradled in her arms. No time to ask her permission either. It's too late for a lot of things; that's why there's only one option left. His stomach had lurched when Claire suggested it. Now it's all he's got. All they've got.

"Load her into the transport container," he says.

Tombstone silence behind him. He turns. It's not just Rupert who's followed him but Thomas as well, and they're both staring at him like a drunk who just demanded his car keys.

"He's shot," Randy says. "The kid's shot right above the heart. He's got no choice but to stay inside the firing window. That means hell on earth for anyone who crosses his path."

"Or he bleeds out if he doesn't inhale in time."

"That's not a good enough reason to sit on our asses," Randy says. "Load her into the container, then load her into the Kodiak." Thinking through the logistics, as always, is a comfort. Sometimes a deceptive one, but at least it focuses him. Their turboprop is technically an off-airport bush plane, but they've never put it through its paces. This sure as hell will. The narrow wingspan, the landing gear that can take a hell of a beating—they can land the damn thing in the middle of a town if they want to. If they wait any longer, that's just what they might have to do.

"A *bloom battle*," Thomas says, "like Claire said. That's seriously what you're proposing? You're going to fly Agatha in and use her like a weapon against Vernon Starnes."

"Call it whatever you want. Vernon Starnes just took out two of our best men. We don't have time to see what he does next. We're going to meet him on the field with something bigger than he is. Get her loaded. Now!"

He starts for the door.

"Where are you going?" Thomas asks.

"To do something I really don't want to fucking do," Randy growls.

"What?" Rupert asks.

"Tell Claire she was right."

He's just reached the barn's floor when he almost runs smack into Ben.

"Poe went over," he says. "Vernon is heading to Spurlock for sure. He unlocked his uncle's phone, found texts about some kind of meetup with the guys who ran him out of town. He pretended to be Johnny, told the guys to meet him at a place called Big Timber Brewpub. Right down from Pelton's Ice Cream."

"Did the bridge close?"

"And then reopened five seconds later. It's like he's vaping the shit now."

"He has to, he's been hurt bad. Vehicle? Dave shot out the van's tires."

"His uncle's Land Cruiser. Poe's not a car expert, but he said it was big and boxy and dark blue and scuffed to shit. The dimensions sound like nineteen eighties to me."

"I'm warning the sheriff in Spurlock. Go get with Thomas and Rupert. They'll tell you the plan. I need you and Rupert to fly to Spurlock with me. Thomas needs to stay here and make sure Claire's OK."

Ben just nods, but he's clearly got a swirl of thoughts about everything Randy just said, and he's struggling to keep quiet.

When Randy heads for the barn doors, he sees Abram Huntley standing there. The look on the man's face is so unfamiliar it stops Randy cold: sympathy. Did Ben let him walk over with him? A little loosey-goosey from a security perspective, but given how screwed things are right now, does it even matter?

"I'm going to fix this," Randy says.

But he sounds pathetic, and Abram nods like he might toward a child.

Then Randy starts for the tech center and the number for Sheriff Jorgensen's station.

I think they're coming up with a new plan, Claire writes.

hope its better.

She's tempted to hide the notepad from everyone else in the room, but there's barely anyone in the dining room now. Margot's still sitting next to her, and Sean, the stylishly dressed one, fills the doorway nearby, eyes on the floor and looking pale, as if the sudden deaths of his teammates have him contemplating his own mortality for the first time.

There are footsteps coming from the adjacent kitchen. Her father's got a strange spring to his step, looks more thoughtful and alert than he has since they all first gathered in this room.

Her hand moves.

Tunnel. Why is he breathing in so fast again should I go back?

"He's been shot," Abram says softly behind her. She feels his hands on her shoulders. "The bloom is stopping the bleeding, but if he stops, he might bleed out."

maybe if i go over there and distract him then he wont breathe in in time and hell bleed to death.

THEN YOU'LL BE STUCK OVER THERE WHEN THE BRIDGE CLOSES. NO, POE. STAY PUT UNTIL WE KNOW MORE.

"There's a new plan." Abram sounds almost relaxed. He's gently gathering her hair in both hands. "For what it's worth, darling, long or short, I've always loved your hair." Startled, Claire turns, and he kisses her gently on the forehead. Then he's backing up, as if he doesn't want to force a tender moment on her. "You want something to drink?"

"I'm fine now. Thanks, Dad."

Thanks, Dad. When was the last time she said those words?

Her hand starts moving again. Her dad withdraws, pats her on the back before he heads into the kitchen. "Going upstairs. Going to use the restroom."

my kingdom for the keys to this guys vault, Poe says.

It's not just about finding the key. It's about what happens once we open the door.

what happens

I don't know I was just the passenger when Agatha did it to me.

Silence, her hand stays still.

one more bad plan and Im going to find out, he writes back.

———

The dispatcher at the Spurlock Sheriff's Station put Randy right through to Jorgensen, which says the man's canceled his sick day and come into work, possibly thanks to Randy's earlier call. Good.

"Well, if it isn't my—"

"Evacuate your town. You've got a dam in your valley just south of you. Activate whatever warning system you got and get everybody out of town and headed north."

"Are you kidding—"

"I am not, sir. I am not kidding you. Vernon Starnes is headed your way, and he's got a weapon that could level your town in minutes.

He just killed his uncle and two of my men. He's driving Johnny Starnes's dark blue Land Cruiser. It's scuffed to shit, early-eighties model, it sounds like."

"A bomb? You're saying Vernon's got a—"

"Vernon found out about a meeting his uncle was planning at Big Timber Brewpub with the guys who helped him drive Vernon out of town. It's scheduled for less than two hours from now."

There's a stunned silence on the other end. Randy would prefer silence to argument. Silence means processing, absorbing.

"So much for taking care of all of this before it got to my door, huh, friend?"

"Here's the most important thing."

"These other things sound pretty fucking important!"

"Nobody shoots him unless he's a good distance from his vehicle and looks normal."

"Normal?"

Randy hesitates. One step of explanation that takes him into woo-woo land and the man on the other end might dismiss him, and every resident of Spurlock might pay the price.

"The weapon Vernon's carrying exposes him to something that alters his appearance. It'll make him look blue. If you see blue, don't shoot. You could blow up everything within several blocks."

"Radiation? Is that kid bringing *radiation* to my town?"

"This is worse."

"Biological? Some kind of gas? What are you talking about?"

"That's about right."

"Who are you, man?"

"You're going to meet me soon enough. I'm on my way. I made you a promise and I broke it, Sheriff, and I'm sorry, so I'm flying there now to clean this up best I can. But if you ignore me, your town's going to pay the price."

"It would help if I knew who you were."

"No, it wouldn't. Do what I say or a lot of people are going to die."
Randy hangs up.

Ben's in the doorway behind him. He's pulled his fleece on and looks ready to travel.

"Loaded up?" Randy asks.

"Yeah, just getting gassed up now."

"I'm going to tell Claire she won."

"Only one guy's winning right now," Ben says.

"You know what I mean."

Ben matches him almost step for step as they cross the lawn. When they enter the dining room, Sean stands at sudden attention in a way that makes it clear he's having trouble staying focused.

"Where's your dad?" Randy says to Claire.

"Upstairs, using the bathroom."

"We're going to go with your plan," Randy says.

Margot says, "You want them to open this guy's vault?"

"*No.* Agatha and I are going to meet this guy. Head-to-head, if you will. Give him a taste of his own medicine. Plane's loaded up. I'd wait around to say goodbye to your dad, but we should be back soon."

Both women are shocked silent. He figures he should consider that a victory. For now.

"Good luck, sir," Margot finally says.

So he's finally earned some small measure of respect from the woman. He just had to get two of his own men killed to do it. Peachy.

As he and Ben leave the house, Randy knows any words out of his mouth will give flower to doubt, so he stays silent as they pass the barn and walk to the shed where they store the Kodiak. They've already rolled the plane out onto the grassy expanse. It's fat on the underside, like a little baby whale, and with one of the shortest takeoff lengths of any turboprop, the little flat stretch of field behind the barn is all they'll need. The wings cross the top of the fuselage, shading the square windows below from dusk's deepening glow. Through the open side door, Randy sees they've removed the back two rows of forward-facing seats to make room for the container. It's a modified coffin, the plainest one they could find, and even then, they had to sand off little ornaments that suggested death and the afterlife. They'd fashioned their own lid and attached it after arrival to allow for some extra space inside. But they don't need it. The interior only needs to accommodate the desiccated tree stump that tore open Agatha's artery and caused her to bleed out. The only time the bloom's separated from the tree stump is when it went for Catherine, and as soon as she hit the road, it returned to its previous position, like a puppy nestling into its mother's belly. As for the bloom itself, it folds up into almost any tight space like balled-up bedsheets.

The container gives off no suggestion of the power within. He places a hand on it, and the men behind him tense up.

Forgive me, honey, Randy thinks. *I tried everything else first.*

He hears the loud thunk of Rupert jumping up into the pilot's seat up front.

"We should get going, boss." Ben steps up into the cabin, pulls the upper and lower flaps of the side door closed behind him. "Our travel time's about the same as his, and he's got a head start."

The flaps close with a resounding clang, and suddenly the propeller on the nose is cranking to life under Rupert's command. Ben urges Randy forward until he's sitting in the front-facing bucket seat right behind the copilot's chair, which Ben takes.

Then the plane's bouncing forward. When it finally lifts into the darkening sky, like it's rising to kiss the mountain peaks all around, Randy thinks what he's thought so many times during moments of incredible risk.

At least we're doing something.

29

One of the many things Dean Jorgensen loves about Spurlock is how the place really does look like most of the photographs posted on the chamber of commerce's website. Coming downhill on Pine Street from the north always offers the same stunning vista of Saint Thomas Lutheran's tall, slender bell tower, set against a dramatic backdrop of the pine-covered mountain flanks that close in on the edge of the valley just south of town, making the whole place feel cradled in mother nature's palm. Newton Dam hides in one of those canyons, out of sight from downtown: an ever-present, if easily forgotten, threat. The dam's a worry for Dean on most days, but his mystery caller's strange exhortation to use its failure warning system to his advantage has been haunting him ever since he hung up the phone.

As he and his favorite deputy speed to the center of town, the red-brick buildings feel less like a historical postcard from the Old West and more like a potential shooting gallery. Most of them house businesses that found a way to ban Vernon Starnes over the years. Which means they're now potential targets. There's Lucy Lowe's little gift shop, Lucy's Treasures, with its front window full of autumn-themed gift baskets and its hand-painted sign above the front door. Just up the street and on the corner is the Sunny Side Up Grill, which—because Dean apparently has the worst luck of anyone today—is still open for dinner and apparently doing a brisk business even though ski season hasn't started up yet and most of the year they just do breakfast and lunch. But the most direct part of the threat was against Big Timber Brewpub, so that's where he heads now.

From the passenger seat of the cruiser, Miles Zander says, "You sure this guy's not a crank?"

"Leadville PD got five 911 calls about whatever went down at Johnny Starnes's house, and they're on their way there now. What do you think?" He double-parks in front of the saloon's big front windows festooned with neon beer signs. Inside, he sees a packed house. Mostly tourists making the most of off-season discounts. "Stay with the vehicle," he tells Zander.

Inside, Dean gets the usual looks he always gets in uniform. Some nods of respect from the locals, but mostly wary surveys and a few barbed whispers from the tourists. Debbie Corbin is tending bar, flame-red hair tied back in a french braid, her bar-branded T-shirt revealing the matching vine tattoos that travel down her pale, fleshy arms. Wearing her trademark toothy smile, she's delivering four sweating mugs of beer at the same time. Debbie's a good egg who runs a good business and treats her employees right, so she's usually happy to see him in her bar. But at the sight of his expression, her smile drops, and she steams toward him, ignoring a customer trying to wave her down.

"You look sick, Sherriff," she says.

"I am, but that's not why I'm here."

"Oh. OK."

By the elbow, he guides her as far as he can from the nearest table. Normally he wouldn't lay a finger on anyone after admitting to a cold, but today is not a normal day. "I need you to close up, Debbie. Right now. We got a threat."

"A threat?" she gasps. "Against the bar?"

"Against the area."

"The *area*? You mean the town?"

"Don't say anything. But it's Vernon."

The woman's face falls. Her breath whistles through her clenched teeth. He's not aware of any trouble between her and the kid, but as with most folks in Spurlock, the name conjures up a strange blend of fear and guilt, the constant anticipation of a reckoning not yet delivered.

"I need you to close up, Debbie. Seriously. The bar's been mentioned specifically."

"Oh God. It's slow season and I've got a full house for the first time in weeks. Can I at least do a last call?"

Dean shakes his head.

"You're killing me, Sheriff."

"Trying for the opposite today. Close out everybody's tab. Zander and I'll wait outside and keep an eye out."

"I told Julia to do something about that boy. I told her to get him some *real* help." She stalks back to the bar. To his relief, she starts breaking the news to her customers.

That's good. But suddenly Dean has the sense of being watched. In one of the shadowed booths at the very back of the bar, beyond the pool tables, three men sit together, silently, expressions tense. He recognizes Flip Morrison, a little shitkicker with the face scars to prove it, supposedly a former UFC fighter if his frequent boasts to everyone on his logging crew are true. Next to him is Buddy Packer, a bearded giant of a man he arrested last year for getting rough with his latest girlfriend on their walk home from this very bar. He's not sure about the third guy. But like his buddies, he's a big menacing-looking dude, and he's watching Dean like a shoplifter who's just managed to stuff a bunch of prepaid phones down his pants before the clerk spotted him acting funny.

Dean's phone buzzes in his pocket. He thinks it might be Zander calling from the car, but when he steps outside, he sees his pie-faced deputy watching him patiently from the double-parked cruiser, hands on his thighs. Dean takes the call, hears gasping from the other end.

"This is Dean Jorgensen."

"Sheriff . . ."

It's the guy he just spoke to down in Leadville a few minutes ago, the nasally police officer who said he was on his way to Johnny Starnes's place. And apparently he's having trouble breathing.

"This Lyle?"

"Lou," the guy corrects him, but it seems to take all his breath.

"What'd you find, Lou?"

"What is this?" The man's tone is shrill and accusatory. "What the hell is this, Sheriff? I mean, this is just . . . *nuts*. I don't even know what to—"

"OK. Calm down and tell me what you found."

"He's been run through a pool."

"A *what*?"

Like the sheriff's an idiot who's also hard of hearing, the police officer continues. "Johnny Starnes has been *run through* the side wall of his goddamn *swimming pool*. Headfirst! I mean, I can't even see how this happened. It's not physically possible, Sheriff. There's no tire tracks, so he wasn't dragged, but his head's just . . . I mean his head, it just went straight through the side wall! And we got two guys floating in the water. One of their faces is gone, the other's head is all messed up . . . Jesus! What the hell is this?"

"I'll call you back."

When Dean enters the bar again, Debbie looks up from the register. "Now," he tells her.

"I'm hurrying," she whines.

"*Now!*" he barks, but he's already moving past her toward the back, where Flip Morrison, Buddy Packer, and their third wheel are suddenly looking like they want to pay their bill. Flip tries to get to his feet as Dean approaches, but Dean grabs him by one shoulder and forces him back to the booth. The man tenses under his touch like a coiled snake.

"You boys have a meeting with Johnny Starnes?"

"No," Flip says.

"Good, 'cause he's dead. Murdered in his own house. Earlier today."

Buddy Packer sucks in a slow, deep breath that raises his giant chest even as the expression on his face looks lifeless. But the only sounds passing between them are an old Martina McBride song coming from the jukebox. Which is suddenly turned off mid-lyric.

"Yeah, that's what I thought," Dean says. "You boys best get out of town or you might end up like him."

Flip says, "You can't just come in here accusing us of—"

"Oh, shut your hole, jackass. I know exactly what you did, shit for brains! What did you think that kid was, a stain you could wipe out of your clothes?"

Flip flinches and looks to the table.

"A service," Packer finally says in that rumbly voice of his. "We did this town a service, is what we did."

"We'll see about that when tonight's over with, asshole. Vernon's on his way here, and he's loaded for bear."

Dean grabs one of their mugs, flicks his wrist. He wasn't trying to douse them with it, just get them moving. And when they see that the splash of foamy beer he's tossed across the table is threatening to pour down onto their laps, that's exactly what they start doing.

"What?" Zander asks when Dean slides behind the wheel of the cruiser. But Dean doesn't answer, just pulls out into a hard, squealing turn, hearing words like *weapon* and *not physically possible*, and then poor Lou from Leadville PD talking about that crime scene like it's his own mother lying on the ground. "What, Sheriff?"

"We're evacuating Spurlock."

"What? *How?*"

He doesn't answer until they're inside the station. When she sees the urgency in their walk and on their faces, Mercedes Anderson rises off her stool at the dispatch desk and starts toward them. Normally, he enjoys her dressed-down outfits. They make for a relaxed and casual atmosphere. Right now, though, her floral-print dress and hot-pink scarf make him feel like they're all yokel amateurs, unprepared for the nightmare to come. "Sound the alarm for a dam failure."

"We have a dam failure?" she asks breathlessly.

"We need to evacuate. Now. The whole town."

"For a dam failure?"

"Just sound the alarm, Mercedes! Please!"

"Sheriff, I'm not trying to question you, but the siren's supposed to be accompanied by verbal instructions. I mean, normally, we tell people it's just a test. But this doesn't sound like a test. So what do I say?"

"I'll say it over the horn in a second, but just start the siren. Now." He turns to Zander. "Get the plate number for a dark blue Land Cruiser registered to Johnny Starnes, probably a late-eighties model. Then put out an APB on it."

Zander nods, hurries to his desk.

Dean's still standing in place when he hears the sound that always makes spiders crawl up his spine, a sound that reminds him of movies about nuclear war that terrified him as a child. A "whoop," they call it, but their town's siren has a more high-pitched wail to it than upward-traveling tones. The dam nearby holds back one helluva reservoir, and some of Spurlock's residential streets snake into mini canyons that take bites out of the surrounding mountainsides. Sound gets weird in those sections, and as he told the town council when they upfitted the thing a few years back, they needed a real screamer. And they got one. It's screaming now.

He turns. Mercedes is a few feet away again. "Sheriff, we're gonna get inundated with calls. We got to be able to tell them something."

Leadville's south. Vernon Starnes, if he's coming, is coming from the south. The dam's south. His caller from earlier told him to have everyone head north. But if he puts out word of a failure, specifically, there's a chance someone from the county could check in with the monitoring stations at the dam directly and override him before he can do anything about it. And even though it feels like a huge risk, maybe the end of his career if he's wrong, he knows there's only one thing to do.

"We've received a credible and urgent terrorist threat against Newton Dam. Everyone needs to follow the dam-failure evacuation plans and head north as soon as possible."

As if on cue, the phone behind Mercedes's counter lights up.

"I guess I . . ."

"Yeah, go answer that," Dean says.

———

what was that thing dad said

Claire's finally been able to get some food down, even managed a few sips of the tea Sean brought her, when Poe starts to tug on her arm again.

Something about my hair, she answers. How he always liked it, short or long.

cause he made that dick comment when you got off the plane.

Maybe. Love you, but need to eat, maybe less chitchat.

i wouldnt be bugging you if youd let me cross the bridge again.

Every time you go over there, we run the risk of him seeing you and hurting someone to make you go away. Remember his threat?

i think this guy is going to hurt people no matter what we do unleeeeessssss

You're preaching to the choir re: the vault. I figure they'll call soon as they get closer to Colorado so they can see where he is. They'll probably ask you to go over again. But you gave them the texts and a destination and that's plenty for now.

not like Im dying to go over to that hellhole just want to end this.

Claire stares at the page. Does their connection allow her to feel her brother hesitating, reconsidering his words? Or is she projecting her own response onto him? Ending *this*, she thinks, and ending Vernon Starnes's killing spree aren't the same thing. Vernon could bleed to death and still her brother would be trapped in some purgatorial realm. Worse, they won't be getting close to what's physically left of him unless they want to trigger some nightmare scenario like in the video Randy showed them of Catherine Caldwell's ill-fated visit to the ranch.

end Vernon I mean, he clarifies.

I understand.

She goes back to eating. Then there's another tug, just like the tug at her waist when Poe was a boy and wanted his big sister to play with him. She gives in, just like she used to then.

wheres dad claire

Margot's studying the notepad with a furrowed brow. "Upstairs, I'm sure. I'll go check on him."

———

The Kodiak's not pressurized, but they're as high as they can possibly fly, pushing close to twelve thousand feet and making decent time. Turbulence has been light so far, and the sinking sun gives a bloodred glaze to the westward-facing flanks of the clouds they pass through as they head south.

Nobody's talking, and it's left Randy to wonder if his men are pissed at him. Is that why Thomas didn't come to see them off? As for Rupert and Ben, they haven't so much as glanced back in his direction since they took off almost forty-five minutes ago.

What else do they want him to do? He's removed Agatha from her lair, broken his ultimate promise to her. The only promise more important is the one he made to always protect her sister from the truth of Thunder Ranch. And to do that he had to threaten to shoot the poor woman.

Surely, the guys can see all this.

Still, maybe he waited too long to act. Maybe he should have sent more guys than just Dave and Zach. Maybe he didn't because he was too preoccupied with securing Claire, Margot, and Abram at Thunder Ranch, and Poe's bloom didn't get the manpower it deserved. But he's making up for that now, isn't he? Flying through the darkening sky with all that remains of the woman he loves in tow.

Could some of that, maybe any of that, earn him a little bit of credit from the guys he's taken good care of for years? Or at least a snippet of friendly conversation?

He's about to break the ice when there's a loud thud behind him. For a second, Randy thinks it came from outside the plane, but the wings are level, and every bit of turbulence they've flown through so far has caused little symphonies of rattles. He didn't hear one just now. Just a thud. And he's pretty sure it came from right behind him.

From the container.

And that doesn't make sense because bloom doesn't thud. It doesn't tap or scratch or sing or yell or talk. It doesn't make any sound at all. Maybe it was the tree stump settling or sliding to one side, but the plane didn't just hit a bump, so why would it do that?

Ben glances back. When he meets Randy's eyes, Randy's not sure what to make of the look he sees there. It's wary, but also knowing and a little ashamed.

The second thud makes Ben wince.

Like someone who's been caught.

"What the hell?" Randy says.

Rupert's staring straight ahead. So's Ben.

If either one of them thought the contents of the container were doing something unexpected at this altitude, they should be reacting. Descending, at least. But they're not.

"What the hell's going on?"

Neither man answers. Randy unbuckles his seat belt, drops to the floor, crawls on all fours to the container. No way should he release a bunch of bloom midflight, but that's what he's about to do, and neither Ben nor Rupert is making any move to stop him.

"Oh boy," Rupert whispers instead.

Randy pops one lock, then the other, cracks it barely an inch just to be safe. No blue light, no bloom. Another inch, then another, and a wave of rank body odor hits him, and there's Abram Huntley, eyes wide, hands already spread out in front of him.

"Hear me out, friend!" he says.

"Are you out of your fucking mind, you dumb son of a bitch?" Randy roars.

"Is that a rhetorical question?" Abram hoists himself to a seated position, rolls his neck from side to side. "Jesus, Mary, and Joseph, I gotta stretch my legs. You guys got a bottle for me to piss in?"

"I should break your damn leg right here! What the hell's going on?"

"You're yelling. In a little plane. And it's really loud."

Randy turns to the men in front. "Did you guys know about this?"

"Seriously," Ben says, "stop yelling."

"I'll stop when you all tell me what the fuck is going on!" Randy yells.

Ben yanks his headset off, squeezes out from between the pilot and copilot's seat. He ends up crouching in the aisle, which makes it look like he's going to spring on Randy like a tiger if he doesn't shut up. "What's going on is that your plan was trash, my friend. Straight-up trash!" he yells.

"Trash?"

"Yes. *Trash.* A bloom battle? I mean, what the hell? We've never seen what bloom from two shifted humans will do in the same room, let alone in a goddamn face-off in the middle of a populated area. It could be a nuclear meltdown, for all we know. *This* we've got some information about."

"*This?* What is 'this'?" Randy asks.

Abram manages to crawl out of the far end of the container. His back rests against the cabin's rear wall. He's smiling nervously, but he's also staring at his bent knees like he's afraid to look Randy in the eye. "*This,*" he says, "will be what you showed us on that video."

It takes Randy a second, but he's only showed them one video all day.

"Catherine," Randy says. "You think . . . you want us to use *you* as bait, so the bloom, your son's bloom, will come after you like Agatha's did Catherine?"

"Seems like a sure-enough way to get it away from this psycho, doesn't it?"

"You saw how it moved in that video. It blew the damn cellar doors off, knocked down everything in its path. Including you, Ben! It cost us a fortune to fix all the damage. What if you can't outrun it?"

Abram looks him in the eye. "I'm not planning to outrun it."

The anger coursing through Randy turns into something softer, but heavier, something that feels like it might tilt him toward despair. At first, he thinks the plane hit a little patch of turbulence; then he realizes he's sagged until his butt's resting on the backs of his heels because he's having trouble sitting up now that the fullness of Abram Huntley's plan is pressing down him.

"Jesus, man," he whispers.

"What do you think would have happened that night if Catherine hadn't finally run?" Abram asks.

"I don't like to think about it."

"Let me, then. It wanted a body. So I'm going to give it one."

"What happens to yours?"

"Guess we're going to find out, aren't we?"

For a while there's only the sound of the churning propeller and the slow and steady rattle it sends through the plane. But Randy can't get up, can't even bring himself to move.

"I know, man," Abram finally says.

"What? What do you *know*, Mr. Huntley?"

"You feel bad about what you've done, and you thought it was your job to fix this. Well, it's not just your job. It's mine too. I've spent most of my life seeing my kids knocked away from me over and over again by something I didn't understand because I couldn't get to them in time. Then I was sitting at your dining room table watching my daughter talk to my son the only way she can. With a paper and a pen. Because if she wants to hear his real voice, she's got to suffer a return trip that churns her guts up. If I can end that, then I have to."

"We've got no proof, *none*, that this will bring Poe back."

"Maybe not," Abram says. "But I'd rather die trying than die not knowing. And if it has the added benefit of getting my son away from this sick fuck long enough for the guy to bleed to death, so much the better."

"Did you tell your daughter what you were going to do?" Randy asks.

"Hell, no. She still thinks I'm using the bathroom."

"You could've told me," Randy says.

"Why'd you fire that gun at Catherine Caldwell that night?" Abram asks.

"To save her life."

"Exactly. You knew when you saw what was coming out of the barn that there was a chance that the woman you loved was coming back. But you fired that gun anyway. You wouldn't give Catherine Caldwell up to it, whatever it really is. And so you never would have let me do this until it was too late to turn back. I knew it, and your men knew it. That's why they helped."

"So much for honor among thieves," Ben grumbles.

"You just stay shut up for a minute until I'm ready to hear you talk again," Randy tells him.

Ben flashes his palms, turns to face forward in the bucket seat he crawled into a moment ago.

"You are one manipulative son of a bitch, you know that?" Randy says to Abram.

"I sure do. Now get me a bottle or something before I piss all over this floor."

———

Margot found the note on the counter in the bathroom where Claire had taken a shower earlier. She brought it to Claire in a trembling hand, and as she shuffled into the dining room, at first Claire couldn't tell if the woman's eyes were wide with anger or fear or both.

The message was short and written in her father's severe block printing, which he always resorted to because his cursive looked like chicken scratch.

NEED TO SEE IF I CAN FIX ALL THIS THE
REAL WAY.
MAYBE ONCE AND FOR ALL.
KNOW THAT YOU WERE THE DAUGHTER
I ALWAYS WANTED, EVEN IF I SCREWED IT UP.
THIS TIME, THOUGH ... FINGERS CROSSED.
LOVE YOU, BEAR

Sean claimed ignorance, said he'd been assigned to the women the whole time and had no idea what had been going on outside the main house. But he's not trying to stop them now as they march in the direction of the barn.

Claire's not seeing the barn that's up ahead. She's seeing the night-vision images in the video Randy showed them earlier, as a rioting, spreading version of Agatha's bloom roared up out of the cellar, driven by what seemed like a singular and unstoppable hunger for her sister's body.

She fights frenzied, panicked thoughts. *Of course he'd do this. The minute we got back together, of course he'd take off on another trip to Crazy Town.* But these thoughts feel childish and petty given the sacrifice implied by his note. Still, why couldn't he tell her? How come, even in the moment, the hallmarks of her family are secrecy and separation? Will this be how it all ends, her family running in different directions in search of wild solutions to a problem they can barely comprehend?

The barn doors are open, but the cellar doors are closed and locked.

"He might not be down there," Sean says.

"He? You mean Abram?" Margot asks.

"No. Thomas. He's the only other guy here."

"They *all* went? Jesus!" Margot snaps.

Sean looks miserable. He seems unwilling to defend this plan, perhaps because he wasn't consulted on it. He tugs his phone from his pocket, taps a message into it. The response freezes him in his tracks. Finally, he returns the phone to his pocket, moves past them to the cellar doors, pops open the storm doors one after the other, then bends down to enter the code.

Thomas sits on a bench just outside the glass wall to Agatha's cell. Inside, the bloom does its same lazy dance, surrounded by the mausoleum of Agatha's old bedroom.

Margot holds out the note so Thomas can see it. He looks to the glass. Finally, he says, "He said if he told you about it you wouldn't let him go."

"Like I've ever had that kind of power over him," Claire says.

"Why?" Margot says. There's a sharp edge to her voice. "Why does he want to go?"

"As if that's not clear," Thomas says.

"Say it anyway," Margot says. "Clarity hasn't exactly been everyone's strong suit around here."

He looks at Claire. "He thinks it'll bring your brother back."

"And you believe him?" Margot asks. "For fourteen years, he thought it was aliens and you knew otherwise, but you just kept watching him and didn't say anything. But *now* you believe him?"

Thomas sucks in a deep breath through his nose. Claire is grateful Margot's doing the talking. Her own emotions are so big and conflicting they've made a logjam in her throat. "Answer me!" Margot barks. "You're the doctor. Tell me what you think is going to happen."

"I think it'll end it," Thomas says. "I think it'll turn your brother's bloom into something that can't be inhaled. By anyone. And I think it's the best plan we got. But will it bring him back? No idea. Sorry."

Nobody says anything for a while. Thomas never looks away from Agatha's bloom, not once.

"Are you in love with her too?" Claire finally asks.

Thomas flinches, looks up at her.

"Randy said three of you visit with her," Claire says. "I assume that's him, you, and Ben. I mean, you're the top three around here, right?"

"You know what it's like to go over there," Thomas says. "It's powerful. It'll change the way you see the world. I mean, you just did it, but give it some time, once you start to process it . . . you'll see. So yeah, I love her. I mean, she's been inside my head. But I'm not *in* love with her. It's different. Like family. And I've never had a great one, to be frank."

"Boo-hoo," Margot whispers.

"Still," Claire says, "you're protective of her."

"That's not why," Thomas says.

Margot says, "So Randy lied to us because he didn't want to fly the love of his life into—"

"No. *We* lied to Randy. By the time he realizes it's Abram in the container, it'll be too late to turn around."

"So you and Ben protected Agatha," Margot says. "Good little soldiers to the end."

"You're a bitch, lady," Thomas whispers.

Margot whirls, so hard and fast Claire grabs her arm instinctively. "And you all are the worst kind of men. Convincing yourself of some higher purpose while you use Agatha like some drug. While you keep all these secrets from this family, from the world, so you can . . . what? Do you have any idea the implications this could have on religions, on disease, on our collective fear of death? Of the unknown? And what? You *what*? You keep it here so you can hoard it! So you can have your little near-death experiences and deal with your PTSD?"

"I didn't have PTSD until you showed up, Ms. Hastings." His eyes meet Claire's. "Your father's doing what he wants to do, and he's doing it for you and your brother. Bloom against bloom? It would never have worked. That whole town would have been decimated."

"Then let's go with my other idea," Claire says.

Margot goes limp in Claire's grip. Thomas stares at her vacantly. Playing dumb, no doubt.

"Open the door," Claire says. "I need to talk to her."

"Randy doesn't want you going anywhere near that kid's vault."

"I don't care what Randy wants. We've been doing what Randy wants for a while now. People are dying, and my father might be about to get himself killed. I'm done with what Randy *wants*. And apparently so are you, because you and Ben just knifed him in the back."

"You start playing around in this kid's vault, the one who'll pay the price is you."

"I want to hear that from her," Claire says. "She's the expert. Open the door, please."

He exhales loudly through his nostrils.

After a moment, he rises, moves to the keypad, enters the code. Then he pulls the glass door open and allows her to step inside.

30

When the waitress brought the check, Claire realized she hadn't heard her father ask for it. If she had, she would have been dreading its arrival. The meal, which she'd hoped would be something special, had consisted of little other than her and her dad staring awkwardly at their food while Poe cracked jokes that were occasionally so inappropriate they'd earn him a "Pipe down now, squirt" and a pat on the shoulder from their dad.

As her dad dug into his jeans pocket, Poe dragged a french fry in lazy, sinuous lines through the little puddle of ketchup on his plate. Slender rivers of ceramic opened before the ketchup closed over them again. "Is blood in the movies really ketchup?" he asked.

"No," Claire said, "it's corn syrup."

"It's always too red, though. Isn't that right, Dad?"

"Isn't what right?" He was counting out bills, maybe flashing them where Claire could see so she'd say something to her mom about how he wasn't broke.

"That blood in movies always looks too red."

"I don't want to talk about blood right now, squirt." When he noticed Claire eyeing his billfold, he looked into her eyes with more focus than he'd studied her with for most of the meal. "Tell your mom I coulda sprung for something nicer, OK?"

Claire wasn't sure what this meant. Didn't he pick the restaurant? It was close to the hotel where they were staying, and it seemed like her dad was eager to get back. Eager to get home too. The few things he'd said during the meal were all digs at LA. How it's impossible to get around, and what's the point of all the sun if it always comes at you through smog? Maybe he loathed the place because it was where her mother's family lived, and they all hated his guts now.

"Can we watch a movie back at the hotel, Dad?" The playfulness had left Poe's voice. He was staring at his plate as if the french fry he kept toying with was about to break some bad news.

"Maybe," her dad grunted.

"Can Claire come watch the movie with us?"

Silence, except for the clatter of dishes in the kitchen that opened onto the restaurant from behind the counter. Two booths over, a pretty blonde woman who maybe looked like how Mom used to look before Claire was born was leaning forward so she could whisper a funny story to the man across from her. Maybe it was a dirty story and she didn't want to be overheard.

Her father's silence was enough of an answer.

Poe's jaw quivered, and Claire saw for the first time how fragile the comic mask he'd worn all through lunch was. And she felt a tightening inside her chest. Her own jaw wanted to quiver too, and she fought it by balling up her little fists and clamping them between her knees under the table. Because she was realizing the same thing Poe was: This lunch was over, and it hadn't been much. Just a thing their parents felt they had to do.

Don't cry, Poe, she thought. *You'll make me cry too.*

Her father's voice was gruff enough to get her attention. "You do good in school, OK? You got a good head and I want you to use it. Keep helping out the other kids. It might be scary at first 'cause you're new, but you're smart enough and they'll see how much you can help them and then they'll—"

"Dad, the movie. Can Claire—"

"I heard you, Poe, and the answer's no. You know what we agreed. It's just lunch." Shamed by his own outburst, he looked at Claire again.

But it was seeming like more and more of a struggle. "And maybe another visit soon."

Poe looked suddenly like he was holding in a sneeze. A tear slipped down his cheek. He'd ground the french fry into a messy glob against the plate.

Claire couldn't speak. She was afraid if she did, her tears would flow, like they were now threatening to burst loose from her brother. And suddenly nobody could look at each other. When her father said, "We're all paid up," they were all sliding out of the booth as if a starting gun had fired, all of them looking in different directions as they went. Poe walked ahead of them so fast their father called his name, then hurried after him out the front door.

When they stepped outside into the wind and traffic sounds, their dad grabbed Poe by one shoulder, but her brother refused to turn around. He didn't want her to see his face.

"Let's say goodbye now," her dad said, and Poe ripped himself out of their father's grip and turned, and that's when she saw her brother was stuttering with sobs.

Poe ran to her and threw his arms around her.

And now Claire sees what she forgot about that day, that their dad held his back to them as they said goodbye because he was crying too.

———

"Claire, tell me what's happening at the ranch."

She'd told herself she could steel herself against the vault's power this time. That she could maintain some sense of the present moment, of who she was today. But she was wrong. As Claire comes out of it, she feels Agatha's arms around her. Maybe because unlike her last visit she's not shaking with anger, not convinced that Agatha deliberately used this memory to manipulate forgiveness out of her. It's no mystery why this memory surged to the front of her vault. The sense of separation from her dad, the revelation of how badly he was hurting too.

But just outside the vault's open door, comfort awaits. Because there's Poe, big grown-up Poe, arm extended. This time she knows better than to look behind her into the void. Agatha helps her to her feet, guides her out into the foggy light where the music still plays and the carousel still glows, and once again, it seems like a miracle that every impossible thing here is unchanged from her last visit.

There's one new addition: a rifle leaning against a nearby bench.

"Claire?" Agatha asks again.

The woman looks much as she did last time: blue jeans and a black-and-red plaid shirt, her hair brushed out like she's entertaining but the guests are old friends. Her brother's the version of himself she assumes is his most recent. Spiky bleached-blond hair and formfitting white T-shirt, little silver studs in his nose and ears, acid-washed jeans. She takes his hand, feels his strange and singular warmth, so unlike anything she's ever felt in the physical realm, and draws him to her briefly.

"Bad, huh?" he asks.

"Rough. Not bad, just rough."

But it's a good thing, she thinks, that there was no steeling herself against the vault's power. It's a sign Vernon Starnes won't be able to either.

"Claire, please, tell me what's going on," Agatha says.

And so she does, the words spilling from her in a rush as she holds Poe close. When she's done with her account, Agatha wanders in the direction of the glowing carousel, the one that spun wildly when Claire first entered this realm through a different avenue, the one offered by her connection to her brother.

Claire almost misses the sign fringed in blue lights. TRAVEL UNDER THE SEA. *The open double doors below, offering glimpses of wavering green.*

"Tell me how," Claire says.

"*How to what?*" *Agatha asks vacantly.*

"*Tell me how to open his vault.*"

"*I'll do it,*" *Agatha whispers.*

"*No, you won't.*"

"*Claire, let her help if she wants,*" *Poe says.*

"*That's not what I'm saying. Look, the doors to his bridge, have they closed at all?*"

"*Since when?*" *Poe asks.*

"*Since the murders at Johnny Starnes's place over an hour ago. Have the doors to his bridge closed at all?*" *Claire asks.*

Poe shakes his head.

"*He's keeping the bridge open because he has to. He has to keep sucking in bloom because he'll bleed to death if he stops. He's shot bad.*" *Claire turns to Agatha.* "*But if you go over, we'll only have the thirty minutes until your bridge here closes and then you'll be yanked back. If we're going to have enough time to do something over there, something that will end this, I have to use my connection to Poe to get here because it's got no time limit. It's why Randy shot me full of adrenaline to bring me back. I was here past thirty minutes.*"

Agatha says, "*We don't think there's a time limit, but we don't know if—*"

"*Look, there's a lot I don't know, and you need to tell me. That's the point. That's why I came to see you first. Tell us how to open this guy's vault so we can stop this.*"

"*Well, first, you have to find the key,*" *Agatha says.*

"*I know that part,*" *Claire says.*

Agatha is struggling with her thoughts. "*This is so dangerous,*" *she whispers.*

"*Why? Why is it so dangerous? Tell me!*"

"*You will join with the other person. You will experience the memory as they do. You'll have no control over what it is or how long it* lasts. *It will last as long as* they *can endure it, not you. And if you resist it, for any reason, if you fight it, no matter how painful or scary it is, you can get lost. And there's only one way out if that happens, and you won't have it."*

"What? What do you mean I won't have it?"

"The other person has to help you. They'll feel it happening, and they'll have to hit upon a memory that you both share. That brings you back to the surface of the vault and resets the process. That's how Randy and I did it the first time I got lost. But, Claire—you don't know this man. He doesn't know you. He won't know what's happening if you do start to get lost, and if he figures it out, he won't help because he won't want you there to begin with."

"I won't resist his memory," Claire says.

"Claire," Poe says.

"I won't resist it."

Silence now, except for the melodic music from the carousel.

"It's harder than you think," Agatha says.

"How? It won't be my memory."

"Exactly! You haven't gone over it a thousand times in your head like they have. You haven't adjusted to it in any way. For you, it'll be the first time. And you'll experience it as they did the first time. And if it's bad, it will be as bad as it was for them the first time. And if everything you're saying about this guy is true, it will be bad, Claire. Real bad."

"And then what?" Poe asks. "So we manage to get this guy out of his vault and on the memory deck, just like you did with Claire, and then what?"

Agatha raises one arm and points to the rifle leaning against the bench.

"How?" Claire says. "Randy said it wouldn't work."

"Randy said it wouldn't open Vernon's vault," Poe says. "That's different."

"Randy's right," Agatha says. "Anything you imagine into being here won't work on Vernon's deck. But it'll work on yours."

Agatha stares down at the rifle as if she's checking its make and model. Claire doesn't know anything about guns, but it looks powerful and big.

"Oh Jesus," Poe finally moans. "You want us to bring that psycho over here?"

Agatha nods.

"It'll be easy," Claire says.

"Easy?" Poe barks. "How will that be easy?"

"He won't understand what's happening to him. We can tell him anything we want. We can tell him we're angels. We can tell him he'll get a thousand virgins if he crosses the bridge with us."

"He's seen me."

"But you were a little boy when you ran over there the first time, weren't you?" Claire asks. "What did you look like last time?"

"This."

"Pick another form," Agatha says.

"Oh, OK. Gee, thanks. No offense, lady, but I've got less experience here than you, and I haven't been so great at controlling it. It changes based on how I'm feeling. I know this won't come as a shock to anyone, but I didn't have a drug problem for most of my life 'cause I was great at managing my feelings."

"You're doing a pretty good job now," Agatha says.

"Yeah, well, what's waiting on the other side of that bridge will test me. It'll test you too, Claire."

"Then don't go," Agatha says. "Wait here. Let Claire bring him over. The gun has to stay here anyway. When they cross over . . . Ready, aim, fire."

"You are a cowgirl, aren't you," Poe grumbles, but he's walking toward the rifle. Agatha moves out of the way.

Poe picks it up, aims it at the foggy sky overhead, and fires.
Claire and Agatha both jump.
"Our guy might have heard that," Claire says.
"Good," Agatha says.
Poe lowers the rifle.
"Claire and I stay together," Poe says. "No matter what."

———

The return trip is as powerful as it was before, and there's no steeling herself against it. But Margot tips her to one side off the pallet on the chamber floor and gets a bowl under Claire's mouth just in time.

Even though Thomas is still wiping her mouth, Claire goes to stand, then keels over. He and Margot catch her and support her and stay with her as she starts for the door.

"Everything you know about Vernon Starnes," she manages, then has to stop to keep her stomach down. "And a mirror. That's what I need. Right now."

Thomas starts doling out details as they guide her toward the cell's glass door.

Stones, she keeps hearing again and again. He put stones on his mother's face after she died. His mother sold stones out of the front of their house in Spurlock, Colorado.

Then suddenly her brother's in front of her, ghostly and translucent. He looks the same as he did moments before when she was ripped away from him. From behind her, Agatha's bloom casts Claire's silhouette onto the glass door, and her brother stares at her from inside it.

"This is good enough," Claire says.

Margot's got one arm around her waist. When Claire turns to look at her, their faces are inches apart, and Margot's eyes are full of tears. "You can't just wait a minute or two? Maybe get your breath back."

"No time," Claire whispers.

Margot kisses her quickly on the cheek. "You are a remarkable young woman, Claire Huntley."

"Here's hoping."

Then Claire raises her finger and reaches for the glass.

IV

Home

Love never dies a natural death.

—*Anaïs Nin*

31

Night is falling by the time Vernon reaches Spurlock.

There's a police cruiser parked at the intersection of Kingman and Powell Streets, just past the old Gas N' Snack where Vernon would sometimes get distracted and wander down to the creek nearby while his mother filled up the truck. It's blocking the southern entrance to downtown, and it looks empty. Vernon slides his foot off the Land Cruiser's brake, inches forward. The closer he gets to the car, the more he hears something strange, but also familiar.

He powers the window down. It's the alarm for the dam, the one that used to always make his mother jump when they tested it the first Monday morning of every month. And he liked that she always forgot about the tests because it made her seem less perfect, which made him feel less stupid for having a different kind of brain than most people.

But now, the alarm's screaming makes him angry. He hopes it didn't drive Uncle Johnny's bad friends out of the Big Timber Brewpub. He's not ready for another plan to fall apart. Not ready to figure out what comes next. His mother is ashes now, and Johnny's friends are all he has left.

With his mind, he pushes the cruiser out of his way, sideways, so its tires make a strange sound along the asphalt that's half squeal, half scrape. *Friction,* he realizes. *There's too much friction.* He imagines the cruiser lifting up into the air. It does, light as a feather. He keeps lifting it and it keeps going, floating over the trees lining the creek, then over the roof of the two-story building a block away that fronts onto Pine Street. The streetlights along Pine Street bathe its undercarriage with an orange glow. He drives slowly after it, keeping it in range.

An idea strikes. He lifts the car over the building's roof, then floats it over the street he can't see. He leans partly out the open window, listening for screams, waiting for people to run through the intersection up ahead to get away from the amazing flying police car.

There's nobody.

Someone has evacuated Spurlock.

And that makes Vernon very angry.

———

"Jesus," Claire whispers. She'd just gotten used to the terrible grating carving sounds that got louder as they crossed the bridge. Now she's stunned silent by the scene before her.

"Told ya, Bear," Poe says. "It's some real shit over here."

She's frozen. Another step and she'll have left the swirling tube of dark green, be standing over the monstrously distorted bus bench with its gnarled teeth. And she's afraid any contact with this foreign ground will cause the intense redness of the place to race up her leg like a terrible fungus. The twisted bus enclosure is covered in smoky images of hooded men with raised arms, men just like the one Poe sent through in his drawing. What their memory deck has in terms of fog, this place has in terms of fire. Given Poe's descriptions, Claire expected the contorted buildings to steal her focus. But it's the burning mountains all around them she can't look away from. The fires covering them are golden, but the tendrils of smoke rising from them are bright red. It's not smoke, she realizes. It's ashes, and they're blanketing the street before her.

In the glass storefronts, she sees a dozen versions of the same image. A police cruiser floating high above sloping rooftops. But the point of view offered by the windows is traveling. It rounds a corner, approaching the floating car from street level. Spurlock, *she thinks. It has to be. The shapes of the buildings aren't the same, but it's the same kind of brick.*

"OK, word of advice," Poe says. "If we've got business to do, don't look at the glass. It can be really freaking distracting. Case in point: my trailhead moment."

"We're looking for something that's got to do with stones, I bet," she says. "The guy was obsessed with them. He put them all over his mother's face when she died. And she sold them for a living."

"So stones, or something you use to work with stones. Like jewelry framing or hot glue."

"Feels like it'll be more substantial than that, but yeah. Is the siren new?"

"New and real," Poe says. "Vernon must be hearing it. I'm not trying to be difficult, but stones is really damn general, Claire."

"Gems, jewels. It was a gift-shop kind of thing, so obviously we're not looking for gravel. We're looking for bright and shiny. They accused the guy of killing his mother, but the cops said there was no evidence. They think he put the jewels all over her face because he thought they'd keep her alive."

"Cool, but, like, does anything here look bright and shiny to you?"

"The fire does."

"We can't get to it. It's like the city buildings on our deck. Just a backdrop."

"I thought you didn't explore this place," she says.

"I didn't. I ran the wrong way the first time I tried to get the hell out."

"OK. Let's start looking for the key."

"Where, though?" Poe asks. "I mean, at least we have real stuff on our deck. I had benches to search. A second level, stairs. Everything here is . . . not what it's supposed to be."

"The surfaces," she says. "We have to search the surface of everything. See if it's blended in."

"But, Claire—"

"I know, Poe. I know what you're going to say."

"If nothing here is what it's supposed to be, how are we going to recognize a key when we see it?"

"We might have to try more than one thing."

"Where should we start?"

"The doors. The storefronts."

"All right," Poe says, "but remember my warning."

"I won't look at the glass," she says.

She starts toward the nearest one before Poe reaches out and grabs her by the arm.

"On your knees," he says.

She realizes why. If they get too close, he'll see them in the nearest reflective surface. And based on their current view into his world, it looks like he's driving, which means there's a rearview mirror right at eye level.

Claire starts crawling toward the nearest storefront on all fours.

———

When Dean Jorgensen was twenty years old, he witnessed a wreck in the opposite lanes of 1-70 that was so bad it sent a pickup flying over the divider and into his lane, giving him only seconds to swerve, saving his life and the life of the girl he was dating at the time.

Now, as he watches the cruiser he had Deputy Zander park on Kingman and Powell fly over Pine Street, his mind's desperately trying to fashion that memory into a frame into which he can put the impossible thing he's seeing. But it's not working. Again, he's hearing that panicked Leadville police officer explaining how the way Johnny Starnes died was "not physically possible," and now he's watching something that *isn't* physically possible, and the words *not physically possible* are starting to feel like a desperate and immature thing a child might say to deny an unavoidable adult reality.

A dark blue Land Cruiser rolls into view. It's battered and old, and from within comes a ghostly blue light, the likes of which he's never seen before. From where he's crouched next to the side wall of Caitlin's Books, across the street and just up the block from the now completely empty Big Timber Brewpub, Dean remembers the strange warning he got that afternoon and lowers his gun. Vernon Starnes is behind the wheel of the big SUV, wreathed in a more translucent version of the light filling up the back of the vehicle. Whatever it was would alter the guy's appearance, the caller warned, and the caller was right. The sight reduces Dean's heartbeat to a chirp and makes the back of his neck feel like it's made of writhing worms.

Dean believes in the value of a primary purpose, especially in situations that threaten to drown you. Military folks call it a mission directive, but it's simpler than that.

Showing up at a party to make your wife happy.

Arresting a drunk on a trumped-up charge because you're sure he'll hurt his girlfriend later that night if you don't. You pick a thing, and whatever happens, you act in service to that thing.

Right now, the thing is to keep Vernon south of town, no matter what.

The north end of town's a traffic snarl verging on chaos. Just as the evacuation plan dictates, they've turned both sides of Spruce Road's twisting path to the state highway into eastbound lanes. But nobody's leaving to the west, probably because the only way out is Pine Break Highway, a terrifying series of hairpin turns that climb the mountain-side. Even though it offers a version of high ground—albeit a terrifying one—years of avoiding it have been hardwired into the town.

If I survive this, Dean thinks, *we are definitely updating our evacuation plans.*

The Land Cruiser slows to a stop just shy of Big Timber Brewpub. Then it starts to turn, headlights penetrating the front windows, falling across the empty stools inside, most of which are still jostled from the quick exodus.

Dean's praying Vernon will hightail it out of there, speeding onto one of the spike strips they've laid before he spots it. Because now it's clear that if Vernon does see the strip first, he can brush the thing aside like a stray hair using whatever crazy magnetic weapon he's got.

Something moves on top of Big Timber Brewpub. A shadow.

A person. Three of them. Like most of the buildings along Pine, it's western false-front architecture with a big square top hiding the gabled roof. That's where that stupid son of a bitch Flip Morrison is crouching with a goddamn gun in hand, and it looks like his buddies are hiding behind him. They didn't evacuate. They fell back, planned to take matters in their own hands, finish the job that caused this mess. Dean's threat didn't drive them off; it just shamed them into further lunacy.

All Dean is hearing now is his caller's earlier warning: one shot at Vernon while he's using whatever he's got in the car, while he's physically altered, and the whole town blows.

But there's Flip, peering over the square top. Some of that crazy blue light shines up on his face, revealing wide, staring eyes. Like most idiots, he's growing more confident in the face of something he can't understand. "Get out of our town, you fucking freak!" Flip screams.

Dean fires before Flip can.

———

Poe is searching the walls of the bus enclosure.

Claire is crawling on her hands and knees along the storefront, running her hands over the gnarled patterns of wood, checking to see

Decimate

*if anything's embedded within. Checking the undersides of what she
thinks are supposed to be door handles but which look more like strange
art pieces.*

Then there's a gunshot.

"Don't look!" Poe cries. "Just keep searching."

She takes his advice.

*But the sound she hears next is a great rumbling. She places her
hands to the ash-blanketed pavement underfoot to see if it's coming
from this place. It's not.*

Don't look, *she tells herself.* Keep searching. Searching is different
from looking.

*The blade-against-wood sound is still there. It hasn't left, but occa-
sionally the sounds coming from Vernon's physical reality have intruded
enough to drown it out. But it's still there, and as she crawls backward
from the window, she wonders if there's more meaning to it.*

*The sound of carving. And that, Claire realizes, is what this whole
place is. A series of carvings. Frenzied and abstract, but the striations
in the wood all around her have the outlines of blade marks.*

Stones and carving, *she thinks, over and over again to herself. Like
a mantra.*

Then she sees them.

*They have long necks and sharp, widely separated wings, like
some unnatural hybrid of swans and eagles. And they're clustered close
together, like an angry but frozen flock. Their eyes are the only hint of
blue anywhere in this place. Flickering with the reflection of the flames
blanketing the mountains. Blue gemstones of some sort.*

Poe is next to her now, following her gaze.

"Their eyes," Claire says. "Their eyes are stones."

*"Fuck," he whispers. Because these strange avian gargoyles—these
carvings with stones for eyes—are gathered around the very top of the
twisted bell tower.*

Which is a hundred feet above the earth.

383

There's no more movement from the roof, but Dean's not sure if he hit Flip or one of his buddies or just drove them into retreat.

The Land Cruiser is backing up now. Slowly, deliberately. Vernon is far from panicked. It looks like he's carefully planning his next move. The fact that he's putting so much distance between him and the front of the bar suggests he doesn't have the slightest fear of a shooter perched on the roof. He's not backing up in Dean's direction either.

Then the front of Big Timber Brewpub is gone.

The noise reaches Dean a split second later. Rattles his bones, tickles his balls.

The front window, the front door, and a chunk of the building's second-floor offices have been replaced by a giant, yawning mouth fringed with split timbers and shattered glass. Office supplies swirl out of the second-floor hole. Debbie's desk, which he knows was pushed against the rear wall of her office, has been blown out the back of the building, it looks like. Dean's never witnessed a force this powerful. And he's never even heard of one that can make that kind of blast without smoke or flame. This was a pure wave of pressure that tore through the building back to front like an invisible meteor, leaving a hollowed-out interior that's now lined with dangling, sparking wires and filled with whirling dust. He's tempted to think it's sawdust swirling through the air, but it's not, he realizes. It's the red dust of demolished brick. If the blast went clear out the back, the staircases inside have been torn to bits. And that means those three idiots on the roof have no chance of escape.

"I'll do it," Poe finally says.

"Do what?" Claire asks.

"Climb it!"

Poe races toward the base of the bell tower. Tries the door. Of course it doesn't open. Every constant door on a memory deck accesses the vault, and the key is high over their heads. But it's insane what Poe's proposing. The bell tower looks like it shouldn't even be able to stand. What will happen if they add Poe's weight to it?

Then she remembers Poe doesn't have any weight. Not now. Not here. No heart, no lungs, no blood, and no veins.

"I'll go with you," she says.

"Bullshit, you will. If we can kill Vernon on a memory deck, you could fall and break your neck. You've both still got bodies, remember? Me, I'm just some kind of Ghostbusters *shit."*

And just like that, her brother starts climbing the side of the tower. Suddenly she sees that all the twists and turns and crazy jagged edges are to their advantage. There'd be no climbing if it was a normal, mostly vertical shape. But in this condition, it's got the lines of a coastal tree gnarled by a lifetime of ocean winds.

Poe crawls over the side of the branching section that juts out over the street, manages to get to all fours on the section's upward spine, and starts crawling forward.

"Oof," he says. "Thought I'd be fine if I looked down, but note to file—a fear of heights will follow you into the afterlife."

"Less talking, more focusing!" Claire cries out.

Poe falls silent and climbs.

———

The gaping hole in the second floor is widening. Shredded boards tear free in big clean sections with splintered ends. They float out from the front of the building, then tumble to the street as if they're being released by giant invisible hands. They make loud sawdust-spewing cracks as they land. Then there's another huge boom that threatens to empty Dean's bladder.

Using a weapon Dean is sure will change the face of the entire world, Vernon repeats what he did to the first floor to the second. And then the real hell breaks loose. The back part of the roof starts to cave in first; then the roof starts collapsing toward the front of the building's shell. The square top Flip was crouched behind earlier starts to go. Suddenly all three men are tumbling through the air like rag dolls swept from a high shelf.

They freeze ten feet from the ground.

Behind them, the facade of the building starts to fall. None of them turn to look because they can't. The only parts of their bodies under their control, it seems, are their faces, rictuses of terror and astonishment, wildly distorted by the blue glow coming from the Land Cruiser. Whatever weapon Vernon just used is not only levitating them but holding them prisoner. In midair.

Slowly, they begin descending. But at just the moment Dean thinks their feet might touch the ground, they stop short of the rubble, Flip Morrison and Buddy Packer flanking the guy Dean doesn't recognize. Then suddenly Flip and Buddy turn, start floating toward the smoke and wreckage. Three different fires have ignited inside the building where the pub was servicing a full house a little over an hour before.

He's going to burn them, Dean thinks. *Vernon's going to burn those sons of bitches.*

Dean raises his gun, not sure what he'll do with it.

A mercy killing, maybe. Will that get him killed too?

But instead of floating the two men into the flames, Vernon pitches them forward. In terrible tandem, they each pick up a broken plank from the rubble. When Vernon turns them to face front again, both men are blubbering, staring down at the arms they can't control.

The third man is still frozen in place, back to his buddies, like someone trapped inside a plaster cast. His friends close in—*float in*—on either side of him and raise their arms. The man starts to scream, but it's choked off by the first swinging, punishing blow of Buddy Packer's arm. Then Flip starts wailing on the guy too, and the blood flies.

———

"Shit!" Poe screams, and Claire hears his voice has changed.

Crawling up the final slope of the twisted bell tower, to where the cupola rises like a finger that's bent back from the rest of a pointing hand, her brother is ten years old again. The Poe of that night, the Poe of the pulse. Gore-Tex jacket and tousled hair.

"What happened?"

"I can't control it. I got scared."

She's trying to think of some advice to shout up at him so he can change back to his adult form when she realizes it hasn't slowed him down any. The intricate gathering of bird gargoyles waiting for him a few yards away might be easier to navigate for someone small.

"Just go with it!"

"Gee, thanks, sis!"

"You volunteered for this, remember?"

"Because I don't have a body, remember?"

There's no forgetting it. As before, she's changed in tandem with him. Looks down to see the bright red jacket she wore that night, mud-splotched hiking boots that seem comically small to her adult eye.

Poe's reached his destination, and she sees she was right. He's small enough to sit on the edge of the cupola and hold the ledge above his head with one arm. "How many?"

"All of them!"

"There's, like, sixteen, Bear!"

"Try for as many as you can."

Poe reaches up. He's standing now in a crouch, feet on the edge. One hand gripping the ledge overhead as his other arm reaches into the nest of carved birds that are almost the size of his ten-year-old body. He's gripping one of its eyes, twisting the stone. It comes free.

"Got one!" he cries. Then he goes for another, and she feels something she hasn't since they first crossed into this hellscape.

Relief.

———

Dean fires.

He watched for as long as he could, and then he fired: one, two, three shots in quick and frightened succession. He's lost track of time, but it feels like a whole minute has gone by since the first man crashed to the rubble, beaten to a pulp, and then, sputtering with sobs, Flip was forced to make his first skull-crushing swing at Buddy Packer.

He's shot both men. They hang lifelessly in the air. No longer alive to receive commands from whatever the fuck Vernon Starnes has in that Land Cruiser.

Mercy killing, Dean thinks.

Then the Land Cruiser starts to turn in his direction.

Dean runs, surging with confidence that Vernon didn't spot him in time. But when the Land Cruiser roars around the corner, headlights falling on him, he realizes he was wrong. Then he's slammed face-first to the pavement by a force he's got no words for, and suddenly he's being dragged backward.

———

At first, Claire's not sure what her brother's doing. She saw him put the stones he was able to pull free in the pocket of his jacket; then he climbed down from the edge of the cupola and onto the back of the twisted bell tower's almost horizontal spine.

"What are you doing?" Claire cries out.

They're still the children of the pulse, but he's tucked the stones inside the pocket of an article of clothing that could vanish in an instant. Will it take the stones with it if it does?

"Speeding things up!" he answers. He tosses the wadded-up jacket down to her. She has to run to catch it, but she does. Then she's unraveling it, feeling the hard lumps inside the pocket, shaking the stones loose into her child-size hand. She drops the jacket, cradling the stones in her hand, races toward the glass storefronts. Grateful to be this short again because it reduces her chance of being seen through the glass.

———

Dean's floating now, floating like the men he just killed.

Feeling what they felt.

A sense of being encased in ice while your body fights to break free. It's like every inch of muscle, every organ inside him, is reacting to a violation it's never felt before, and he worries that this alone might tear him apart before Vernon's mad weapon can do him in.

"Vernon!" he shouts, and he hates the groveling sound of his voice.

Dean's hopes of being brave in a moment like this are dashed. In the end, he realizes, fear does the talking for you. *The greatest indignity of all,* he thinks.

"It was wrong what was done to you, Vernon. You're right to be angry. You've got every right, Vernon."

He can see the kid's face behind the windshield. It's not easy with the reflection thrown off by the blue light. Vernon's eyes look dead, the whites of them the same color as the light.

Dean's floating closer to the nose of the Land Cruiser, like he's being studied. Inspected.

"I told him not to," Dean chokes out. "I told your uncle not to bury your mother. I told him to wait until you were out to give her a proper funeral."

There's silence, and then a familiar voice says, "But you're the reason I was there."

The windows are rolled down, so it's easy to hear him, and Dean wonders if Vernon rolled the windows down just so he could hear the screams of his dying attackers. And what can Dean say to this accusation?

"You're the reason I couldn't stop him," Vernon says.

"No, Vernon. Please—"

"You're a bad man too, Sheriff Jorgensen."

"Vernon, I did what I had to do. That's all. We only held you—"

"He took my mother away when I was in there. Because of you, Sheriff Jorgensen. He took my mother away, and I couldn't do—"

Dean crashes to the pavement so hard, pain thunders up both sides of his body. He realizes it's firing out of his knees, which he landed on. He crumples, the wind knocked out of him. But when he jerks from the terrible pain, he's got control of his limbs again. And suddenly it seems like a good thing, a very good thing, that Vernon Starnes stopped talking midsentence.

Head spinning, Dean rises to his feet. The Land Cruiser's horn is blaring. He stumbles sideways out of the headlights until he can get a good look through the driver's side window and sees Vernon slumped over the steering wheel, the horn screaming from the pressure of his chest.

Vernon Starnes, for all intents and purposes, has been knocked out cold.

Dean runs.

32

After his mother set off for work each morning, the grassy backyard at Uncle Johnny's house became Vernon's universe, and that was how his mother wanted it. She'd given him plenty of toys to play with outside because Uncle Johnny didn't want him in the house when his mother wasn't around.

"You go off into your own little world when you're with your army guys, sweet pea. And that's exactly where I want you to be when you're home with Uncle Johnny, OK? Just go outside and be in your own little world." Technically they were called "action figures," but he called them army guys because the army was apparently something important, and he knew this because Uncle Johnny told him the army was something he could never join because he was too stupid. Vernon knew that boys who were only four years old probably couldn't join the army anyway, but he also knew Uncle Johnny thought he could never be in it. Not ever. Not even when he was grown.

The ant pile, the grassy shade offered by the evergreen that sprouted from the alley behind his house, and the enormous sidewall of the pool nearby—these were the landmarks of his own city, a place where no one stared or asked questions he couldn't answer. A place for his army guys to roam. In his head, he called it Vernonville, and when he told his mother this, she laughed and held him close and kissed his forehead and called him "clever."

The morning of the bad game, he said goodbye to his mother just inside the front door, which was how she wanted it because she was afraid if they said goodbye out on the porch, he would try to follow her all the way to historic downtown Leadville, which was really just a few blocks away but sounded like a magical place. She gave him a big hug and kiss, then called out to Johnny to tell him she was leaving. But as usual, he didn't say anything back. Then Vernon was alone, and he was nervous suddenly because he couldn't remember where he'd put his army men after he got done playing with them last time.

He looked on the back porch, on the window ledge near the porch swing where he thought he put them last. But they were gone. He searched the grass, even getting down on his belly and moving his eyes level with the dirt to see if any of them were lying flat and hard to see otherwise. Then he saw where they were, and his heart skipped a beat.

They were in a bad place. They were where he wasn't supposed to ever go. The rim of the swimming pool, way up high. His mother had made him promise he wouldn't go anywhere near the pool when he was alone. She would give him swim lessons when they had the time, but right now, he could only get in it with her.

But she'd also told him to play with his men while she was gone. He couldn't do that if they were way up high. Still, the distance between the ground and the swimming pool's rim seemed like the height of the Empire State Building. It confused him, gave him a little sick feeling in his stomach, to see his army guys up there because he knew who probably put them there, and it didn't seem right. His mom didn't do it. Miss Clara, the woman who cleaned for Uncle Johnny every other week, wouldn't either; she always lined them up neatly on the window ledge next to the porch swing. She was nice to Vernon, sometimes helped him with words he couldn't understand. So it had to be Uncle Johnny. But why? Was it a game?

He placed his hands on the metal ladder and started to climb.

Something small and hard ricocheted off the side of the pool. A second later Vernon felt a biting pain in his shoulder. A rock, maybe.

But it was going so fast there was no way it could have fallen out of the sky. It was thrown, and a grown-up had to have thrown it because that's how hard it hit him.

But his army guys were more important than stupid rocks.

He started climbing again. The next rock struck him right between the shoulder blades. He wasn't expecting it, but the pain was much worse than the first. A little jerking cry went up from him. A sound a baby would make, not a big boy like him. And his mother wanted him to try to act like a big boy when he could.

But this time the rock felt hard and round. And that's how he definitely knew it was Uncle Johnny who had thrown it. Because it wasn't a rock, it was a marble, and his uncle had a tin of them. Just the week before, he'd made a joke to some of his friends who were over. "I better keep some on hand since my sister's kid lost all of his the second he was born." And then his mother had come in from the backyard with an angry look on her face, and everyone had gotten real quiet.

He realized that if this was his uncle's idea of a game, then it was probably meant to make him more normal. Because that's what he always yelled at Vernon about—being more normal. Sometimes when his mother wasn't there, Uncle Johnny pushed him away from things he wasn't supposed to have, sometimes hard enough for him to hit walls. But that only happened when he took too many of something they needed to share, something they might run out of.

Not his army guys. His army guys belonged to him, so it didn't make any sense that Uncle Johnny would take these from him. Unless Uncle Johnny finally wanted to play a game with him, and this was it. And so Vernon thought he should play along because he knew it made his mother nervous to leave them alone together, and so, if they could find a game to play, even if it hurt, it might make things easier.

Vernon started climbing again.

Then suddenly it felt like his right eye had caught fire. He couldn't see out of it. The next thing he knew, he'd fallen to the dirt. A marble had whacked off the side of the pool and hit him in the face.

I don't like this game, Vernon thought. *I don't like this game at all.*

He didn't get his army men. Instead, he started back toward the house, and he tried to keep his head down as he walked in case Uncle Johnny threw another marble, but he couldn't resist looking up, and when he did, he saw a shadow move in Johnny's bedroom window.

Then Johnny left. He wasn't supposed to. He made promise after promise to Vernon's mom that he wouldn't leave Vernon alone, but sometimes he left for an hour or two and came back with funny-smelling breath. Vernon, knowing there was more of something called danger when he was alone, would sit in a small room and rock back and forth, because the movement made the thoughts in his head slow down, until Johnny returned.

He didn't do that this time. Instead, he went to the closet in the kitchen where Miss Clara kept the things she cleaned the house with. He was remembering her accident from a few weeks before, how she fell and Vernon's mom had to bring her water and they almost called a doctor. Later, he asked her if she'd had what they called a heart attack, and she said no. Explained to him that she'd made a mistake and that's why she fell down. She had accidentally poured bleach into a bucket that had something called ammonia in it, and it made something called fumes, and these were bad. She breathed them in through her nose, and they made it so she couldn't stand up right, and that's why her mom had to help her. Miss Clara had taken him to the closet, showed him the little mask she started using while she cleaned—*Just to be safe,* she said—and showed him the bottles and said, "These two. Never mix these two, OK? It can be a very, very bad thing, Vernon."

A very, very bad thing was also a good way to describe what Uncle Johnny just did to him.

And that's why he put on Miss Clara's mask and took both bottles up to Uncle Johnny's room and poured some of one and then the other inside the little metal case that was something called a lunch box. When he was done pouring the things the cleaning lady told him never to mix, the marbles in the lunch box turned white like bones, and so he closed the lid of the tin box real tight and ran away fast. And he wondered if he'd just done what his mother would call a bad thing. But she also taught him that games were supposed to be fun and fair. Was that still true if you were bigger?

A few hours later, Uncle Johnny got home. He was walking in the slow, unsteady way he always did when he went out with his friends in the middle of the day. And after a while of listening to him clomp around upstairs with his big grown-up feet, Vernon waited until it sounded like he was in his bedroom; then he went for his army guys again. When he put his hands on the ladder and started to climb, his palms were sweaty. And this meant he was feeling something called fear, and maybe that was good because his mother said sometimes he needed to have more fear about certain things.

There was a loud, scary sound like the ones Uncle Johnny sometimes made when something in the football game he was watching didn't go the way he liked.

Vernon turned, looked up at the window, saw his uncle bent over and gasping and wiping spit and maybe a little throw-up from his mouth with one forearm.

"I win!" Vernon cried.

When his uncle exploded out the back door, Vernon realized winning might not be a good thing and he took off running. Then Uncle Johnny grabbed him with both hands, and Vernon was flying. He saw a glimpse of the pool's sidewall before he hit, then something bright that streaked across his vision that reminded him of cartoons where little stars circled the head of a cat that had hit its head really hard. And he knew something that big and bright inside his head might change him forever and make him more different than he already was.

He hears a girl's voice then, but he doesn't recognize it. "Molded, not broken," she says.

———

When he gradually appears in the darkness just beyond her reach, Claire moves to the little boy and takes him into her arms. It was her plan all along, but she didn't anticipate how right Agatha would be, how deeply the shared memory would meld her to him, despite the nightmares he's unleashed in the world. On her knees, she cradles him in both arms, stares down at him, trying for the best beatific smile she can manage. Through the vault's half-open door, menacing red light falls in a single band across his stunned cherubic face, one wide brown eye staring up at her. Blinking.

She only meant to think the words—molded, not broken—her mentor's old mission statement, because there's no denying it: the boy in her arms now, and the monster inside him, were made. That's what his memory told her. And the boy knows, and that somehow makes it even worse. He knows his uncle's abuse—the final, devastating moment of it, at least—damaged him irreparably, maybe in ways that unleashed the full fury that came roaring out of him the second he got Poe's bloom.

She has to move now. Thirty minutes is almost no time at all when the reality you're moving through might betray you with some new quirk at any moment. She rises to her feet, holding the little boy in her arms. She's Claire again, adult size.

"Can you please tell me where I am?" Little Vernon asks, and his voice sounds hollow. Like he's emulating an adult he's seen on TV.

"You're safe, Vernon. I'm taking you to see your mother now."

"Really? She's here?"

Claire doesn't want to cry, but it's a struggle. Agatha was right. The memory became hers. The little boy's confusion, his burning desire to do things right in a world of damaged, struggling adults. The terrible shock of realizing the pain that had torn through his little body that day had been wielded by an adult, a grown-up who was supposed to protect him, but who had tormented and tortured him instead. It's one thing to describe a loss of innocence like that to a therapist; it's another to have it resonate through your soul.

If she wants to move more quickly, she should sit him up against her chest, hold him around his back. But she's afraid she'll lose his trust if he can't see her face. Propped with his chin on her shoulder, he'll be forced to take in the fiery hell of his own mind without her as a distraction. And a deception. So she carries him bridal-style toward the yawning green hole inside the bus enclosure. Poe is gone, and she realizes why. He couldn't control his form, and Vernon would recognize him as the man who hurled himself at something inside his mind during the attack on the trailhead.

"You're sad," he says.

Molded, not broken, *she thinks, but sometimes the molding hands can break you.*

"I'm sad because I know how much your mother's missed you. But she's going to be so happy when she gets to see you. She's missed you, Vernon. She's missed you a whole bunch."

"Did I die? Did the sheriff man kill me?"

"No, sweetie. Your mother decided she didn't want you to hurt anymore or be confused, so she sent me to take you to a happier place. It's where she's waiting for you."

"She was nice. You seem nice too."

"Your mother is nice, Vernon. She's a very nice woman, and she loves you very much."

"I'm not nice, though. I'm different."

Has Poe made it back to the other side already? Is he standing with the rifle raised? Will they have to watch this ghostly little boy take a gunshot like he took his uncle's wailing fists that day? She keeps walking, worried she might not be able to manage the weight of him all the way across the bridge. And will he stay so placidly cradled inside her arms once he sees the massive sharks swirling through the green?

"No, you're a very nice boy, Vernon. Your uncle just did a bad thing."

"He hurt my head," Vernon says.

"I know, honey."

They're a few paces from the bus stop and the entrance to the bridge. Little Vernon turns his face to look at it. "What's that?"

"That's where we're going, honey."

"It's dark."

"Just for a minute, that's all. We're going to walk through it to get where your mother is."

"Why can't she come here?"

"Because it's safer for both of you on the other side."

"But I don't want to."

"But your mother wants you to. Don't you want to see your mother again?"

"She should come here. I tried to save her. She should come here."

The sharp pitch of defiance is headed someplace worse, she knows.

It's now or never. She sits him up, clamps one arm around his tiny back, and starts running. Into the wavering green. Shadows circle the tunnel, and she realizes her mistake too late. She didn't warn him the way Agatha warned her, and now Little Vernon has looked one of the sharks in the eye, and it's roaring toward the edge of the tunnel, releasing a nightmarish bellow that seems to echo through the vast depths all around them. Jaws agape, it barrels toward them, then turns at the last minute, giant pectoral fin slashing through the tunnel's edge, spraying them with water that dries and effervesces instantly. Vernon screams, *his voice ramping from a little boy's wail to a grown man's bellow. Suddenly he's impossibly heavy in her arms, and they crash to the floor.*

Poe's at the far end of the tunnel, backlit by foggy light. He's got the rifle. Vernon—grown Vernon, now—scrambles away from Claire back toward the opening they just passed through.

"You're a liar! You don't know where my mother is! My mother is ashes. She's ashes! You're a lying person."

Poe is running toward them now, rifle raised. He's testing how far down the bridge he can bring it, she's sure, and so far it hasn't vanished or blipped out of existence or whatever the hell it might do next. But Vernon's back on his deck.

Claire hurls herself at his back, slams him to the ground. Instantly, he's four years old again and she tells herself not to care, orders herself not to see a child as she closes her hands around his throat. He stares up at her with stark terror in his eyes. But she can't let go. She heard the nightmares he was making in the town beyond the glass. She heard the gunfire, the screams and the agonizing sobs of grown men.

She brings her face to his and squeezes his throat as hard as she can. "Listen to me. Listen to me, Vernon. You have to stop! Do you understand me? You have to stop what you're doing! What you have, what you took from that crash, it is not a thing. It is not a toy. It is a person. Do you understand me? What you have stolen is a person, and he is not yours to play with."

Vernon's wail becomes a pathetic, furious gurgle under the force of her hands.

"He is not yours. He is my brother. And he does not belong to you. He will never belong to you. And if you don't stop using what's left of him to hurt people, I will hurt you, Vernon. Do you understand? Every time you breathe him in, I will be right here, and if you don't stop, I will find a way to tear you apart, Vernon Starnes. Do you understand me? I will tear you apart!"

"CLAIRE!" Poe's voice.

She looks back and sees him standing just inside the bridge. He's still got the rifle. He's made it this far with it, and he's trying to tell her she only has to drag Vernon a short distance before he's within firing range. Claire drags the boy to his feet, and suddenly a grown man's arms are swinging at her. A punch lands on her jaw and sends her skittering backward.

"You are NOT nice!" Vernon roars.

He's barreling toward her when suddenly he slams to his knees, eyes wide. For a second, Claire thinks Poe fired, but he hasn't. Vernon's been struck by a blow none of them can see.

Standing inside the end of the bridge, Poe fires. The bang is loud, but what follows is like a puff of air, a speeding bullet popping out of existence only seconds after leaving the rifle's barrel and entering the memory deck. "Dammit!" Poe wails.

But Vernon is still on his knees.

"What's happening?" he moans, eyes wide, staring at Claire as if he expects her to give him answers even after he'd decked her. "What's happening to—"

A door nearby had swung open, and suddenly Vernon is sucked backward through it. It slams shut behind him with more power than the rifle shot.

———

Vernon jerks awake, hears the Land Cruiser's horn go silent the second he sits up.

The light all around him has gone crazy. It's not the right color blue anymore. It's more silver. And when he looks behind him, he can't even see the airplane seat because it's like everything in the back of the SUV is a big, roaring ball of gray.

He hears a sound he doesn't recognize at first.

It reminds him of the motor scooters some people would drive through town on Sundays. But it's louder.

It's a propeller.

———

Dean and two of his deputies watched the plane swoop in low over the spreading fire on Pine Street. He's been ignoring the slew of questions from both panicked men. Just repeating the same thing over and over again. Some sort of weapon, possibly electromagnetic. They have to keep evacuating. No one goes south. And then the propeller plane came down out of the night sky and everyone stopped yelling, and some of the people in the cars stuck on the street nearby lowered their windows to watch its perilous flyover.

And then suddenly the plane was gone, but there was no boom or blossom of fire above the rooftops, and Dean thought, *Holy shit. They landed.*

———

Vernon races around the back of the Land Cruiser. There must be something close by that's ruining his mother's gift.

It's not your mother's gift, you FREAK. It's that girl's. The girl in your head.

But he doesn't see the girl anywhere. And he's still here. So the power is his, and that's what he'll call it now. So it's not a gift. It's a power, and it will be his for as long as he can use it.

But when Vernon opens the cargo doors, a wave of pressure shoots him backward, and he lands on his ass on the pavement. And he can't see the airplane seat anymore because the light inside the vehicle is getting so bright, and it's making a really fast thumping sound. And he knows that's wrong because the power has never made any kind of noise at all before, and if it's making noise now, it means something's really wrong.

"Hey!"

It's a man's voice, a shout, and it's coming from a block away. It's not the sheriff. It's a man Vernon's never seen before, and he looks wide-eyed and afraid but he's also smiling. And he's walking toward Vernon like he's not afraid of what Vernon can do.

The Land Cruiser's cargo door flies sideways away from the SUV, and Vernon wonders if he did it without meaning to. And then the side windows blow outward in matching showers of glass. Something pours out of the back of the Land Cruiser that's thick like smoke but smoother. The blue is gone. It's the color of skin now, and it's flying over Vernon as if it doesn't care about him anymore. He whirls and throws one hand out, thinking he'll be able to make it stop, but it keeps going.

A block away, the strange man who just shouted at him falls to his knees, his arms thrown out as if he's embracing the air. But there's terror in his eyes, and it looks like he's crying.

Vernon has no name for whatever this thing is that is firing down the street toward the kneeling man. It is not a gift. It is no longer his.

What was once Vernon's fuel, his power, his only hope, slams into the man like the angriest, craziest cloud Vernon's ever seen, and then the man is gone. Gone and not gone. A flickering impression inside a light storm that seems to contain all the colors of the rainbow. The man's arms drift to his sides from where he'd braced them over his bent head right before the cloud struck him. The substance spreads around him like a blossom veined with little lightning bolts. As it unfolds, the man finds the courage to raise his face, but his face is shifting, shifting back and forth between the faces of two men, neither of whom Vernon recognizes.

"Claire!"

It's her brother's voice. She runs to the opening of the bridge.

The rifle's lying at her feet. Poe dropped it because his arms are being sucked backward. It's as if the tunnel's become a ventilation shaft and all the air's rushing back toward their memory deck. In another second, his bent, tensed legs won't be enough to hold him in place. She races to him. Nothing fights her, no suction pulls on her body. Just his. But when she's a few feet from him and he goes to grab her hand, he slams chest-first to the tunnel floor and flies backward. She runs after him, screaming his name. His desperately reaching arm leaves a trail of a color she's not used to seeing in this realm—bright gold. And then he flies backward out of the tunnel.

When she bursts onto Pier 39, the carousel is spinning madly, and her brother is on it. Racing between the horses. He's ten years old again, in his bright Gore-Tex jacket, and he's screaming her name as the carousel spins faster and faster, so fast its horses are becoming a blur. And when she runs toward it, it moves so quickly her brother becomes a blur too. It's clear he can't jump off, that something's holding him in place.

Something is taking him.

The force that sucked him backward down the bridge has gathered on the carousel into something even more powerful, something that's spinning her brother into oblivion.

Her screams leave her throat raw. And finally, the carousel begins to slow, the horses begin to come into greater definition.

And her brother is gone.

Vernon raises his hand, but he already knows what to expect. Even though he still glows, his power is useless against the light storm a block away and the strange man at its violent center.

And then Vernon sees the strange man has also raised one arm.

In a voice that echoes inside Vernon's head, the man growls, "Get away from my kids."

Blood squirts from the fingers of Vernon's outstretched hand. He sees the blue light that's sustained him for so long peeling away from him, taking skin with it like a Band-Aid ripped off too hard. Not peeling, he realizes. *Pulled.* Pulled from inside him. From his whole body. The velvety, weightless feeling that filled him every time he breathed in more of the gift from heaven has now been replaced by fiery agony, and that's when he realizes what's happening in his arms and hands is happening all throughout his body.

By the time he hits his knees, he can taste blood in his throat, his nostrils, and the last glimpse he sees of his arm is more bone than shredded skin, and the last thing he hears is the sound of his own skull crunching and splintering.

———

There was no stopping Deputies Zander and the new kid Frye from following him, and now they're all standing a block away from the smoking remains of the Land Cruiser, its back door blown open like some mouth with all the teeth punched out.

Like a ghost is being pulled out of Vernon's body, Dean thinks. *No other words for it. It looks like someone's pulling a damn ghost out of Vernon Starnes.*

Staring down Pine Street, he can see the plane that flew over earlier. It landed two blocks past the burning remains of the pub, and just beyond the flames stand three shadows. One of them's got some kind of cowboy hat on. Like Dean and his men, they're frozen by the sight filling the intersection of Pine and Alexander.

And then it stops.

What's left of Vernon is a gnarled mass of splintered bone and gore, like a body that's been dropped off a roof and then run over ten times in a row.

But there's something else in the intersection. Something that hasn't taken shape yet.

And to Dean's astonishment, the three men from the plane are walking toward it.

The one in the cowboy hat takes up the lead, and his eyes finally meet Dean's, his face lit by the flames. There's some kind of scarring around the man's right eye, but he looks calm and focused, and Dean's willing to bet a fortune it's the man who called him earlier today. He raises his hand, like he's telling Dean and his men to stand down.

Or maybe the message is something else. *Trust us. We'll take care of it.*

If the guy is the caller from earlier, he's been right about everything else, and so who is Dean to question him now?

"Sheriff," Zander gasps. "*Sheriff?*"

"Nobody move," Dean says. "Just stay right where you are."

And he knows it might be a stupid thing he's doing, letting these men from the sky collect whatever mess is left in the intersection a block away. Not wrong, necessarily. Just foolish to believe they can take all the consequences of this night away with them forever. As much as he'd like them to.

———

Claire isn't prepared for the horror of how this place will feel without Poe. This drifting fog and the lonely foghorn. The sound of cheerful music from the carousel is a taunt, as if the whole contraption is reminding her that it just somehow took her brother from her.

"Bear?"

She recognizes the voice, and it doesn't belong here.

Her father's standing behind her, but he's wreathed in the same shade of gold that spilled from her brother's reaching arm as he was dragged down the bridge. There's a calm that radiates from him. It's such a stark and sudden counterpoint to her despair that she moves to him, and when his arms close around her, she feels something more intense than the heat of pure spirit that came off her brother. She feels suddenly enclosed in something that moves gently through her entire form.

"What happened?"

"Looks like this is my memory deck too," he says.

"No," she says, realizing.

"Afraid so, honey. I got here the old-fashioned way, I think."

"No."

The floorboards all around them brighten suddenly, and when they look to the sky, she sees the fog is parting, and out of the even dome of blue a golden halo spreads outward, and the shafts of light pouring down from the sky above look alive. All around them, the glass storefronts are suddenly as blue as the sky overhead once was, and the shadowy people take on faces and features and form. Suddenly the pier appears sunlit and alive, and the laughter does not echo. It is here, it is present, it is alive. Or that's how it looks and sounds anyway.

Like an amusement park and no one knows how to turn on the rides, *she remembers her brother saying.* Only now someone's turned them all on, and this place, this memory deck, is working as it should, greeting her father's entry into the afterlife the way it was designed to. And that can only mean one thing, and it forces a sob from her.

Death comes for the dead.

"Well, darling," her father says, "if it's not your time yet, I think you should try to get out the way you came in."

"No. I don't want to. I don't—"

But her father is guiding her toward the carousel, and the closer she gets to it, the faster it begins to turn.

"I know, honey. I know. But it seemed like the only way. And I can only hope it worked the way I wanted."

"Dad, but we just . . . You and I, we just . . ."

"Get on the carousel, honey. If everything went according to plan, then your brother's going to need you. You'll take care of each other better than I ever did. And know this, OK? I need you to know." They're not arms that wrap around her, but a kind of light, a power, that holds her to him in a halo of gold. Her feet leave the boards. "Just because I let you go doesn't mean you weren't everything I ever hoped you'd be."

A light shove, and suddenly she's drifting backward in between the horses, which rise and fall around her as the carousel turns. She drops to the carousel's floor, and suddenly she's spinning away from him. But on the return trip, he's still there, smiling at her. Again and again, and as the carousel speeds up, and as the scenes of the pier beyond its borders start to become a blur, Claire sees what her father has not yet seen. That her mother stands behind him next to one of the benches, with a gentle, loving smile that seems full of the peace brought by knowledge, knowledge she seems poised to share, and she's holding her lost necklace in one hand because it is the key to everything that comes next.

33

Two Weeks Later

Maybe he's just a Montana man through and through, but Randy's never quite understood the appeal of Jackson, Wyoming. It's too touristy, for one, and it can't seem to make up its mind if it's a mountain town or a prairie town. Also, he's never been much for skiing, and Saddle Butte rising to the northwest looks like a bulbous slag heap poised to consume the web of streets below. And then there are the arches made out of elk antlers in the town square that seem like either horror-movie props or a self-conscious attempt to provoke those who get sentimental about wildlife. And then there's Catherine Caldwell. Now Catherine Caldwell Devlin, who's made this place her home for decades now and whose presence here probably lends everything about it a negative charge in Randy's mind.

He's brought her various suitcases full of cash over the years, some of which she's quietly accepted, others she's tried to reject and play games around. Even though she's never said so to his face, Randy imagines the woman has always battled the temptation to plow the payments from her sister into her husband's numerous political campaigns. But given the shadows Agatha placed around the money's source, her sister is worried doing so might link her family's political fortunes to a criminal enterprise. And she'd be sort of right.

But this time, he hasn't brought money. He's brought a leather satchel full of files and photographs, and some videos loaded onto a memory stick.

The scene looks mostly the same as it did when he was here last, except for the prayer circle gathered in the town square. The men and women are all dressed in white, hands linked, singing softly under their breath around white pillar candles that ring several poster boards featuring an enlarged photograph from a video that has redefined the term *viral*—a video taken by a passenger aboard Ascent Airlines Flight 62 that shows exactly what happened to Poe Huntley the second several pieces of ceiling tore free and speared him through the chest, causing him to shift in a single, blinding instant. The video was uploaded before impact, then shared with the world by the astonished wife who discovered it on their family's cloud drive several days after the crash. Bloom, once a secret of Thunder Ranch, has now been shown to the world.

Accordingly, some of the storefronts Randy walks past now have signs in them that say CLOSED FOR THE END OF THE WORLD, attempts to make light of the fevered madness that has come to grip the planet.

When he steps into the campaign offices of Catherine Devlin for State Senate, he's surprised to find the place mostly empty. The office has about ten or twelve desks spread out over the bullpen, but only three of them are occupied.

"May I speak to Ms. Devlin, please?"

At the sound of his voice, Catherine emerges from a windowed office where all the blinds have been pulled. It's the first time Randy's visited her anywhere besides her backyard or an isolated diner or a rest stop ten miles from town. The mix of confusion and hurt in her expression reminds him too much of the terrible expression on Agatha's face as she prepared to shift in his arms. She's got the same big, round blue eyes as her sister, the kind that always make her look vaguely sympathetic, even when she's furious. But her hair looks perfectly in place, ready for the cameras, a medium-length bob.

"What do you want?" The ice in her tone makes her staff members go rigid.

"To talk." Randy's dressed light, no outer layers, and his shirt's tucked in tight, his jeans belted. All attempts to make clear he isn't concealing any weapons, which he emphasizes by lifting his arms to stretch his shirt taut against his torso. "And apologize."

She pulls out her phone. "I'm calling my husband."

"OK. I'll be happy to apologize to him too."

Surprised, she looks up briefly, then turns her back to him, speaking in hushed, frantic tones into her phone. Then she hangs up, a sure sign her husband's now on the way. Then they're staring at each other while her few riveted staff members stare at them.

"Not the best time to be launching a campaign, I guess," Randy finally says to cut the tension.

"My communications director just quit. She's moving to California to be with her family because she thinks the Rapture's coming."

"Most people think it's already started."

"A Rapture for one person? That's certainly not what we were promised."

One of the staff members stifles laughter. But from where Randy's standing now, he can see their computer screen, sees they're monitoring the news. Which is what most people have been doing in the two weeks since filmed evidence of events defying explanation started winging through the mass media networks that now connect the globe. The "Colorado Events" is what the media's calling them, a name Randy finds self-consciously benign and ultimately misleading, a term that absolves everyone who uses it of the fact that they have no idea what the events involved actually mean. They've got the evacuation of Spurlock to thank for that. Nobody with a camera phone was anywhere within view of the demise of Vernon Starnes.

A pressure is building in Randy's chest. His palm burns around the satchel's handle. Catherine's eyes are glued to it. Suddenly, in a professional voice, she says, "You guys go on and get some lunch. I'll text you when I need you back."

They hesitate, give lingering looks as they head for the door, but in another few seconds they're gone, and suddenly he's alone with her for the first time since he fired a gun over her head.

"Are you out of your goddamn mind bringing money here?"

"It's not money." He sets the satchel on a nearby desk. "And it's heavy, so if you don't mind . . ."

"What is it?" she asks.

"The truth. If you want it."

"I want to know what happened to my sister."

"That's in there," he says, "along with a lot of other things."

"First you try to shoot me, then you bring me this?"

"I was protecting you."

"From what?"

Randy gestures toward the satchel. Catherine approaches the bag, but her hands stay planted on her hips.

"This was supposed to be my turn," she finally says. "I've been the good political wife for fifteen years. Now it's my shot, and here I am trying to start a campaign during the end of the world, and now you come, laying this all on me. Finally."

"I'm not laying it on you. I'm giving it to you. You can decide what you want to do with it."

"My sister's dead, isn't she?"

"If I had an easy answer to that question, I would have given it to you years ago."

He hears a rumbling truck's engine behind the building, and then the back door of the office flies open and Kyle Devlin enters, tall and imposing and moving swiftly despite the fact that he walks with a cane. He's gained a considerable amount of weight since the boat accident that jacked up his right leg, the same one that entailed a lengthy recovery and took the taste for politics from him, clearing the way for his devoted wife to run for his seat. Despite the limp, the speed and momentum with which he approaches now suggest he's fully capable of beating Randy half to death with his cane.

"Who are you?" Catherine asks.

Randy reaches for the words he's rehearsed countless times over the past few days. "I'm a man who loved your sister more than I thought I could ever love anyone. And so I made her a promise. A promise that I'd always protect you from the real reason your father went missing when you were a baby, from the real reason your mother had no eyes. From the things your sister kept in the cellar under the barn. From the reason she hired me. All of it. And I've kept that promise as best I can. And I'll still keep it. Once you've heard and read everything I've got, I'll destroy it all if you want, or I'll keep my mouth shut if you do. But your family's past won't be a secret from you anymore. It'll be your choice what to do with it. And given how things have gone for me of late, that seems like the best thing I can do."

"Why now?" Kyle Devlin asks.

"Let's just say I've taken too many choices away from too many people."

"Or you think the Rapture's going down out there and you want to unburden yourself," Catherine says.

"I know exactly what's going on out there," Randy says, "and you will too if you listen to what I have to say and read what's in that bag."

The color drains from Catherine's pale face. After what feels like an eternity of silence, Kyle jerks, a sign he'd shifted most of his weight onto his cane-holding hand without realizing it and the pain there suddenly caught up with him.

Without another word, Catherine gestures for them both to follow her into her office, but she's moving slower, and her hands are at her sides.

Ten minutes into the story, she's sobbing in her husband's arms, leaving Randy to wonder if he's doing the right thing. He reminds himself he's doing the only thing.

And it's what Agatha told him to do.

34

Six Months Later

They told Claire the trailer could withstand a bomb blast and a wild-fire. Considering that, she thinks everything inside it looks fairly homey and bland. They'll only be here a short while, which is why all the trappings of living have been removed. There's no bed in the back room, and the shower doesn't have water pressure or a glass door.

Randy's sitting at the banquette dining table when she enters; Margot is leaning against the window opposite, trying to get a glimpse of the drones circling lazily above the treetops, like they're warming up for what's to come.

Voices come from the trailer's back room, one of them comfortingly familiar, even if it is raised in argument.

When they notice her arrival, Margot turns from the window and Randy slowly gets to his feet.

"I figured you guys would have fallen back already," Claire says.

"Another few minutes, they said." Margot moves to her and brushes hairs off her forehead. "Needed to clear your head?"

"Something like that." Claire manages a smile that hurts her face.

Margot says, "Well, honestly, I wouldn't fall back at all if they'd let me, but . . ."

"Let's not have that argument again," Claire says.

"Fine. Stubborn as your dad."

Margot kisses her on the cheek, and then Claire is facing Randy. They haven't quite moved up to the hugging stage yet, but his smile's warmer than most of the ones he's given her in the past. To cut the awkwardness, he takes out his phone, holds it up so Claire can see live footage of crowds gathering in Times Square.

"Trying to give me stage fright?" she asks.

"Or make you feel supported."

He looks tired. Maybe it's relief, but on a man of action like him, it looks like fatigue. The ranch's cellar was cleared out months before. Three weeks after the plane crash, Catherine Devlin, formerly Catherine Caldwell, gave a press conference alongside her husband, revealing the contents of the files Randy had given her, the agonizing twists and turns of her family's involvement in the Colorado Events, and their true source, a family's ranch in Montana.

"How you doing?" Claire asks.

Startled, Randy looks to her. "I'm hanging in there."

"They let you visit her, right?"

"Oh yeah. That part's just like old times. Except my body's hooked up to a bunch of machines during an inhale so that they can . . . 'get to the bottom of what she can do' is how they're phrasing it."

"And how is she handling all of this?" Claire asks.

Randy shrugs, looks to the floor, a flash of pain in his eyes before he does.

"Sorry," Claire says. "That's between you two, I guess."

"Atonement's never easy," he says finally. "It's not supposed to be."

Claire's not sure what to say to that.

"She thinks you're very brave," Randy adds, "and so do I."

There's a warning knock on the trailer door, and then it opens to reveal one of the many men and women who've been scouring the forest around the trailer with instrument readers of all kinds for days, scientists and agents of so many different government agencies, Claire has trouble keeping track. This woman wears a sleek, formfitting hazmat suit, except for the headpiece, which she's removed to reveal a sweat-matted ponytail. "We're at twenty minutes. Time for visitors to clear out." Her polite but firm voice brokers no disagreement.

Margot takes Claire's hands, kisses her gently on the forehead. "It'll be fine," she says, but it sounds like she's trying to assure herself. "Your father would be proud."

Claire gives her a fierce hug, feels a light pressure on her shoulder. It's Randy. He's clasped her shoulder as he moves past her, the most they've ever touched. Now she's alone with the two voices coming from the back room.

When she opens the door, both men look at her.

She has no reason not to believe that the slender blond guy with the slightly pug nose and rounded chin is her brother. He's in possession of a storehouse of his memories. Still, every time she lays eyes on Poe now, it's a struggle not to remember Randy's account of what they had witnessed on the streets of Spurlock, Colorado, that night, the stunning violence of the bloom slamming into her father's body, contorting his flesh and bone into the man standing before her now. To hear him tell it, it played out as if the bloom itself housed a blueprint for everything essential about her brother, and all it needed was the draw of genetically related flesh to create a brand-new physical version of him. Physically, however, his new body isn't a perfect replica. Poe's head is a little longer than it was before, his brow heavier and more pronounced, his eyes a little less round. And he's a full inch taller. Why that is, along with countless other questions, will eventually be answered by the team of doctors studying him now, doctors like the man Poe is currently arguing with. Claire recognizes him; he conducted several interviews with her when they first turned themselves over to the government. Ken An is his name.

"Claire," Poe says, "please tell this nice gentleman I'm not going to wear this ugly, horrible suit."

"And please tell your brother the request isn't coming from me."

"His name's Ken," Claire says, "but I'm not going to wear one either. Sorry, I think it's dumb."

Ken sighs. "The level of protection this suit will offer both of you is unrivaled by any other technology we—"

"It's a little late to be protecting us from what's in the cave, isn't it?" Claire asks. "I mean, isn't that the whole reason he and I are the ones doing this?"

Ken turns to Poe. "We have reason to believe that the cellular material that makes up your body has undergone substantial changes since you were exposed to the pulse as a child. Now if you would like to re-create those changes and introduce abnormalities into your current body, then by all means, don't wear—"

"I'm way past the point of being normal, handsome." Poe gives the guy a wink.

"I will inform the president that you are denying her request," Ken says, folding the hazmat suit primly over one bent arm.

"Throw in that I think she's really cool and I voted for her twice."

"However, the cranial sensors are not optional. That said . . ." Ken reaches into his medical bag, removes a case, and pops it open. It reminds Claire vaguely of those face-hugger things from the movie *Alien*, but it's designed to fit around their skulls. This model has little shiny bits of platinum studding the spidery legs. "We did get you a special designer version because we know how worried you'd be about all the cameras."

"What am I?" Claire asks. "Chopped liver?"

"We get what we ask for in life, Claire." Poe pops the cranial sensor on like it's a tiara, then does a little curtsy.

Ken looks at both of them. "Good luck. Both of you. It's not lost on any of us what you're doing."

"Good," Poe says. "Then can we go out sometime?"

"Let's see if you live," Ken says, and then he departs.

"He's funny," Claire says.

"Was that sexual harassment?" Poe asks. "Asking him out like that?"

"He doesn't work for us. He works for the government."

"And we basically work for the government, so now we're kinda coworkers, which means maybe that was sexual harassment. But the point is, they're sending the cute ones around all the time now because they think I'll do what they say. So I'm trying to call them out on it. It's kinda homophobic, if you think about it."

"Maybe stop hitting on them, then?" she asks.

"I'll take that under advisement."

"So doctors are your type now?"

"Well, it used to be drug dealers, so I figured I should trade up. New life, new body. All that."

Claire laughs.

She takes his hand. It's something she does a lot now, but she's never prepared for how the warmth of his flesh will affect her. And then there's the scar, or more appropriately, the ghost of a scar, that snakes along his forearm. Whiter and vaguer than the scar that marked their father's forearm in exactly the same location, but its serpentine path is the same, its constant presence a reminder of Poe's rebirth. Of their father's sacrifice.

Hands linked, they listen to the growing silence outside. The workers who've been scouring this patch of forest for weeks have ceased operations now, fallen back into what's been designated as the safe zone, the same place they've taken Randy and Margot, where Benjamin Running Creek and Thomas Billings, Rupert, and Sean are waiting along with Catherine Devlin and her husband and scores of scientists from all over the world. Melissa and Phil are there too. Front-row seats to an event that might change the world even more than it's already been changed.

"But we don't have to do it dressed like walking condoms, and that's why I was a bitch about the suit, OK?" Poe says.

"I'm on your side here, brother. You don't have to convince me."

"We should probably put our earpieces in," Poe says.

Just then a voice comes through the speakers affixed throughout the trailer. *"That's correct. Put your earpieces in."*

That morning, in a live televised address carried on all networks, the president of the United States described the event scheduled for the afternoon as the first step into a new realm of human understanding. "Today, we begin a new exploration of our place in the cosmos." For the first time, and without equivocation, she acknowledged that the Colorado Events not only challenged humanity's understanding of Newtonian physics but strongly suggested than an idea many had always believed in and hoped for might now be supportable through measurable evidence—that the end of physical life might not be the end of human consciousness.

She praised the bravery of both Agatha Caldwell and Catherine Caldwell Devlin in laying bare their family's profoundly painful connections to these revelations, and emphasized that history must not erase the tortured combination of warfare, hate, and division that made the path to these discoveries a perilous and winding one. But in the end, the president called for unity. "For all those who have believed and who have hoped that death is not the end," the president said, "let the Colorado Events, the discoveries on the Caldwell ranch, and the opening of the cave at Lake Michele today unite us as we take this first of many steps on a new journey of discovery into the nature of our existence."

The evacuation orders covered the entire state of Montana and spilled over into neighboring states. Plenty have chosen to ignore them, some of them massing along highways with signs proclaiming either their excitement over the revelations to come or their fear of them. Air traffic over the continental United States has been grounded, and most Americans have been told not to come in for work, opting instead to gather in groups.

Crowds are gathering not just in Times Square but all over the world. Claire watched them on television all morning. They were gathering in churches and in public plazas. In school auditoriums and raucous bars. There are protesters, of course, making wild claims that the opening of the cave is the latest in a Nazi plot that stretches all the way back to World War II, and others who claim the cave is the home of a devil who cloaked himself in the trappings of science. After all she's been part of, Claire thinks the level of organization and plotting these theories require bears no resemblance to the mad jumble of desperate secrets and shame that actually built the conspiracy of lies that began to unravel the minute Ascent Airlines Flight 62 fell from the sky.

Now, she and Poe are walking the same path they walked that long-ago night before the pulse brought their family to its knees. Only now it's daylight, and the leafy branches around them are hung with dozens of electronic eyes, thermometers and instruments taking readings beyond her comprehension. And in the skies above, the drones that were circling earlier now hover, no doubt having arrived at the best angles to broadcast everything happening below to the entire world.

They've now traveled farther along the edge of the lake than they ever did that night, and when they finally arrive at the great mound of granite, shining in the sun like the remains of a ruined temple, Claire is stunned by the array of rovers and drones prepared to do the work humans are still too afraid to do.

As soon as Poe's done his.

"Ready?" a voice says in both of their ears.

"Yep," Poe says.

The yep heard 'round the world, Claire thinks. Maybe later she'll make this joke to Poe, but for now her focus is on the countdown playing in their ears.

Poe raises one arm, fingers spread. And then, thanks to the gift left to him by his miraculous rebirth, by their father's sacrifice, a crack appears in the center of the largest fallen stone, forming cleanly and with determination, with none of the violent chaos of weather, cataclysm, or human rage. As the stone falls away, as a new doorway opens on the secrets within, Claire sees a flickering deep inside like a humble and forgotten fire.

The ghost of a machine, she thinks.

The drones lined up before them rise into the air, propellers whirring. They fly forward through the newly opened crack. The rovers follow. But despite this dazzling display, she can sense her brother's attention.

"Love you, Bear," he says, with the voice she never thought she'd hear on solid ground again.

ACKNOWLEDGMENTS

For my obsession with near-death experiences and theories of the afterlife, I have my mother to thank. The minute I told her I was working on this novel, she sent me almost every book that had been published about NDEs. Thanks for the new library, Mom. And the support.

My best friend, producing partner, and podcast cohost, Eric Shaw Quinn, gave this one a wonderful editorial read. As always, his feedback made the final draft deeper and more compelling. Our podcast, *TDPS Presents CHRISTOPHER & ERIC*, and our special series, *Christopher & Eric's True Crime TV Club*, are the highlights of my pretty great life. Our discussion—at Eric's suggestion—of a documentary entitled *Crazy, Not Insane* directed me to the growing body of research suggesting sadistic psychopaths are formed through a dangerous marriage of preexisting mental illness and traumatic brain injuries sustained in early life, typically as the result of repeated physical abuse. Those ideas, while still evolving (and controversial), very much informed my construction of Vernon Starnes. You can find that discussion and all our episodes at www.TheDinnerPartyShow.com. Additional thanks to our amazing TDPS sound designer Brandon Griffith for keeping us going during the pandemic.

For answering my (sometimes loony) questions about commercial aviation accidents, I'm eternally grateful to Christine Negroni, whose brilliant book *The Crash Detectives* is one of the best I've ever read about plane-crash investigations. Christine is an excellent journalist who speaks truth to power and uses a methodical analysis of evidence to unravel baseless alternative theories but also to substantiate others. When she responded to my emails, I had a bit of a fanboy moment. That said, any factual errors on the topics that appear within these pages belong to me alone.

My good friend, the talented writer Kristen Proby, first introduced me to Montana, opened up Glacier National Park to me, and immediately made a U-turn on Going-to-the-Sun Road when she saw my fear of heights was about to give me a heart attack right there in the front seat of her car. Together with her husband, John, she answered many of my questions about the park, bears, camping, and lightning storms.

And for working with me on excellent—if disturbing—translations of German to English, I'm indebted to my dear friend Marcus Rettig.

For sterling editorial guidance, my profound thanks to Liz Pearsons and Caitlin Alexander. And once again, a huge thanks to everyone on the Thomas & Mercer team, especially editorial director Grace Doyle. A text exchange with Grace about a particularly wacky episode of television (which shall remain nameless) pulled *Decimate* together into something that felt like a novel.

For excellent lawyering in all things, a huge thanks to Christine Cuddy.

Thanks also to Cathy Dipierro and Christine Bocchiaro, Unreal pros, for amazing web support and graphic design, and to Lynn Nesbit, for various agenting.

ABOUT THE AUTHOR

Photo © 2016 Cathryn Farnsworth

A *New York Times* bestseller since his first publication at the age of twenty-two, Christopher Rice is the author of *Bone Music* (an Amazon Charts bestseller and the first novel in the Burning Girl series) and its sequels, *Blood Echo* and *Blood Victory*, as well as the Bram Stoker Award finalists *The Heavens Rise* and *The Vines*. His second novel, *The Snow Garden*, received a Lambda Literary Award. He is an executive producer on the television adaptations of *The Vampire Chronicles* and *The Lives of the Mayfair Witches* by Anne Rice, and he also collaborated with her on *Ramses the Damned: The Passion of Cleopatra* and *Ramses the Damned: The Reign of Osiris*, two sequels to her phenomenally popular novel *The Mummy, or Ramses the Damned*. Together with his best friend and producing partner, *New York Times* bestselling novelist Eric Shaw Quinn, he runs the production company Dinner Partners. Among other projects, they produce the podcast and video network TDPS, which you can find at www.TheDinnerPartyShow.com. As C. Travis Rice, Christopher writes tales of romance between men. Learn more about Christopher at www.christopherricebooks.com.